MADGE SWINDELLS

Edelweiss

WARNER BOOKS

A *Warner* Book

First published in Great Britain in 1993
by Little, Brown and Company

This edition published by Warner Books in 1994
Reprinted 1994, 2000

Copyright © Madge Swindells 1993

The moral right of the author has been asserted.

A CIP catalogue record for this book
is available from the British Library.

ISBN 0 7515 0942 6

Printed in England by Clays Ltd, St Ives plc

Warner Books
A Division of
Little, Brown and Company (UK)
Brettenham House
Lancaster Place
London WC2E 7EN

Also by Madge Swindells

SUMMER HARVEST
SONG OF THE WIND
SHADOWS ON THE SNOW
THE CORSICAN WOMAN
THE SENTINEL
HARVESTING THE PAST
SUNSTROKE
SNAKES AND LADDERS
WINNERS AND LOSERS

Author's note

Edelweiss was the name of a Catholic student resistance group founded in Bavaria prior to the war. Broken up many times by Gestapo informers, the students re-formed and similar groups sprang up all over Germany. Organisations like The White Rose, the Werner Steinbrink movement, the Alfred Schmidt-Sas group, Die Meute in Leipzig, the Kittelbach Piraten in the Ruhr, the 07 Group in Munich and the Anti-Nazi Verband in the foothills of the Alps, opposed the Nazis every way they could.

Three months before Adolf Hitler took power as Chancellor of Germany, on 30 January 1933, over sixty-five per cent of the German population voted against the Nazis. For them, the next twelve years became a time of agony. As freedom of speech and individual rights were swept away, the Nazis introduced a system of control, based on a network of informers, that bound the population in a web of fear. The people became cogs in the mighty German war machine that goose-stepped through Europe from the Atlantic to the Volga.

'My country right or wrong', was the patriotic spirit of the age, but amongst German youth a new concept was dawning ... that an individual's first responsibility was to God and to justice, that no one should obey laws that were immoral, and that a corrupt government must be challenged. These thoughts were like beams of pure white light in the stygian darkness of the Nazi era, but they brought savage reprisals upon those who dared to say: 'This is wrong.'

So widespread was the youths' underground opposition to the Nazis that a concentration camp, called Neuwied, was hastily established for 'subversive' students, while a special youth section was created in the RSHA (headquarters of the Gestapo, or secret police) in Prinz Albrechtstrasse, Berlin.

Many were executed, thousands were imprisoned, but the spirit of Edelweiss could not be destroyed and eventually the Edelweiss flower became the symbol of student resistance throughout Germany.

This story is about the Edelweiss students and what they did in those twelve terrible years. Although the characters are fictitious, the thoughts and deeds and courage belong to those who died and those few who survived the concentration camps.

Edelweiss became a cry for freedom.

Part One

September 1937 – September 1942

Chapter  1

IT WAS A GLORIOUS AUTUMN MORNING, the air cool and sparkling, the sky clear blue, and the distant peaks of the Bayerische Alpen shone dazzling white in the sunlight. When the train entered the forest the sunlight shone in scattered beams on russet and brown leaves through drifting mist. Bill Roth, standing quietly by the open window, experienced a sudden sharp pang of nostalgia for boyhood days of hiking through forests and mountains. His dark blue eyes gazed moodily at the scene and at that moment he saw himself as his own prisoner, caught up in a self-imposed, obsessive mission. He longed to get off at the next station and tramp through the forest, but he had set himself a tight schedule. I'll take a break and come back, he told himself, but he knew that he would not. There was always another pressing story to write, a new lead, some major crisis that he had to cover, and never enough time. Then the train shot out of the forest into blinding light and patches of snow and the mood was lost.

Bill's destination was a village outside Hallein, not far from Salzburg. During a chance encounter with a nurse the previous weekend, he had stumbled upon a brilliant lead. The nurse had heard rumours . . . nothing firm, mind you, but the hospital was full of Gestapo officers and there had been an internal inquiry. Even she had been questioned, although she worked in the

3

geriatric ward. A day spent on the telephone had thrown up enough evidence to make the trip seem worthwhile to Bill.

As the train began to slow, Bill glanced at his watch. It was almost 10 a.m. He put on his tie and jacket and gathered his gear together. Most of his bag was full of equipment: a camera, folding tripod, flashgun, special lenses and a notebook. Other than that he had a change of underwear, a volume of Hemingway's *The Sun Also Rises*, to pass a couple of lonely evenings, and his hiking boots. Who knows, he might get some time to himself.

The station master eyed him curiously as he stepped off the train. Bill was well over six foot and lean, with a loose-limbed, loping walk. His dark hair was short, his clothes were foreign and casual. Noting the watchful eyes and rugged, sun-tanned face, he labelled him American, and probably a journalist. He had a shrewd idea why he had come here.

Bill was aware of the scrutiny, but pretended not to notice. The inn was only ten minutes down the road, the porter told him, so he set off, enjoying the walk.

When he reached the place, a pretty, Alpine chalet with dark wooden beams and overhanging windows, he heard the sound of children's voices. His steps quickened and he realised for the first time that he had not really believed the rumours. Skirting the building he paused by a low gate, watchful and intent. In the garden five youngsters were squabbling over a swing, one was crippled. Could it be them?

'Don't fight,' he heard someone say softly, in a low voice. 'You know it's Bertl's turn. Push her gently, don't frighten her. That's better.'

The speaker, who had her back turned to him, was sitting on a low tree stump. She was hugging her knees, and he could see her slim waist, flaring to boyish hips and the graceful long curve of her neck. Her hat, blouse and skirt were of blue linen, and several dark blonde curly locks had escaped from the confines of her hat. He experienced a sudden instinct that when she turned she would look as lovely as he imagined her to be.

When she did turn, Bill gasped. He had never before seen such a striking woman. Her face was too wide to be classically beautiful, her eyebrows were too thick, slanting up like bat wings, her nose too snub, her mouth too wide, but still she was lovely. Her eyes were deep blue, the most tantalising eyes he had ever seen, so that for a moment he felt overwhelmed by her and stood rudely staring. It made her scowl at him.

'Please forgive me for intruding,' he blurted out, without noticing that he had spoken in English. 'I'm Bill Roth, freelance reporter from Berlin ... The truth is ... I heard rumours ... forgive me ...' He sounded like a bumbling schoolboy and he cursed himself for being so gauche. He began again in German.

'We can speak in English. It makes no difference, none at all,' she interrupted. 'What do you mean, rumours? Where did you hear about us. We have been so awfully careful.'

Her English was perfect, her pronunciation too perfect. Her skin was smooth and glowing with just a sprinkling of freckles over her nose. Her lips were full and wide and a second ago, one side of her mouth had tilted up, as if in a half-smile. Yes, she was definitely smiling at him now. That was encouraging. He struggled to concentrate.

'Someone who works at the hospital ... a friend ... tipped me off.'

'And you came all this way on a rumour? What dedication! But what exactly are you dedicated to, Mr Roth?'

'Exposing the Nazis for what they really are ... not the false face they show the press.'

'Then we have something in common. I don't know how much you know, but I am not alone and I have to get permission to talk to you. That might take a while. You probably know that I am stuck here without exit permits, they confiscated them while they make up their minds what to do with us, so we can meet later, if you like.'

'I guess I should book in, anyway,' Bill said. He reluctantly turned away. After depositing his bag in a clean but primitive bedroom, he wandered around the inn and the village, which consisted of three cobbled streets, but he didn't see the woman or the children in her charge.

After lunch he came across her sitting on a chintz sofa outside
the children's bedroom. Mellow light, reflected from the low
ceiling, glistened on her lustrous skin and shone in her eyes. A
thin gold chain hung around her long neck and she was
fingering the pearl that hung from it with sensitive, restless
fingers. She was trapped here, yet she remained calm and docile
and he wondered just how much strength that took. The door
was open and she put her finger to her lips.

'Shh! They're sleeping,' she whispered.

'May I?' She nodded and flushed slightly as he sat beside her.
'I'm hoping you'll tell me your name,' he began.

'To a reporter? That would be foolish of me, wouldn't it?'

'Not even if I promise never to use it in my story?'

'Oh, so you do have a story, do you?'

'Only if you have permission to talk to me. Do you?'

She hesitated. 'You may write about the children and their
predicament. I'm going to take them for walk when they wake.
You can come with us if you like. We'll leave from the back door
in about half an hour. They like going through the orchard
because the innkeeper lets them eat his fruit. You may
photograph the children. In fact, Mr Roth, my superiors know
about you and they seem to think that you are just what we need
. . . a world platform to help us bargain with the authorities.'

Bill went to fetch his camera.

Half an hour later, while the children were munching apples
in the orchard, she turned to him and said, 'How lovely they
look. So normal, so happy. You must describe them just as you
see them, Mr Roth. Write about why they had to leave
Germany.'

'Bill . . .'

'All right, Bill it is. I'll try not to be emotional, but it really hurts
. . . these children . . . these harmless, helpless little mites . . .' She
broke off and bit her lip, and Bill pondered again on the very
Englishness of her words.

After a while she took a deep breath. 'Sorry! Let me try again.
These orphans would have been put to death by the Nazis
because they're not quite up to Aryan standards. We were able

to obtain permission from some of their nearest relatives to remove them from the country. It took time . . . and time almost ran out. One is Austrian by birth, three have living relatives, one has a guardian . . . the whole matter is very complex and we were almost too late, so finally we simply snatched the children from the hospital. The Red Cross are waiting on the Austrian side of the border at Salzburg to take the children to Zurich, but the authorities have cancelled our travel permits. I was forced to leave the train at Salzburg, so I came here to wait.'

'Tell me about the children.'

In response she beckoned the children to her side. 'This is Heike, and she's two years old.' Then added in a whisper, 'She's epileptic.'

Bill looked at the sweet blonde girl with a freckled face and winning smile and tried to smile, but his lips seemed to have frozen. He had difficulty trying to be relaxed as the children were introduced to him in turn. Dieter, five, was crippled, his right leg twisted and ending in a club foot, forcing him to walk on his toes and setting his spine askew. Chubby, lovable, wistful Hermann was nearly blind and his snub nose almost touched 'Auntie' each time he spoke to her. Bertl, six, seemed normal, but she was also epileptic. Inge was clearly retarded, at six she behaved like a toddler and Bill was touched to see how gently 'Auntie' looked after her. Bill was well aware that the Nazis could arrive at any moment and take the children back to the hospital and then to the gas chamber. And what would be the fate of this heroic girl?

'They were taken from various orphanages to a hospital for tests and documentation prior to euthanasia,' she was saying. 'We kidnapped them. That's all there is to it. '

'And how did you get them out of hospital?'

'I can't answer that question, except to say that there are many of us. So now we wait here while the Church battles with the State. You have probably guessed that the Archbishop of Munich is behind this. He detests the Nazis' euthanasia laws, but you must not name him in your story.'

They walked for a while enjoying the hot afternoon sunshine

and the birdsong, while the children were enchanted by the antics of the squirrels, and Bill took photographs of their play.

There were berries in the brambles which Bill picked for them and the 'girl in blue', as he'd decided to call her since she refused to tell him her name, poured lemonade from a flask she'd carried in a knapsack. She was so young, he thought, watching her playing tag with the children, and too vulnerable. She needed looking after herself and he felt irrationally responsible for her.

'Listen,' he said anxiously, as they turned back towards the Inn. 'I'm sure I can help you. I can call on the assistance of the American Embassy. I have good contacts. And you must move away from here, they know where you are . . . you're sitting ducks . . . please,' he pleaded. 'Let me help.'

'Just write your story, Bill,' she said. 'Make it so poignant that your readers erupt in fury and their governments can't ignore what is happening. The Third Reich won't dare to push their fanaticism in the face of world criticism.'

She shyly refused his invitation to dinner. She was tired, she said. She would sleep in the children's room and she wanted them to go to bed early.

Bill let her go, full of fears for this extraordinary young woman. The Third Reich would make an implacable enemy, she might survive this time, because the Archbishop was a powerful man, but from now on she would be a marked woman.

Despite his professional armour of a newspaperman, Bill had fallen under the spell of this enchanting girl. It was not only her beauty that had captivated him, but the humour which shone in her eyes, and the goodness that was all about her. He was awed by her courage.

Bill couldn't sleep, what he had learned that afternoon had left him tense and brooding. He tried to write the outline of his story, but he could not get to grips with the concept of killing children . . . it was far beyond his understanding, macabre and utterly unbelievable.

Perhaps he should start the story by describing the girl who was defying the mighty Third Reich? Could he write that she was as kind and brave as she was lovely? That she joked in the face of mortal danger? No. That would be melodramatic.

Or should he write about the five little children and how they had trembled so fearfully at the sight of the SS guards they had seen in the distance, guarding the station?

Or perhaps he should begin with the Archbishop of Munich and his courageous, outspoken denunciation of the programme of euthanasia from the pulpit of his cathedral, week after week? How he had encouraged Catholics to stand up and be counted and do all they could to stop this unholy programme.

Bill had known about the Nazis' insane 'mercy killings' for some time. The Law on the Protection of Hereditary Health was part of the Nazi concept of breeding a pure 'master race' by eliminating those they considered unfit. This operation, known as T4, was confined to the incurably handicapped and mentally deficient and it aimed to cleanse the racial stock. There had been plenty of rumours recently, triggered off by the unexpected deaths of mental patients in hospital, but there was never any proof as the bodies were not made available to relatives for post-mortem, because they had been sent for cremation.

No one seemed to know how to stop it until now. Perhaps this group had found a way. If so, Bill feared for the only one of their members he had met.

He dozed off into a restless sleep and woke much later to the soft clip-clop of hooves on the cobbles outside his window. He looked out but everything was obscured by the thick mountain mist. In the morning he learned that the girl and the children had left. He questioned the innkeeper, who feigned ignorance.

'They've left, that's all I know,' he said. 'Their bill was paid in advance, so they were free to leave if they wanted to.'

Bill tried to convince himself that he wasn't the least bit depressed. After all, he had his story.

Chapter  2

BILL ROTH RETURNED TO BERLIN still in awe of the bravery of the girl in blue. He made inquiries through the Red Cross and learned that the children had arrived safely in Switzerland. Then he filed his story and tried to put it out of his mind. There was so much work to do, so many leads.

Until now Bill had been living out of suitcases and working from seedy hotel rooms all over Europe, but increasingly in Berlin. This was where the news was. He had been self-supporting for some months and he knew it was high time he found an apartment in Berlin. He was lucky to find something suitable not far from the Kurfürstendamm in Kantstrasse; five rooms plus a kitchen and bathroom, overlooking the park and dam. It was old, but the large rooms appealed to Bill and he happily signed the lease.

He was far too busy to furnish or refurbish the place, instead he asked his friends to recommend a good interior decorator. Taube Bloomberg was at home when he telephoned, and she agreed to come and see him later that day.

Before she arrived a telegram came in from Reuters in New York, asking Bill to cover the Spanish Civil War. Their regular man had been shot. They would get a permanent replacement out soon, but they could not promise a date. For Bill, this was a chance in a million.

When Taube Bloomberg walked in, he was already packed and itching to leave. He tried not to show his impatience as he sat down to talk to her. She was slender, poised and beautiful in a Mediterranean way, with long black hair swept up on her head. She was wearing a superbly tailored grey suit, a white lace blouse, grey suede shoes and carrying a large briefcase. Bill could see from her scrap book that she was right at the top of her profession, although she didn't look much more than twenty-eight. She was too good and expensive for him, Bill felt. He told her so bluntly, but it seemed Miss Bloomberg wanted the job.

'I'd thought of dividing it like this.' He took out a rough pencilled sketch. 'Two offices, for myself and a secretary, plus a bedroom, a lounge and a spare bedroom. Make it cheap and light,' he said. 'Oh and try for a telephone. Two lines if you can. If possible have them installed before I return.'

She stared at him with her mouth open. 'You must give me some idea of price ... give me a limit.'

Bill wrote out a cheque. 'That's the limit,' he said, then hesitated before continuing, 'Look ... I hate to ask, but could you do me a favour and put an advertisement in the paper for a secretary, shorthand typing in German and English, long hours, knowledge of French, responsible person, that sort of thing?'

Taube Bloomberg nodded.

Bill picked up his gear and left.

Bill's footsteps had hardly faded out of earshot, when Taube burst into tears of relief. In the past few months she had walked her feet off trying to get any sort of a job. Her own profession was barred to her, because she was a Jewess. She could take only menial work, but no one wanted to employ an untrained woman even as a maid. Recently, centres had been set up to teach Jewish girls laundry, sewing, and cooking. Taube had been prepared to suffer this 're-education programme', for the sake of her parents, but she wasn't prepared to stop trying for something better.

Now Bill Roth had given her a job. Was he Jewish? No, she

thought, probably not, but he wasn't the usual Anglo-Saxon type. His skin was darker, his dark brown hair was cut short and brushed back vigorously, but this had not eradicated the tight waves. He had a brooding, intent look about him: his long bony face might have seemed harsh if it weren't for the warmth in his blue eyes, and the lurking smile around his sensuous lips. He was good-looking in a way, but shy. She guessed him to be around twenty-four.

He'd rescued her, there was no doubt about that. There and then, she vowed that his apartment would be the best thing she had ever undertaken.

Count Frederick von Burgheim, Austrian Minister of Foreign Affairs, paced his office in Plechy Palace, Vienna, before turning abruptly to face his daughter, only to step back before her implacable gaze. How stubborn she was; her chin was tilted up, her eyes were wide open, but giving nothing away, while her lips curled on one side into a half-smile as she scanned his face in silence. She would say nothing, he knew that, and wait for him to trap himself. When he did, she would pounce and it would be over. He could not help thinking that if he had not loved her so desperately he might have brought her up with more respect for her elders and betters.

He tried again. 'Our family has the misfortune to be always under public scrutiny. As my daughter, your behaviour must be exemplary at all times. A month ago you involved our family in a confrontation with a friendly, neighbouring state. Your behaviour was unacceptable, even for a matter of . . . compassion.' Still that silent stare with just a touch of scorn in her eyes.

'Don't look at me like that.'

'I'm sorry, but your choice of words . . . "friendly neighbouring state". Well, really. I've heard you describing the Nazis quite differently.'

The Count eyed his daughter warily. He thawed a little as she put her arm around his waist and hugged him.

'Let's forget the lecture, Father. You would have done the same in my shoes. Why not admit it?'

'No . . . never. I'm too old to be so headstrong, or so foolish. You begged me to give you four years . . .'

'I didn't beg. I never beg . . .'

'You wanted to drop your title and live like any ordinary student, but I warned you that the spotlight would always be on you. Hitler has vowed to destroy the Habsburgs and he will not hesitate to crush you . . . us . . . if you openly oppose the New Order in Germany. It would be better for you to go to England . . .'

'But, my friends—'

'Don't interrupt . . . learn to co-exist. Close your eyes to what you don't like, as I must. That is how the Habsburgs survived, by compromising—'

'. . . by compromising their moral integrity?' she asked innocently. 'For us Habsburgs, expediency counts more than morality? Is that what you're saying?'

The Count felt his anger rising and struggled to control himself. He took a deep breath. 'What I'm saying is keep out of trouble. And in particular keep out of the press.' He flung a newspaper across his desk.

It was the *Chicago Herald*.

Special report from Bill Roth, in Salzburg, she read, and then gasped as she turned the page and saw a large photograph of herself with the children. It had been taken in the orchard. Admittedly she had her back turned to the camera, but her clothes and her watch had revealed her identity to her father, but surely to no one else, she thought with a sigh of relief. *One who dares* . . . the headline read. *Munich's Catholic Students back the Cardinal's protest against euthanasia* . . .

She had a sudden vivid recall of that friendly American journalist with his expressive, sensitive face and kind blue eyes. When had he taken that shot? She had thought he'd only photographed the children. 'At least it doesn't show my face,' she said, looking up apprehensively.

With his head bent forward, his huge brown eyes peering from under his wide, wrinkled brow, his lopsided face topped with thick, tousled black hair, her father looked like a tired old bull awaiting the *coup de grâce*. She melted instantly. Crouching beside him, she flung her arms around his neck. 'I'm sorry I worried you, Father, but what else could I do? It's not only me. There's a few of us, and they were going to gas the children. Can you believe that?'

'I can believe anything, nowadays. I want you out of Germany.'

She wasn't listening, he could see that. Her fingers were clutching the newspaper as she reread the report. The Count eyed his daughter apprehensively. His fears were heightened when she blushed and gazed up guiltily. 'He's a very good writer,' she said softly. 'A highly intelligent man. I liked him.'

'Marietta,' he said, as sternly as he could. 'Never forget that your four years of freedom will end all too soon. You will return to take up your responsibilities and to make a fitting marriage to a Habsburg, or possibly into royalty. Sometimes I wish there had been a male to inherit your grandmother's vast fortune. Then, perhaps ... Ah well, the Cardinal saved you. Did you know that?' he said, switching back to his first worry. 'He's a brave man. He said you were acting under his instructions. Were you?'

'I can't answer that.'

There was a knock and Marietta turned to see her brother standing in the doorway.

'Louis! What are you doing here?'

'I was sent for.'

Louis, tall, lank and intent, watched them impatiently. She knew how he hated family dramas. Lately, he had acquired a world-weary, cynical expression which he used as a shield.

Marietta loved her half-brother deeply and knew him for what he was, an introverted, caring, over-sensitive boy, caught up in the trauma of being Count Louis von Burgheim and facing a future of State affairs and family responsibility. All Louis cared about was music.

'You are to keep an eye on your sister in Munich,' the Count said. 'Spend more time with her. That's an order. You may leave now. We'll talk about it over dinner.'

'My own brother must spy on me ... ?' she called over her shoulder as she left with Louis.

'Relax, Marietta. Let it be,' Louis said. He caught hold of her hand and pulled her round to face him. 'Let's have a look at you. You're growing up fast. Father's right, of course. You know that, don't you?'

She turned away, feeling angry, but unwilling to fight with someone she loved and saw so seldom. 'Have you had breakfast?'

'Jan's gone to organise something in the kitchen.'

Louis watched her uneasily. He felt inadequate to protect her. What could he say to his idealistic sister? 'We're Austrian,' he said finally. 'The New Order has nothing to do with us.'

Evidently that was the last thing he should have said. They were locked in mortal combat for the rest of the day. The family feud continued throughout dinner until Marietta went to bed.

Chapter  3

MARIETTA WAS TOO ANGRY TO SLEEP. Although she had stood her ground, she was disturbed by her father's and Louis' condemnation. Were family responsibilities more viable than her own conscience? Had her fortune lost her the right to guard her own soul? Her grandmother had said on her deathbed, 'You are only a link in a chain, be a strong link ...' Surely she was entitled to more than that?

How well she remembered that traumatic week when her responsibilities had settled on her shoulders like a hideous black crow. She could still feel the cold chill of death and smell the heavy perfume that permeated her grandmother's bedroom. How unprepared she had been, returning from England with Ingrid in expectation of a wonderful holiday, but the longed-for holiday had never happened.

The final exams had ended at last. She and her cousin, Ingrid, were sitting in the common room of their English boarding school comparing answers. It was dusk, the lamplight shone on Ingrid's hair, and her pale cheeks, making her look ethereal and pure. At nineteen her cousin had grown into a rare beauty, she was petite and slim, with a lithe figure and long ash-blonde hair.

'D'you remember when Father left us here, six years ago?' Marietta asked, looking out at the old red brick building with the ivy creeping over it. 'I thought we'd never survive, but we have, and soon we'll be out in the world. A brilliant new adventure.' She squeezed Ingrid's arm affectionately.

'That's easy for you to say,' Ingrid murmured, pulling away. 'You have your future mapped. Uncle will expect you to marry into royalty, or something close to it. I have nothing to look forward to. For once in your life, try to understand that the future's not going to be brilliant for me, although I'm sure it will be divine for you.'

Marietta looked up sharply and caught Ingrid's expression, a mask of envy and dislike. She felt shocked and sad.

'I know it's difficult for you, Ingrid, but you have me right behind you, and Father, too. You have nothing to worry about. Whatever I have, I'll share with you equally. Let's think about the holiday. We've earned it and we're going to have a wonderful time.'

'Spare me your charity,' Ingrid murmured.

Marietta made up her mind to try and understand Ingrid's fears and to reassure her, but an hour later news came that her grandmother, Princess Lobkowitz, was dying.

Two days later she reached Prague after an exhausting journey across Europe. Jan, her grandmother's driver, was waiting at the station to meet her.

'The Princess is holding on for you,' he greeted her. 'She's tough and determined, but it is only a matter of hours.'

Marietta sat in the car in a daze of impatience and grief, hardly noticing the kaleidoscope of farms, fertile fields, small stone bridges, forest and lakes, church spires and mediaeval villages which they were driving past. They followed the route of the Vltava River southwards. It was wide and swift-flowing, and there was an occasional glimpse of a passenger steamer.

Twenty miles south of Prague, Jan braked on a hillside and turned the car down towards the river, and there, almost hidden by the dense forest, rose the turrets and ramparts of Sokol

Castle – her home. She sighed as the car crossed the river towards the old gate, topped with crumbling gargoyles.

'Hurry, Jan,' she whispered. She *had* to see Grandmother before she died.

Minutes later they were pulling up in the courtyard by the old stone steps, smoothed and hollowed by centuries of wear.

When she stepped into the vast castle hall, the chill of death wrapped round her like a cloak. She shuddered as Max, the household manager, gave a low mumble of condolence. He looked anguished. Then her father came hurrying towards her.

'We'll talk later,' he said, hugging her. 'There isn't much time. You must go straight to the princess.'

The sight of her grandmother shocked her, her skin was ashen and her eyes were deeply sunk in their gaunt sockets.

'Grandmother!' Scalding tears blinded her momentarily.

The old woman made a heroic effort to reach for Marietta's hand. 'It's up to you, my child,' she muttered. 'Think only of the family. Hang on to what is ours. Make it grow. Do your duty.' Her voice sank to a hoarse whisper. 'I always hoped for a male heir, but your mother let the family down. I know you'll never do that. Sacrifice yourself. That's how the Habsburgs became great. Promise me you'll play your part.'

'I promise, Grandmother. I won't let you down.'

The princess fell back exhausted. Marietta leaned over her and listened to her breathing.

'Don't go. Please, Grandmama ... I've been longing to see you. Talk to me.'

'Always remember, child ...'

'Yes ... yes, I'm listening ...'

'You are a link between the past and the future. You must be a strong link. You must safeguard our wealth and our power. You are the trustee for future generations.'

'Yes Grandmother, I promise.' Marietta felt scared and over-awed by the gravity of her responsibilities.

'Times are changing. Difficult times are coming. Be brave!'

Her voice grew faint. She was slipping away. 'Grandmother ...

Can you hear me? I want you to know how much I love you. You were more than a mother to me and I love you very dearly.'

'Love ...' the old woman's lips twitched. *'Forget love! Remember only your duty...'* She closed her lips firmly, as if she had said all there was to say, and quietly died.

The next few days passed in a blur of activity. Marietta had to meet managers, lawyers, farm foremen, bankers, investors, security advisors, managers of the breweries and the wineries, accountants, government officials and forestry chiefs. There was so much to do, and all of it seemed to increase her feeling of unreality. How could all this be hers? When Marietta realised the extent of her inheritance she felt inadequate and there was little comfort to be taken from the thought that she was merely the custodian. As the days passed she realised what she must do and squared her shoulders for a confrontation with her father. She had wanted to choose her moment, but he spent so much time locked in his own study sorting out his affairs in the wake of the Princess's death, that she was forced to confront him just before breakfast, which she knew from bitter experience was not the ideal moment.

'Father, I want you to know that I promised Grandmother I would do my duty and run the estates to the best of my ability.'

'I would expect no less of you.'

'But Father I'm not trained to run anything. I need to study economics, farm management, modern methods of agriculture, forestry, marketing ... frankly, the list is endless. I need to learn so much. I want four years off to prepare myself. Think of it as a time to equip myself properly for the future,' she went on desperately as she noticed his frown and his fingers ominously tapping the desk. 'I have to be free. I want to live my own life.'

'You're entitled to live your own life,' he said eventually, 'since no one else can live it for you, but this *is* your life.

'Freedom won't play much of a role in it. You have wealth, power, the entrance to a brilliant future, but little freedom. It is part of the price you have to pay. I shall appoint managers with expertise in all the areas you've mentioned ...'

'That's fine for now,' she snapped, 'but for the future, I'll never be content with the role of a figurehead. You would not have tolerated a male heir to conduct his affairs in such a way, and I do not accept such a position merely because I am a woman. I need four years in which to study. That's all. I am going to enrol at Munich University where they have a course in estate management. While I'm there, I'd like your permission to drop my title and live like any other student.'

The Count looked so belligerent, that she was sure he would refuse her request. Instead, he sighed softly and in a resigned tone said, 'Perhaps you could persuade Ingrid to go with you.'

Marietta hadn't realised she had been holding her breath, she released it slowly. She'd won. 'Thank you, Father.' She flung her arms around his neck and hugged him. 'Ingrid wants to go to a finishing school in France. She longs to become a famous society hostess.'

'A pity,' her father said ruefully. 'She'll have to marry wisely. Remember, Marietta. After four years you'll have to get on with the serious business of being a countess and an heiress.'

'Oh Father, of course I will,' she promised lightly, hugging him again. 'Thank you.'

Lying in her bed in the Plechy Palace, she mused that it was only a few months since her grandmother had died, yet overnight the carefree schoolgirl had vanished, and her promised freedom had become a mirage. Huh, freedom! It's not fair, she muttered miserably.

Eventually she sat up and put the light on, looking around for something to read ... anything that would distract her. A letter from Ingrid was lying on the table. She picked it up and read it again. Ingrid wrote of parties, fashions and the young men she had met. She had been flirting with an Italian count and he seemed to be serious. *Yesterday, I overheard the famous designer, Schiaparelli himself say, 'a lovely girl is an accident, a beautiful woman an achievement'. From now on, I'm going to model myself on Mrs Wallis Simpson.*

Marietta smiled, despite her gloom. How exactly did one set

about flirting, she wondered? She considered some of the boys she had met so far. A few kept trying to court her, and of course, she'd danced with some, but the idea of kissing any of them was revolting. Yet lately she was filled with curiosity and strange, undefined longings. Would she ever fall in love? She was seventeen, almost eighteen, and she had never been kissed. She'd led such a sheltered existence she simply didn't know whether she should care or not. She remembered the journalist, Bill Roth. Did he think of her at all? She sighed and switched off the light.

After a restless night, she wrote her father a note and left it on his desk before returning to Munich.

Forgive me, Father, but I must be guided by my conscience. You brought me up to do my duty and I cannot shirk my moral responsibilities. Your loving daughter, Marietta.

Chapter  4

BILL ARRIVED IN SPAIN IN MID–OCTOBER, as General Franco tightened his grip along the eastern front of the country, and he was sickened by the savagery he saw as Franco's troops swept the battered government forces before them. He wrote about the bombed civilians, the starving and the destitute; he wrote about mothers who shielded their children with their own bodies, of the slaughter of hundreds of disarmed soldiers in the bullring at Badajoz, of women and children in rags, their faces yellow and gaunt, showing their suffering so clearly. There was no shortage of such material and Bill kept filing stories day after day. He had little time for sleep, but in the odd snatched hours between battles, his dreams were invaded by visions of the girl he had met in Salzburg. Bill was only too glad when, in mid-November, the new permanent correspondent arrived to take over. He was afraid of becoming too used to the atrocities and the cruelty.

Back in Berlin, Bill found his apartment in Kantstrasse looking like an advertisement in *Vogue*. It wasn't just fine, it was breathtaking. The clever use of mirrors made the narrow entrance hall appear huge. The bare boards were gone. White marble tiles, mirrors and plants had turned his humble apartment into a millionaire's pad. The furniture looked expensive and modern. There were bookcases filled with books, framed black and white engravings of old Berlin on the walls, a blue and white ceramic vase on the table was filled with golden autumn flowers. The bedroom was breathtaking, white and grey with a crimson silk cover over the bed. The office looked far more spacious than he remembered. Bill couldn't take in every detail: he was in shock as he tried to work out the cost.

He saw with relief that there was a telephone on the desk in the white and olive office, and using it summoned Taube Bloomberg to come round to the apartment immediately.

By the time she arrived, the contents of his suitcase had spoilt the orderliness of the bedroom, and his papers had comfortably covered the highly polished desk.

He faced her awkwardly. 'Thanks for getting this organised.' Bill gestured towards the telephones and typewriters. 'Look,' he went on, trying to brace himself for a fight with a woman, 'I don't want to make a big thing out of this, but I gave you a limit on what you could spend.'

'Yes, you did.'

'You couldn't buy those tiles for that price, let alone have them laid,' he said bluntly.

'They're secondhand, as is the furniture. It's amazing what you can pick up these days. Here are the receipts. You can see exactly what I paid for everything.' She handed him a folio of annotated bills.

'Who did the work?'

'An odd job builder. A Jew,' she said carefully. 'You can get Jewish labour quite cheaply if you don't mind having Jews around.'

Bill felt furious and disgusted with her, then belatedly the truth dawned. 'Are you Jewish?'

'Any objections?' Now her aggression was like a palpable force between them.

'Just what are you made of, Miss Bloomberg? How could you beat down one of your own people?'

'Oh!' She let out her breath audibly. 'It was my brother, actually. And I didn't beat him down, he was glad to help me.'

'Please thank him for me.'

'He has left Germany . . . thank God,' she added softly.

Bill immediately regretted his brusqueness. 'Miss Bloomberg, you did a wonderful job. I think you're some kind of a genius. When I walked in I couldn't believe what you'd achieved and I thought you'd overspent. I'm sorry if I offended you.'

She was still looking nervous. 'I have overstepped my authority and hired a secretary for you. She seemed so right for this job.' She broke off. 'You look all in. I can see you're exhausted, I'll make coffee.'

'The fact is, I haven't slept properly for days.'

'You go ahead and sleep.' She was very anxious to please him, but Bill was too tired to wonder why. 'What time would you like your secretary to wake you?'

Bill had the impression that this was not the way an interior decorator should behave, but he was too damn tired to care. 'Tell her to keep the noise down, hold messages and wake me at 6 p.m. with coffee. I've a heck of a lot of last-minute notes to write up.'

After what seemed only five minutes of sleep, there was a knock at the door. Bill looked at his watch, it couldn't be six already, but it was. He made his way to the bathroom. It was too much effort to run a bath, so he rubbed his face with cold water and brushed his hair. When he returned to his bedroom a plate of sandwiches and a pot of coffee had been placed on a table. This girl knew her business. With a cup of coffee in one hand and a sandwich in the other, he walked through to the secretary's office. Taube Bloomberg was sitting there, looking fierce, although he sensed a certain desperation about her.

'Why are you still here?' he asked.

'I'm the new secretary, sir,' she said.

'But why you? You're not a clerk, you're right at the top of your profession. I guess you know that.'

'I'm good, I admit it, but there's no profession for me to be top of, because, as you guessed, I'm Jewish. Please, Mr Roth. I'll work very hard. I'll even accept half pay.'

'That won't be necessary,' Bill said gruffly, feeling more

sorry than he should. 'The job's yours.'

'It is illegal for you to employ me in any professional capacity, and since I'll keep your apartment clean as well, I registered myself as your maid.'

Bill flinched and walked out of the room to hide his sadness.

Now that he was back in Germany, Bill set out to discover the identity and whereabouts of the 'girl in blue', whom he could not get out of his mind. Who was she, he wondered, what gave her so much nerve? And why were there so few like her? He knew the answer to that question ... there were dozens of concentration camps in Nazi Germany and they were filled to overflowing with gypsies, petty criminals, Protestants, Catholics, priests of every religion and all those who had showed even slight opposition to the Nazis' New Order.

Armed with a photograph, Bill visited the Archbishop of Munich's secretary. The priest denied all knowledge of the girl or any involvement in the rescue of the orphans, but Bill was granted an appointment with the Archbishop. The interview gave him an excellent story, but no more information about the girl in blue. He seemed to have reached a dead end. Bill tried to put his obsession aside and for a while he succeeded, with the help of Taube.

It was wrong to mix business with pleasure, he knew, but he was lonely and so he took her to the theatre several times and they often had dinner together. Taube was a great asset to his career, Bill soon discovered, she had a flair for sensing news and she knew so many people.

For Taube, working for Bill was like manna from heaven. She felt that she owed him a great debt, but she quickly realised she enjoyed the world of journalism and they soon established a close professional relationship. It wasn't long before he told her about the girl he had met in Salzburg and showed her his cuttings. Taube knew immediately that Bill had fallen heavily in love with the anonymous saviour, but she recognised that Bill was totally unaware of how transparent his feelings were.

A week later, she came up with a tip that some students from

Munich University were planning to demonstrate against the
sacking and deportation of their professor. She gave Bill the
details. 'It's being organised by a group of Catholic students
calling themselves Edelweiss, but they're hoping for support
from non-members, too. By the way, they're backed by the
Cardinal of Munich.' She wondered why she felt sad when Bill
rushed out of the apartment to make his travel arrangements.

Chapter  5

WHEN HE GOT TO MUNICH, Bill found a restaurant in Ludwig-strasse, chose a table next to the window and placed his camera and bag under it. He sat and watched the wind buffeting the trees in the gardens opposite. The branches were almost bare and the last leaves were blowing in every direction. After he'd eaten breakfast and lingered over a second bowl of coffee, Bill asked the waiter to look after his gear for a while.

He located the ousted Professor's graceful old house in the Schwabing area, opposite Moses' fountain. A heavy furniture van was parked in the street, its contents being unloaded under the supervision of a pot-bellied workman. A Brownshirt and his family were moving in. White with anger, Bill took a few photographs, pretending he was interested in the fountain.

By 10 a.m. he was back at the restaurant, sipping at another cup of coffee when he heard a car draw up with screeching brakes on the other side of the square. Through the trees he saw a girl step out. Opening the boot, she removed a tin of paint and a brush. The driver, a dark-haired girl, crashed the gears and for a few seconds the ancient convertible moved forward in noisy lurches. Bill switched his gaze to the girl with the paint and caught a glimpse of her face under her hair, blown awry by the wind. With a jolt of intense excitement, he stood up and, grabbing his camera, signalled to the waiter that he'd be back. Could it be her?

As he started across the square, she moved to the wall and with hurried strokes began painting a slogan. Bill crossed the square swiftly, adjusting his camera. By the time he reached the wall she had finished her task and he read: *Release Professor Cohen – racism offends justice.* His flashgun exploded and the girl jumped, spilling paint on her shoes.

'You again!'

He had found the girl in blue. Above her cornflower blue eyes her perfectly arched eyebrows met ominously as she frowned at him. 'Why are you here? How dare you follow me around?' She was visibly shaking – with anger or fear, he wondered?

'Don't you remember me? Bill Roth. I met you in Salzberg,' he said.

'Unfortunately I remember all too well. You photographed me when I specifically denied you permission. We don't want the press here. Go away.' She glared at him.

'You have nothing to fear from me. But I don't think you should be doing this. It's too dangerous. You've got to get out of here.' He grabbed the tin of paint and the two wrestled with it. 'Damn,' he said, as the paint sloshed over the pavement. 'If you want to fight the trolls, go underground. You're sitting ducks ... all of you.' He shut his mouth firmly. He'd said enough ... more than enough. Holding on to her arm, he pushed her towards the restaurant.

She seemed more amused than angry. 'Look here, Sir Galahad. Go and find someone else to rescue. I'm busy.' She pulled her arm free and fled.

Well, at least he'd got her away from the painted wall. Bill walked back, paid his bill and collected his gear. Slinging his camera over his shoulder, he hurried towards the library where he found a crowd rapidly gathering.

*

Marietta found her friend Andrea on the library steps. Breath-lessly, she explained about the American journalist and the photographs he had taken.

'National headlines could prove embarrassing, or even fatal,' Andrea muttered. 'We'd be hand-picked for martyrdom.'

Marietta felt scared, which made her angry. 'If we don't like the risks we shouldn't be doing this,' she said. 'In a way he's offering us a loudspeaker to the world. We can't expect to be both good and safe. It's one or the other, isn't it? I mean ... it always has been.' She began to regret her words.

Andrea looked as if she'd been slapped in the face. 'All hail to Joan of Arc,' she retorted. Marietta flinched. She loved Andrea who was her closest friend. The truth was, she loved everyone in the Edelweiss movement and she didn't want them to be harmed. Now suddenly here was Bill Roth offering them a worldwide audience and a passport to a Gestapo cell.

On the other side of the square, Bill saw Marietta climb up between the statues of Greek Gods, and lean over the balcony. Her clear voice rang out with surprising strength.

'Citizens of Munich,' she called. 'Professor Cohen was a good man, and a profound thinker. We knew him as a wonderful teacher, but he's been sacked and deported with his family, simply because of his religion ...'

Her words were tough and determined, but she looked shy and disarmingly beautiful. The hecklers could not leave her alone. She flushed bright beetroot at each vulgar remark, but carried on determinedly while the wind played with her hair.

'Professor Cohen is only one of thousands who disappear from our cities every year ... thousands of human tragedies ... Is this what we want here? In our heart of hearts don't we all feel deeply ashamed? Don't we long to call out – *no more.*'

In the distance Bill saw more troops approaching. The Brown-shirts were closing in. Some men in the crowd rushed to help the girls, but they were attacked by the baton-wielding stormtroop-ers. A group of students fled up the steps of the library, white-faced and shocked. A boy fell under a vicious blow from a baton, blood spurting from a cut on his face.

'Look at them now ... we've got to stand up to these thugs, and stand together, or else we are lost ...,' she yelled, as armed police raced towards her.

Hands were pulling at her ankles as she hung on to the statue of Sophocles. She kicked them off and retreated higher, clinging to the philosopher's head.

Bill tried to push his way up the steps. 'Run,' he yelled. 'Get back into the library and run for your life.' Then something struck the back of her head and she fell limply to the ground. Bill watched helplessly as two men half-dragged her towards the cars, her legs trailing on the cobbles.

Bill tried to fight his way towards the car, but he felt a stunning blow on his ear and another on his neck. The Brownshirts were stamping his camera into the cobbles. Bill was fighting mad, but he was badly outnumbered. A third blow sent his world spinning off into darkness. His last conscious thought was regret. He still didn't know her name.

It seemed like only a split second later when Bill came to. He hung on to a lamppost to drag himself upright. The crowd was rapidly dispersing and no one came to his assistance. His camera was a mangled wreck and Bill kicked it into the gutter in disgust. He made his way slowly back to the restaurant, feeling dazed and disorientated. The waiter fetched him black coffee, and ice for the bump on his head, all the while urging him to leave as soon as he could.

Bill felt in his pocket for the first reel of film he had taken. It seemed undamaged. Thanking the waiter for his help and tipping him generously, Bill made his way to the offices of the local newspaper, and there persuaded an acquaintance to allow him to use their facilities. Two hours and three beers later his report was filed and the photographs developed.

He had also developed a massive headache and he gratefully accepted the local man's offer of a bed for the night.

He woke early and after several reviving cups of strong coffee made his way to the central police station. It was Bill's first introduction to the Gestapo at close quarters and he had to admit it was an intimidating experience. The building reminded him of a spider's web. Once you had blundered in, you were trapped. He presented his credentials to the first guard, who was stationed inside the front entrance, and asked to speak to whoever was in charge. He was ushered into a lift which took him into the bowels of the earth. At the fourth basement level he was told to alight and was led into a large room. There a Gestapo official took down his details and he was instructed to wait. It didn't take genius to see that he was stuck.

After a tension-filled hour during which inhuman whimpers echoed from the floors below, he was shown into an office and told to sit down. An SS captain walked in and Bill disliked him on sight; the man's unblinking gaze sent a thrill of repugnance through him. He was tall and and gave off an aura of immense strength. His eyes were large and of a strange, light amber colour, set wide apart under heavy lids. His hair was dark brown and plastered close to his skull, his eyebrows were thick and nearly met over the bridge of his wide nose, his skin was olive brown and oily. Everything about him was larger than life. His powerful appearance, plus his black Gestapo uniform, was intimidating.

'I am Captain von Hesse, Mr Roth. I understand you have come about the subversive students we arrested. Which one are you concerned about?'

Bill hesitated, but only for a instant. 'No one in particular, I just want to check the facts ... I've got a good story here: brutal beatings ... innocent girls being knocked out and dragged away into detention ... explicit pictures ... Pretty girls, too – bound to make headlines overseas. And the story's been filed,' he added, as the Captain picked up the file.

'They're not innocent,' the Captain said. 'What exactly is the point of this meeting?'

'As I said I need to check the facts,' Bill said. 'If those students were released today, I'd have to advise my editor to kill the story and he prefers his staff to file substantiated news.' Bill shrugged. 'After all, I know how hard you're trying to present a different kind of image to the public overseas.'

'Very smooth,' von Hesse said. He smiled and folded his hands. 'Well, you'd better call your editor, Roth, because the students are about to be released.'

'I'll advise him to put the story on hold, just in case.'

'As you wish. Now let us discuss you, Mr Roth.' The Captain's eyes narrowed. 'Why are you working as a journalist when you are a major shareholder in a company that manufactures arms in the United States?'

'That's none of your business.'

'It might be. Some of us feel that masquerading as a journalist is a clever way of infiltrating our munitions factories and spying for your country,' von Hesse said with a smile which didn't touch his eyes. 'By the way, are you Jewish?'

'What the hell has that got to do with you? What I am is an American citizen and an accredited journalist.'

'So you say,' von Hesse said smoothly. 'And a perfect cover for investigating German manufacturing.'

Bill could feel the menace of the man, his skin was pricking and the hair was rising on the nape of his neck. 'Don't try to intimidate me, Captain. You'll find I'm a tough nut to crack, and one who has the backing of the American Embassy and Reuters. If those students aren't released I'll raise such a stink this whole damn place will need fumigating.' He stood up. 'I guess I'll be getting along,' he said.

The Captain shrugged. 'I will overlook your threats this time, but don't try to blackmail the Third Reich again. It would be – er – uncomfortable for you.' He stood, then added with a leer, 'By the way, which of the girls are you sweet on, Roth?'

Bill ignored him. He was led by the corporal through a series of passages to the lift at the end of the building. As they ascended, Bill was unable to suppress a deep shudder.

A floor below the office Bill had just left, Marietta sat on a plain wooden chair in front of a desk facing a barrage of lights, behind which sat the interrogators.

'Who gave you permission to use the University printing

department?' There was silence. Then, 'Who gave you the key?'

'I won't answer your questions. You're wasting your time.'

The blow was swift and savage. It landed on her bruised shoulder. The pain made her feel sick. She flinched as she waited for the next blow to fall. This time the baton cracked across her neck. She stifled a cry as she fell forward. Oh God help me. What if they break my neck? They wouldn't care if they did.

'Someone must have helped you to do the typesetting.'

The rubber truncheon smashed on her fingers which had been gripping the side of her chair. She gasped and nursed her hand. 'It's better for you if you talk. All the others have,' her interrogator persisted in a smooth, high-pitched voice. 'You won't be telling us anything we don't already know.'

'Then why bother to ask?' she retorted, in a small tired voice. She leaned back and closed her eyes and momentarily drifted into unconsciousness. A bucket of ice-cold water brought her to her senses. She looked up and glared at the man bending over her. 'Are you ready, or do you want another soaking?' He was a young man with staring green eyes and blond hair greased to his skull – the archetypal Nazi.

At that moment an SS guard walked into the room and stared at her curiously before whispering urgently to the blond man. Her tormentor gave her a regretful glance and left the room.

Marietta sighed with relief at this temporary respite. She leaned back and closed her eyes. Her entire body was a mass of pain. Was it just bruises, she wondered, or did she have a few broken bones? Despite her discomfort she had the feeling that she could hold out for ever. She knew why, too. It was because she despised them so much.

Chapter  6

SHE DIDN'T KNOW HOW LONG she'd been slumped in the chair when the door opened. Her guards leaped to their feet and gave the Nazi salute as Captain Hugo von Hesse walked in. When he bent over her, Marietta half-rose from her chair with the shock of recognition. 'Good God! Is it . . .? Hugo! I can't believe my eyes,' she gasped.

He gazed at her gravely, his lips pursed. Then he switched off the large desklights. Marietta blinked, unable to see for a while. 'Bring some water,' Hugo ordered.

As the implication of her step–brother's SS uniform sank in, she began to feel nauseous. 'Hugo,' she muttered. She was disgusted by the sight of him clad in the insignias and swastikas and all the paraphernalia that the Nazi officers wore to make themselves feel élitist and powerful.

'How did you know I was here?' she said fiercely, after a long silence. 'Are you in charge of beating up students? Is this your job?'

'No,' he sighed. 'Thankfully not, but I am in charge of security. They called me when they learned who you were. You look a sight, Marietta,' Hugo went on. He frowned, gestured at the guards and the room emptied. When they were alone, Hugo perched on the edge of the desk. 'Have you any idea what the time is?' he asked her.

'I guess around midday.'

He smiled. 'Nine a.m. Not a bad guess. Sometimes people imagine that it's days later.'

'Don't try to be pleasant, it won't help. I have no intention of answering any questions.'

'Really? Well, I don't have any questions for you.'

She scowled at him. 'Aren't you ashamed of yourself supporting this regime when Father brought you up to believe in goodness and human decency?'

'Lessons I hope I learned well.'

'I doubt that. What happened to your law career, Hugo? Did you qualify?'

'Yes, I qualified, but none of you took the trouble to find out, did you? When Father threw me out of the family, the Nazis took me in, so nowadays I advise them on legal matters ... amongst other things,' he muttered.

'It seems you've devoted your life to a creed which is wicked beyond ...' While words failed her, her eyes were glinting with fury.

'You know very little about it,' he said, and to Marietta's surprise he was not annoyed, merely impatient with her. 'As a student, you should open your mind.'

Why am I so surprised to see him here in this terrible place? she wondered sadly, her anger slowly fading. In a way it makes perfect sense. Wasn't Hugo always full of anger and bitterness? Everyone knows the Nazis attract all the sadists and thugs in the Fatherland. To think that he's my stepbrother! How shameful! It will destroy Father. Hugo is ... was ... one of us, raised under the same roof, and now he's a Nazi thug. What will Louis and Ingrid say when I tell them? If I ever get out of here.

'You don't look well, Marietta,' Hugo said. 'Would you like some water?'

She nodded.

He handed her a full glass which she drained. 'Marietta,

listen to me carefully. I seem to recall that you once collected a special prize for Sokol's Landrace sows. You went to the show because Grandmother was ill. Remember?'

She stared at him in bewilderment. 'Of course,' she said, 'Why on earth—'

'Tell me about those pigs.'

She replied hesitantly, unsure of where the conversation was leading. 'They're specially bred in order to get far more bacon from them. Better quality bacon, too.' She smiled tightly, determined to humour him. 'Now for your next silly question.'

'This superior strain was developed by selective breeding?' Hugo persisted, ignoring her remark.

'Why not?' Now she could see which way he was headed. Not very subtle, she thought.

'I have never been able to understand why scientific breeding is extensively used by man to improve his livestock and even his vegetables, yet man allows his own species to degenerate. He keeps the sick and the infirm alive with expert medical care and even allows them to propagate. In fact, the poor, the stupid, and the inferior have the most children. Tragic, don't you agree?'

'No,' she said.

'You think it's clever to breed more inferior beings than intelligent ones?'

'People are not pigs. You can't treat them like animals.'

'Why not?' he went on without waiting for her answer. 'We believe that Homo Sapiens can be bred into a race of godlike men with superior intellect and physique ... Aryans! That's what Nazism is all about.'

'And the rest?' she asked quietly.

Hugo scowled at her. 'They will be put to work in the factories, the foundries, the mines and the fields.'

'Worked to death, you mean.'

He shrugged. 'You send your runts to market.'

Marietta struggled to control her rising fury. White-faced and stiff with rage, she dug her nails into the arms of her chair. 'It's no good trying to convert me to your cause,' she spat. 'I abhor all you stand for. I should feel sorry for you, Hugo. Your talent and energy are wasted. I thought you were a Catholic.'

'I am.' Watching his step-sister's eyes, so zealous and compelling, and her voice ringing out clear as a church bell and twice as self-righteous, Hugo felt his own fury rising. Who the hell was she to judge him? And why was she always so sure of herself? How dare she have the courage to oppose him.

'The New Order is here to stay. It's going to wipe our enemies off the face of the earth. And that will include the Habsburgs.' A note of triumph echoed in his final sentence.

'And I shall oppose you all the way,' she promised, tight-lipped and furious.

'We'll see.'

He sat down behind the desk and toyed with a pen, making an effort to regain his equanimity. Why couldn't he stop caring what she thought of him? The great irony of his life was that however much he hated Marietta and the family, he longed for them to acknowledge him.

He knew he was wasting time. 'Like most people, you are not capable of grasping the greatness of the Führer's vision. He is five hundred years ahead of his time.'

'How dare you be so arrogant,' she shouted, close to losing control. 'You've forgotten what civilisation is all about. It's not about better bacon, or taller people, it's about the progress of ethics and morality. It's a system to safeguard people not destroy them.' Flushed and furious, she gasped for breath. Hugo was scribbling in his notepad. 'Forgive me if I have recorded some of your thoughts a little sketchily. You spoke so fast. But it's a fair record of your beliefs.'

'I'm not afraid of you,' she hissed. 'I shall do my utmost to resist you and your kind at every opportunity.'

'Harsh words, Marietta. Some might call them treason. I won't insist that you sign this statement, since I'm sure you haven't the courage.'

'Oh, but I have. Oh yes, I have!' She reached forward, grabbed Hugo's pen and signed the sheet with a flourish and without reading it.

'To hell with you, Hugo,' she said, flinging his pen down. 'Now are you going to keep me here, or are you going to let me go?'

'Soon,' he muttered. 'I've decided to be lenient; after all, we're family. You'll be home before supper.'

Hugo watched Marietta being led back to her cell, before returning to his office. Arrogant as ever he thought, like Father, and now it was only a matter of time before the Count contacted him. He was looking forward to hearing him beg. For seven years he had waited for the opportunity to repay the humiliation he had endured at their last meeting.

As a child he had been aware of how unfair his stepfather had always been to him. He'd never been appreciated, the harder he tried the more he was put down. He'd been thirteen years old when he found out why this was. Their Scottish nanny had smacked him for shaking spoiled little Marietta. 'When I'm the Count, I'll fire you,' he had told her, rubbing his hand.

The girl had laughed. 'Louis will be the next count, not you.' She had sniffed derisively. 'You don't have an ounce of blue-blood in you. You don't even bear the Count's name. How could you ever sack me?'

Later he had cornered Father in the library and learned the truth. Louis *was* the heir. He, Hugo, was a penniless interloper, a mere stepson, although he'd always thought of the Count as his real father. At the time his stepfather had looked concerned and promised him that he was setting up a special fund for him, but it had all come to nothing. He had been thrown out of the family, and all because of blabber-mouth Ingrid. She was part of the score he had to settle.

He shook his head. The Count would live to regret his cruelty . . . time was on his side.

His adjutant came in and saluted. 'Heil Hitler! The Austrian Minister of Foreign Affairs is on the line, Captain von Hesse.'

Hugo shivered with pleasure. He knew exactly how to manipulate the conversation. He would be invited back into the bosom of the family, with its castles and uniformed flunkies and a style of living which he had missed bitterly. Life was like fencing, he thought. To win his game he must stay within striking distance, and now Marietta had conveniently played into his hands.

'Father,' he began simply. It's good to hear your voice ...' When he replaced the receiver five minutes later, he knew that he had won the first round. It would be a long fight and the stakes were high, but Hugo intended to destroy the powerful von Burgheim family and take all that they owned.

Marietta was asleep on a hard cell bed. Despite her exhaustion, the moment the cell door clanged open she sat up in alarm. Then she gasped. Her body seemed to have set into a rigid mass of pain.

'Get up. You're wanted. Come quickly,' the wardress barked.

She could hardly bear to stand, every muscle screamed in protest as she moved. She staggered along the corridor, clutching on to the walls for support, and was pushed into the lift. They were going up ... and up.

Moments later she was handed her watch, her purse, her shoes and belt and thrust out of the main door. Dazed and grateful, she stood on top of the stairs looking round. Surely fresh air had never smelt so sweet. The air of freedom! She breathed in great gulps of it. Then she heard a shout and saw Bill Roth standing on the pavement, looking up at her.

'Oh hello!' she said shyly holding the railing as she limped down the steps feeling dizzy and sick. 'Have you been interrogated, too?'

Bill caught hold of her and examined her. 'I guess you're not too badly hurt,' he said, his voice husky. 'I was so afraid.' Suddenly she was in his arms.

She pulled herself together quickly and stepped back. 'How many were arrested?' she asked. 'Who's still inside? Do you know?'

'I think you're the first one out.' Bill said. 'Some creep called von Hesse told me you were all going to be released today.'

'Oh ...' she said, flushing with shame. 'Thank heavens!' She would die rather than admit that 'the creep' was her step-brother.

'Are you really all right?' The way he looked at her made her feel warm and wanted.

'What about you?' She touched his swollen jaw.

'Don't worry about me. It's nothing. Boxing was my sport once.' He touched her cheek. 'I'm glad you're safe. You were so brave. I'll never forget the sight of you clinging to Sophocles and yelling at the Nazis. Are you going to carry on with your Edelweiss group?'

'Of course! We can't stop now, but maybe we'll lie low for a while.' She tried to look braver than she felt.

He took her hand and held it between his. 'Can I see you again? How about telling me your name?'

'Marietta von Burgheim, and yes.' She laughed shakily.

'You're in the arts faculty, I assume,' he said.

'Agriculture,' she said. She broke off as she saw Andrea hobbling down the steps.

'Oh my God! Andrea!' Marietta tried to run towards her friend, but failed and winced with pain. Bill swore as he noticed her friend's swollen black eye and helped her down the steps and into Marietta's arms.

The students were all emerging, one after the other, looking dazed and bewildered. All had been beaten, but none too badly. Moments later they were hugging each other and swopping experiences. Marietta could see they were in a mild state of shock, as she was, and very grateful to be free. When she next looked for Bill she found he had gone.

That night the Edelweiss students were wild and emotional as they made light of their beatings, told the same stories over and over, and showed off their bruises. Everyone had been badly frightened. Marietta tried to feel happy, but failed. Guilt and shame kept her eyes smarting and her hands trembling. She was free, but only because of Hugo ... that hurt far more than her bruises.

Chapter

7

THE FOLLOWING AFTERNOON, the Edelweiss students met in Marietta's apartment to decide whether or not to continue in the face of the Gestapo's brutality. Marietta sat on the rug by the fire listening to the arguments, hoping that most of the students would remain together, for they had built up a wonderful bond. Lately, they numbered twenty-four ... a good sized group. They were having fun, too, and they used words like 'Fascist swine', 'Nazi pigs', 'the Trolls', and 'the blonds', and they joked about the danger of cocking a snoot at the authorities. Her flat had become known as a haven of free speech and thought, and a favourite meeting place for liberal students and lecturers. The position was ideal, for hardly anyone noticed strollers slipping in from the park. Sometimes they stayed for hours, working on speeches, plans for demonstrations, or simply laying out the pages of their newspaper. The place was beginning to take on character, Marietta thought, looking around as the debate went on and on. There were books by Leon Feuchtwanger, Jakob Wassermann, H.G. Wells, Zola and Proust, all of which were banned. Marietta had added paintings and photographs of the wild life and scenery of her beloved Bohemia. Andrea had added a bust of Mozart and an engraving

41

of Mendelssohn. Thanks to their housekeeper, Frau Tross, the furniture glowed with attention and the air smelled of polish.

Finally the students ceased their discussions and held a ballot to decide whether or not to continue. There was a one hundred per cent vote in favour of carrying on. However fond she was of them all, Marietta was glad when the meeting ended and people drifted off to their own homes. Her body still ached from her beating and she desperately needed time to herself.

It was nine the next evening when Louis walked through the park entrance, enjoying the moonlight shining through the bare branches of the trees. As he approached the stone steps leading to Marietta's flat, he heard someone playing the piano quite beautifully. For a moment his hand remained poised over the door knocker. It was Granados' *Goyescas* and he was caught up in the emotional interpretation. He lingered for a while before creeping in.

The sitting-room was in shadows except for the glow from the lamplight at the garden gate. A dark-haired girl was sitting in front of a piano, her thick curly hair falling over her shoulders and obscuring her features. Her hands were beautiful as she ran her fingers over the keys, as if unsure of what she would play next. She strummed a bar from one piece and then another, quite unaware of Louis' presence.

Then the moon rose swiftly over the trees. It was lustrous and huge and its light illuminated her face. As the pianist broke into *Clair de Lune*, Louis gazed longingly at her. She was very young and very lovely.

She caught sight of him and gasped.

'Sorry! Don't stop. I'm Marietta's brother. I'm invited to dinner, but I'm late. I don't want to interrupt you. Please . . .'

'Oh.' She smiled uncertainly and Louis was beguiled by her eyes. They were large, deep-set and brown, and they were glowing. She was quite lovely, he decided, but not obviously so. He had the feeling that he alone had discovered her beauty and that other men would miss it entirely.

She played on, and Louis listened quietly. He had the strangest feeling as if his soul flowed out and merged with hers and intertwined with the moonlight and the music.

Eventually she stopped and sat in silence gazing at the keys. He knew that she felt the same way as he did, for they both sat on, sharing the night, unwilling to break the spell.

Suddenly the door opened and slammed shut, light flooded the passage and Marietta rushed towards them.

'My God, you're sitting in the dark. What's the matter with you two? Andrea, this is Louis, my brother. Louis, this is Andrea, my friend and lodger, but anyway I see you've already met. Good! I'm so sorry I'm late. Just look at this bag of cones I've collected. Enough for the evening.' Her face was pink and glowing, her eyes sparkling as she threw some cones on to the fire. They hissed and spat and flames roared up the chimney. 'Don't tell me, Father sent you. It doesn't matter. The point is, you're here.' She flung her arms around her brother and hugged him tightly. 'It was wonderful in the park. I've been feeding the ducks. What's for supper? I'm starving.'

As the girls rushed around laying the table and coaxing Frau Tross into warming up dinner, Louis sat quietly by the fire, the music still alive in his head. Strangely without appetite, he sipped the warmed-up soup, and picked at his food.

Andrea's eyes glowed mockingly, laughingly and moodily in turn as they discussed their day. Louis listened to their chatter and felt increasingly depressed. Not only were the girls continuing with their group, but they were producing another newspaper.

'I promised Father to look after you, Marietta,' he interrupted, looking intently at her. 'Please give up these politics. Concentrate on your studies.'

'You call it politics. I call it humanity. I'm sorry, but I have no intention of being turned into a coward by these thugs,' she snapped.

Listening to them both, Louis couldn't help admiring them, despite his fears. They were passionately dedicated to their ideals. He had never felt that strongly about anything.

Andrea changed the subject abruptly, wanting to know what Louis studied.

'Piano. A long-standing ambition of mine,' Louis explained, 'but first Father made me graduate at a military academy.'

'That can't be true.' Andrea looked sceptical. 'I haven't seen you in the music faculty. He's teasing me, isn't he, Marietta? So tell me then, what's your favourite piece?'

'*Clair de Lune*,' he told her, trying to look romantic.

Andrea burst out laughing.

'Oh, but that's not true,' Marietta said, smiling at him. 'You prefer jazz to the classics. You told me so, often.'

'Absolutely untrue,' Louis protested.

'Oh, yes, you did. How can you change like the wind? That's Louis for you,' she said shaking her head.

'Last week was another era,' Louis said. 'Whatever happened before tonight is utterly insignificant.' Watching them, Marietta felt amused. She had never seen Louis try to flirt before. He wasn't too good at it, she observed and went off to study, leaving them together.

'Play something,' Andrea said. 'Anything to convince me. I still think you're teasing.'

Louis moved over to the piano and sat down. He badly wanted to impress Andrea but he felt nervous. He began a tune from Cole Porter's musical, *Anything Goes*. He hit the wrong keys a couple of times and looking up, saw her agonized expression. When he felt more confident, he switched to jazz. He began 'Honky Tonk Train'. All at once Andrea was next to him.

'Move up, let me play. That's my favourite,' she said, eyes shining with excitement. 'I'll improvise down this end.'

'D'you know this one?' he said a few minutes later. He strummed the opening bars of 'One O'Clock Jump'.

'Do I know that one?' Andrea laughed her low, thrilling laugh. They were at one with each other as they played their way through the jazz hits of Dixieland and New Orleans. They had no need to speak.

Andrea's forehead was damp. To Louis she had that look of

a woman who has just made love. Louis, suddenly serious, reached over and stared intently at her. 'You're not engaged or anything like that, are you?'

Andrea did not reply. Instead her dark, expressive eyes gazed at him with trust and affection and a hint of sensuousness. There was pleasure in them, and happy anticipation. He felt he would be able to draw her face from memory: her smooth brow under a low hairline, her nose, which was a trifle too sharp, her full, expressive lips, the lovely line of her cheeks, her thick eyebrows over deep-set brown eyes. Strength and delicacy were mingled there. Passion and virtuousness. Louis knew that he had found himself a rare treasure.

Bill had learned to value Taube and to rely on her superb efficiency, so he was uneasy when she did not arrive on time the following morning. It was half-past ten when she walked in, looking pale and apprehensive. She took off her coat with the yellow star on the sleeve and sat at her desk. Then she burst into tears. Bill gently coaxed the story out of her ... a crowd of thugs had roughed her up, threatened her, told her she wasn't wanted and tormented her. The Brownshirts had stood by laughing. She was badly scared, but unhurt.

'Taube,' he said when she had dried her tears, 'take my advice, get out of Germany while you still can. I'll help you. You can work for my uncle for a while.'

Taube put her head in her hands. 'Oh Bill. I've tried so hard to get Father to leave. The trouble is, he's not at all Orthodox. He sees himself as a Berliner, not a Jew. Besides he belongs to the CV, that's shorthand for an unpronounceable cultural German–Jewish organisation which is supposed to support us, and they keep advising him to be calm and wait for things to get better.' Her voice was verging on hysteria.

Bill poured her a drink. 'Keep going,' he said. 'I want to hear everything.'

'It's not so easy to find a place to go to, Bill. If you're young and you have some skill or profession, then probably you'll find a country willing to give you refuge eventually, but for the old people there's nowhere to go. Unless you have money hidden overseas, but we don't. All Father's capital is bound up in his business. It's the best music shop in Berlin with a huge range of stock. But the Nazis take all you own as the price of their wretched exit permits.'

She bent her head and sat shaking for a few seconds. 'My brother has just paid the equivalent of twenty thousand dollars to get out. He'll arrive in New York with nothing but the clothes he's wearing and he'll be one of the lucky ones.'

'Why don't you follow your brother?' Bill asked gently.

'I cannot go without my family. To be honest, I've been doing the rounds of the Embassies, but so far I've drawn a blank. There's no point in badgering Father to leave, if there's nowhere to go. And there's worse to come if we have to stay. Early this year, Father was told that all Jewish-owned small businesses must be sold to Aryans. He had to list our assets: property, businesses, stock, cash in the bank, jewellery, paintings, everything. We are to be robbed of all we own. How shall we survive?'

She began to shake again. Bill put his arms around her. 'Don't give up, Taube,' he said. 'I'll contact the American Embassy. Let's see what the situation is. If you have a position to go to, maybe they'll take a different attitude.'

'Why don't you come home to supper on Friday? Just so you can meet the family. Father's so proud. You'll see for yourself how stubborn he is. He seems to have retreated into unreality. Perhaps he would listen to you.'

'I'm driving down to Munich on Friday, Taube. But next week would be fine.' He waited until she was calmer, then went into his office and called an old school friend who worked at the Embassy. 'It's not as easy as you might think, Bill,' Andy Johnson said. 'There are thousands of the poor bastards wanting to get out. We're swamped. We try to take those with the skills we need, particularly those young enough to work and to adapt ... or those who have family in the States ... There's all sorts of rules and regulations. You'd probably have to stand security for them.' He sighed. 'I'll make inquiries anyway.'

'Do that,' Bill said.

*

That night, the Edelweiss students gathered in the University printing department at midnight with a barrel of cheap white wine, to celebrate the printing of their manifesto. They congratulated each other solemnly. They were impressed with their layout and their professionalism, and feeling awed by the gravity of their own words when transposed to print. The newspaper had been put together and printed on campus after hours through the connivance of their English professor, who had written a leader exhorting students all over Germany to expose what was going on behind the Nazi scenes.

Marietta had written one of the articles and she was proud of it. The heady feeling of success was better than champagne. She walked home bubbling with joy and floating on air. If only that American reporter, Bill Roth were here to read her efforts. She'd been longing to see him again, but didn't know for sure if she ever would.

Two days later, the Nazis' reaction to the Edelweiss newspaper was swift and savage. The staff of the University printing department were brought in for interrogation. Some hours later, their professor appeared in the lecture hall, seemingly unaware of his black eye, cut lips and swollen face.

Chapter  8

BILL WALKED INTO THE BLOOMBERGS' SHOP at seven the following Thursday and found Taube's father still working, mending a clarinet. He was a tall, stooped, thin man, and Bill's first impression was that he was not in the best of health. His hair was grey, there were deep shadows under his red-rimmed eyes and his cheeks were hollowed. But when he smiled, his face lit up and he looked years younger. Bill reckoned he was around sixty, if that, and that he was consumed with tension.

The shop looked prosperous enough. It was stocked with every type of musical instrument, one wall was taken up with stacks containing musical scores, and behind the main shop was a small workroom for repairs.

'I do most of them myself,' Anton Bloomberg explained as he showed Bill around.

Bill then followed his host upstairs to the family's apartment. The living-room was large and comfortable with fresh flowers and a few good antiques, but what struck Bill most forcefully was the peaceful atmosphere. It seemed that the aggression of the New Order could never penetrate here.

Odette Bloomberg was remarkably pretty, with a delicacy and

femininity which was most appealing. Bill liked her on sight. She had curly blonde hair, soft blue eyes, bright red lips that smiled most of the time, and that indefinable Berlin chic. She wore a straight tunic-style dress of navy and white with starched white collars and cuffs and little embroidered flowers down the front. She looked fresh and sweet and years younger than she was. Taube's olive complexion came from her father, Bill saw, but the combination of their genes had produced a rare beauty.

Odette said, 'I'm glad to meet you, Mr Roth. Taube's been so happy since you gave her employment.'

'I guess I'm pretty satisfied, too,' Bill said.

Odette beamed with pleasure and began to question him about his home. Bill realised that she thought he was a suitor for her daughter. He wasn't quite sure how to put her straight.

While Taube and her mother made supper, Bloomberg played some old records he'd bought. 'I always despised East European music,' he said, looking apologetic, 'but now that I'm forced to discover my roots, I've found some real gems. Listen to this.' He played a haunting melody that sounded vaguely Slav. The two men liked each other. Before they were halfway through dinner they were on first name terms. Anton had three degrees in music and could speak six languages. He was also an incurable optimist and he loved his fellow man, particularly Germans. 'They're good people at heart,' he told Bill several times. 'They're being browbeaten by the Nazis, but this madness will pass. You'll see. Things will get better.' Bill respected his sentiments, but thought them a dangerous weakness.

Later, when he got home, Bill reflected on the evening. He had felt at home with the Bloombergs, perhaps because Anton reminded him of his uncle. At the same time, he was shocked by the degree of self-deception that was going on in the family. Why wouldn't Taube's parents face the facts? Because they dared not? Because there was nowhere to go? Or perhaps because they wanted to live normal lives for as long as they had left? It caused him nightmares, but he vowed to visit them again.

When he did a week later, he heard the sound of a scuffle round the corner from where he was parking his car. There were thuds, a hoarse scream, people shouting ... Bill raced from his car in time to see Anton being kicked into the gutter. 'Dirty Jew,' two thugs yelled. Bill dived into the ruckus, knocking one headlong and rounding on the other. The men fled and Bill pulled Anton to his feet.

'They wanted my wallet and they've got it,' Anton said, when he'd recovered his breath after being helped upstairs. 'Every thief and thug in Germany uses anti-semitism as an excuse for their crimes. That's all. It has nothing to do with hating Jews.'

'I'll call the police,' Bill insisted.

'You'd be wasting your time, Bill. Beating up Jews has been legalised by our so-called government. The police won't do a damned thing to stop it.'

'Listen, Anton,' he said, holding a handkerchief over a cut on the older man's forehead. 'You can't stay here. I've just decided that the Roth plant is going to expand into musical instruments. Eventually you can buy back the business from us out of your share of the profits as and when you like. You'll need to advise us on our new operations in the US, so visas won't be a problem.' Bill tried to sound businesslike.

Odette's face crumpled and she burst into tears. 'Oh ... Bill ...' she sobbed. 'You're saving our lives ...'

'Shame on you, Odette,' Anton said. He turned to Bill. 'I'm touched by your gesture, Bill, but I'm not yet desperate enough to take charity. This madness cannot last for much longer.'

'Please Father,' Taube burst out forcibly. 'Listen to Bill. Listen to me. You must say yes ... for all our sakes.'

'It's not philanthropy,' Bill argued. 'America needs people like you.'

'You don't know what you're saying, young man. You don't understand that we're getting to the age when things break down. We'll soon be too old to work. Already Odette has a weak heart, and I have high blood pressure. A new shop might take ten years to pay for itself.'

'Be reasonable ... ,' Taube begged.

'This is the sort of thing we discuss in private, Taube. The subject is closed.'

Taube was furious with her father and the following morning, she determined to force him to face reality. 'Father, you must come to terms with the truth. Our situation is pitiful here. We must leave.'

The family were sitting at the table. Since the delicatessen owner had been arrested, their traditional breakfast of chopped herring and hard boiled eggs had been replaced by toast and coffee.

'I'd be robbed if I tried to sell the shop now. You know that.' He stared at her reproachfully over the rim of his cup.

'But you are forced to sell. We've been notified. Had you forgotten?'

Anton went pale. He stood up, knocking over his chair and walked out of the room.

The two women stared at each other for a few minutes. 'Lately, he's putting things out of his mind,' Odette said sadly. 'He can't cope with this hell, so he simply ignores it.'

'We were talking about leaving Germany,' Taube said fiercely, then realised her mother was in tears. She crouched beside her. 'Don't cry, Mother,' she said. 'We must accept Bill's offer and we must accept it very quickly.'

'It would kill Anton to live on charity. He's never borrowed, never depended on bank loans, everything in the shop is paid for, it always has been. This young man doesn't deserve to be saddled with us. We hardly know him. It would be different if he and you ... well, you know ... But still ...' she dabbed her eyes. 'We have no other choice.'

'Chile,' Taube muttered. 'I know we stand a chance there. I'm seeing the consul soon. Mother, listen!' Taube put her arms around her mother and rocked her backwards and forwards. 'You must speak to Father. He must agree to Bill's offer. It is charity, I agree, but Bill is very rich and he doesn't mind.'

'They're not arresting ordinary people,' Odette said looking childlike. 'Just the misfits, those with criminal records and antisocial tendencies, particularly the Communists.'

'Stop lying to yourself, Mother.' Taube shouted. 'Don't be like Father. You must face up to reality. You must make Father face up to it, too. Promise you'll try.'

'All right, I'll do my best.'

Chapter  9

MUNICH HAD STILL TO FEEL the winter. The air was pleasantly warm on Friday afternoon when Marietta emerged from classes at two-thirty, to find Bill standing under a tree. She saw him, before he saw her. His brooding blue eyes were solemn, almost sad and he looked tired, as if he hadn't slept. His hair was growing into tight curls and she guessed that was why he usually kept it cut so short. His face spelled out strength and stability, but there was a sensuousness about him. Then he saw her and his eyes lit up while his lips curled into a soft smile. It was an intimate smile, as if they had shared secrets. He ambled towards her and put one arm around her shoulders. Stooping, he planted a kiss on her cheek.

Her heart seemed to leap into her mouth and something stirred in the pit of her stomach. Warmth was shining out of his eyes as clearly as a beacon on a dark night. He was holding a silly bunch of drooping flowers in his hands. He held them up, but their heads fell over like drunks after an orgy.

'They seemed okay when . . .'

'They need water . . .'

They had both spoken at once. Now they smiled at each other. 'There's so much useful information you can send via a smile,' she thought. 'So much simpler than talking.'

'Well ... Hi ...' Bill said. 'Hope you don't mind me waylaying you unexpectedly. One of the girls arrested with you told me I'd find you here if I tried hard enough. It's a lovely day for a walk,' he said. 'Are you free?' He put his arm around her waist and she shyly pushed hers around his and there they were, side by side, their steps in perfect unison as they set off to explore the old town, the cobbles echoing underfoot.

They window-shopped and lingered a long time over coffee and cakes in a quaint old restaurant they discovered. It was dusk when they reached the park. They sat on a bench by the edge of the lake and watched the mist drifting across the water and talked about the books they had read, and the music they liked as they searched for common territory. When she shivered, Bill wrapped his arm around her and hugged her close against him. The touch of his thigh against hers and the warmth of his body was spellbinding. He was so strong and he smelled deliciously of tweed and wool and soap and something else, masculine and inviting. She couldn't help noticing his long suntanned fingers with thick dark hairs along his knuckles and wrists, and the curly black hairs on his chest where the collar of his shirt lay open.

When the cold forced them to leave the park, they found a nearby restaurant where the waiter persuaded them to order the restaurant's speciality, *Wotan Lustbissen*, which, he said, was slices of beef fillet cooked with mushrooms, ham, sweet peppers and served with a tangy cream sauce and rice. He brought them Bavarian beer and lit the candles. When the waiter had left, Bill reached across the table and took her hand in his. As they gazed into each other's eyes it seemed to Marietta that all her lifeforce was flooding into him.

'Funny isn't it ... ?' she said awkwardly.

'This feeling that we belong?'

'Yes, I suppose that's what I meant. Us being so close ... I mean, like this, yet we are strangers.'

He laughed. 'No, we're not. I know all I need to know about you.'

'You don't even know where I live,' she laughed.

'You're beautiful, resourceful, wise, hard-working, brave, compassionate . . . I can go on all night. Anything else would be inconsequential.'

'You make it sound so easy.'

'What?'

'Getting to know someone. Do you always judge by first appearances?'

'Yes. Don't you?'

She hesitated. 'I don't really know. I haven't had much practice. You see, this is the first time . . . well, to be more precise, this is the first time I've dined out without a chaperone.'

'Honestly?' Bill laughed aloud. 'Then we're going to celebrate.' He called the waiter. Ignoring her pleading he ordered champagne.

'Well, I don't have the same advantages as you,' she teased as she sipped her champagne. 'I only know that you're good at tracking down girls you want to date. You're a flirt,' she said, feeling strangely light-headed. 'I suppose you think that all this flattery will impress me.' She pressed her lips together and shook her head. Suddenly she hiccupped and flushed with embarrassment.

They both laughed. 'I also know that you can't hold your liquor and that I can't take you anywhere,' he added.

'Shh! You don't know any of those things. Not true. You're trying to make me drunk, so that I forget to ask about you. I want to know about your life. I want to catch up on everything I've missed. I want to know you.'

Suddenly she realised that she was being too serious. She flushed even deeper and pulled her hand away.

'Don't. Please don't,' he said, snatching it back. 'It belongs here. Can't you feel it's made to fit?' He pressed it tightly between his two palms.

She gasped slightly, a soft 'oh' which told him that she felt as he did.

'You're the most sensual girl I've ever seen.'

'Oh, but now you're really being foolish. Why, I haven't even been kissed. Not ever.'

'Tonight's the night for all these "firsts",' he said. 'I'll call the waiter again.'

She giggled. 'Not him. Have you seen his moustache? His wife must hate it.'

'Aha, so you noticed and you thought about kissing the waiter. I'm hurt. And you're very red. Caught out, huh? I am getting to know you rather well. Don't you think so?' At that moment the waiter arrived and leaned over the table. 'Is everything all right, Sir?'

She looked up at his handlebar moustache and bit her lip to hold back her laughter.

'There is one thing,' Bill said, staring hard at her. 'The lady here would like . . . a glass of water.'

'Ouch!' he said. 'You pinched me. That hurt.'

'Serves you right. Now we are going to be serious. You have teased me too much. Why do you speak German so fluently?' She asked the question out of the blue to try to move them back to serious topics. 'Where is your home? Tell me about your brothers and sisters.'

He sighed. 'I suppose I might as well get it over with.' For a few moments he toyed with his food, looking grave and frowning slightly. 'My family manufacture armaments. I used to hate that. In fact, I hounded my family about it. They said I was a rebel, but I think I just felt guilty. Uncle sent me to a German school so I'd be useful in the marketing team.'

She laughed. 'And now you're a journalist.'

'It's a temporary reprieve,' he said shortly.

Marietta felt jolted by the similarity of their situations. It's as if I've known you forever, she thought, gazing dreamily into his eyes, but we were separated by some accident of birth, and here we are together again.

She squeezed his hand with both of hers, feeling daring and wicked as she savoured little thrills of pleasure from his touch.

'Please, carry on . . .'

'It's a long, boring story.'

'No, not for me.'

So she learned of his childhood in France. How his father had run away from the tedious life of American industry to become a painter and married a Parisian interior decorator. They had both been killed in a car crash when he was seven and shortly afterwards his uncle had flown over to take him home to Baltimore. He tried to explain the fear of being left alone, how the police had taken him to the orphanage, and then his relief at finding relatives he never knew he had. He'd never told anyone this before and he was surprised how much it affected him and how he wanted to convey the precise and factual feelings he had experienced. He paused, remembering ... Uncle Henry had looked so much like his father, it had been easy to confuse the one with the other and eventually they had merged in his mind. He'd been a father to Bill in every sense of the word and Bill loved him. Aunt Lorna had been as good as any mother, and he'd do anything for her. Then there was Irwin, his cousin, and the two of them were as close as brothers could be, except that they were complete opposites. Irwin would never settle down to run Roths. He hated the plant.

He tried to paint the picture vividly, so that she could she could see their factories, and their home and the ranch in the mountains, which was Aunt Lorna's passion, and his horse, whom he missed so much.

'I guess it all worked out okay,' he said gruffly much later. 'They're great people.'

He broke off as the waiter brought them two laden plates of Black Forest gateaux, sprinkled with Kirsch and served with a bitter cherry compote and whipped cream.

'I won't be able to stand up,' Bill groaned.

Then he told her what he was trying to do with his life now. Bill was a serious young man with a firm awareness of family responsibilities. He had come to Europe to prove he could make it on his own, without the help of his wealthy family, and he'd begun to make his name as a foreign correspondent, but his future was with the plant. He felt he was not an inspired writer, but he had an instinct for finding the truth and he was painstaking and concise, with a flair for research. He'd been self-supporting for some time, but lately he'd begun to understand exactly what the Nazis intended to do with the people and the countries in Europe and this had frightened him, so now his self-imposed mission was to warn the West. He worked all hours, interviewing by day, writing most evenings, filing stories by the score, never letting up.

Around eleven, he grinned and squeezed her hand. 'So there you have it . . . my life story. One of these days I have to go home and run the plants. Meantime I have a few years of freedom.'

Like me, she thought, but said nothing, and Bill, who had noticed that she was strangely reticent about her home, decided not to press her.

They took a cab back because Bill had left his car at the University. He asked the driver to wait while he said goodbye. It had turned cold and the wind was strengthening. He folded her in his jacket and they stood close together in the doorway, obsessed with the nearness of each other, hands clasped, legs touching. She felt his hands pressing against her back, pulling her hard against him. Suddenly his lips were on hers. Desire surged through her blood and tenderness fled as she succumbed to passion. Her fingers gripped the back of his neck as she pressed her lips hard against his.

'Hey wait a minute,' he said, drawing back. 'Lesson time. Open your mouth, just a little, like this, make your lips soft, relax.' When his tongue touched her lips she almost passed out with the force of longing surging through her. 'Oh, oh,' she gasped. 'So this is kissing. What have I been missing? Oh Bill.'

'Not bad for a beginner,' he said, holding her back. 'I said you were the most sensual girl I'd ever seen. It's stronger, because it's underground. All this hidden passion waiting for Mr Right. You're really something special, Marietta. Oh heck, what a mouthful. Can't I call you Marie?'

'Yes, you can,' she whispered. 'If you kiss me again.'

'No. Not this time. I'm not a eunuch.' Bill ran his fingers through her hair. 'You're a lovely girl,' he said. 'I want to see much more of you. How about if I drive down overnight Fridays and spend some weekends in Munich? Would you be free some of the time?'

She nodded, too breathless to speak.

After Bill had gone, Marietta went inside in a daze, filled with strange longings and needs.

She was disappointed to find Andrea asleep. She had so much wanted to talk about her evening. She slept restlessly and dreamed of Bill, waking repeatedly, murmuring his name, her body hot with longing. She felt dizzy with happiness. Bill cared for her. He was coming most weekends, he'd said. The future stretched forward invitingly. There was only one flaw in her happiness and that was the knowledge that she and Bill could never be together in the long-term. One day they would both have to return to their individual responsibilities. But right now, four years seemed like forever.

Chapter  10

MIDNIGHT IN THE KURFURSTENDAMM. The moon rose and hung like a golden orb above the roofs, newly-washed by an evening shower. Around the buildings the shadows lay like dark pools of unknown and treacherous depths.

Hugo was leaning against a wall in the deepest shadow. His uniform, his gloves, boots, hat and eyes were black. Only his olive skin showed dimly and the whites of his eyes glittered as he gazed around. The night enfolded him in its gentle bosom and caressed him.

He breathed in deeply, then glanced left and right. He badly wanted a cigarette. The seconds passed slowly. A cat picked its way delicately along the top of the wall and rubbed itself against him. He stroked it absent-mindedly while studying his watch.

Twelve-thirty. As if on cue, he heard the rasp of heavy locks. On the other side of the street, doors swung open. Hugo stepped forward and gave the signal, a brief flash of his torch. A block away from Fasanenstrasse, he heard engines starting up. Two half-tracks and three lorries emerged, concealing a squad of storm-troopers. Across the road, in the synagogue, a rabbi from South Africa had supposedly been lecturing on Maimonides. Hugo knew that the real purpose of his visit was to hand out South African visas to over a hundred skilled workers who were under

thirty-five, together with their families. The door of the synagogue opened a cautious crack. Twelve men slipped out and
passed quickly along the pavement, keeping to the shadows.

Good. They were staying together, so it would be easier to
round them up. The Jews were out of sight, but shortly
afterwards he saw his lieutenant's torch flash and heard the
engine of the first lorry move off into the night. So far so good.

Hugo called the next squad. His troops moved into position,
but too fast and too soon. One of the Jews called a warning and,
as if pre-planned, they scattered in every direction. There were
shouts, gun shots and a howl of anguish. Every man was yelling
and struggling as they were forced into the waiting lorries. The
women's shrill screams echoed in the night and mingled with
gunshots. Hugo could smell blood and sweat mingled with the
jasmine. He strolled towards the synagogue. There was blood on
the sidewalks. Those damned Jews should have gone quietly. It
was the rabbi's fault. He had given them hope; something to
fight for. Foolish of them to try to escape. The Third Reich
needed their labour and their skills. Their accumulated wealth,
their businesses and all their possessions would help to fill the
coffers of the Nazi Party.

When Hugo returned to headquarters there was a message for
him to see SS Security Chief, Reinhardt Heydrich. It was
almost midnight, but Hugo knew he might have to wait until
dawn, because Heydrich often worked all night. Hugo could not
stifle the painful twinges of unease that ripped through his
stomach periodically. He knew that was foolish. Heydrich had
always helped him, even on their first fateful meeting. When
was it? July, 1932, Hugo remembered, for he had recently
gained his first degree. His results were outstanding, but his
triumph was soured because he could not gain a position as a
legal clerk. After tramping the streets of Munich for a month,
Hugo went to the Party's headquarters. Eventually, Hugo found
himself face-to-face with Reinhardt Heydrich, chief of Reich
Security, a momentous meeting for him.

Within days, Hugo was working for the Nazi party's firm of

lawyers. Since then his rise through the ranks had been
meteoric.

But it had all begun much earlier. To be precise on New
Year's Day, 1932. How cold and hungry he had been as he lay
awake in the early hours of the morning. His stiff and swollen
member had brought back memories of Ingrid and for a few
minutes he'd allowed himself the excitement of remembering
how she had been. Thinking of the von Burgheims living in
luxury, gorging themselves nightly in their ornate dining-room
at Plechy Palace, made him feel murderous. It was fourteen
months since Father had turned him out, but he was just as
bitter as on the day he had left. His paltry income from the
count went nowhere in Munich, so he was alternately starving
or working himself to exhaustion at any odd job he could find,
while studying at University all day.

Hugo had washed and shaved in ice-cold water. He looked
around in disgust at the small room he rented in a dilapidated
boarding house in Pfister Street. Gazing at himself in the
cracked sliver of mirror, he noticed how thin he had become,
but starvation had merely accentuated his strong features.

He sauntered out into the street, wondering where to go,
what to do and how to get a meal, or even a crust of bread. At
the corner, he was caught up in a crowd pushing their way
towards the stadium, and for the first time he heard the voice
of Adolf Hitler. Hugo stood around and listened only because
he had nothing better to do. He was drawn to the man. Here was
masterly oration; here was genius. More to the point, here were
words he wanted to hear.

'We want to make a fresh beginning based on truths,' the man
screamed. 'The first truth is this: our future lies only in our own
strength and our courage.'

As Hitler spoke, he punched the air, bunched his fists,
writhed and shook with passion, his intensity affecting everyone
in the crowd. There was nothing imposing about his face or his
physique, but Hugo sensed the fanatical power that flowed out
of this shabby-looking man.

'We are the Master Race. All other races must be subservient to us ... and we have sworn to destroy all that is decadent in our society.'

Hugo stood there entranced for more than an hour. He knew instinctively that he was listening to a man who would lead Germany to a great destiny.

'... the concept of nationality is meaningless. Race transcends national boundaries. *We shall unite the German folk, scattered and abandoned throughout Europe. United, we shall conquer the world.*'

Hugo walked home in a daze, Hitler's words whirling in his head. Now he knew what he had always suspected, his stepfather, Count Frederick, had sinned by marrying a Czech, princess or not. Marietta had tainted blood and was not a fit custodian for all that wealth. Only true Aryans should control such vast resources. Hugo realised that his future was in his own hands. Hitler's New Order would give him the power to take what he wanted. The thought was like a revelation. His skin tingled, and he felt his blood surging with triumph.

Feeling heady with power, Hugo went back to his room and began to jot down his own ideas on a series of laws which could ensure that Germany's resources remained in the hands of true Germans. He wrote day and night; when he delivered it to headquarters, he joined the Party.

A week later Hugo was called to the Nazis' headquarters to meet the local bosses. They had a legal problem, but Hugo soon found a solution. Before long, the Nazi Party were consulting Hugo regularly. He was their young lion: a genius at finding solutions to tricky problems, a tireless worker, and a fanatical Nazi. From then on, while Hitler plotted to seize absolute power, Hugo worked tirelessly, together with Himmler and Heydrich, planning how best to institute *Gleichschaltung*, the laws which would pave the way for securing the Nazi State and brainwashing all Germans, as soon as the Nazis gained control. He was involved in the creation of the Nuremberg Laws which, step-by-step, would deprive Slavs, Jews, Gypsies or anyone with one-sixth 'mixed' blood in their veins from official positions, from the professions, and eventually from any

participation in economic life. Then on January 13, 1933, their
Führer was proclaimed Chancellor of a coalition government of
Germany. The time had come to put all their plans into
practice.

That night Hugo was intoxicated with success. From his
window, he heard the jackboots vibrating on the cobblestones,
saw the torches held high in traditional German manner. As he
stood at the window watching the stormtroopers below, he knew
that a new world was dawning – a world where he would hold
all the aces.

He was still reliving those early days when a guard saluted and
led him to Heydrich's office. The room was austere, but the
furniture was antique. Hugo knew from which Jewish banker's
office it had been confiscated. There were two old Masters
hanging on the walls, a Bruegel and a Vermeer. If he remembered rightly, they had both come from the same bank.
Heydrich was wearing his black dress uniform, which set off his
pale skin and blond hair. He walked towards Hugo and patted
his shoulder.

'I have good news for you, von Hesse,' Heydrich said, as he
poured them both a brandy. 'Hermann Göring has suggested
that you are his choice for creating and enlarging *Reichswerke
Hermann Göring Corporation*.'

Hugo tried not to show his elation. This organisation
currently controlled Germany's steel production and industries.

'Göring wants to establish an empire that will eventually
bring all essential industries under State control. You must have
heard heard of this. What are your views?'

'Dangerous. Far too much imbalance of power ...' Hugo
broke off. Had he gone too far?

'My thoughts exactly. I knew you were the right person. You
and I are mutually concerned with the State's security. I can
relinquish you for this post, just as long as I can be sure of your
loyalty to me.'

'That goes without saying. You launched my career. My

allegiance will always be to you.'

'Good. I'll recommend you. Leave it to me. By the way,' Heydrich said, 'you've been promoted. From tonight you're a major in the SS. My congratulations.' He refilled Hugo's glass.

'There's one more matter, von Hesse. I've heard that you used your power to release the Edelweiss students, one of whom is your step-sister. The Führer feels that they are a subversive influence which must be eradicated. Countess Marietta is particularly dangerous.'

Hugo looked up and smiled softly. 'The Führer is hoping to annex Austria. Four of these students are Austrian. Imprisoning the daughter of the Minister of Foreign Affairs for giving a speech might cause unpleasant repercussions. We mustn't forget the Archbishop's influence either, or overseas publicity. I intend to arrest them on far more serious charges than public speaking . . . put them away for good . . . not yet, but soon.'

Heydrich nodded approvingly and the atmosphere became more relaxed as the two men discussed the gossip of the Nazi hierarchy.

It was nearly dawn when Hugo left Heydrich's office. Overnight, his personal horizons had become limitless. He had the chance to become one of the most powerful men in the Third Reich, as long as he kept on the right side of Heydrich.

Chapter  11

IT WAS THE FIRST FRIDAY in December and bitterly cold outside, but warm and cosy inside the girl's apartment. Marie watched Bill thawing out by the fire after his long drive from Berlin. 'Did you get your Learner's Licence?' he asked.

Bill had been teaching her to drive in country lanes for the past six weekends, but she had not bothered to get her licence and she knew this had annoyed him. 'Yes,' she said, smiling at his surprise. 'Yes . . . yes . . . yes . . . Happy now?'

He acknowledged her laughter with a chuckle. 'It's very quiet here,' he said.

'Frau Tross has gone home for the weekend, and Andrea is out with Louis,' Marietta said, in a rush. Then she flushed a deep scarlet. 'We'll have to get our own supper,' she stammered.

'We could go out . . .'

'Oh no! I'll just warm something up.'

Bill watched her curiously. For the past two months they'd spent most weekends with Andrea and Louis and they'd had fun together. They got on well. Louis and Andrea were obviously in love, and Bill guessed they might want to be alone sometimes, but this evening Marie's guilty expression made him suspect that she had engineered this evening together. Bill decided not to comment as Marie went into the kitchen.

Lighting the gas stove was frightening. The flame lit in the pipe and roared ominously. She jumped, switched it off and started again. Hearing her fumble around the kitchen, Bill wandered in and perched on the edge of the kitchen table. She felt self-conscious enough to believe that he was laughing at her. She glanced up accusingly, but his expression was neutral. She pushed back her hair and tried to look calm and collected.

'Sure you know what you're doing, Marie?' he asked as she placed mincemeat patties into buttered rolls and popped them into the hot fat in the frypan. 'I've never seen it done that way before,' he said, and smothered a laugh behind his hand.

Flushed and furious, Marietta turned and glowered at him. 'Please . . . go and open the wine . . . and you're in charge of the music,' she snapped.

Smoke rose from the gas stove. 'Oh, no,' she wailed. Then the fat spilled over the pan and caught alight.

'What was that supposed to be?' Bill asked as he doused the pan in the sink and put out the flames.

'Hamburgers. Frau Tross said I only had to fry them lightly.'

'I guess your mother spoiled you,' Bill said.

'Uh huh!' she said. She'd learned that useful, non-committal sound from Bill. 'There's plenty more food in the pantry,' Marietta muttered, trying to change the conversation, 'but I'm not sure what . . .'

'Scram, Marie! I'll prepare something. Just keep out of the kitchen or you'll burn the whole place down.'

Banished to the sitting-room, Marietta felt swathed in guilt. She had never thought of herself as incapable, yet now she felt as though she'd been exposed as a liar and a cheat. Absurd! Did it matter that she was a countess, an heiress, and never saw the inside of a kitchen from one year to the next?

By the time Bill arrived with a tray of ham sandwiches, pickles, salad and wine, she was feeling wretched.

'Bill, there's something I haven't told you.' She stared at him anxiously. 'My family is quite rich. I actually have a title. Archaic, isn't it?'

'Lady Marietta. Sounds pretty nice to me,' he said smiling. 'Is that what you are?'

'Actually I don't want to talk about it. At least, not yet. But I don't want you to feel that I'm deceiving you. You see, Bill, I'm very fond of you.'

'Is that all that's worrying you?' he said, bending over her, suddenly tender. 'Don't worry about it. I love you, Marie.'

'I love you, too, Bill,' she said wonderingly.

He put his arm around her. 'The strange part of it is, we have so much in common,' he pulled her closer to him and felt her gasp slightly.

They sat in silence, hunched in front of the fire.

Marietta sighed deeply, 'I got rid of everyone because I wanted to be ... I thought ... well, that we could have a romantic evening ... We never have the chance to be alone.'

'I'm all for romantic evenings.' He took her chin in his hand. Lifting her head, he smoothed his hand over her hair. His mouth pressed over hers and she felt his tongue on her lips. Then he moved back.

'Oh,' she sighed. 'Don't stop.' She reached out passionately and wound her arms around his neck, which felt taut and sinewy. His mouth was pressed on to hers again. His hand was moving, exploring, caressing. She leaned back on the hearth rug and Bill leaned over her, staring into her eyes; he moved closer and she closed her eyes, totally obsessed with the exquisite feelings that had taken control of her body.

Her desire to touch and be touched was almost unendurable. She felt his fingers at the buttons of her blouse, the back of his hand brushing her breast.

'Undress me,' she murmured.

Bill's hand stopped its fumbling and he drew his head away.

'You probably think I'm old-fashioned, but I think girls should be married before making love.'

She opened her eyes in surprise at his words. 'I want to feel you, feel your skin against mine, feel your—'

She stopped abruptly as he gently placed a finger on her lips.

'You are younger than I sometimes remember. You are lucky

I love you enough to be responsible,' he muttered hoarsely. He gently pushed her shoulders against the sofa, easing her clothes off her taut body with a delicacy he hadn't known he possessed. In moments his clothes had joined hers in an untidy heap and her skin felt like satin against his, her hair spilling through his fingers like silk.

Marietta yielded to unimaginable pleasure, part physical, part emotional, as if drifting in time and space, as Bill kissed and stroked her. She longed for more, much more of him. She closed her eyes and tried to imagine what it must be like. This act, which was shrouded in mystery, but for which she longed.

The autumn term was drawing to a close. Bill felt that he and Marie were about as close as two people could be without being married. He wanted her for his wife, but was hesitant about proposing. He was disappointed by her decision to return to Bohemia, to spend the Christmas holidays with her family, particularly since she had not invited him. Was she ashamed of him? He'd suggested they go skiing in Switzerland for a month, or even a week ... anything! Or tour Germany, or France, or any damn country she liked. Then he'd proposed a trip back to the States to meet his folks, but Marietta wanted to go home. She was homesick, she admitted. Besides, the family always spent Christmas in Bohemia.

'I'm longing to see Ingrid,' she said. 'Look, I had a letter from her today. She sent these photographs of herself at a ball. Isn't she lovely? And so sophisticated. I can't wait to see her.'

Bill tried not to sulk.

On their last evening together, Louis and Bill were invited to dine with the two girls at their apartment. After dinner, Louis produced two invitation cards, complete with the von Burgheim crest.

'It's Marietta's birthday in January, Bill,' he said.

Bill nodded. He'd already bought her a bracelet. Now that she could drive, he'd even found a suitable car which he intended to buy as soon as she gained her licence.

'Father and I have organised a house-party and a birthday

ball. We should like you both to come,' Louis said formally.

Bill looked at his invitation. The party was for three days. 'Is this correct?' he asked, astonished. 'A three-day party?'

'It's very remote. It will take you a day to get there,' Louis said.

'Sure I'll come. Thanks!'

Andrea looked less certain.

'There's a music room and a piano, so you can practise as much as you like,' Marietta said. 'Please come, Andrea. You can even bring your oboe. Greater love hath no friend.'

Andrea looked towards Louis, a frown hovering.

'Please come,' he said quietly.

'All right. I'll come. Thank you,' Andrea said.

Marietta smiled in delight, but it seemed to Bill that she was nervous about his acceptance.

'Don't you want me to meet your family? he asked, when they were saying goodnight on the doorstep.

'Of course I do,' she said. 'It's just that . . .'

'Come on. Tell me what's bothering you.'

'When you see how wealthy I am, you'll think I'm just a spoiled socialite. You won't want to know me anymore.'

He laughed. 'Silly goose,' he said. 'You're worrying about nothing. I'm honoured to be invited. I was dreading the weeks without you. Knowing I shall see you in January will get me through Christmas.'

He tried to dispel her anxiety with a passionate kiss, but she remained stiff and tense and remote. Bill went home wondering what had got into her.

Chapter  12

ANDREA WAS WAITING at the bus station as arranged. It was 10 a.m., but there was no sign of Louis, so she walked over to a kiosk and bought herself a cup of coffee and a newspaper.

She heard Louis' voice calling before she'd more than glanced at the headlines. 'Andrea. I'm sorry I'm late.' He hugged her. 'You look marvellous,' he said, examining her red skirt and black jersey under her duffle coat. 'New?'

She nodded and flushed.

'I'm so glad you're here. I hate family gatherings, specially our family, but this time it will be different. I missed you. Did you miss me?'

'Oh, yes . . .' She grinned happily as Louis picked up her case. Arms around each other's waists, they sauntered across the road.

When Andrea saw the car, she gasped. It was a brand new, white Bugatti touring car. A chauffeur, dressed in a bottle green and gold livery, limped forward to open the door.

'This is Jan, our chauffeur,' Louis said awkwardly. 'Jan is driving my car back. I should perhaps explain that Father is a bit old-fashioned. Rather pompous, in fact, maybe because he's the Austrian Minister of Foreign Affairs.' Louis tried to ignore Andrea's shocked expression and plunged on desperately. 'We

don't let our hair down in front of him, because his subsequent
long-winded lecture simply isn't worth enduring. The right way
to address him, just so you know ...' he said over-casually, 'is
Count Frederick, not Count von Burgheim. Well, that's that.'
He let out a low whistle and started the engine. The Bugatti
surged forward.

'So one day you'll be a count?' Andrea queried.

'Actually, I already am,' Louis mumbled. 'Like it?' he asked
her, patting the dashboard after a long silence.

'I'm impressed. Whose car is it?'

'Marietta's ... a birthday present from Father. I took delivery
this morning. That's why I was late, they kept me waiting.
Father's so excited about it.'

Andrea was quiet for a few miles. The reality of Louis' family
was hard to absorb. Then she felt Louis' hand on hers.

'You'll meet my cousin, Princess Ingrid. Please don't let her
intimidate you,' he said awkwardly, trying to ease her obvious
anxiety. 'She'll try, I promise you that. She's beautiful and witty
and great fun to be with ... bitchy, too, and rather superficial
to my way of thinking. She'll try to impress you with her title,
but don't take any notice. She's just Ingrid, whatever she says.'

'I feel intimidated already and I haven't met her yet.'

'I'm going to tell you a secret,' Louis said, coming to a quick
decision. 'Please don't let on that you know, but just so you
understand the family a little better.' He smiled, put his arm
around her shoulder and recited, 'Once upon a time there were
two beautiful Hungarian princesses ... Marianna and Beatrice
Szapary. They both had blonde hair like moonlight and blue
eyes like the sea, and the palest of pale skins—'

Andrea giggled. 'Oh, come on Louis. This is too much ...'

'No, bear with me. Hear the story as I used to hear it, when I was
a child, *ad nauseum*. Both princesses grew up and married. One
chose Prince Gustav Lobkowitz, whose estates and castle were in
Bohemia, now a part of Czechoslovakia. That's where we're going
now, by the way. Her sister married a Russian prince.

'Well,' Louis said, 'here comes the sad part. The Russian
princess had a lovely daughter who became Ingrid's mother, but

both she and her husband were shot by the Bolsheviks. That's becoming a habit with the Habsburgs, by the way. Ingrid was rescued by the family housekeeper who pretended the toddler was her granddaughter. She put Ingrid in a local orphanage and it took Father years to find her and get her out of Russia.'

'That's a sad story,' Andrea said.

'Sadder than you may think. I'll never forget the first time I saw Ingrid ...'

He broke off, the scene as vivid in his mind's eye as if it were yesterday ...

The von Burgheims had been waiting at the station in Vienna in a straight, self-conscious row, out of step with modern times. Louis knew this, and so did the passing travellers, for while the platforms were crowded, there was a conspicuous pool of space around them.

At last the train clattered into the station. His stepmother turned to their new Czech chauffeur. 'Go and find the princess, Jan.' As Jan limped off, the Countess von Burgheim shrugged impatiently. 'Every lost dog knows where to find a home,' she said scathingly, loud enough for Jan to hear.

'My dear, he drives perfectly well,' her husband said, 'his affliction harms no one, but himself.'

Louis squirmed with embarrassment for Jan. He disliked his stepmother and he felt Jan's humiliation.

Jan limped down the platform, peering into every carriage, then retraced his steps, searching more slowly. Eventually the whole family joined in the search. Louis was the first to recognise Ingrid, perhaps because he had no perception of what a Habsburg princess should look like. She was huddled in the corner of a carriage, wearing a dress three sizes too big for her and a threadbare coat that was too small. Covered in sores, head shaved, eyes scared and lost, she looked like a street urchin.

He read the label tied around her neck: *My name is Ingrid Graetz. I speak Russian. I am unaccompanied and travelling to Plechy Palace, Vienna.*

She had the largest blue eyes Louis had ever seen, like ice crystals. Her face was pale under the grime, except for a bright red spot on each cheek, she looked bruised and wary. He tried to take hold of her hand, but she pulled away and lashed out, kicking his shins hard, her face contorting into an ugly mask as she backed into a corner.

Despite her kicks, Louis swung her on to his shoulders; she weighed no more than a sack of coal. A moment later he was bitterly sorry for his actions as she had wet her pants. The smell of urine was nauseating.

'She's peed all over me,' Louis said in disgust, as he tried to hand her to his stepmother. Unintelligible shrieks almost drowned his words.

'Oh, my God,' the Countess whispered. She clapped a perfumed handkerchief over her mouth and stepped away.

Father lifted Ingrid down. He took off his coat and wrapped it around her. 'My, my, she's frozen,' he said. He rubbed her hands in his. 'This poor child has suffered dreadfully. I blame myself. It took too long to find her. Now her troubles are over, for we shall take care of her.'

Louis felt shocked by this glimpse of a world beyond his own home and family. His romantic concept of the Bolshevik revolution was shattered by its reality.

'Why are you shivering?' Andrea demanded.

Louis brought his thoughts back to the present and smiled sadly. 'I was just remembering . . .'

'Tell me everything about your family. I feel I hardly know you.'

'We're part of the Habsburg monarchy, which was dissolved eighteen years ago. Many of us retained our property, but we don't always fit into today's national pigeon-holes, although we should. Our roots are German, so we're German by culture; our home was Vienna, so we're Austrian by nationality; our property is all over the place and we'll probably lose most of it before this century is out . . .'

Once Louis began on the family history there was no

stopping him. Andrea soon began to wish she hadn't asked.

The needle of the speedometer crept higher, but the black Mercedes held the road magnificently despite patches of black ice. The driver looked like a man in a trance. Head thrown back, he was obsessed with the joy of speed and the thrill of handling this powerful machine. They might have been one – one throbbing, surging, glittering beast, tuned to perfection.

Like the car, its driver, Major Hugo von Hesse, was handsome and strong, a purely German creation. He was magnificent in his black uniform: his peaked hat piped with white denoting the SS, the aluminium cords showing his officer status. On his tunic he wore the coveted gold sports badge, showing that he was both a shooting and fencing champion.

He sneered at the passing Czechoslovakian countryside, the tatty jumble of chickens and goats running wild, pigs gleaning acorns, land lying fallow and unused. Well, that would soon change. Hugo had the precise production output of the area in his mind. It could be doubled. As for labour, there were tens of thousands of teenagers lounging in youth clubs and sports grounds. In time they would all work the factories and industries of the Third Reich. This fertile land was crying out for colonialisation. Rounding the next bend Hugo drew up and lit a cigarette. The sight of Sokol Castle brought back the past with a surge of emotion. He was blundering back into the family's fairy story, created ten centuries before, with its castles and uniformed flunkies and a style of living which he missed bitterly. Hugo's throat constricted with envy. Life was like fencing, he thought. To win his game he must get the measure of his opponent, and stay within striking distance. His SS rank, his Nazi-backing, his intelligence would combine to destroy the powerful von Burgheims.

It had been raining, but soon the sun broke through the clouds and the river banks glistened in the bright winter sunlight. Bill and Marietta could smell the fragrant damp earth and wet grass. Marie took off her glove and Bill felt her hand sneak into his.

They drove in silence, happy to be together.

Bill could not help thinking about the past three days as he drove towards the Upper Vltava valley. The time had flown. He and Marie had avoided the crowds and explored the lakes and mountains of Bohemia, skiing, riding, and walking by day and sleeping in the family's hunting lodge high in the mountains. They had become even closer and he was sorry that the holiday was almost over, for they for they were on their way to Marie's home for her birthday ball.

Fifteen miles south of Prague, Marietta indicated that he should turn off to a narrow track which wound steeply downhill. As Bill rounded a sharp bend, he saw a castle of such grace and beauty, yet of such massive dimensions, that he stopped the car and stared silently. 'Wow! Look at that!' Bill gazed at the battlements and ramparts and the flag flying high on a steeple. 'It's magic,' he murmured.

'Hurry, there's another car behind us,' Marietta said tersely. He glanced at her curiously. Surely this couldn't be . . .? They crossed an old bridge spanning the river, drove under a granite archway into a cobbled courtyard within the castle walls. As soon as Bill stepped out, a uniformed servant slipped into the driving seat and drove the car away.

Bill felt bemused. The castle was as big as a village, but it seemed, from Marietta's breathless explanations, that it was only one of their many homes. As an engineer, he was amazed that those early artisans could reach this degree of symmetry and aesthetic grace, working in such massive dimensions. Altogether, Bill reckoned the soaring turrets and square ramparts covered close on two acres. As an economist, he marvelled at the cost of transporting all that granite, those exquisitely-dressed slabs and the intricate stained glass. In front of them stood millions of dollars of baroque art, massed together to create the structure which Marietta casually referred to as 'our Czech home'.

Marie was eager to show him round. He followed her through courtyards and passages and dusty halls to more courtyards and more passages; past stuffed heads of long-dead animals, glassy-eyed and accusing; stained glass windows set with semi-precious stones; carvings, statues, portraits and still more portraits.

He began to feel claustrophobic and the smell of damp decay depressed him. Bill had always thought his own background to be stifling, with his family's stern adherence to social and business obligations. Marie's was a hundred times worse. He trudged behind her, pondering on the irony of their situation.

They had so much in common, both of them were struggling against their predestined family roles. And what the hell was Marie babbling on about? He just *must* see inside the summer pavilion.

'Princess Grimalda, my great aunt. She was fourth in line to the Hungarian throne,' Marie said, stopping in front of an ornately framed portrait and sounding like a museum guide.

Bill gazed into two ferocious eyes set into rolls of fat on a porcine neck choked with jewels. 'Grimalda! That figures! The family resemblance is uncanny.'

She giggled.

'Marie, give it a break, they're dust now. I have a longing to breathe fresh air. I'm suffocating. Oh heck! Don't be mad at me.'

'I'll show you to your room,' she said tritely. 'I presume history wasn't your favourite subject.'

'You're damned right.' Then realised that to her history was part of her life.

Chapter  13

HUGO LOOKED AROUND at the leather armchairs, the shelves of rare books, the Count's desk littered with papers, the air redolent of expensive tobacco. Nothing has changed, he thought. It's all exactly the same as the last time I stood here. But on that occasion I was shaking. I was being flung out of the family by that sanctimonious old pig I'd always thought of as my father. Well, he mused with deep satisfaction, the tables were now turned. He was no longer the immature boy who had been so easily dismissed at their last meeting. This time, the Count would be shaking.

Despite his bravado, Hugo had a sudden vivid image of himself as a boy. What a pathetic figure he must have looked; he flushed with shame and, reaching forward, grabbed a cigar just as the Count walked into the room.

'Ah! Hugo. Help yourself, my boy. Help yourself.'

Hugo flushed and gritted his teeth.

'But not a boy now, rather a man. Welcome home, Hugo. I'm glad to see you haven't forgotten your family. Thank you for your influence in freeing Marietta and her friends. Of course, they're only children playing at politics, but it could have been misinterpreted.'

The Count turned and patted Hugo on the shoulder ... a

gesture which Hugo had once prized.

'So what would you like to drink, Hugo?'

'Brandy,' he said.

I prefer him as I remember him, Hugo thought: arrogant, harsh and very straight. The old boy's behaviour is as false as hell. He's scared, Hugo realised with a jolt. He watched the Count pour two glasses of vintage brandy, hatred suddenly coursing through his veins, as he recalled the way he'd been abandoned to poverty in Munich.

He sniffed his cigar and struggled to regain his poise by concentrating on the Count's appearance. He looked older, Hugo thought. His eyes were ringed with dark shadows. His skin was pale, his eyebrows thick, black and bushy. His features were all larger than life, but seemed to blend together. The overall effect was of a studious giant. Yet he was neither as large, nor as intimidating as Hugo remembered him.

From the Count's patronising, but friendly manner, Hugo guessed that he intended to follow the ritual of the return of the prodigal son.

'I've been following your career, Hugo. My congratulations. I'll be honest and admit that I would have preferred you to choose another route to high places, but . . .'

'But without capital,' Hugo grimly interrupted, 'or any influence behind me, there was no other route I could take. When you threw me out, Father, another family took me in, which was just as well, since I nearly starved to death.'

'Well . . .' The Count seemed at a loss for words.

A lowly pittance was all he'd received from his stepfather. The first instalment had been flung across this very desk at him, with the words, 'One hundred marks a month is all you'll get out of me, and only until you finish your education. If you ever try to come within a mile of Ingrid, I'll have you horsewhipped and the money will stop. Is that clear?'

Without wanting to, Hugo now relived that embarrassing scene. The Count had used every cliché of a betrayed Victorian patriarch, his voice trembling with emotion.

'You have despoiled my niece,' he'd stormed. 'You are a

blackguard and a monster. You will leave my house today and you will never darken this family's doors again.'

'Nothing happened between us. I swear it, Father,' Hugo had whined. 'Ingrid called me in the night because she'd had one of her nightmares.' Even as he had spoken he heard how unconvincing his denials were, and at the memory he felt himself flushing again.

His story had made the Count even angrier. He had lunged over his desk, his mouth moving, but no words forming, as he grabbed Hugo's lapels, shaking him like a terrier with a rat. 'Blackguard,' he had roared.

With an effort Hugo blocked out the memory and brought his attention back to the present. He sipped at his brandy, aware that he now held the reins of power. The thought made him smile.

'I was surprised to hear that you wanted to see me,' the Count began. 'Very surprised.' He gave his curious, lop-sided smile which to Hugo's mind, always made him look like a blood-hound. 'You mentioned that you want to talk about money. So let us discuss your inheritance,' he said softly.

Hugo laughed aloud, and took his time relighting his cigar. 'Actually, I came to warn you. You know as well as I do, that the Führer has sworn to destroy the Habsburgs, so I've decided to put our past differences behind me and do everything I can to protect your holdings,' he paused. 'In the meantime, I must warn you that some of your Bavarian estates are about to be to be expropriated. The State requires the land for a new airfield and an aircraft manufacturing base. Of course you will be compensated.'

'At a fraction of the real value, I have no doubt.' The Count stood up and began pacing in front of his desk.

'Furthermore,' Hugo went on, enjoying the Count's fury. 'Your light aluminium factories and ball-bearing plants outside Munich are also to be bought by the State. We are at the start of a new era, Father. We shall soon see the transition from the old private enterprise system to a Nazi-controlled economic empire. I am in charge of expropriating these strategic industries. Businessmen, such as yourself, are considered unfit to control vital resources. The State's military machine can never be at the mercy of private enterprise.'

The Count seemed to physically crumple and Hugo's lips curled in amusement. He spread some papers on the desk, indicating that his father should examine them.

'I shouldn't be showing you these, but it will give you a chance to gather your resources. One of my staff from Minister Göring's *Reichswerke Corporation* will be contacting you soon. He will want to know which of your holdings are in the hands of foreign shareholders. Naturally he will have more difficulty in expropriating those. You have about three weeks' grace, Father.'

Glancing through the papers, it did not take the Count long to discover that the terms were most unfavourable.

'What if I refuse to sell?'

'It is not in your power to refuse,' Hugo said softly. 'Any industrialists who prove themselves enemies of the State will be severely penalised. They could lose their freedom, quite apart from the financial penalties.'

'I'm in your debt for the second time this month, Hugo. But tell me, why are you helping me?'

'We're family, Father. And let us say I have a promise to fulfil.' He stood up, saluted and walked slowly towards the door.

Several years ago he had paused in the same doorway, pocketing the hundred marks. Enraged and humiliated he had vowed: 'I'll pay you back, Father. As for my "inheritance" – I will own this castle. I will own everything. I'll stand in this room and see your family destroyed.'

'The ravings of a rabid dog,' the Count had said.

'Rabid dogs have a deadly bite,' Hugo whispered now, but the Count turned away, looking baffled and very disturbed.

Chapter  14

INGRID WAS AWARE that her looks electrified every man at the party and that in her ice-blue pleated voile suit and matching hat she was the most fashionable woman present. After only one term at her Parisian finishing school, she was quite transformed. Her make-up, her hair, her grooming, her deportment and her clothes were perfect. Her French had always been exceptional, but lately she had acquired a Parisian accent. She knew how to conduct herself at any social function, and now she flitted from group to group, enjoying the compliments which she felt she deserved, while her eyes searched the guests anxiously. She knew everyone. They were all close friends or relatives, but there was no one here she could set her cap at. Disappointment flooded through her. Ingrid knew that her face was her fortune and she had spent hours preparing herself, hoping that some of Marietta's eligible Habsburgs would turn up.

Disappointment made her feel quite limp and it was an effort to keep her bright smile in place. To the world at large she was Princess Ingrid Mignon von Graetz, but to the family she was just cousin Ingrid, poor little thing, a disinherited princess brought up in the lap of luxury, but with nothing to call her own. Daily, her penniless plight churned her stomach.

She looked back towards Marietta's American journalist. He was handsome in a homely sort of way. But a *journalist*. Ah well,

Marietta could afford to indulge herself with poor beaux, Ingrid thought with a sudden, fierce shaft of jealousy, while she could not. Eventually her fortune would enable her cousin to marry anyone, no matter how old she was. She, on the other hand, would probably have to settle for someone much older, and she'd have to hurry. It was wealth she needed, not love.

She felt a hand on her arm and glanced round with a happy smile. Then all her sophistication fled. 'Hugo,' she gasped. 'But why ... how can you be here ... ? Go away, go away.'

She turned as if to flee, but Hugo caught hold of her wrist and pulled her back to face him. 'It's all right. I'm invited. Yes, I am. Father has welcomed me back into the bosom of the family.' He laughed unpleasantly, but Ingrid hardly noticed. She was shivering all over. The memory of the fascination of his extraordinary maleness and his power flooded through her. It was almost as if she were hypnotised, just like before. Hugo looked taller and even stronger. His eyes were deeper set and more amber than she remembered. The impact of his masculinity and his wilfulness recalled a dozen memories and she felt her cheeks and eyes burning.

I'm not the young, impressionable teenager he seduced, she told herself fiercely. Then she shuddered. She doubted if any other man would thrill her as Hugo once had. It was his subtle, underlying cruelty that brought her skin out in goosepimples. He must never find out how he still affects me, she thought. She drew back abruptly. The past must stay dead and buried.

She searched for something scathing to say, but before she could think he said, 'I must congratulate you for growing into the most beautiful woman imaginable, for being so gracious and so poised ...'

He's overdoing the compliments and he sounds so damned gauche, she thought.

'What are you doing here?' she whispered. 'I wouldn't like uncle to see us together.' She gestured at his uniform and said, 'So you're a Nazi. I might have known. But how could you wear your uniform here? Good God. You know how uncle feels about the New Order.'

'My dear Ingrid, the Nazis are the powerhouse of the future, and I'm climbing to the top. I told you I'd win, didn't I? You should have believed me. Dance with me,' he said peremptorily, 'I want to be close to you.'

'No, Hugo. The past is behind us. Let it stay buried.'

Hugo appeared not to hear her and unbelievably Ingrid found herself moving slowly around the room in Hugo's arms.

'For old times' sake, I'll tell you a secret,' he whispered. 'The richest man in this room is Bill Roth. Marietta thinks he's just a journalist.'

'Isn't he?' she whispered back, knowing her cheeks were scarlet again.

'Yes, but he's also joint-heir to one of the biggest arms manufacturing corporations in the States. It seems he's afraid of his wealth and wants to make his own way.'

The music stopped. 'Good hunting,' Hugo said mockingly, then bowed and turned away. Moments later Ingrid was engrossed in her plan of attack. Marietta didn't need another fortune. She already had more than enough.

Leaning back against the mahogany seat, her hair streaming in the breeze, enjoying the gentle sway of the steamer, and sipping the wonderful sparkling wine from Sokol's vineyards, Andrea wished the day would last forever. She glanced lovingly at Louis, who was briefly greeting his relatives. He seemed to feel her glance, for he turned and smiled and beckoned her, but she shook her head.

Andrea turned as she felt someone sit down beside her and found herself gazing into the sad eyes of the Count. She had only met him briefly when they arrived and she'd liked him on sight. She smiled warmly at him.

'How are you enjoying yourself?' he began awkwardly.

'I'm in a daze. I seem to have wandered into a fairy story.' Andrea smiled again, hoping to see him smile back. 'All this . . .' She waved her hand vaguely in the direction of the castle. 'The strangest thing of all is that Louis and Marietta never hinted at their wealth. They are modest, kind, caring, down-to-earth people . . . both of them. And I love them both dearly . . .'

She broke off, struck by the serious and troubled look that had crept into the Count's eyes. 'I mean . . . ,' she stammered, embarrassed by her frankness.

'I know what you mean, my dear,' he said. 'I see it in your face. Unfortunately, all these privileges also demand great dedication. Take Marietta. A lifetime of selfless devotion to her family lies ahead of her. She asked my permission to be free for four years, but when she gains her degree she must return to take up her responsibilities.'

The Count was looked intently at her and Andrea felt a twinge of unease. What was he trying to convey to her?

'Of course, her grandmother was a stickler for tradition,' the Count went on. 'She used to keep a file of suitable young men . . . royalty most of them . . . absurd, I thought, but the truth is, there are only twenty men eligible to marry Marietta. One day she must make a fitting marriage and devote herself to looking after her inheritance. For this she'll need a partner with the same background and training. The same goes for Louis. He, too, faces a lifetime of service to his country, either in the government, or the army, plus the strict protocol that goes with it. He's a bit of a rebel, but everyone is at his age. Later, he'll take his rank and fortune more seriously and choose a wife brought up to this type of discipline.'

Watching her turn pale, the Count stood up. 'Good heavens, I'm monopolising you, and stopping you from dancing. Can I fetch you a drink, my dear?'

The Count looked wretched, she thought, through the tears which were flooding her eyes. She bent her head, excused herself and rushed to the toilet where she blew her nose vigorously several times. She felt sick. The Count had gone out of his way to warn her that Louis could never marry her.

'Oh God. How can I bear it? Louis, I love you,' she whispered. Louis would never be able to marry someone like herself. The Habsburgs married other Habsburgs, or royalty, or anyone but the likes of her. She shivered again. 'Oh Louis . .' she whispered in anguish.

A feeling of humiliation began to well up inside her. She could not keep up a pretence of happiness in front of Louis. She decided to leave at once. When the steamer docked, she would say that she had to return home urgently.

It was a rush to get back to the castle, bath, change and be downstairs by seven, as arranged, but Bill just made it. He found himself sitting next to Ingrid, listening to truly fantastic flamenco being played across the room by four guitarists. There was the sound of laughter and the clatter of feet, some of the guests were trying to dance to the music and making idiots of themselves. It was warm and peaceful and Bill was euphoric. He'd had a wonderful afternoon in Ingrid's company and he'd decided she would make a superb sister-in-law.

Jan, who was acting as barman, handed Bill another Scotch. Louis was sitting in the shadows, looking deflated because Andrea had decided to go home for some unconvincing reason.

Then Marie made her entrance in a clinging sheath of midnight blue silk that left one shoulder bare and hugged every curve of her body. Bill stood in admiration and bowed formally over her hand. 'Are you safe in that dress?'

She laughed. 'It's straight from Paris. My aunt sent it to me. Do you like it?' she asked. The lights caught the glittering diamonds at her neck and ears, and Bill was suddenly reminded of her wealth and status.

'Yes,' he said grumpily. He preferred her in student clothes, with her hair untidy and blowing in the wind. He caught hold of her hand. 'Come and dance.' She stepped easily into his arms.

'You don't like the dress, do you?' she said, sensing his mood.

'There's nothing wrong it, it makes you look like a countess ... fit for a king. I have a vision of you leaning over the fence back home, watching your favourite horse going through its paces; somehow, the dress doesn't match that dream.'

He kissed the tip of her nose. For a moment it seemed to Bill that they were alone.

Ingrid watched their every movement, her face twisted with envy.

As the music came to an end, everyone stared towards the door. Looking round, Bill saw von Hesse stride into the room wearing his ceremonial black uniform. At the sight of him Bill's stomach contracted in a painful spasm. But this is Czechoslovakia, he told himself, and the Nazis had no power here.

'What's that bastard doing here?' Bill whispered to Marie, furiously. 'Last time I saw him, he was a captain. Now he's a major.'

Marie did not answer. She looked angry and embarrassed.

Von Hesse crossed the room. Louis stood up and held out his hand. 'Welcome home, Hugo,' he said. 'Sorry I didn't see you on the steamer, but I hear you were there briefly.'

Home. Bill was astonished.

Von Hesse flung up his arm in a Nazi salute. 'Heil Hitler,' he snapped. Then he shook hands with Louis and turning to the girls, bowed to them with a strange twisted smile on his face.

'Bill, do you know my stepbrother, Hugo?' Louis said.

Bill had to force himself to stretch out his hand and summon a smile. The evening had taken a macabre turn, and he felt he'd been deceived. He scowled at Marie in shock and disappointment.

Feeling sick with embarrassment, Marietta wanted to puncture Hugo's assurance. Father had explained why he'd allowed Hugo back into the family fold, and they had fought about it. Eventually she had given in and promised to keep politics out of her party, but her temper was now getting the better of her.

'Really, Hugo, bringing those dreaded symbols into my home shows contempt for all our feelings. I loathe that uniform.'

Hugo laughed. 'So you don't like the uniform?' He put one hand on her shoulder, a proprietary gesture that infuriated Bill. 'That's stupid, Marietta. Within a few months every factory, every institution, every district and every street in Austria will be run by people in uniforms like this.'

Marietta was so shocked she could hardly talk coherently.

'Oh God. No. Never. Not so soon . . . surely?'

Watching Marie's reaction, Bill felt completely confused. What the hell was going on? He seemed to have stumbled on to the wrong set, wrong dialogue, wrong occasion.

Hugo neatly appropriated a cognac from a passing waiter. 'Happy birthday, Marietta,' he said, lifting his glass. Then he turned to Bill. 'You see Roth, you had nothing to worry about. The welfare of my little sister is of vital concern to me, although keeping her out of trouble seems to be a full-time occupation.' He lifted his glass. 'To the family.' He tossed back his drink. 'My God, it's good to be home.' Then he stood with his back to the fire, legs astride, looking as if he owned the place.

Bill gritted his teeth. It was a sordid picture of double-values and insincerity played out at the highest level of society, and Marietta was the worst of the lot, Bill reasoned. She'd been playing the fashionable heroine in safety while other Edelweiss students had been at risk. And to think he'd been so worried about her, while she'd known she was safe, because her brother was 'something' in the Nazi Party, making sure that nothing too terrible happened to her. No wonder the students had been released so quickly.

Bill didn't like his thoughts, but he could not banish them. He shot her a look of angry despair and noticed that she had the grace to look embarrassed. Then the band began playing again and she motioned him to dance with her.

Bill joined her reluctantly. 'How come you never mentioned your brother, never mind his position in the Nazi Party?' he growled.

'Oh, Bill, the first time I knew Hugo was in the Nazi Party was when they called him into my interrogation. It was a shock . . . but then, when I thought about it, it made sense. I mean, he'd always been at odds with the rest of the family.'

'Ah, come on, Marie. I can't believe you didn't know his position. All right, I grant that you're ashamed of his beliefs, but that doesn't alter the fact that you knew you were safe to demonstrate . . . and rescue the children . . . and publish your damned newspaper . . .'

Marietta turned pale. 'Is that what you believe of me?' she stammered. 'Truly? Are you calling me a fraud?' She felt sick with humiliation. Her legs felt rubbery, her mouth was dry and there was a lump in her throat so large she thought she might choke. Bill had called her a liar. The word echoed in her mind as she sought words to convince him of her sincerity, aware that pride was preventing her from speaking.

'I guess you need a Nazi in the family. Someone has to protect the old fortunes and castles,' he muttered. 'I've always admired survivors. You really had me duped, Marie. Oh, for God's sake.' He almost shook her in frustration.

'Why should you think your opinion matters to me one jot?' Her eyes flashed in annoyance and she lifted her foot and brought it down hard, stamping his toe with her heel. 'You are a mean-spirited, suspicious, disloyal . . . Oh, you're despicable.' And, holding her head high to prevent her tears falling, she swept through the crowd leaving him in solitude.

Chapter

15

BILL WATCHED MARIE LEAVE, then limped back to the bar with a sour taste in his mouth.

'A lover's tiff?' Hugo's voice boomed beside him. 'Ingrid, be a good hostess, dance with our guest, won't you?'

More to get away from Hugo than from any desire to dance with Ingrid, Bill took her hand and led her on to the dance floor. He moved around the floor like an automaton, feeling miserable. When the dance ended everyone applauded Ingrid and she twirled her full skirt in acknowledgement.

'You're a good dancer,' Bill said gracelessly.

'Am I?' Ingrid smiled wickedly. 'Let's have a nightcap.'

She drew Bill to a quiet corner of the room. She sat so close to him that he could feel the warmth of her thighs through the silk fabric of her dress. 'Don't be miserable, Bill. You Americans can never understand the pressures and responsibilities that people like Marietta have to shoulder. I don't suppose you know that she is one of the richest women in Europe ... maybe she is *the* richest. Who knows? There are only twenty men sufficiently eligible to marry her.' She giggled. 'Once, when we came here years ago, Hugo stole the list of those eligible men out of the old Princess's study so that I could set my cap at one of them. The silly goose! But then *I* can marry for love. The only reason to marry, don't you think Bill?'

He mumbled unhappily.

'Uncle is hoping she'll marry into royalty – did you know that the blood of almost every royal family in Europe runs in her veins? Well, my veins, too. I am even higher born than she. My father was closely related to the British royal family, but there . . . he's dead.'

She sighed and looked so forlorn that Bill reached out and took her hand in his.

'Don't pity me, Bill. It happened long ago. Of course, I can understand Marietta wanting to be free as a bird, but it was selfish of her, too. She insisted on dropping her title during her student days. Uncle was furious, but she's very spoiled and she always gets her own way. She doesn't care if people get hurt – she knows *she* will always be all right.'

Bill wished that Ingrid would keep quiet and he began to wonder how to leave her without being rude, but she was well into her theme.

'Right under our feet, in the vaults below, is the most prestigious and priceless collection of jewels in Europe – the Lobkowitz collection. It's all hers. Of course, Marietta is the sole heir to the whole Lobkowitz fortune, the breweries, mile after mile of farms, factories, industries, just about everything . . . spread over Czechoslovakia, Austria and Germany. Then she'll have a slice of her father's wealth, too, although Louis will get the lion's share. So you see, Bill, she has a duty to protect her fortune. Part of her wants to be a free spirit, but most of her knows she is destined for much greater things and she is reponsible for the future of the family.'

'But why should Marietta inherit all this?' Bill asked, feeling wretched. 'Why not Louis?'

'It is from her grandmother, Princess Lobkowitz. Marietta was the only child of the marriage of Uncle Frederick and Princess Anna. Her mother ran away from the responsibilities of being the heiress and the Count's wife, and she was killed later in a car crash in Switzerland. But Marietta is made of sterner stuff, she will never run away.

'Sometimes I thank my lucky stars that my family lost everything. Freedom is worth a lot, don't you think?'

'Yes,' Bill said with a sigh.

'Well, I need my beauty sleep. Tomorrow will be tiring. Goodnight, Bill. I look forward to a repeat performance on the dance floor.' She reached up and kissed his cheek and then she was gone.

Bill stayed where he was, almost too tired to move. He idly watched Hugo walk towards the musicians, say something before sitting at the piano. The guitarists shrugged and stopped playing as Hugo strummed the notes of the Nazis' *Horst Wessel* song, while singing raucously:

> *The flags held high! the ranks stand tight together!*
> *SA march on, with quiet, firm forward pace.*
> *Comrades who, though shot by Red Front or Reaction,*
> *Still march with us, their spirits in our ranks.*

Bill wanted nothing so much as to punch that bastard, but who was he to interfere? He was the stranger and Hugo was part of the family. This evening Bill had discovered just how much of a stranger he really was.

Hugo came to the end of his repertoire. He stood up, lifted his glass and roared: 'To the Führer! Heil Hitler!'

Some of the dancers and the four guitarists raised their voices for a round of enthusiastic 'Heil Hitlers'.

What a bitch of an evening, Bill thought. He drained his glass and left.

Bill woke with a hangover and a feeling of gloom which deepened as the day dragged on. The girls were closeted somewhere with hairdressers and whatever else it was they did before a ball. Finally he went for a long walk and came back feeling refreshed but still foul tempered. By now the castle was crowded with extra staff, arriving guests, drivers, waiters with drinks, musicians tuning up. The great reception hall looked like Grand Central Station in the rush hour.

Bill was now determined to leave, but longed to see Marie one last time. He must say goodbye at least, he persuaded himself. He went to change for the ball, aware that he was being weak. This was not his world. Marie was not for him and he had no right to feel cheated and sore.

He heard a knock on his bedroom door. Feeling sure that it was Marie, he flung it open, but it was only the chambermaid with hot water. The richest family in Europe, he thought, and nothing spent on the plumbing. He finished dressing and went downstairs.

Sokol's ballroom had come to life with a glitter and brilliance that Bill had never seen in his life. Now the extravagance of the ostentatious art form, which had seemed passé in daylight, became flamboyantly alive. The gilded saints and cherubs gleamed from the rosy-hued ceiling; chandeliers sparkled with light and the women's jewels winked back. The orchestra was playing a Strauss waltz in the minstrels' gallery and the women's skirts glittered and swayed to the rhythm of the dance, while the ancestors, in their gilt frames, seemed to be watching the dancers in approval. This was what money was all about, their eyes seemed to say. This was living!

Feeling out of place, Bill lingered on the fringes of the crowd. Then Marie appeared as the band played 'Happy Birthday'. She looked pale, but extraordinarily beautiful in an off-the-shoulder white dress that billowed and floated around her. He tried to get close enough to wish her happy birthday, but clearly she was avoiding him. She looked his way only once and he saw the hurt in her eyes.

He knew he must go. He would leave a letter in Marie's room, he decided, together with her birthday present.

But he stayed on, drinking quietly in the corner, refusing Ingrid's exhortations to dance. He watched the guests milling past and heard snatches of their conversations. The music ebbed and flowed around him. He was filled with a strange sense of unreality. Was he hallucinating? This feeling of being a part of everything, yet not really there, gave him goosepimples. Was he real? Were they real? Or were they fragments of history, drifting in time? He turned to go, but paused in the doorway. Looking back, he had the strange impression that he was walking out of a lavish illusion.

Chapter  16

MARIETTA READ AND REREAD Bill's curt goodbye letter dozens of times and spent the last days of her holiday in a daze of misery, punctuated by outbursts of bad temper. It was a relief to return to Munich, but she arrived to find Andrea packing to leave.

'You're early. I'd no intention of being here by the time you arrived,' Andrea said.

Deeply shocked by Andrea's curt words, Marietta said, 'What? Why are you going? Andrea, please, we are friends. What is going on?'

'Friends don't lie to each other,' Andrea hissed. 'Now, *Countess* Marietta, will you please go away.' She did not look round as she spoke, but continued to cram clothes into her suitcase.

Marietta sat on the floor by the radiator, hugging her knees and feeling totally depressed.

Andrea looked at her friend and suddenly wondered which of them felt the worst. 'You must understand that you're playing a game,' Andrea said, regretting her outburst. 'So is Louis. When the holidays come, you pack up your dedication and your liberal ideas together with your corduroy trousers and your shabby old jackets and it's back to your castles and liveried servants.

'Your world is not my world,' Andrea added, speaking more gently. 'I felt that I'd been used when I found out about your title ... and everything.' She paused. 'How many times have we shared a meal to eke out the pennies, or turned off the heating to cut the bills? We even walked to school, three mornings in a row, because we didn't have the money for tram fares. You were playing with me. You've never been short of anything in your life.'

'My father warned me that it wouldn't work,' Marietta replied, shame slightly slurring her words. 'What was I to do, Andrea? Once, when you were broke, I offered to pay for you, but you were furious. I just wanted to share your world.'

'But I can never share your world,' Andrea said softly. 'Louis is out of reach for me. Heavens!' She smiled. 'I didn't even know if I was supposed to curtsey to you and Ingrid.'

Marietta felt comforted by Andrea's weak attempt at a joke.

'Everything you've said is true, but Andrea why should all this make you leave? Surely we can remain friends?'

'It's not you I'm running away from,' Andrea said moodily. 'It's Louis. Counts only marry titled women, the rich marry the rich and the Habsburgs marry Habsburgs. Oh God! I'm making such a mess of this. I've fallen in love with Louis and I can't bear to lose him.' She leaned forward and buried her face in her hands.

'Andrea! Oh, dearest Andrea! Don't cry.' Marietta knelt beside her and put her arm across her shoulders. 'To be honest, I don't know what Louis thinks about tradition and class-consciousness,' Marietta began, feeling helpless. 'Of course, Father would expect him to marry a Habsburg, you're right about that. But Louis's different—'

'It was Count Frederick who spelled it out to me.' Andrea interrupted fiercely. Between sobs she explained what the Count had told her, adding: 'He's probably a kind man. I could see he didn't want to hurt me, but he said what he thought was right.'

The two girls were silent for some moments.

'Please stay, Andrea,' Marietta said at last. 'We need each other. Bill's walked out on me. He was furious when he found out that Hugo von Hesse is my stepbrother.'

Andrea gasped.

'Yes, it's true. Bill was so angry. He accused me ... ' She buried her face in her hands. 'You can probably imagine what he thought.'

Andrea looked bewildered. 'Surely you don't mean that von Hesse is Louis' brother?'

'Half-brother.'

'Why didn't you tell me?'

'We lost contact with Hugo after he was thrown out of the family in disgrace. I was eleven when he ... he was discovered in Ingrid's bed. She was only thirteen at the time. You must never, *ever* mention that. I hadn't seen him since. I didn't even know he was a Nazi, never mind in the SS, but Bill was so sure I knew all about Hugo's position that he didn't wait for an explanation.'

The words seemed to be tumbling out of her in relief at being able to talk about it. 'I knew that we would have to part eventually, Andrea,' she said sadly, 'but I kept pretending to myself. I know I can't abandon my birthright and responsibilities. There's no future for us ...'

Andrea stood up and took a carafe of wine from the shelf. She filled two glasses, handed one to Marietta and lifted the other. 'To our lost loves,' she said, the tears trickling down her cheeks. 'It's crazy, but I really love that brother of yours. It's as if we've known each other for ever. I thought we had so much in common.'

She gave a long sigh and squared her shoulders. 'I am not ashamed of crying,' she said aggressively, wiping the tears away with the back of her hand. 'I've lost something very precious. I'm going to stop seeing him. We can never be together and I don't want to get hurt any more.'

'And I've been a fool,' Marietta said. 'I shall never speak to that pompous fool, Bill, as long as I live. He's so naive, so damn

American. What gives him the right to judge me?' She slapped one fist into the other palm and burst into tears again.

Andrea reached out and hugged Marietta. For a few minutes the two girls clung to each other again. 'I don't understand any of you,' Andrea wailed. 'You're all so – so out of this world. I mean ... take Ingrid, why is she a princess? And why is she so arrogant and conscious of her title? Why is it *your* castle? Why are you working so hard here, while Ingrid learns to be a society hostess? And why has Louis never mentioned Hugo?'

'Father married twice,' Marietta began sipping her wine. 'His first wife was a penniless, widowed noblewoman, Agnes von Hesse, who had a two-year old son ... Hugo. His father, an army officer, had been killed in a brawl. Agnes had been living in a grace-and-favour cottage on one of Father's estates before he married her. She died when Louis was born. Two years later, Father married my mother, Princess Anna Lobkowitz. He adored her, perhaps too much, I don't know, we weren't very close, and then she left ...'

Marietta broke off and stared at her glass, twirling the wine round and round.

'As long as I live, I'll never forget that night,' Marietta said in a whisper. 'I always longed for Mama to come and kiss me goodnight, but she never did. Then one night I woke to find her bending over me, just as I had always dreamed.

'"Dear little Marietta," she said. "I've come to say goodbye. I'm leaving ... for my health. I haven't been a very good mother." When she smiled I saw tears glistening in her eyes.

'"You're the best. The best mother in the whole world and the most beautiful." I remember saying that. I tried to hug her, but she pushed my hands away. "Mind my hair, darling," she said. "I'm not happy here. I'm going to live in Switzerland. Be a good girl and do your duty. After all, you are your father's daughter. Don't be like me. Be strong. One day soon you'll be able to take my place. Forgive me."

'Then she was gone, leaving a wisp of lovely perfume all around and a chiffon scarf lying on the floor beside my bed. I still have that scarf. For years I longed for her to visit me, but she never came and then, when I was about thirteen, she was killed in a car crash.'

Marietta felt obsessed with memories. Once upon a time, she had lived in a world that had seemed so safe . . . so beautiful . . . then Ingrid had come into their home, bringing with her a glimpse of another, cruel world. Did that orphaned waif still exist beneath Ingrid's sophisticated façade? And Hugo hadn't always been evil. Had he?

Bill sat at his desk, trying to write an article, but the muse wasn't on his side lately. He felt restless, miserable and lonely.

He had returned to Berlin determined to forget the false and treacherous woman who had deceived him so blatantly, but so far he had failed to do so. She still monopolised his thoughts and ruined his concentration. Had he misjudged Marie? He remembered little things she had said and done that seemed to prove that she was innocent. No, not misjudged . . . that was too weak a word. He had been rude and self-righteous . . . unforgivably so. But why hadn't she mentioned von Hesse after her interrogation? Once again his thoughts spun in a tormented circle.

Two days before, he had telephoned Marie in Munich, but Andrea had relayed the message that Marie would not speak to him, and he was too proud to try again.

'Forget her,' Bill told himself, and tried to get on with his work.

It seemed to Bill that the whole world was closing its eyes to the truth. Adolf Hitler, Chancellor of Germany, was a man of extreme cunning, ruthless ambition, and a shrewd judge of human nature. He had conned the world into believing that he only wanted to unite the *Volksdeutsche*, those oppressed German-speaking people exiled outside Germany's borders. In Austria, Nazi agents were whipping up riots and street battles between German-speaking and Slav Austrians.

Bill had spent several days there, reporting the riots and describing the fears of Austrians as their country was plunged deeper into political and economic chaos.

He picked at his typewriter keys, groping for words and phrases to describe how Hitler was conning the world.

Anschluss, or the union of Germany and Austria, is a word which either strikes terror or hope into every Austrian. To the Austrian Nazis, Anschluss means the first step in their dream of uniting the German people to become the strongest force in Europe. To the millions of non-Germans who have made Austria their home, Anschluss means the end of freedom. Harnessed to the Nazi machine, they will become second-class citizens in their own country . . . to the Jews . . .

He stopped, realising that he was losing his objective focus.

What would *Anschluss* mean to people like Marie, he wondered? He rubbed the back of his neck which was stiff with tension. 'Oh Marie,' he murmured. 'I miss you.'

His misery was disturbed by the European editor calling from Paris. He told Bill to get his ass back to Vienna to cover *Anschluss* at first hand.

'By the way, Roth, do try to get off your bloody soap box,' his dry, English voice went on, 'our readers want news not lectures.'

Bill replaced the receiver feeling angry. No one wanted to hear the truth.

Chapter  17

AT DAWN ON MARCH 14, 1938, German troops, together with the Austrian legion, began to pour across the border from Germany. Behind them came the ranks of uniformed men who would control Austria: the Gestapo, the SS troops, SD agents, and the Brownshirts.

Sitting at a top floor window in Cöbenzl Castle, Major Hugo von Hesse watched the SS troops goosestep past. On either side of the road, joyous Nazis lined the route to give the troops a tumultuous welcome.

As he watched the columns of infantry and tanks pass beneath him, Hugo tried to think of anything which might have been left undone. There were shadows under his eyes, and he looked haggard. Working day and night for the past two months, Hugo had been brilliantly successful in setting up the Nazis' undercover control of Austria and organising the riots that had brought the government to its knees. As in the Fatherland, a network had been established by which the Gestapo could supervise every sphere of life. All Jews, Jewish sympathisers, Communists, and everyone who might be expected to oppose National Socialism, had been carefully documented. Within hours, six thousand of them would be taken to specially constructed concentration camps.

Moments later, on the radio, Hugo heard the broadcast of the Austrian chancellor, Doctor Schuschnigg. 'We have yielded to force,' he said brokenly, 'because we are not prepared to shed blood even in this terrible hour. I take leave of the Austrian people with a word of farewell, uttered from the depth of my heart – God protect Austria.'

It was time to arrest Schuschnigg. He was going to a concentration camp, too. As for Father . . . Hugo thought about his fate for a while, toying with his pen. Once inside the camp, the Count would be beyond Hugo's reach. He might even survive. Hugo reached for his pen and crossed the Count's name from the list.

Marietta woke with a sense of alarm, but she wasn't sure why. For a few moments she felt confused, until she remembered, she had returned to Vienna to be with Father and she had been here for a week. Just seven days during which the foundations of her life were cracked wide open.

Nothing had changed, yet everything had changed, Marietta thought, feeling sick with despair. The boulevards were crowded with excited shoppers, most of whom were German. For the first time they could enter Austria without permits to buy up goods they hadn't seen for years. The theatres were still crowded, but the Jewish actors had been replaced. They had either fled or been arrested. Queues of frightened people stood waiting their turn for exit permits and Nazi troops stood around in groups, guarding the population.

Dr Kurt Schuschnigg, former Chancellor of Austria, had been arrested and imprisoned. So had many other government officials. Father had expected the same fate. He had been dismissed from his post as Foreign Minister, but he was still at liberty. The change in him was frightening, he seemed to have crumpled from the inside out. He walked around as if in a dream, hardly acknowledging her, but wrapped up in his own gloomy thoughts.

Rumours were rife: it was said that thousands of unwanted citizens were being removed to concentration camps by special trains before dawn each morning. Marietta was desperate to know the truth.

She got up and dressed warmly in old slacks and a sweater. Determined but frightened, her hands shook as she went downstairs and borrowed Louis' car. By 5 a.m. she was outside the station. The platforms were guarded by troops and she was not allowed to enter, so she hung around trying to keep out of sight, shivering in the darkness.

Ten minutes later she heard the sound of lorries approaching in a convoy. A deeper chill entered her bones as they drew up outside the station, and dozens of armed troops rushed to them, shouting commands. The backs of the lorries were lowered and the nightmare began.

The people were bewildered and slow. Some were very old. They stumbled under the soldiers' batons and sometimes fell. The troops wanted them to hurry. There were terrified shrieks, howls of anguish, the guard dogs were barking, children were crying. The civilians were herded sheeplike on to the platforms. She glimpsed windowless carriages and heard doors scraping across their rollers, bolts being drawn, whistles blowing.

Another wave of people ventured timidly out of the lorries. They were well-dressed, cultured people, some clutching their children, some their wives, and many showed signs of having been beaten. Suddenly they, too, were running before the guards like pigs to slaughter. *You send your runts to market.* Hugo's words echoed dully in her head.

She put her hands over her ears to drown the terrified cries and the arrogant orders of the soldiers. A train moved forward and gathered speed, then another. The silence that followed was like a blessing.

Marietta was trembling violently and she felt sick. 'Oh God! Oh God, how can this happen?' she muttered.

Another train was approaching in the distance. She heard its whistle as it entered the tunnel. Then she was aware of more lorries arriving.

Dead on time. The Nazis' efficiency was truly terrifying. More people tumbled out, pushed from behind, and dragged

from the front. Suddenly a woman broke away and ran to
Marietta. She hung on to her, sobbing hysterically. Something
was pushed into her pocket. Then she sprawled on the ground
from a blow from a soldier's baton, stumbled to her feet and ran.
Marietta saw her agonised face gazing over her shoulder, and
her mouth framing a silent plea.

'Are you a Jewess?' An SS guard caught her shoulder and
spun her round.

'No.'

'What are you doing here, Fräulein?'

'That's none of your business,' she said angrily, shaking off
his hand.

'Papers!' He held out an immaculately gloved hand.

Sullenly, she handed over her identity document. Some of his
arrogance faded as he studied it. Almost reluctantly he saluted
her. 'It would be wise to keep away from the station, Countess,'
he said, as he handed her papers back. Quivering with fury,
Marietta returned to Louis' car, but she waited until she had
driven out of sight of the station before fumbling in her pocket
for the woman's note. It was written on a sheet torn from a
diary. *If you love God, save my child. Her name is Hilde. She is
six years old and all alone.* There was an address. Nothing more.
Marie changed direction and drove rapidly southwards. She
knew exactly where to get help.

Bill was outside the Austrian parliament taking photographs of
the official Nazi takeover and the jubilant crowds waving. He
finished four rolls of film and pushed his way back to his car. He
was stopped several times by SS guards, but his position as an
American correspondent ensured him free passage. The Nazis
had all been well-briefed . . . foreign journalists, many of whom
never looked behind the window-dressing, were Hitler's most
valuable tools.

He was hungry. He glanced at his watch and saw that it was
almost eleven. Perhaps he could find a café nearby. As he walked
along by the shops, he heard someone call his name.

'Bill . . . Bill . . .'

He turned and smiled with pleasure as he caught sight of Ingrid. 'My goodness,' he said, giving her a quick kiss. 'You look tremendous.'

Sophisticated and beautiful, her hair was swept into a loose chignon at the nape of her neck, her perfect features accentuated by expert make-up. She was wearing a navy blue and red outfit with a matching hat; its blue veil, with red blobs on it, hid her eyes. Bill pushed the veil up over the brim.

'That's better,' he said. 'Now I can take a proper look at you.'

'You've just ruined a Schiaparelli hat,' she said, laughing happily. 'Those silly red blobs make me feel dizzy. All the same...' She rearranged the net. 'I was going to take a stroll past the shops, and perhaps have some coffee and cake. You would like to come with me? Yes?' She smiled coquettishly.

'People are rioting round the corner,' he said warningly.

She made a little deprecating gesture with her mouth, as if blowing the problems away. 'There's the most divine orchestra at Sacher's. And their coffee is wonderful ...' Her graceful, ringed hand gestured her approval. 'Come, or we might not find a vacant table.' She swept ahead of him and Bill decided to play along.

Ingrid chattered away while he ate a huge breakfast. She told him about her finishing school and the parties she had been to. She could keep going all night, he reckoned.

'I'll be twenty on April the thirteenth,' she confided, 'but by then I'll be back in Paris, so I'm having my party next Friday. Please come. Really ... I would love you to.'

Why not? Perhaps if he saw Marie he would realise that it was all over and stop pining for her. 'Thanks Ingrid,' he said. 'What time shall I come?' He tried not to notice how happy Ingrid looked.

Chapter  18

THE TWO COUSINS WERE SITTING in the breakfast room, a pleasant place decorated in blue and yellow with a French door looking on to a small private walled garden. The morning sun glinted in Ingrid's hair, her pale face looked ethereal and her eyes were sparkling as she smiled as if at some secret joke.

Marietta looked exhausted and scruffy in old slacks and a crumpled blouse. Her hair hung lifeless and dirty, and there were deep shadows under her eyes.

'You look a sight, Marietta,' Ingrid said. 'When are you going to learn to look after yourself? Why are you eating that disgusting English meal?' She wrinkled her nose at Marietta's plate of eggs and bacon. 'You're building up bad eating habits. You'll be sorry when you're fat. Not that anyone would notice in those dreadful clothes you wear.'

'I'll worry about it if and when I get fat,' Marietta said vaguely, not paying much attention to Ingrid's silly chatter.

She took another helping of crisply-fried bacon and carefully laid the strips on to a piece of buttered toast. She was taking a large bite when Ingrid dropped her bombshell.

'Guess who I met yesterday?'

Marietta shrugged. She couldn't have felt less interested.

'Bill Roth.'

The toast fell on to Marietta's lap. She retrieved it and put it on to her plate. Suddenly she wasn't hungry.

'I invited him to my party, but I thought I'd better check with you first.'

'What party?' Marietta said.

'Oh, really! I've told you a million times. I'm having a birthday party next Friday.'

'Sorry. I forgot.'

'Well, what about Bill?' Ingrid sounded peeved.

'No, you should not have invited him here. Where did you see him?'

'He was walking past the hat shop near Parliament last week. You know the one I like . . . I saw him through the window.'

Marietta frowned and tried to hide her agitation. The thought of Ingrid setting her cap at Bill was hurtful. 'I really don't want to see him again,' she said.

'I don't suppose he wants to see you either, since he was in such a hurry to leave you. Don't be a dog in the manger, Marietta. I like Bill. I really do,' Ingrid said defiantly. 'And if you don't want to see him, you can't mind if I do, can you?'

'No . . . no . . . of course not.' Oh damnation, Marietta thought, why do I care? Why does it hurt?

'Good, because he's coming.'

For a moment anger dimmed her self-control and she felt like lashing out at Ingrid.

Ingrid put her head on one side and smiled up from under her new hairdo. Marietta frowned.

'Please be straightforward,' Ingrid said. 'He is available, isn't he?'

'I detest him.'

'Well then,' Ingrid said, as if that solved their problems. Marietta left the breakfast room feeling disturbed and depressed. Bill Roth means nothing to me and I don't care who he goes out with, she told herself several times, trying to ignore the twinges of genuine pain in her stomach.

Friday came all too soon. It was almost six o'clock; the guests were arriving, but Marietta was pacing her room. She peered anxiously into the mirror. A pale and angular face stared back at her. Surely her nose was too long, her mouth too wide, her eyes too dark. She sighed and rifled in her drawer for the make-up kit Ingrid had given her, but which she had never used. She tried foundation to give her face some colour, and lipstick to shape her lips, then she smoothed on eye shadow. When she had finished, she took a long, hard look at herself. 'My goodness, make-up does make a difference,' she murmured.

Why am I bothering? Let him have Ingrid. She's welcome to that disloyal American. With frenetic energy she searched her cupboards for the third time. Ingrid was so sophisticated nowadays and she had such lovely clothes. Marietta gritted her teeth; she only had one Parisian dress and she had never worn it. It was a short, clinging shift of dark green silk, with fringes around the tiered skirt. They shimmered and shook when she moved. Just right, she thought.

Bill was feeling claustrophobic. Palaces did this to him, he had discovered recently. He was acutely reminded of his last evening in Sokol Palace. It was only three months ago, but it might have been another era, so much had happened since then. Too much horror and fear. He felt years older than the naive boy who had stormed out of the ball.

God, but this place was overstocked with antiques and paintings. How could people live like this? They should ship them to the nearest museum, he thought, as he peered around every statue and potted plant for Marie.

Distracted by Ingrid showing him off to her friends as though he were her latest conquest, Bill began to think Marie wasn't coming. Then he saw *her*. He caught his breath in wonder. She was no longer a girl, but a woman, and she was surrounded by a sea of dinner jackets. He hung around, noting how her every movement was full of grace, how her eyes glowed with genuine warmth. The force of his desire made his hands tremble. Ingrid clutched his arm and whispered in his ear. 'Marietta has a secret. He's standing next to her right now. He's always here, and they steal out together at night. Father would be furious if he found out. Perhaps she's going to elope.'

Bill felt shocked to the core. He gazed at Marie's companion more closely. He was quite old – pushing forty; he looked Scandinavian with his pale skin and near-white hair. The two of them seemed to have plenty to talk about. When had she met him? Was he one of the eligible twenty? He turned away in secret agony and trailed behind Ingrid, listening wearily to her frivolous chatter. 'They say Picasso painted his *Guernica* within weeks of the German bombing. It's a sensation in Paris. Marietta and I drove there for the opening of the exhibition. Quite extraordinary.'

Infuriated by her shallow prattle, he left Ingrid anchored to a group of actors and made his way doggedly back to the source of his pain. Marie was still talking to the same man. They know each other well, he thought, feeling empty and alone.

'Marie!'

She seemed to freeze. Her shoulders tensed visibly, and she turned slowly.

'Bill.'

'Oh Marie ... How are you?' His voice was hoarse, and he cleared his throat. For a moment their eyes met, then Marie forced a taut smile.

'Ingrid told me she had invited you. I hope you and she have a lovely evening.' She turned away.

'I came to see you,' he said quietly. 'I over-reacted at your birthday. I'm a stranger here and I don't really understand the way you think about ... about certain things.'

Marie listened to him with a haughty and disdainful expression on her beautiful face. He stumbled on with his prepared speech. 'I realise now that I had no right to judge you. I'm sorry. Yes, truly sorry. I apologise.' There, he'd said it! Bill could count the number of times he'd apologised on the fingers of one hand.

'Apologise? Good heavens! Whatever for? It's lovely to see you again. I hope you and Ingrid have a wonderful evening. Please excuse me, Bill.' She turned back to her companion, who was looking embarrassed.

Bill stood there feeling astonished and very wretched. 'Stop fobbing me off, Marie,' he muttered, grabbing her arm, all too aware that he was being rude.

Marie quickly excused herself to her companion and drew Bill aside. 'Go away,' she said.

'I think you were wrong not to tell me about von Hesse, but that doesn't stop me from loving you,' he said quickly.

'And your apology doesn't stop me from thinking you're a pompous, self-opinionated fool. And you're using Ingrid to see me. Just how mean can you be? There's no future for us, Bill. There never was.'

'I'd use anyone or anything to see you, if that's what it would take. And who the hell is that creep?'

'He's a man I admire, which is a lot more than I'll ever say of you.'

She turned back to her companion and Bill could think of nothing to keep her. In a temper he went to find Ingrid. To hell with Marie. He flirted with Ingrid all evening and danced with her for hours, hoping that Marie was watching, knowing he was monopolising the belle of the ball and taking vicious pleasure from the admiring glances.

Bill left around midnight, having given up hope of seeing Marie again and disgusted by the way all the guests spoke of everything under the sun except reality. What would life be like under their new Nazi leaders? He decided to return to Berlin at once, and bury the memory of Marie forever.

Chapter  19

AFTER HUGO'S SUCCESS IN AUSTRIA, he was given the under-cover task of whipping up hatred between the *Volksdeutsche* and Czechs in the Sudeten areas of Czechoslovakia. He installed himself in Hirschen Manor, a lovely old gothic home situated outside a small Austrian village near the Czech border. It had been owned by a family of Jewish merchant bankers, who were now resident in a labour camp.

There was one room which he assumed had been the family room, for it was situated in the sunniest wing of the house. Hugo called this his planning room. Here he paced the floor far into the night perfecting his plans.

So far he had succeeded brilliantly, thanks to his team of hand-picked plain-clothes agents, all of whom spoke Czech fluently. Nightly, they slipped across the border into Sudeten-land in various disguises. Today's newspaper had recounted the sad story of a *Volksdeutsche* glass-blower who had been dis-missed from his job simply because he was of German roots. He was found hanging from a rope in his garden the following night. In vain, his Czech employers explained that he had been sacked for theft and that his wife suspected that he had been murdered. No one wanted to know. Hugo carefully pasted the story in his scrapbook. The incidents were multiplying. Hatred

111

was spreading like a forest fire, as Germans and Slavs rioted and fought each other in clubs and bars.

It was Monday morning and, like all good German housewives, Heide Smeidt was hanging her spotlessly white, freshly laundered linen on the washing line in the garden where she lived, two miles outside the village of Volary, in the Sudetenland area of old Bohemia. It was one of those perfect summer days that seem to banish all cares and Heide was singing an old German folk-song as she worked. Before her stretched a field full of barley, with patches of deep red poppies here and there. Beyond was the stream, and on the far bank, an old mill by the forest.

The mill had been abandoned for years, so Heide was surprised when the door swung open and a man came out. He looked like a labourer, but whatever could he be doing here, she wondered? As she watched him approach the stepping stones across the river, she felt vaguely uneasy, but she was not sure why. She picked up the laundry basket and went into the house. On second thoughts she slammed home the bolt. 'Silly,' she muttered to herself. 'How silly you are. It's just a worker crossing the river. That's all.' She glanced through the kitchen window. Why was he moving so purposefully towards their cottage? Her husband, Jan, worked at the foundry, five miles away, and two of her children were at school. The other, a two-year-old boy, was playing on the sitting-room floor.

There was a knock on the door. 'I'll go, Jan,' she called, pretending her husband was home. She glanced through the window. There were two men. Where had the other one come from? 'Hello.' She opened the window. 'D'you want my husband? He's upstairs.'

'Yes,' the first one said. 'We're from the Union. There's a special meeting tonight. Here's the address.'

'Oh!' Relief flooded through her. 'Is that all?' She reached through the window, but a strong arm caught hers and slammed it hard against the frame.

She screamed with pain and fright. 'Let me go!' She might as well have pulled against a steel bear trap.

She heard the second man kicking the door. The wood splintered and smashed, and she heard her child wailing.

'What do you want?' she screamed.

In answer the man punched her hard in the face. She heard her nose crunch sickeningly. Pain dimmed her fear as she gagged on the blood. She fell back on to the floor and hit her head on the table, passing out momentarily. When she came to she was spread-eagled on the floor, her skirt around her neck and they were dragging her into the sitting-room. One of them saw her open her eyes and kicked her savagely in the ribs and the face.

'Oh God, help me. God help me,' she sobbed. 'Why are you doing this? Who are you?'

'Czechs,' they said. 'Czech patriots. Go home, you German whore. You and your race are not wanted in Czechoslovakia. This is our land.'

They stripped off her clothes as she kicked and screamed. Then they raped her, taking turns to hold her down. Opening her eyes she saw that there were more of them. Was it five, or six? She could not see clearly for the blood was running in her eyes and she couldn't think for the pain which was everywhere. Each time there was a new pain. She screamed when they bit off her nipples and then again when they sodomised her over the kitchen table. And then when they broke her arm and smashed her ribs.

Later, they dumped her naked in the river and left. She managed to crawl to the river bank, where she lay, bloody and broken for hours until the children came home from school.

That night she recovered consciousness briefly in hospital. She repeated to her grieving husband and the doctor what the men had said. She did not recognise any of them, she muttered.

One was huge, with frizzy white hair, an albino. One had been very dark with a cast in his eye. The others ...? She tried to remember, but died before she could.

It was a beautiful evening. Dappled sunlight fell across the planning table, but Hugo hardly noticed as the sun set and dusk changed to darkness. Soon the moon rose and its light sparkled on the fountain by the roses.

It was time for the news. Locking away his files, Hugo switched on the radio and heard the Führer vow to save the 'innocent and oppressed' Czech Germans by force of arms, if necessary. 'I will have justice for the *Volksdeutsche* in Czechoslovakia!' he screamed to the world.

Hugo stretched and bent over his planning table again. He began rearranging a line of black dominos. Each represented a train with twenty cattle trucks. He knew from past experience in Austria that he could squeeze sixty men into one cattle truck.

Hitler was demanding massive inflows of Czech male and female slave labour to arrive within the first few days of the occupation. As well as farm livestock, dismantled factories, even the Czechs' new railway sleepers were to be shipped back to Germany. Hugo thrust his hands into his pockets and began to pace the floor. The transportation problems seemed insurmountable. He was disturbed by the shrill ring of his telephone.

'Heydrich here. How are you, von Hesse?'

As soon as he heard Heydrich's voice sounding clear, calm and friendly, Hugo knew good news was coming his way.

'I was working on transportation plans.'

'Certain plans have been pushed forward. October the first is the date scheduled. You must finish your research before then. Oh, and by the way, you've been appointed to the rank of colonel. My congratulations, von Hesse.'

Hugo gasped and he heard Heydrich chuckle. Shortly afterwards, Hugo replaced the receiver feeling elated. He went back to his desk. He had not been there long before he heard soft footsteps outside. He tiptoed swiftly across the room and swung the door open.

Freda, his new Bavarian housekeeper, nearly fell on her face with shock. She was carrying a tray with coffee and biscuits.

'Heavens, you scared me, Major,' she said shakily. 'I woke up and realised that you were still working. You said you mustn't be disturbed, but you've had no supper. I thought you might like something to eat so I came down. I hope you don't mind my gown. I didn't want to waste time dressing.' She smiled coquettishly.

She was lying. Her nightdress was uncreased and she had brushed her hair and applied some pink lipstick. When she leaned forward to put the tray on the table her negligée fell open, revealing her breasts. Rather a gauche attempt at seduction. Well, he'd prefer not to have a genius poking around his home. He reached forward and pinched one fat pink nipple.

'I have to leave for Berlin at seven. My driver and three men will be here for breakfast. Will you be able to cope?'

'With anything you want, Herr Major,' she said, her eyes gleaming with laughter.

'Are you sure?' He caught hold of her so swiftly that her feet lifted from the floor. While he held her with one arm he swept his hand under her loose gown and cupped one pendulous breast. It felt good . . . heavy and maternal.

She had found her feet, so he slipped the other hand under her buttocks. He was surprised how firm they were. She would be good in bed. He knew from her small, moist lips, her heavy-lidded eyes and her trim, muscled body which was soft only in her breasts. Her hair was blonde, her eyes were blue, and she was twenty-two years old. He laughed and slapped her backside. 'It's Colonel now. Let's celebrate. Play your cards right and you'll be set up for life.'

'It will be a pleasure to serve you, *mein Colonel*,' she said. She had obviously made up her mind about him some days before. 'You go up, I'll bring coffee.'

'Bring champagne. And hurry, I hate lonely beds.'

Two men were meeting in a rented hotel room in central Berlin, one of them a well-known economist and mayor of a thriving German city. A middle-aged man with iron-grey hair and a military moustache, there was nothing outstanding about his appearance, but he was known for his liberal views, his indomitable will and his stern opposition to the Nazis.

The other was Count von Burgheim, who was pacing the shabby room. 'There are so many of us who hate the Nazis, my friend. There is no shortage of recruits. I've been talking to left-wing politicians, trade union leaders, journalists and church leaders; they're only too keen to join us, but I'm convinced that a civilian uprising could only fail. Civilians could not last against the tanks and flamethrowers of the armed forces. Hitler has a genius for self-protection. By training his own SS army, he can defeat an uprising. Unless . . .'

' . . . we had the entire German army with us,' the Mayor said. 'Exactly. Between us we have the contacts and the power to bring the top generals together and sound them out. There must be many who think as we do.'

'And many who would betray us,' the Mayor went on. 'So we must be careful. We must try to find out which generals would be with us, without revealing our plans.'

'I'll start with close friends,' the Count said.

For two hours they pored over lists of names and connections, speaking in low tones, falling silent at the sound of footsteps in the corridor. Finally satisfied they'd done as much as they could, the two men shook hands and left separately.

From then on, the nights took their toll of the Count's stamina. For the first time in his life he was deadly afraid. Not for his own safety, but for his children's. The Nazis were never content with merely executing traitors. They destroyed the entire family. Nevertheless, in solitude, he pondered about the near-impossible task of staging a putsch to overthrow the Nazis.

Chapter  20

THE SUMMER OF '38 was an uneasy time for the von Burgheims. Too many Austrian aristocrats were being stripped of their wealth and possessions. Count Frederick expected to be arrested at any time, but inexplicably he remained at liberty.

Louis was particularly worried. The Edelweiss students were heading for destruction, any fool could see that. Louis had promised Father he would look after Marietta, but she was headstrong and wilful. Nothing he could say would make the two women he loved more than anything else in the world take care of themselves. His rift with Andrea was a constant source of pain and misery.

After weeks of frustration, Louis decided to enlist Marietta's help and he waylaid her in the campus and hustled her to the dining-room. Louis was struck by the change in Marietta. She was growing up fast. She was wearing a navy cotton skirt, a white blouse, tennis shoes and socks. She wore no make-up or jewellery and her hair was pulled back into plaits which were wound around her head. One plain watch with a black leather strap completed this image of a serious student. She was hungry and Louis couldn't help being irritated with her single-minded devotion to gobbling cakes.

'Are you going to tell me what's going on, or are you going to eat forever?'

'Sorry! I haven't eaten today. Anyway, you did invite me. Father cornered Andrea on the boat, the day before my birthday and gave her the whole bit about duty and what it means to be a Habsburg. He said that you must marry someone from the same background. Well ... something like that ... She didn't tell me word for word. I wasn't going to tell you, but now that I see how unhappy you both are ...'

'Damn Father!' Louis exploded. 'At least her behaviour makes sense. I'm not losing her for the sake of primitive "duty".'

'There's no point in blaming Father. He didn't invent the system,' Marietta said.

'But he's turned it into a blessed religion.'

'You've never really understood Father,' she said sadly.

'All too well. It's absolutely crystal clear to me now. Thanks! By the way, I don't hear much about Bill nowadays. Did he get the same speech?'

'I have no wish to see that arrogant, self-opinionated, distrustful, disloyal, rotten pig—'

'In other words you're still pining,' Louis interrupted mischievously. Looking closely at his sister, Louis decided that she was eaten up with a misery she didn't recognise. 'What a mess,' he sighed.

Louis was furious with his father, yet he had to acknowledge that there had been some truth in his words. His future wife would look forward to life of strict protocol and exhaustive duties. Would Andrea cope? More pertinently, would she want to? Would it be fair to her? Nevertheless, he missed her warmth, her candour, her low, thrilling laugh and her love of music. Torn between two worlds, Louis decided to visit the parish priest in Munich and talk to him about his problem. But when Louis attended a service at the Catholic church nearest to the University the following Sunday, he was disgusted to see that the Christian cross had been replaced with a swastika. On the altar there was a copy of *Mein Kampf*, and a sword. The altar cloth was a large Nazi flag and a larger-than-life picture of Hitler was placed behind the altar. He turned and walked out, his stomach churning.

The presbytery was occupied by a Nazi official. The priest had been arrested during a nationwide purge against the clergy and the church had been converted into one of Germany's first *Ahnenhalle*, or national churches dedicated to Nazism.

For Louis, the next week was a period of bitter introspection. He had never been interested in politics or in civil disobedience, but this was a question of ethics. Eventually he came to a decision ... Marie was right, Father was wrong. Ethics had to be guarded, with your life, if necessary. It was time to take a stand. Finally Louis had the commitment and strength to join Edelweiss.

The pull towards Marie became too much for Bill to resist. May and June had dragged by endlessly and in July he wrote to his bureau suggesting that he should cover the post-*Anschluss* Austrian scene. He was pleased, but not particularly surprised, when they agreed. In Vienna, Bill made a point of visiting all the places Marie was likely to go to during the University vacation, but it seemed that a chance meeting was not to be. Finally inspiration struck and he called Louis and invited him for lunch 'to discuss the local scene'.

'Viennese society seems determined to hold back the clock,' Louis told him with a detached smile as they sipped aperitifs. 'Despite the New Order and the austerity, the Establishment are hanging on to their privileged existence. Look at them. . .' He waved his hand dismissively at the crowded restaurant. 'The same parties are still being held, there's the same flamboyant attendance at the theatre and the opera. People are ignoring the changes, betting they will then go away. It won't last. How can it?'

Over coffee, Bill turned the conversation to Louis' family and, of course, Marietta.

Louis said: 'Bill, my friend, it's none of my business, but I'd like to put you right about Marietta. There's nothing false about her. None of us knew that Hugo had joined the Nazis until

Marietta was arrested and interrogated. Since then Hugo has used his power to force Father to welcome him back to the family.'

'I wish I could wipe the slate clean.' Bill sighed and signalled for brandies.

Bill was overjoyed when Louis invited him to join the family at the opera and dinner afterwards. They were to meet for drinks at Plechy at six. Bill arrived first and hung around in a state of nervous excitement, keeping one eye on the door. He longed to see her, sure he could make everything come right again.

Then Ingrid hurried in wearing a black velvet trouser suit with a Mandarin collar. It glittered with sequins and made her look older, sophisticated and very lovely. She rapidly made it clear that Bill was to be her escort and that Marie was not coming.

His disappointment was almost impossible to hide. 'What happened to Marie?' he muttered to Louis when he had the chance to speak privately.

'Sorry, Bill. I did try, I promise.' He shrugged.

Later that night, when Bill was leaving, he saw Marie hurry out of a car and enter the palace by the servants' entrance. Was that to avoid him, he wondered? Looking hard at the driver, he recognised the tall Scandinavian he'd seen at Ingrid's birthday party.

From then on the invitations came regularly and Bill reciprocated by inviting the family to whatever fascinating entertainment he could devise for them. He always hoped that Marie would change her mind and join them, but she never did. Wasn't she jealous? Didn't she care that he was seeing Ingrid? Or did she know that he was only seeing Ingrid by default?

Why was he doing this, he asked himself after each occasion? It was unfair to Ingrid and surely to God he could take the brush-off from an obstinate foreign countess. Marie, it seemed, only had eyes for her Scandinavian. Was she having an affair? This question kept him awake and in torment most nights.

*

Berlin was not a good place to be that summer, and Bill's absence made it worse. Taube missed the security of having him around.

He had called her from Vienna and given her the morning off, but she felt guilty about leaving the office. As she hurried along the pavement she kept her eyes straight ahead. Like a horse with blinkers on, she never looked to either side. She did not want to see the many signs in offices, restaurants, theatres, and even benches in the park and public toilets saying: *Jews forbidden*. Her stomach was knotted with painful lumps, as it always was lately, for she lived in a permanent state of terror and tension. Consequently, her legs were stiff, her eyes burning, her neck aching, but worst of all were the cramps in her stomach.

Nowadays, she had to wear a yellow Star of David on her arm. The penalty of breaking this new law was immediate removal to a concentration camp. She could not take this chance, for she could be asked for her papers at any time. But wearing the yellow armband invited every lout to abuse her.

At last she'd reached her destination, the Chilean Embassy. She hurried into the gates with a sigh of relief, but then her fears returned. What would they say? Had her application been successful? Seconds later she was standing at the end of a long queue of anxious people, all Jews, most of them elderly. They looked resigned and hopeless, as if they knew there was no escape. It was past ten before she reached the desk, where a Chilean woman with large hazel eyes and a kind expression said: 'Your name and reference number, please.'

'Taube Bloomberg.' She passed the number through the slot and sat there quietly, unashamedly praying, embarrassed by her youth.

The woman was gone for a long time. Taube tried to relax.

'It will be all right,' she whispered to herself. 'They will take us. It has to be . . . they're desperate for settlers.'

This was their last chance. Taube had plagued every foreign embassy for the past eighteen months and drawn a blank everywhere. No one wanted old, unskilled penniless Jews, as both of her parents were classed.

The woman returned with her file and an anxious expression on her face. She avoided looking at her, which, Taube had learned from experience, heralded bad news. Her heart sank.

'Miss Bloomberg, *your* application is successful,' the woman said brightly.

'And my parents . . . ?' Taube's voice faltered.

'Unfortunately we cannot accept responsibility for your parents. They are too old to be useful immigrants. We need young, strong people who can work the fields and turn the land into profitable farms. Your parents don't seem to be quite what we're looking for. They would become a – a burden on the State. I'm afraid we're not a . . .' The woman's voice tailed off uncertainly.

'But I did explain,' Taube said. 'I cannot abandon them.'

The woman folded her hands and gazed at them. She seemed to be a kind person. She listened to Taube's long tale of despair without interrupting her.

'I'm sorry, but there's no hope,' she said at last, months of similar interviews had not totally extinguished her compassion. 'Unless, of course, you could find sponsorship from a Chilean family.'

Taube shook her head despondently. 'I would support them,' she whispered. 'I've told you that.'

'You would if you could, but there is no guarantee. Perhaps if you were to go first, they could follow when you had accommodation and employment and could prove financial support for them.'

'They should live so long,' Taube muttered. She felt feverish and did not know how to handle this latest, possibly final, blow. Last week, they had been told that the authorities were going to force all Jews to hand in their passports in October. That gave her three months to escape, but only with her parents.

'Eighty per cent of the German Jewish youth have already left Germany,' the woman was saying. 'Your parents would understand. They are old. You are young.'

'I can't leave them. Don't you understand that? Mother

would never cope without me. Please help me,' Taube said desperately. 'Please . . .' She shouldn't beg. That was inexcusable, she knew. It put too much burden on a civil servant who had no power, but who was trying to help. 'Forgive me,' Taube said quickly. 'It is not your fault. I had no right . . .'

The woman was looking stricken, flustered by the situation, aware that she might not have the strength to be as selfless if their roles were reversed. 'Perhaps if they sold their shop. If they had enough capital, they would be acceptable immigrants.'

Taube almost snorted in despair, she might as well ask for the moon. Yet another new law was forcing Jews to sell their businesses and property to non-Jews for whatever they were offered. Besides, the cost of an exit permit was all you possessed. Thanking the woman gravely, she walked back to work. There were no solutions now beyond Bill's charity. Her father would have to accept it. No matter how tactfully Bill voiced his concern, it boiled down to charity. He, personally, would have to stand surety for her family and pay their fares, their settling-in expenses, their rent, her mother's medical bills, the costs were endless. Oh God!

Obsessed with her problems, she stumbled into a group of Brownshirts who were rounding up Jews to clean the pavements. Before she knew what was happening to her, she was forced down on her knees with a pail of water and a brush, to scrub out the gutter. Bitter tears of humiliation scalded her cheeks.

'Don't cry! Just work,' the old woman next to her whispered. 'Don't argue. Don't look up. They beat you if you refuse or if you're slow. That's what this is all about, a chance to beat people, so just scrub. They get tired of it after an hour or two and let you go.'

It was the most terrible morning of her life. People stopped to jeer at them. She became wet and muddy and terrified that she would be taken away, never to be heard of again, as so many were.

She got back to the office tired, filthy and close to hysteria. She put a call through to Bill in Vienna. She hadn't intended telling him everything, but every detail of the day poured out.

'Bill. You said once you would help us get to the States. Father was too proud to accept your help, but Bill, I accept on behalf of all of us. I'm desperate. Somehow I'll force Father to leave.'

'I'll telephone the Ambassador now, Taube,' Bill promised.

Chapter  21

OBSESSED BY HIS PURSUIT of the elusive Marietta, Bill allowed himself to be drawn into the whirlwind that was Ingrid's world. It seemed there wasn't a function in Vienna which could take place without the patronage of the beautiful Princess Ingrid. For Ingrid it was obligatory to attend every first night of every fashionable opera, concert or play. He sat through hours of heavy drama in the national repertory company's Burgtheater. More hours of modern drama at the Hofburg. Ingrid became totally absorbed by every performance, emerging like a sleep-walker and only much later pulling herself together to deliver scathing criticisms or condescending praise. All Ingrid's energy was thrust into the joy of living. Every night there was a gala occasion and some nights as many as three. Bill wished he had her stamina.

July ended with a magnificent party at Plechy Palace. This time Bill was sure he would see Marie, but once again she was absent.

'Where is Marie?' he complained to Ingrid and saw her face become taut and her eyes narrow.

'I told you, she's in love. She disappears for half the night quite often. I don't know why the Count allows it,' Ingrid replied, and turned away.

That night Bill lay sleepless, fretting at the mess of his life. What was Marie doing? As for Ingrid, had he been thoughtless and irresponsible, or was he the fool? Despite her beauty, Bill knew he could never love Ingrid. Like her city, Vienna, she was sophisticated, gifted, beautiful, but built to endure: beneath the joy she was solid granite. He'd have to return to Berlin and acknowledge his failure to win back Marie. He knew he had lost something infinitely precious. Furthermore, it was his own fault.

At two in the morning, Bill received a call from Andy Johnson, an old friend, who worked at the American Embassy in Berlin. 'Bill, last week we issued permits for sixty-five Austrian Jewish children to enter the United States. Some of them are orphans, but most of them were left behind when their parents were arrested and taken away just after *Anschluss*,' Andy said.

'Certain Nazi authorities received a massive bribe from unknown sources to look the other way. The children's train leaves Austria at 5 a.m. this morning. Sorry to give you such short notice, but everything's so damned clandestine, it's hard to know exactly what's going on and when. They'll be accompanied by Red Cross officials and some members of the Austrian underground, who were responsible for finding and rescuing these kids. Most of them were in hiding. God knows how many more there are left alone.

'We'd like a story. Would you be prepared to do us a favour? It must only break after the kids reach neutral territory, for obvious reasons. No word about bribery, of course. The point is, we have to find foster homes in the States, and we need an emotional piece, something to pluck the heart strings. Can you cover this?'

'Sure. It'll be good to write about something positive for once.'

'And can you guarantee your report will be syndicated throughout the States?'

'It so happens that I have a few favours owed to me.'

'Thanks. This is where you must be at 4 a.m.'

*

The children were scared, miserable, bewildered and unwilling to leave the country without their parents who, in most cases, had simply disappeared without warning.

Looking at the sad eyes and pale faces of the shocked, stumbling little mites, Bill was acutely reminded of his own childhood when he had lost his parents. He shared their grief and shock, but realised his experience was soft in comparison.

Bill found the Red Cross official in charge, an older man who was blinking hard to keep his composure. 'I'll tell you all I can,' he said, 'which won't be much. We were contacted three days ago and told that by some miracle sixty-five children had permits to leave Austria, plus temporary Swiss visas. The Red Cross in Geneva will look after them until they leave for America. Transport was needed, plus international supervision, so we came along to help.'

'Only sixty-five?'

The official nodded. 'I know . . . I know. They tell me that it's not so easy to find them. We just pray to God that the Resistance unearth them before the Nazis do.'

'I'll do my best with my story,' Bill said gruffly, trying to control his emotions. 'Who's in charge here?'

'Sorry! I can't tell you that. You can say the Red Cross, but confidentially, this has been organised by students claiming to be members of an Austrian Resistance movement. Some of them are very high-placed and a lot of money has changed hands. They must remain anonymous. Photograph the children, please, but not the organisers. If you get an accidental shot, destroy it. Someone's life could be at stake.'

Suddenly, without any doubt, Bill knew exactly why Marie had been missing for so many days and nights. He swore long and silently.

He found her, as he'd known he would. She was sitting in a carriage with a group of toddlers. Eight pairs of frightened eyes stared up at him. Some of them were crying, but Marie was reading them a story, trying to make herself heard over their dismal sobs. They were huddled closely against her, as if touching her made them safer.

Marie looked exhausted. There were shadows under her eyes, her face was grimy and she was scruffily dressed, grubby, nervous, pale-faced and thinner than ever. Her hair hung limp and unwashed and her fingernails were chewed. She was still the most desirable woman he had ever seen. What was this vital ingredient which made him love her so much? Her goodness, Bill decided. Goodness shone out of her, transcending everything else.

Why the hell had he been traipsing around those futile society functions when the woman he loved was risking her life, night after night, and giving all she had to give? 'Sweet Jesus,' he muttered, watching her. 'What sort of an idiot am I?'

He said: 'May I take a photograph, please? Turn your back away from the camera. I don't want to show your face.'

She looked up, relief shining in her eyes. 'Oh Bill, it's you. Thank God! I knew someone was watching us. I thought it was the Gestapo . . . but it's you.'

Bill couldn't speak for the lump in his throat. He reached forward, took her hand and squeezed it. For a long time they gazed into each other's eyes.

'Marie, there's so much I have to say, but now is not the time. Forgive me, Marie. I love you.' He touched her lips with his fingers.

The small child tucked closely into her arms looked up at him curiously. 'Who are you?' she asked.

'My name's Bill. What's yours?'

'Hilde. Hilde Stein.'

'Hello, Hilde,' Bill said.

'Do you like my new coat?'

'Yes, very much.' he said, hoarse from emotion.

'Auntie Marie bought it for me.' She shot Marie a glance of pure devotion and pressed closer against her.

'We're going to America,' Hilde said.

'Yes, I know. That's where I come from. You'll be happy there.'

Sleepily, the child snuggled into Marie's lap.

'How did you get involved with this?' Bill asked quietly. 'I mean ... that's why I'm here ... for a story. The Embassy called. How did it begin?'

'It all began with Hilde here. She came first.' She gave the child a quick hug. 'I was at the station early one morning ... just before dawn. Hilde's mother thrust a note into my pocket ... But that's a bigger story, for now just write about the children and their longing to be safe and free and their hopes that their parents will one day come and find them.

'Tell them how we desperately need entry visas and immigration papers. It's difficult to get these things. That's why we need publicity. We've had a lot of help from the Church of Sweden, but I don't think that you should write about that.'

'Marie,' he muttered. 'You're someone very special to me. I want you to know that if you ever need me ... for anything ... I'll be ready. I'll wait for you forever, if I have to ...'

'Not now, Bill, don't sound so serious, please. You're frightening the children.'

He stood up as the train began to jolt and whistles blew. 'When will you get back?' he whispered.

She shrugged. 'As soon as possible. I'm going through to Switzerland. I don't trust the border guards. We have the necessary permits, but there's a suitcase full of dollars up above me in case of problems.'

The train began to move. Bill stood poised in the doorway. 'Take care of yourself,' he said hoarsely.

Chapter  22

BILL STOOD ON THE PLATFORM feeling dazed. He had found Marie. There was hope for them. He knew now that he loved this woman with all his heart. He could never love anyone else. He was awed by her heroism. He watched the train until it moved out of sight, longing to be with her. Obsessed with images of her and the children, he blundered into someone, knocking them flying.

'You look as if some coffee would do you good, Bill,' a voice boomed in his ear. 'Come with me. I'm Eric Perwe.'

Goddamit, it was that tall Swede Marie had been seeing. What the hell was he doing here? His temper surged, but behind his male ego was a journalist and Bill sensed a story. He'd play along, he decided.

The Swede lived in a small cottage next to a church ... Church of Sweden, Bill read. As they walked up the path between the flowers, a woman in a white apron came running out.

'Pastor, come inside. The Brownshirts have been hanging around. They've gone now, but they'll be back. Scum ... Scum ...,' she muttered. She rubbed her hands on her apron and closed the door behind them.

Pastor?

Eric was gazing into the mirror adjusting his clerical collar. He smoothed down his hair and turned with an apologetic smile. 'It just doesn't help to walk around in a uniform nowadays, particularly this uniform. I'm a marked man as it is.'

For a moment Bill lost his tongue. He felt bewildered and then pleased. A pastor! Not a rival after all. Just another good man risking his life to help the children ... and helping Marietta, too. Bill felt ashamed of his jealousy.

'I'm not worried for myself,' the Pastor was saying. 'I have the Church and Swedish Embassy behind me, but I worry about those people who are seen in my company. Particularly Countess Marietta, who is altogether special.'

The cottage smelled of comfort: polish, coffee brewing, newly-baked bread, the heady scent of roses in a bowl in the hall. Bill allowed himself to be tempted to breakfast and moments later they were sitting around a large table in the breakfast room, the housekeeper plying them with fish and minced herring, coffee and warm bread.

'How did you know about Marie and the children? I've been worrying ever since I saw you. Is our security slipping so much? Tell me.'

'The American Embassy needed a story, so they contacted me. I had no idea Marie was involved until I saw her on the train. I'll focus only on the children ... no mention of Nazi corruption or who organised what. Just an emotional piece about orphaned children who need foster homes back in the States.'

'Good! Excellent! Screen your pictures carefully. The Nazis will, I can assure you of that.'

'Yes, I've been warned.'

There was sudden crash from below, the sound of splintering glass, footsteps pounding in the hallway. Eric hustled his housekeeper into the kitchen. 'Stay there,' he said, as he bundled her into a cupboard.

'Don't go out,' Bill yelled, but Eric was already running to the hall, arms outstretched.

'My friends,' he began, foolishly, Bill thought.

Bill reached the doorway in time to see Eric fall from a blow to the back of his head. He was kicked as soon as he collapsed. Time turned to slow motion. Bill lurched at the group of burly, thug-like figures in brown SA uniforms who were kicking Eric. He kneed the nearest man in the testicles and brought his hand down hard on the back of his neck as he tumbled forward. A face leered towards Bill and he drove at it, hating it, sticking his thumbs into the eyeballs, using his strength to pin the man against the wall and feeling pleased at the howl of anguish. Bill fought his way towards the priest. He saw Eric spread-eagled across the threshold.

All the frustrated anger Bill had bottled up for months came frothing out. He lunged forward, felt the power of rage surging through him, dulling pain. He heard his voice yelling. His vision was failing through a sea of red mist. He didn't know why. He felt nothing. Just joy at hitting and kicking everyone within reach. It all came to an abrupt end with a searing white flash. Then a sense of floating.

Chapter  23

BILL REGAINED CONSCIOUSNESS AT MIDNIGHT. After a few moments of confusion he realised that he was in hospital. He remembered the attack and felt surprised that he was still alive. The ward was quiet and the night light was on. Bill wondered if his kidneys had been kicked out of place. It sure felt like it. He was desperately thirsty, but when he tried to call out his voice was a faint croak. He heard a noise and a woman bent over him with a glass of water. It was Ingrid. He smiled up at her.

'Only a sip,' she said as she tilted the glass. Her eyes were haggard and her face was pale. 'Oh Bill. I've been here for hours. I've been so worried about you. What happened?'

'How did you know I was here?' Bill whispered.

'Pastor Perwe called uncle.'

'But I thought ... The last time I saw Eric he was knocked out and covered in blood.'

'Just a bruise and a cut, or so he said. The Brownshirts left him in the garden, but his housekeeper called the doctor. You were both brought here, but he's gone home now. The Count's been here and so has the American Ambassador. You should feel very important.' She smiled tenderly.

'I feel sore.' Bill struggled to sit up, but the pain in every part

133

of him was too intense. 'It was very quick. A couple of minutes from beginning to end.'

'How did you get so badly beaten?' she asked. Her eyes filled with tears, but she dabbed them with a handkerchief and a minute later she was bravely smiling.

The little woman bears up, Bill thought cynically, and hated himself for it. 'I don't know,' he said. 'I was too busy trying to hurt them. I feel as though I was run over by a steam engine, but I don't think there's anything seriously wrong.' He desperately wanted to get up, but knew he couldn't.

'The doctor says you must spend the night here.'

'Fuck the doctor. Why are you here ... ?'

'Where else should I be? I care ... Bill, must you stay here in Germany? I mean ... I would love ...' She flushed.

Bill cringed. He had to face up to Ingrid and the awful thing he'd done to her. It might as well be now. Best to get it over with and tell her about Marie. He sank back on to the pillows. 'Ingrid, we must talk.' Bill reached out towards her and Ingrid took his hand in both of hers and sat squeezing it, while her eyes oozed love and happy anticipation.

'I've been selfish ...'

'Shh!' She put her finger over his lips. 'Why don't you go to sleep? We can talk about the future in the morning.' There was a world of caring in her eyes as she gently placed his hand on the blankets.

'I feel so close to you, Ingrid, sort of brotherly. You seem like family to me,' he began clumsily. 'You're a beautiful woman, Ingrid, but for me you're Marie's sister, and I love you because of this.'

Bill watched her face change. The sparkle went out of her eyes and the dim night light accentuated her cheekbones and her lovely slanting blue-green eyes. Underneath that pretty exterior was a sad woman.

'Why don't you give me a chance? Give us a chance? Please, Bill,' she babbled. 'I'm ideal for you. Furthermore, I'm free. Marietta will never be free. Not for you.'

'But I love her,' he said quietly. 'Forgive me, Ingrid.' He tried to hold her hand, but she pulled it away.

'All right, Bill,' she said, tucking her bag under her arm and pulling on her gloves. 'Enjoy your silly dreams. Do you think that Marietta would give up her estates and castles, to live in America? Or are you planning to live in Czechoslovakia as some sort of a Prince Regent?'

'The question doesn't arise. At least, not now. We haven't talked about the future.' He closed his eyes and for a few moments was only conscious of the pounding in his head.

Watching him, Ingrid felt anger stirring. What cowards men were. He'd led her to believe that he was going to propose. He'd made a fool of her. Good God, half of Vienna had been congratulating her for weeks. He was a thoughtless bastard ... a rotten liar ... a cheat. She had longed to go to America. Watching him, she began to feel bitter and vengeful. Everyone would laugh at her. She was poor little Ingrid again. Marietta would get everything, as usual. But that wasn't the worst of it by half. She loved this worthless bastard.

She stood up, shaking with rage and hurt and genuine fear of the future. 'You're a fool, Bill. You should have fallen for me. I'm free of all responsibilities.'

'Oh God, Ingrid,' Bill groaned. 'I wish I had. Believe me.'

'You pompous, lying fool,' she said.

Marie arrived later the following day. When she saw him she flushed and smiled shyly. She came to the side of the bed and held his hand. For a while they sat in silence gazing at each other.

'You look awful,' she said eventually.

'Awful!' There was that British boarding school again. Bill reached forward and pulled her down over him, smoothing her hair with his hand.

'But not as bad as I had expected,' her voice was muffled by the bedclothes. 'Let me up. Someone might come. When Father told me, I was so frightened for you. I've been so wrong,' she said. 'Oh Bill, I've been such a fool. We don't have to destroy the present, just because we don't have a future.'

She leaned over him and gently kissed him on the lips.

'I'd be beaten up anytime just to hear you say that,' Bill said happily.

Chapter  24

LOUIS WAS SITTING IN THE COLD and draughty utilitarian hall of the Corn Exchange Buildings in Prague, which was used for workshop concerts to launch unknown musicians. Only the first six rows were filled.

Andrea was to play the solo in Telemann's Oboe Concerto. The final movement was a stiff test for the soloist's virtuosity and Louis admired her courage at choosing the piece. As he sat listening to the orchestra tuning up, his palms grew damp in apprehension. When she emerged from the wings looking drawn and nervous she was wearing a black dress that was absolutely wrong for her.

'Oh God, Andrea, what have you done to yourself?' Louis muttered, appalled by her hair crimped in the latest Marcel wave and her pale pink lipstick. He leaned back and tried to relax. It was nothing to him if she made mistakes, he assured himself, nor was her lack of fashion sense; he had come to listen to her debut.

By the end of the concert Louis felt light-headed with pride. Andrea's playing had been inspired; not faultless, far from it, but brilliant in her emotional interpretation and delicacy. Louis rushed out of the hall, bought a basket of flowers from the vendor and retraced his footsteps, stiff-legged with tension. No

one challenged him as he entered the stage door and made his
way to the dressing-rooms. Andrea, surrounded by her family
and friends, was laughing with joy. But when she saw Louis in
the mirror, her expression changed to shock, then anger. Louis
placed the flowers on the dressing-table and bent over her. 'I
have never enjoyed the concerto so much before. Tonight I
realised what it's all about. I have you to thank for that,' he
finished awkwardly.

'You shouldn't be here,' Andrea muttered. 'Why can't you
keep away?'

'Why can't you trust me?' he said, tight-lipped and furious.

'It's not a question of trust . . .'

'Andrea, forget what Father said. He's out of tune with the
times. Listen to me,' he snapped as she turned away, leaning
forward impulsively, catching hold of her shoulder, forcing her
to face him.

'Damn you, Louis.' In one violent gesture, she swept the
flowers to the floor and shook off his hand.

Andrea's mother came forward, her face twisted with curiosity and embarrassment. 'Aren't you going to introduce us to
your friend, Andrea?' She turned to Louis. 'I'm Frau Soltys and
this is my husband, Charles.'

Louis was about to speak but Andrea interrupted. 'He's not
a friend,' she said too loudly. 'As a matter of fact he's slumming
it tonight. Have you met Count Louis Burgheim, Father?
Didn't you conduct concerts at Sokol Castle for Princess
Lobkowitz, his late grandmother? He's studying music at
Munich University because he has nothing better to do.'

Her mother gasped. 'Andrea! How could you be so rude?'
She turned to Louis and curtsied.

Louis cringed.

Her father stepped forward and bowed apologetically. 'She's
not like this usually, believe you me. She's the kindest girl. This
was her first solo and she's feeling the strain. We'd be honoured
if you would join us at home in a small celebration. I was very
impressed by her performance. What did you think?' Herr
Soltys prattled on, assuming acceptance of his invitation,

diplomatically gathering the party together.

In the darkness of the corridor, as they all filed out, Andrea whispered fiercely in Louis' ear: 'Don't you dare to come. I can't bear to see them fawning. Oh, I hate you. I'll never forgive you for coming.' Then she grabbed hold of a young man and went off on his arm. Feeling hurt, but determined, Louis ushered six members of the Soltys party into his car and followed the convoy home.

The house was elegant, modern, and devoted to the musical careers of the family. It seemed miraculous that they all fitted into the tiny rooms around the grand piano, the conservatory, the statues of Mozart, Beethoven and Bach, and the various musical instruments lying here and there.

Her father was a short thin man with a great intensity of movement and gesture. Beneath his nervous posturing, he was a kind and pleasant man. He had pale eyes and blond hair which kept falling over his forehead, while his thin white hands kept smoothing it back again.

His wife was overawed by Louis' visit. She was tall and thin and appeared surprisingly young. Louis thought she looked elegant and fashionable, watching her trim figure dart amongst her guests, ensuring everyone had food and wine.

As Andrea studiously avoided Louis, her mother fussed over him. She told Louis about Andrea's gypsy grandmother, her *husband*'s mother she emphasized, who had been a famous dancer and singer in Prague. Andrea's grandfather, a pianist from Budapest, had fallen madly in love with her and married her against his family's wishes. It was clear that Frau Soltys was not altogether happy with her late mother-in-law. Louis also learned from Madame Soltys that her husband was still waiting to achieve fame and fortune through the pieces he had composed, mainly concertos based on Czech folk-songs.

When Louis said he would like to hear them, Frau Soltys obligingly put on some records at high volume in the music room. Louis sank into an armchair listening as he observed the many aunts, uncles, cousins and friends in the pleasant but small house on the outskirts of Prague. He felt himself both an outsider and also at home with everyone there, bound by their love of music.

The compositions came to an end at last and Louis knew he should go, but could not bring himself to do so. He tried to prolong his stay by discussing the music with Herr Soltys. Anything to stay longer, when he heard excited chattering and a crowd of young people waved goodnight as they passed. Andrea's parents hurried after them and moments later he heard voices at the front door raised in farewell. Andrea stood in the doorway, hand on hip, brown eyes smouldering balefully.

'Go,' she said, striding across the room to grab his wrist and pull him towards the door. 'Go home, Louis. Go home and never come back.'

He tilted his head, churning with fury. 'Who's the boyfriend you've been hanging on to all evening?'

'It's nothing to do with you.'

'Yes, it is. You were mine from the moment we met and you know it.' His words were an angry growl.

Her eyes filled with tears. 'How dare you be so possessive! No one will ever own me, and there are plenty of better men in the world. Xavier could teach you a thing or two about manners for a start, you arrogant ...' she spluttered in outrage and half-pushed him down the corridor towards the door, showing amazing strength.

'Which one was Xavier?' he wondered looking over her shoulder at the three men left in the living-room. One was staring at Andrea, quivering with anger, but her mother had him pinned in the corner beside her.

He caught hold of her, shaking her roughly. 'Listen,' he said hoarsely. 'Swear to me by all you hold sacred that you feel nothing for me and I'll never trouble you again. But don't lie to me, because it's too important.'

'Why should I? Why should I lie ... ? To make you feel better about your stupidity and selfishness ... you and your sister ... you never thought how others might get hurt. And what was it all for? Just to prove you two could survive without your bloody chauffeur ... and fifty thousand uniformed flunkies for a month or two? Get out!' She gave him a sharp push and he staggered back, taken by surprise.

Suddenly Xavier was bounding towards him, fists clenched and held high in front of his chest – a stupid stance. Louis kicked his feet from under him and punched his jaw as he lurched off balance. He fell awkwardly, and remained prone on the floor, blocking the tiny passage.

Everything seemed to be happening in deathly silence. Andrea was backed against the wall looking furious. Her father's expression changed from mild incredulity to menace, and even Madam Soltys looked offended.

There was a pregnant silence. Manfully, Louis threw all he had into it. Three magic words: 'Marry me, Andrea.'

Chapter  25

SURPRISINGLY, FATHER GAVE IN without much of a fight. Louis went straight back to Plechy Palace to confront the Count. He found him nervously pacing his study, a glass of brandy in his hand, a notebook and pencil on the desk where he had been jotting down his thoughts.

'I'll marry Andrea whether you like it or not,' Louis began without much preamble. Father looked surprised, but not angry.

'I'm prepared to leave all this ...' he gestured around vaguely. 'I can earn a living ...'

'You won't get far as a concert pianist, my boy,' his father said gently.

'No, you took care of that for me. I couldn't practise, I was too busy being "brought up".'

The Count crumpled. His face seemed to droop and his lazy eye wandered away as if to avoid this confrontation. Then he reached out towards Louis. 'Forgive me, Louis. You were born into the wrong family.'

'Look Father,' Louis said, stepping away from his father's groping arms. 'I'm prepared to face family and State duties, but only with Andrea as my wife. That's final. She's strong and beautiful and good and brave .... If I searched the world I wouldn't find better, but all that is beside the point. The fact is, I've chosen her.'

'Yes!' The Count looked distracted. 'Very well.' He swung forward the portrait on the wall behind his desk and fumbled with the combination of his safe. For a few moments he fumbled amongst its contents, then he withdrew a small box and handed it to his son.

'Here you are Louis. I accept your choice, and not only because I have no alternative. The truth is, I like Andrea. I felt very sorry . . .'

'You had no right.'

'Yes, yes, perhaps. I'll be honest with you. Once, in my false pride, I thought there were only twenty men sufficiently eligible to marry Marietta and that you would have to choose from amongst the Habsburg women. I brought you both up with that belief, too. It's too late to change the past, but fortunately you and Marietta have more sense than I, and take account of the future. Life never neglects to teach its bitter lessons.

'Lately, I've been thinking about this obsession to be the favoured few, the superior or the élite, the Master Race, the world's aristocracy, the richest or the best. This desire has always trapped mankind and the path leads downhill straight to evil. It's a simple choice we have to make: on the one hand the brotherhood of man, on the other the creed of elevating the powerful few above the remainder. It doesn't seem like a choice between good or evil, does it? But it is. Step on this path and there's no turning back. I shudder for humanity.'

Louis was only half-listening. In his hand was the von Burgheim betrothal ring – a huge emerald surrounded by sapphires. It had been in the family for centuries. His step-mother had always worn it, and presumably his own mother before then. It hadn't brought either of them much joy, he reflected and was tempted to hand it back, but instinctively he felt that such a ring would symbolise family acceptance of Andrea.

'I'm rambling,' Father was saying. 'Forgive me. That's one of my biggest faults. Louis, listen to me. You must go now. I have a guest arriving. Things are happening ... matters which I cannot discuss with you. There are many people in Germany who hate the Nazis and I am one of them. I have never made a secret of it.' He broke off and clapped Louis on the shoulder.

Louis felt astonished as he walked out. What did Father mean? Was he involved in a conspiracy against the Third Reich? But no, of course not. The nearest he would ever get to subversive activity would be writing a letter to the newspaper. Even then it would be so erudite as to be incomprehensible, silly old fool, he mused affectionately. Despite their deep differences he loved the old man. The thought came unbidden and it was strangely shocking.

Ingrid hardly left the palace after Bill's sickbed confession. She gave in to the despair and rejection that was gnawing at her. What would become of her? Who would want to marry her? In one brief conversation, Bill had taken away her love, her future home, her security, her feeling of self-worth ... everything!

Bill loved Marietta. He always had. He had only used Ingrid to keep in with the family. How dare he play with her, lead her on and let her believe that she was the reason for his visits to the palace? How could he be so manipulative? While she, like an idiot, had worn her heart on her sleeve.

Autumn came and Ingrid became increasingly bitter and vengeful. She lost weight, her hair hung lank and dull, her skin erupted in blemishes and her eyes looked haggard. Worry gnawed at her. She'd wasted her first season on Bill. Now she was twenty and penniless. She was practically an old maid. Eventually it was Hugo who came to her rescue, persuading her to meet him for lunch.

'You've been avoiding me, or so it seemed. Perhaps I have offended you?' He made a show of affection and complimented her on her appearance when she arrived promptly at one.

Hugo had chosen a discreet, Italian restaurant where they

were unlikely to meet anyone they knew. In his grey suit with navy shirt and Paisley tie, he looked distinguished and fit. His hooded eyes gleamed with suppressed amusement as he examined Ingrid's face.

She had dressed with care. In her navy classic Chanel suit and white straw hat she felt that she looked sophisticated and beautiful. Closer inspection, she knew, would reveal her chewed fingernails, the shadows under her eyes and her pale face, which she had made an effort to hide with rouge and lipstick.

'So it is Marietta Roth loves, after all,' Hugo said, without any pretence at subtlety. 'He used you to be with her. Marietta's just as guilty, she was playing games. All your life you've been used. Poor little Ingrid.'

Ingrid flushed and bent her head. 'Ancient history, Hugo,' she said with a touch of bravado. 'What was, *was*.'

Hugo laughed. 'You wouldn't have liked living in America. Much better to stay here.' He bent forward and whispered. 'Listen to me carefully. Eastern Europe is destined to join the great German empire. One of my less important briefs is to investigate claims of those Germans who had their property stolen by the Bolsheviks. It is possible that some estates will be restored to the rightful owners by a grateful nation . . .'

'Grateful?'

'For services rendered to the Führer.'

Ingrid tried to look unconcerned, but her mouth was pulled taut and her fingers were white as they gripped her glass. He's lying, she thought. Nothing has ever worked out for me. Why should this plum fall into my lap?

'Join us, Ingrid,' Hugo said urgently, 'and help our heroic armies to restore to you what is properly yours.'

She said coldly: 'I don't believe you, Hugo.'

'Why not?'

He could be vicious, Ingrid realised, noting the raised eyebrow, the narrowed eyes, the tenseness of the man.

'Hitler is intent on despoiling the aristocracy, not reimbursing them. Why should your Aryan soldiers shed their blood to restore property to a Russian-born princess?'

'That's my Ingrid,' Hugo enthused. 'Observant, courageous and shrewd. You're also a survivor. That's why I've had my eye on you for some time.'

'What do you mean?'

'Order your food and we'll talk,' he said.

'Let me be specific,' Hugo began when the waiter had left. 'I need the assistance of a clever and well-connected woman who can infiltrate anti-Nazi circles at the very highest level. You would be perfect. In return for passing on certain information I would pay you well.'

Ingrid began to believe him. All her life she'd had to fight and manipulate to get what she wanted, now Hugo was offering her the chance to do exactly that. 'And how would I explain away my sudden wealth?' She tried to hide her eagerness.

'I'll arrange for one of our banks to contact you about an inheritance. Our story would be that before his death, your father deposited certain funds in a Swiss bank, from which you will now receive interest.'

'It's a little late to find out about an inheritance, don't you think?'

'No! Parents often bequeath fortunes for their heirs to inherit when they reach twenty-one. You're almost twenty-one, and with the new discretion laws no one can query such an arrangement.'

It all seemed so plausible, Ingrid thought as she sipped her wine. Hugo didn't want much for his money, either. She sat in silence for a few moments. Marietta was obsessed with her philanthropic activities, the Count was too distracted to take much notice of the family nowadays, and Louis was seldom at home.

'A spy?' she said, testing the word.

'No, not a spy. Never a spy! You'll merely be helping me with my research.'

Ingrid was no fool, but if Hugo wanted to give her job a spurious title, she wouldn't argue.

She smiled and said 'yes' and listened intently while Hugo explained how she must set about her task. He told her exactly what it was he wanted her to do.

She thought about his instructions as she ate her sorbet. Of course, Hugo had not mentioned the biggest payoff, which was the chance of avenging herself on Marietta and Bill.

Chapter  26

MARIETTA OPENED THE FRONT DOOR of her flat with a sense of relief. This was her first real home and she loved it. She was glad to be back in Munich for the autumn term. As she stepped inside, the heady scent of roses wafted down the passage. 'Heavens!' she gasped. A florist had emptied his van here. Was a new boyfriend hovering? The thought was strangely unwelcome, but Andrea had been so miserable this year and she deserved to be happy.

Andrea was sleeping. Marietta looked in and saw long dark hair tangled over the pillow. One hand was thrown over the duvet and as Andrea stirred Marietta saw a ring glittering on her engagement finger. She gaped in surprise and tiptoed closer. How many times had she watched that gigantic emerald glittering on her mother's elegant hand? For a moment she was lost in wonder ... Louis and Andrea! All her pre-conceived notions of birth and class and the rightness of things, which had been drummed into her since early childhood, surged into her mind. This wasn't allowed! Louis must marry a Habsburg, mustn't he? Yet there was Mother's ring. Father must have agreed to their engagement, to hand over that betrothal ring.

Marietta dropped to her knees beside the bed and took Andrea's hand in hers. Andrea stirred and opened her eyes.

'What time is it?' She smiled softly. She was all dewy-eyed and languid with love.

'So we're going to be sisters,' Marietta said, smiling at Andrea. 'I could never have hoped for such good fortune.'

Andrea burst into tears.

'Why . . . what have I said?' Marietta said in alarm.

'Louis told me that I might lose you as a friend. He said that you put duty first and love far down on the list of your priorities. He said,' she smiled, 'that he didn't know which you were the most zealous about, your Catholic faith or the family tradition, but that you kept both well-concealed from everyone behind your liberal front.'

'He said that about me? How stiff-necked and old-fashioned I sound. Perhaps it's true, too. Andrea, I'm very happy for you both, truly. It's just that . . .'

Andrea sat up and gazed searchingly at her friend. 'You're not being honest with me, Marietta.'

'I was only thinking that if Louis can, surely I . . .' she broke off. 'Tonight we'll throw a party for all our student friends, if that's agreeable.'

'It certainly is agreeable,' Andrea teased. 'But Marietta, how did you know? Did Louis call you?'

'You mean you don't know about this ring? My mother wore it, and my grandmother. The bride of every von Burgheim heir has worn it for six centuries. One of these days I'll tell you its history, or maybe Louis should.'

She found herself flushing under Andrea's relentless scrutiny. 'It's going to be a bit more complicated than Louis said, isn't it, Marie?'

'Yes. It would be wrong to lie to you. Very complicated, but no more difficult than playing Telemann solo in public,' she said flatly. 'You'll manage. We'll all help you. And you'll always have Louis beside you.'

She went into her room and shut the door. She took off her coat methodically and hung it in the wardrobe. Then she sat on her lonely bed and shuddered. If Louis could throw duty to the wind, why shouldn't she? Bill was the only man she would ever love. Yet for her, there was no choice. Love was a joy, a gift, a luxury. It was not something solid on which you could base your life ... her life was based on duty. She had been brought up to shoulder her responsibilities, she couldn't take the selfish way out. Mother had done that, leaving a trail of heartbreak. Louis was wrong, but she loved them both, and if that was what they wanted, she would back them all the way. And, of course, Louis was a man, he could combine duty with love, a choice not open to her.

'Well, Count von Burgheim, here I am. What is it that you want to discuss in particular?'

The Count's visitor was General Hans Dietz, Deputy-Head of the Central Bureau of the German Intelligence, *Abwehr*. He had travelled all night to meet the Count in Vienna after an urgent message from a mutual friend.

The Count had not met the General before, but he knew that Dietz was reputed to be a man of considerable intellect, imperturbable in danger, and a brilliant military strategist. With his parade ground bearing and crew-cut grey hair, he looked every inch a soldier, too. He was sitting across the table, his chin resting on a clenched fist, elbow on the table and he was watching the Count with a bemused, puzzled expression.

The Count had never felt so scared in his life. He had chosen to approach Dietz first because he was known as a free-thinker, a rebel and he was closely associated with men the Count needed. But could he trust him? And if he could, would Dietz keep his mouth shut?

The Count cleared his throat and gazed at the table. This was his moment of truth, he would not get another chance. This was his self-appointed role and it was too late to turn back now. He said: 'I was with Schuschnigg at Berghof. I endured fifteen hours of non-stop rhetoric from our strutting Führer. To my mind the man should be committed to an insane asylum, he is not fit to be a head of state. He will lead us into terrible disaster.'

He looked up slowly and gazed searchingly at his companion.

Dietz had flushed red, but he could read nothing from the man's eyes.

'And so . . .?' Dietz said gently.

'I believe we share the same views.'

'Half of Germany's intellectuals share this view.'

'True, but unfortunately, Dietz, most Germans can do little about it. We, however, can.'

'Which is?'

'To bring together men who hate the Nazis as much as we do, and who have sufficient power to overthrow them.'

The Count turned away to disguise his fear. The die was cast. He had chosen a dark and dangerous path that would lead him perhaps to death and only God knew when he would ever see the end of it. He only knew that he would never stop until either the Nazis or he were destroyed.

It seemed that a century passed before Dietz answered him.

'I'm with you,' he said.

Much later, after Dietz had left, the Count poured himself a brandy and went through the recent negotiations he had held with those in high places. So far he had recruited thirteen brave and powerful men, mostly army generals. Between them they had the means to combat the SS divisions. Soon they would be able to start planning where and when and how best to convince the German people of their worth. The Count felt that he was getting somewhere.

Chapter  27

IT WAS A RAINY SUNDAY AFTERNOON, late in September and unusually cold. The wind was buffeting the trees in the park and it was overcast and almost dark, but in Marietta's apartment it was warm and well lit. The two girls were sprawled on the hearthrug, engrossed in their books, when the doorbell rang.

It was Pastor Eric Perwe, and he looked worn and wretched. He was even thinner than before; his cheeks were hollowed, his eyes haggard, and his forehead was deeply lined.

'It's getting rough,' he said, when the girls had helped him off with his overcoat and scarf and poured him a brandy. 'I've lost two safe houses. I'm desperate. I hate to ask you, but I need your help. Please ... I have a young woman ... It wouldn't be for long. You could pass her off as a student friend. Right now I have twelve young people on my hands and no place for any of them. My own house is overfull and no longer safe.'

It was accepted nowadays that they were always bargaining and bartering, he had helped them many times with exit permits and contacts for the orphans, and now they must help him. She had never seen him look so depressed. While he talked, she was considering the possibilities ... Louis had a spare bed for a male. She and Andrea had a spare room ... two could share it.

'I'm sorry, but this is an emergency. She's sitting outside on the park bench.'

'She must be frozen.'

'I'm sure she is. Can you help?'

'Yes,' the girls said without hesitation.

'Then I suggest you both go out into the park and pretend that you know her. Bring her back for supper and persuade her to stay the night, simply because it's late. That should satisfy your housekeeper. I'll find another place by tomorrow morning. I promise.'

The Pastor drained his glass. He looked ashamed. 'I'm sorry to do this to you,' he said. 'I am running out of friends.'

One look at the frail young woman shivering on the bench was enough to know that she was Jewish, a fugitive, frightened and very sick. How could they pass her off as a student?

Her name was Stella, and she had been studying to be a doctor until she was deprived of the right to study. Now she was on her way to Brazil, via the Pastor's chain, where she had been accepted as a farm worker.

The girls did their best to make Stella feel comfortable and safe.

It was after ten that evening when the doorbell rang again.

'I'll go,' Andrea said, turning pale. 'Stella, go to your room.'

Marietta stood frozen by the living-room fire as Andrea went to the front door. Then she heard Ingrid's voice in the passage, and relief surged through her.

As usual, Ingrid looked as if she had just stepped out of a fashion show in her turquoise slacks and cashmere sweater, topped by a mink jacket. She swept in, dropping the jacket on the back of a chair, and glanced round critically. 'What an atmosphere! Brr! So gloomy! So stuffy!' Ingrid pouted. 'I can see I'm not welcome.'

'What are you talking about?' Marietta snapped. 'Of course you're welcome, we weren't expecting you, that's all. Why didn't you let us know you were coming?'

'Yes, I'd have put some champagne on ice,' Andrea said

flatly. Marietta shot her friend a scathing look.

'I haven't yet congratulated you on your engagement, Andrea,' Ingrid purred. 'Isn't that ring a little large for you?' She smirked at her nails. 'Well, I'm teasing. It's just terrific . . . we'll be one happy family.'

Only, as usual, I'll be the poor one and you'll both be stinking rich, Ingrid thought, struggling to control her spite. Hugo was teaching her the art of manipulation and she knew she must appear warm and affectionate. Not a very good start.

'I came to ask you a favour.' She settled into the armchair nearest the fire.

'Ask away,' Marietta said.

'I've made up my mind to enrol at the University. I've discovered what I want to do. I'm going to be a writer.' Ingrid flashed a nervous smile at them both.

'Why not compose a symphony in your spare time?' Andrea snarled.

'Sorry if I've trodden on your artistic toes,' Ingrid said contritely. 'The point is, I've almost certainly got a place to read literature, even though term has started.'

Marietta frowned. 'Please don't snipe at each other.' She was relieved that Ingrid was moving towards the idea of a career. 'I think that's a splendid idea. You shouldn't fritter your life away in Viennese salons.'

'But where can I live? I have to throw myself on your mercy and beg a roof over my head until I can find rooms of my own.'

Marietta forced herself to appear relaxed. 'Ingrid, I'm afraid a fellow student is staying in our spare room tonight. She's leaving in the morning. In fact, we had thought of dispensing with our housekeeper and that would make two more rooms available, but it's Andrea's apartment as much as mine. Please excuse us while we discuss this.' She drew Andrea into the bedroom. 'We can't say no. She's family. We have to help her. All my life I've felt so guilty about Ingrid. Now that she's chosen a career, it's up to us to back her all the way. I know it's going to be awful, but what else can we do?'

'I'm worried,' Andrea said slowly. 'I know she's family, but

I don't trust Ingrid. Anyway, I'll leave it up to you. Whatever you decide is all right with me. I'm going to bed. I'll work better there.'

'Don't worry,' Marietta said. 'She's prone to sudden urges. She'll soon get fed up with studying.'

'You can move in tomorrow,' Marietta told Ingrid. 'You can have my bed tonight, if you like. I'll sleep on the sofa.' To her surprise, Ingrid insisted on taking the sofa.

After a few weeks, Marietta realised how she had under-estimated her cousin. Ingrid worked hard and never missed lectures. For the first time she was becoming interested in other people's problems. She spent hours talking to the girls about the plight of the Jews, consequently, Marietta was not surprised when Ingrid decided to join Edelweiss. From then on, she worked all hours. It didn't matter how menial the task was, Ingrid was prepared to help out. She collected cheques from sympathisers, stamped and addressed envelopes, carried heavy parcels to the post office, learned to operate the printing machine, attended their meetings and read all the right books.

When the students held their next editorial meeting, to plan their forthcoming newspaper, Ingrid was there.

'Let me help,' she said to the editor. 'After all I intend to be a writer.'

'Pass on whatever you write, we'll use it if we can,' he said.

'Well, here's the first. That surprises you, doesn't it?' She took an envelope out of her bag and tossed it onto the table. 'If you don't want it, throw it away,' she said mutedly.

'He doesn't need your permission to do that,' Andrea said, looking amused.

Ingrid had several good ideas, but she wasn't sure who to interview to get the facts she needed.

'I just need help to find some contacts. For instance, who gave you this information?' She did not look up as she flipped through past issues.

'Don't be dumb. How can we tell you that? Write what you feel, Ingrid. You'll gradually make the contacts.'

From then on Ingrid brought articles regularly and the editor used most of them. Everyone was amazed at her dedication and talent, only Andrea remained tight-lipped when Ingrid was around.

'I wish you'd get to like Ingrid,' Louis grumbled to Andrea.

It's my damned gypsy blood, Andrea thought. She makes the hair stand up on my scalp. I can almost feel the malevolence surging out of her. But I can't say that to Louis and Marietta.

'I'll try,' she said aloud.

'Andrea suspects me,' Ingrid said to Hugo. She was calling him from a public telephone near the park. 'She's always watching me. I don't trust her. I'd rather leave their flat.'

'You can't. If she makes trouble, I'll deal with her. Now I want you to spread your net as wide as possible. You say they took the last Jewess to the paper wholesaler. Are you sure of this?'

'Yes, of course I'm sure,' Ingrid snapped. Her guilt was making her bad tempered.

'I'd need to identify more of these subversives. Why don't you volunteer to help move the fugitives.'

'I have. They refused,' Ingrid said flatly.

'Keep trying. I have another batch of reports for their newspaper, and some statistics for Roth. When can you get here..?'

'Tonight? They're both going to a concert.'

'Usual place then.' A sharp click terminated the conversation. Ingrid walked slowly through the park. Working for Hugo was like stepping into a bog, you were trapped and sucked down and there was no way out. Meanwhile, Ingrid seemed far away from achieving her ultimate reward.

Chapter  28

INGRID ARRIVED IN BERLIN on the night express. She found a
taxi and gave the driver Bill's address. She looked divine and she
knew it, but not even her new blue woollen suit with matching
hat and gloves, could make her confident. She leaned back, lost
in her thoughts. It was a lovely morning. The sun had just
appeared after an early morning shower. Autumn mists hung
around trees and hedges and every building shone clean and
sparkling from the rain, but Ingrid only saw Bill's face and the
way he had looked at her in hospital. Once again she forced
herself to relive her torment. Ingrid longed to make Bill as
miserable as she was and Hugo had given her the means. In her
handbag she had enough statistics to incriminate Bill as a spy,
all she had to do was plant the evidence on him. He would be
deported, Hugo had promised her. Nothing more. The prospect
of Marietta's grief had brought Ingrid joy. Would Bill sense her
hatred and be warned? She forced herself to smile.

Bill was up early. He switched on the radio and listened to the
news while he made coffee. Hitler had called for a four-power
conference to be held at Munich to discuss the Czech crisis. No
one wanted war, Bill knew, but surely Britain and France would

take a stand against Hitler's demands if they understood the kind of New Order that Hitler had in mind for Czechoslovakia. He leaned over his typewriter and reread the article he'd been writing at midnight.

...*Germany's age-old dream to own vast colonies in Europe is about to be realised. The Germans call this dream, Lebensraum, which translated means: living space. Czechoslovakia has been targeted as Hitler's first objective. This will bring thirteen million Czechs and Slovaks into the Reich. They are destined to become slaves under Nazi rule. Czech soil will soon be handed over to German settlers piecemeal. The fat cattle and farming produce will be loaded on to trains and sent to feed the German people.*

Only two things can save Czechoslovakia now. First, the Bohemian fortifications, strongest and most modern in Europe which allied to the Czech fighting troops (known to be the best equipped in Europe), makes Czechoslovakia a tough opponent. Second and more important, the hope that Britain and France will stand by their treaties and protect this country from invasion.

The door bell rang. Bill glanced at his watch. 7 a.m.! It couldn't be Taube. He went to the door and cringed at the sight of Ingrid. But what a lovely sight she was ... all in blue, with her ash blonde hair falling in waves over her shoulders; she looked soft and feminine and very alluring, except for her eyes which glittered like ice crystals.

She stepped forward to kiss his cheek and Bill was enveloped in an aura of costly French perfume, while her hair tickled his cheek.

'Mmm!' she said. 'What a gloomy expression.'

For gloomy read guilty, Bill thought. He stammered a greeting and led her inside.

'God, it's cold in here. How can you bear it?'

How slender she was, Bill noted with a pang, as he switched on his only heater; her thinness accentuated her high cheek bones and slanting eyes. Like an overbred filly, she was full of swift, sudden movements. Twisting and turning she paced the room, one jewelled fist pummeling her hand in tiny, suppressed spurts of energy.

'I've been hearing about your new career,' he said, flushing. 'Marie keeps me up-to-date with the family. She said you've got a lot of talent, Ingrid . . . that's just great. Maybe I can help you to get your work published.'

Did that sound brotherly? Or patronising? If only he could be spontaneous and warm, but his mind and his mouth and brains had fossilised at the sight of her.

He made Ingrid coffee and then some toast and more coffee, while she chattered away about her new friends and her hopes and dreams. 'Bill, I've been silly,' she said eventually. 'Let's be friends again. I value your friendship and I want it back.'

'Of course I'm your friend,' Bill mumbled.

'Then take me out to lunch. I want to spend a lovely day with you. A new beginning. I'm sorry I'm so early, I travelled overnight. Let's go out,' she said beguilingly. 'How about a walk in the park? Please, Bill.'

Perhaps because Bill felt so relieved to be let off the hook, he threw himself into enjoying the day. They walked for hours, lunched at the park, danced until teatime and walked again in the gathering mists, by now it was dusk and Ingrid showed no sign of leaving, so Bill took her to dinner.

Halfway through the meal, Ingrid put a large white envelope on the table between them.

She turned as white as the tablecloth and lowered her eyes as she said, 'That contains some very important information.'

Bill shuddered. 'What is it, Ingrid?' he asked awkwardly.

She tried to smile, but failed. 'I hate the Nazis,' she whispered, 'and my hatred is killing me.' She took the papers from the envelope. 'The German rearmament programme . . . it's for you.'

Bill smiled indulgently. She was unlikely to have obtained any classified information that he, with his excellent contacts, had not yet uncovered, but she was insistent so he scanned the pages.

Moments later Bill scooped the pages back into the envelope. Then he gazed around the restaurant carefully. No one was watching them, so he slipped out one sheet and read it slowly.

It gave precise details of the battle cruisers under construction in top secret German shipyards; next there were drawings of the prototype of a fleet of submarines being made covertly for the Nazis in Finland, Holland and Spain; plans of fighter aircraft being made in Russia, which he had known about, and precise numbers of Nazi troops being trained inside Russia by German Chiefs of Staff. He'd known about that, too, but the statistics turned mere rumours into a red hot certainty.

Ingrid leaned back and sipped her wine. Hugo had told her that Bill would be hooked by his bait and he was. She stifled a smile of triumph.

'Jesus, Ingrid! This is classified material. This could get you into prison.'

'It fell into my lap. Can you use it?' she asked sweetly.

'Use it?' He laughed softly.

'I had to pay for this material,' she began, suddenly overcome with nervousness.

'Fair enough! I'll pay you back.'

'All right,' she said, as if in huge relief. 'I thought you'd want it. I didn't know how to tell you how broke I am. How much is all this worth to you?' She gestured towards the papers.

'I normally pay a flat rate for information, as suggested by my bureau,' he said, feeling awkward that she was short of money. 'But obviously, I won't let you be out of pocket. First, tell me where you got hold of all this.' He tapped the envelope.

'... a close friend of Uncle's ...' she recited the fictional details Hugo had versed her in and gave an inward sigh of relief when Bill took out his cheque book.

'I don't want the cash for myself, Bill,' she flushed and looked ashamed. 'The truth is, I keep borrowing from Marietta and I'm never able to repay her.'

'I bet Marie doesn't give it a thought.'

'But I do, Bill. That's the whole point of the matter. I care, so if you could just make out the cheque to her ...'

'What a funny goose you are,' Bill said. He made one cheque out to Marietta and another for Ingrid. 'That's your commission,' he said. Ingrid seemed more relaxed as they sipped their brandy and listened to an entertainer singing the blues.

What a strange girl Ingrid was, Bill thought. He didn't really know her or understand her. Would he ever? He took her to the station in time to catch the last train back to Munich. Then he went home to work through the night.

'You're not achieving enough, Ingrid.'

Hugo paced up and down his study after Ingrid had been shown in. Eventually he turned abruptly and leaned over her. 'Try harder,' he said.

Looking into Hugo's implacable, brooding eyes, Ingrid shuddered. 'I brought you Bill's cheque,' she argued. 'I told you about the Jews Marietta and Andrea are sheltering . . .'

'But you can do more . . . much more. Listen to me. I want you to understand the Nazi dream, so that you'll feel as inspired as I do.'

Hugo stood gazing out of the window, shoulders straight, head high. Ingrid couldn't help thinking what a magnificent looking man he was, but lately she did not find him attractive, she was too afraid of him.

'If the world imagines that the Führer will be content when he has united the Germans, they couldn't be more wrong,' he said softly, in his deep, vibrant voice.

'The genius of the Führer has won a giant victory for the Fatherland without a shot being fired. Britain and France are going to hand over the Sudetenland areas of Czechoslovakia to us on a plate. The rest of Czechoslovakia will be unprotected. In a few months time, we'll walk in unopposed. Next Poland, then the Ukraine . . . Yugoslavia . . . Russia . . . . That's when you get your family's estates restored to you, Ingrid. Isn't that a dream worth fighting for?'

He's mad, thought Ingrid, but I need to believe him.

The thirteen men sitting around the table in the Count's Berlin apartment, were also aware of Hitler's dream for a European Empire. The ravings of a maniac, they privately considered, a maniac whom they intended to execute to protect the Fatherland. Between them they controlled most of the German Army, the Wehrmach. They had enough power to arrest the top echelon of the Nazi party and hold Berlin against SS army attacks for days if necessary. They had been meeting for weeks and now their plans were finalised.

They would strike when Hitler issued the order to invade Czechoslovakia. The army generals would arrest the dictator and bring him to trial. He would be charged with recklessly pushing Germany into armed conflict.

Time was running short, they knew. The world was teetering on the edge of war. Britain had mobilised her fleet, and France had called up her reserves to man her border defences. Surely, France and Britain would back their treaties and stand firm against the Nazi threat. A meeting would be held at Munich on September 30, to hammer out an agreement in the face of Hitler's demands.

The Count stood up and said: 'Gentlemen, I pray to God that the British and French will hold firm against Hitler and that we shall succeed in bringing this evil man to justice.'

Shortly afterwards a long-distance call came through from their contact in the German Embassy in London. The Count looked stricken as he listened.

Minutes later he looked on the point of collapse as he turned to the members of the Conspiracy. 'Gentlemen . . . bad news . . . the West intends giving Hitler what he wants without a fight . . . in fact, more than he asked for . . . so now . . . how can we arrest him on the charge of endangering the Fatherland? The people will turn against us. Our plans have become farcical.'

The Count was filled with despair as he watched the meeting disband. Would no one take a stand against evil? Would the Nazis be allowed to impose their terrifying New Order all over Europe?

In the black days that followed Allied appeasement, it seemed to the Count that the only sane British politician was Winston Churchill. In his speech to the House of Commons, he said: '*We have sustained total and unmitigated defeat. We are in the midst of a disaster of the first magnitude. The road down the Danube ... the road to the Black Sea has been opened. All the countries of Middle Europe and the Danube Valley, one after another, will be drawn into the vast system of Nazi politics radiating from Berlin. And do not suppose that this is the end. It is only the beginning.'*

Chapter  29

THE NIGHTS WERE BECOMING longer and colder and the Bloomberg family were plunged into despair. It was a bleak October and their fears made it worse. Money was short, for hardly any customers patronised the music shop and they were living on Taube's earnings. Then came Bill's good news. They had been accepted as immigrants to the United States. Their permits would be available by the end of the month. Bill had not told them what strings he had had to pull, nor what it had cost him.

On October 25 a news broadcast informed all Jews that they must hand in their passports at the local police station within twenty-four hours. The Bloombergs did not, hoping against hope that the visas would come early.

At seven the following evening they heard hammering at the door downstairs.

'I'll go,' Father said, looking stricken. He returned looking haggard. 'They've come to fetch our passports.'

Odette began crying quietly. 'We're trapped,' she whispered, as she unlocked the safe. She clutched her husband and hung on to him. 'We should have made Taube go without us,' she muttered, between her sobs.

The doorbell rang again, but it was Bill's special ring. They clustered around him, sure that he could solve their misfortune.

Bill had never felt more inadequate. His contacts and his fortune and all his influence as a journalist were useless to help his friends. The futility of battling against inhuman and faceless red tape made him feel apathetical, but he knew he could not quit now. He was all they had. He made a show of being confident.

'We won't give up,' he said. 'Your visas will be through any day now. I have a friend who's intimately connected with the Austrian Resistance. They can buy exit permits. I'll contact them at once.'

Taube guessed that the friend was Countess Marietta, but she knew better than to comment.

From then on, the Bloombergs endured a traumatic time of nerve-jangling suspense. Each day seemed to last forever. The nights were fearful, every creaking floorboard, every footstep in the street a possible harbinger of the Gestapo.

On November 9, they heard on the radio that a seventeen-year-old German Jewish refugee had shot and mortally wounded Ernst vom Rath, the Third Secretary of the German Embassy in Paris. The youth's father had been among ten thousand ex-Polish Jews deported to Poland in boxcars shortly beforehand. Taube felt sick. This would provide a catalyst to set in motion more anti-Jewish riots.

At eight o'clock on the night of the tenth of November, Odette was darning a sock under the table lamp, trying to get the best angle in the dull light. She looked up, blinked and rubbed her eyes. 'Your father's working late. Put the kettle on, won't you, Taube? He should stop now. I can't see that his stocktaking is all that important anymore.'

'Did you hear thunder?' Taube stood up restlessly and went to the window. After a few minutes she flung it open.

'Oh, no, dear. You're letting all the warm air out. How could you?'

'Shh! Listen! And look over there. Flames ... and I can smell smoke. Can't you?'

They strained to hear what sounded like dull thuds, muffled shouts and then a scream, but the sounds were too far away to be identifiable.

Almost immediately there was the rumble of marching feet. Then a sound that could be glass breaking, followed by a shrill scream, although the sounds came in snatches in the wind.

Odette stood up and her mending fell forgotten to the floor. 'Fetch your father,' she said. She stood there, pressing both hands against her midriff. 'Hurry, will you? Tell him to lock and bar the shop straightaway.'

Taube began to run down the circular stairway.

'Oh God ... oh God ... Help us.' Her breath came in shallow gasps and there was a vice-like grip around her chest.

'I must be calm,' she muttered. 'For their sakes I mustn't crack.'

She stumbled on the last step, ricked her ankle and bruised her elbow as she fell against the banister. 'That's what panic does,' she said aloud, picking herself up and smoothing her hair. Her hands were shaking badly.

'Father, where are you?' The shop was empty. Then she saw him standing on the pavement with David Herschel from the bookshop next door. Father had opened the shop bars enough to pass through.

'Father, quickly, shut the shop. I'll help you. Mr Herschel, you must go inside and bar your windows.'

Mr Herschel usually stayed open until eleven, for he did most of his business in the evenings. '... thousands on the march ...' he was saying.

'Upstairs it sounds much louder, much nearer,' she said.

At that moment a van swung round the corner and several men in Hitler Youth uniform spilled out of it.

Taube screamed. Her father caught hold of her and with the help of Herschel pushed her into the shop, dragging the bars across the doorway.

The men hardly glanced at them. They had a job to do and

they were in a hurry. They pushed long sticks through the bars, shattering the glass which fell in jaggard shards over the inside of the shop and the pavement. One of them was carrying a pot of paint and a thick brush which he used on the wall.

Father and daughter stood stunned amongst the glass and heard the van drive further down the road. Soon the street was empty, but the thunder of the crowd was coming closer.

Mr Herschel was keening monotonously. Anton gently shook him, unlocked the gate, and half-carried him to his shop.

Taube followed, trying to help support the old man. It was then she saw the large red 'J' painted on their wall.

Herschel suddenly recovered his wits. 'Go back to your own home. I'll lock the shutters from the inside. Hurry!'

'They've marked us for the crowd,' her father said grimly. 'They don't want their nice, gentile-owned shops destroyed. This is a well-organised pogrom. I'm going to try to wash it off. I have some paint-remover . . .'

'Please, Father.' She tried to quell the hysteria in her voice. 'Come upstairs. Think of Mother. Please come.'

She stood arguing, wringing her hands, but suddenly Father made a dive at her and threw her bodily on to the stairs. She heard the door being bolted behind her as she sat rubbing her shins. Her limbs felt leaden as she walked upstairs.

When she opened the door to the living-room, the horrifying sound hit her like a steam engine. The total impact of shouts and screams, breaking glass, and the rumble of feet and vehicles, sounded like some voracious beast rampaging through the streets. Rushing to the window, Taube saw the crowd surge into their road. Brownshirts . . . Hitler Youth . . . crowds of civilians, some of them women . . . but they were like one unit, moving in unison, tearing down shutters and bars with pickaxes, breaking windows, dragging out the occupants and beating them in the gutters. Three trucks came hurtling down the street, horns blaring, and the victims were thrown on to them.

Her mother was becoming hysterical. 'Go and get your father, *now*.'

'Father's locked us in.'

'So, why doesn't he come up. He's gone mad.'

Below them, men were running towards their shop door
carrying a long pole. There was a dull thud and the sound of
wood and iron shattering. Now the footsteps sounded from
inside the shop. 'Father!' Taube cried.

The noise downstairs was terrible. Thuds as if someone was
being beaten. A groan. Angry shouts.

The door from the stairs was kicked open. A Brownshirt
burst in. His eyes were wild and grinning like a madman, his
brown hair flattened on his scalp with sweat, a bestial grimace
on his lips. With a shock she recognised their postman.

'Aha, Fräulein Bloomberg, I've always wanted you,' he
snarled, his voice hoarse with excitement. 'Let's have a look at
your tits.' He lunged at her.

'Don't touch me.' She gasped and backed away towards the
fire escape. She would have made it, but she stumbled on the
fallen needlework and he caught her arm, pulling her back
towards him. She could smell brandy and garlic and something
rotten on his breath. One hand ripped her blouse open and
wrenched up her bra. She screamed as his thick fist fumbled and
squeezed her nipples. Then she was fighting like a wild cat,
scratching, kicking, biting, trying to escape, but there were
more men. Many more and they pinned her back against the
table. 'No . . . no . . . no . . .' she sobbed.

She recognised their newsagent's boy, a pimply, dim-witted
youth, his large red penis pulsing in his hand. 'This is for you,'
he said, laughing crazily.

With a surge of strength, Taube lunged away from the table
and snatched up the poker, smashing it down on the postman's
head.

He fell to the floor yelling obscenely at her. The other men
angrily grabbed her, knocking her heavily over the table. They
pulled her skirt up over her head and tied it there, pinning her
arms inside her dress. Blinded and helpless, half-suffocated, she
felt her pants and stockings being ripped off.

Her body was bent back, her legs were forced apart and she
felt a violent pain in her crotch. Nausea and self-loathing welled

through her. She felt abandoned and worthless. She could not see or breathe, she was suffocating and she wished she could pass out, but the pain went on and on. Was it six, or seven? She heard someone making strange, inhuman noises and realised it was herself.

Eventually they left. There was no sound or movement in the room, just the rumble of shouting and destruction coming from the street. Bruised and bleeding, it took all her strength to roll off the table. She fell on the floor dazed, struggling feebly to loosen her belt through the thick woollen fabric of her skirt. Eventually she clawed her way into the fresh air. Where was Mother? She took a deep breath and, clutching the legs of the table, struggled to her feet, the pain in her back intense. She looked round, but the door to the study was still closed. There was no sound. 'Mother,' she cried.

It was then that she saw the Brownshirt sitting in the armchair by the fire. He had a glass of her father's brandy in his hand. He lifted it. 'That was a very good performance,' he said. 'You were very good, too. Now you must go down to the truck with your mother. Unless you want an encore, that is.'

Taube backed away towards the fire escape. She looked back, panic-stricken, and saw him lunge towards her. She jumped. She was falling . . . out of control. Then she clutched the railings and pulled herself on to the steel steps. She ran down and down, her mind filled with the sight of those savage eyes and the big hands reaching towards her.

Chapter  30

SOMETHING WOKE HIM. Bill sat up and switched on the light, glad to be freed from his nightmare. Then he shuddered. There was no comfort in waking, the nightmare was invading his days. It was real. The Bloomberg family were destroyed, Anton was dead, Odette 'resettled' in some camp in the East, he'd been unable to find out which one, and Taube was missing. He'd searched for her for days.

Bill shivered. His pyjamas were drenched with sweat and his blankets were on the floor. He stumbled into the kitchen to make coffee and was appalled to see how his hands were shaking. Gazing in the mirror, he hardly recognised his haggard face and swollen eyes. It was guilt that was driving him crazy, he reckoned. He should have got them out sooner. In disgust, he thrust away the insidious thought that there was nothing he could have done; the Nazis had all the power.

Then he heard the sound that must have woken him, like a kitten mewing. He put down his cup and went to the passage. He heard it again. Bill flung open the door and saw a body slumped against the wall. As he bent over it, he nearly gagged on the stench of blood, vomit and stale sweat.

'Oh my God . . . oh dear God . . .' He couldn't stop muttering as he half-carried and half-dragged Taube into his passage. Was she alive? How had she got here? She was so cold ... as cold as death.

His first reaction was to call an ambulance, but in this crazy New Order, they'd just ship her off to the camps. He got her into his bed, packed the blankets around her and turned on the heater. What the hell else could he do ... Then he remembered that a doctor or some sort of specialist lived on the same floor. Leaving the door ajar, he ran and woke the man, who came at once, with a raincoat thrown over his pyjamas. Bill made coffee while the doctor was closeted in his bedroom. When he emerged, his eyes were like stones, his mouth a thin line. He seemed to have trouble speaking coherently through his anger.

'You should be horsewhipped ...' he began. 'Men like you should be castrated. I intend to report you to the police. Is this how you get your kicks? Can you never get enough of it?'

'She's a Jew,' Bill said, his voice flat. 'The Brownshirts attacked her family. Her father is dead, her mother on some train to a camp. I thought she was dead too. I don't know how she got here.'

'Of course, I should have guessed.' The doctor blushed slightly. 'My apologies.'

'Does it matter?' Bill snarled.

'Not to me, my friend,' the doctor said. 'There'll be no charge. I've never set eyes on her, nor you. I've given her an injection. She's suffering from shock, exposure, rape, hunger, bruises ... Need I say more? Keep her safe, warm and fed for as long as you can. A strange world we live in, my friend.'

After a week of nursing and hiding Taube, listening for footsteps, avoiding the neighbours, and fearing for her life every second of every day, Bill set about trying to get Taube out of Germany. He offered to marry her, but Taube refused.

'I never felt particularly Jewish before,' she said, 'but now I do. I can't marry you, not even to save my life. Besides, it would be so unfair on you.'

Bill argued for days, but Taube would not give in.

Aware the Embassy would not bend immigration rules on his

account, he decided to contact Marietta. Frustrated by not
being able to speak to her immediately, he left a garbled message
with Andrea.

Bill was asleep when the phone rang. The sound of Marie's
voice brought an onrush of joy. Glancing at his watch he saw
that it was past midnight.

'What's wrong?' she asked.

'I need to help Taube . . .'

'Tell me what happened.'

After Bill had related the details of the attack on the
Bloombergs and how Taube had come to him, there was a long
silence. Then Marietta said: 'She shouldn't be with you. That's
the first place . . .' She broke off. When she spoke again, Bill
thought she'd taken leave of her senses. 'I'm planning a family
party at Boubin for my birthday. Please come.'

'Marietta, for Christ's sake, what are you thinking of? I don't
feel like celebrating. I'm not calling you for a social engagement.'

'Bill, it's all interconnected. I need you . . . with a capital N.
Truly!'

'All right. I'll be there. But there's a problem. I have to go to
Sweden for a few days. It's vital. I should leave the day after
tomorrow . . . I dare not leave . . .'

'We'll collect long before then.'

'I'll ring you when I get back.'

He replaced the receiver with relief. He knew that Taube
would be taken to a safe house where she would stay while her
forged papers and passport were being created. Then she would
join the Pastor's chain to get out of Germany. For the first time
in days he slept dreamlessly.

It was 6 a.m. when Bill awoke to the sound of a car drawing
up outside his apartment. He leaped out of a bed and peered
through the curtains, dreading the sight of a Gestapo van.

He saw an old man with a beard, wearing a clerical collar and
a black suit. The man identified himself as a Pastor in the local
Church of Sweden and affiliated to the Red Cross. He started
at every sound, anxious to be gone. In the nervous tension Bill

and Taube barely spoke. When she had gone the apartment was as silent as a tomb.

Bill had stumbled upon news which scared the hell out of him. From contacts high up in the Third Reich, he had been told that a German physicist, Otto Hahn, had developed a method to exploit the energy in the atom, following the discovery of a new radioactive process called nuclear fission, which could create unimaginable energy. Hahn's former assistant, Frau Lise Meitner, had fled to Sweden taking Hahn's research with her.

This was the reason for Bill's trip and the following morning, he flew to Stockholm and managed to contact Lise Meitner through the Jewish Board of Deputies. She spent several hours with Bill and gave him copies of her notes to send to the States.

Bill wrote a series of articles and took them, together with Meitner's notes, to the US Embassy, for transportation to the relevant authorities, via the Embassy bag.

He flew back feeling scared and depressed. War was threatening. If this new form of energy were to be used to make weapons, the West would be at the mercy of the Nazis. Once more he fought the thought that the Third Reich was indeed invincible.

Chapter  31

IT WAS THE DAWN OF 1939, but in the Bohemian mountains it could have been a century before, or millenium, Marietta thought. Nothing changed here. A narrow country road meandered south through slanting stony fields with patches of snow under hawthorne hedges. Soon the road reached the Upper Vltava Valley, a place of mists and marshes and mystical vistas of wild, haunting beauty. To the right lay calm, grey lakes fringed with snow, with patches of ice on their sullen surfaces. To the left, the Plechy Mountain rose to a sharp, serrated peak. Around the mountain, virgin forests shone white with snow. The only sound was the wind whining through the trees as Andrea and Marietta were driven by Jan towards the Boubin Manor. Jan parked the car by the roadside without being asked. The two girls shivered and eyed each other questioningly. Then, in the distance, they heard singing.

'Oh!' Andrea said. 'How beautiful.'

'Listen carefully,' Jan said, 'It is important that you understand what is happening here.'

Marietta eyed her driver curiously. He had undergone a subtle metamorphose, from humble servant to ... well ... what exactly? She wasn't sure. He was almost a fellow conspirator.

But he knew nothing of their plans, did he? Had he been spying on them?

The singing was coming from the woods, and through a fire break they could see a camp fire, a frozen lake, woodsmoke and meat sizzling – and boys – a hundred or more – were singing with the voices of angels. Their eyes glowed as brightly as the flames in the fire. It would have been idyllic, except that each boy wore the Hitler Youth uniform and held a pole with a swastika hanging from it.

Jan beckoned the girls to leave the fire, and as they walked down the path, their footfalls deadened by a carpet of pine needles, a handsome, bearded man stepped on to an upturned log and began talking to the boys. He looked as if he sprang from the land, a man of courage, with his noble features and blond beard. A Viking! He told them of the glory of the Nazi party and the wonder of their Führer who had been sent to unite them with Germans all over Europe. Together with their blood brothers in Germany they would become the greatest and most powerful race in the world. Soon they would conquer Europe and impose the glorious Nazi New Order wherever they went.

When they'd returned to the car, there was anger in Jan's eyes. 'This is how it begins,' he said. 'They feel called to a noble cause. They don't understand that they're being moulded to serve the Third Reich. This is what we are up against, Countess. Never trust any German-speaking Czech family. They have children . . . as you can see, the children are being contaminated. Trust no one.'

Marietta and Andrea exchanged uneasy glances as they drove on. The two girls, both so different, invariably thought alike, Marietta through her reasoning, Andrea through intuition. Here was another Jan. So who was the stranger they thought they'd known so well?

When they approached the next village, Marietta could not recognise the shops for the mass of swastikas hanging from every window. Bohemia had changed forever, she thought with a heavy heart, I thought it never would.

'They're only human, therefore greedy,' this new Jan said,

unexpectedly. 'When the Sudetenland was annexed, all Czechs of Slav descent were given forty-eight hours to abandon their farms and businesses. They had to leave their cattle, equipment ... everything they possessed. *Volksdeutsche* Nazis were rewarded with land and businesses. Rich pickings! Look around, Countess. You'll see how many of your neighbours are new and German-speaking.'

Jan had never talked, Marietta suddenly realised, merely answered. She experienced a sudden wave of guilt as she acknowledged that she had never had a conversation with him, although she'd virtually grown up with him. She'd always taken his humble attitude for granted. Then anger surged. Which of his two roles portrayed the real Jan?

Later, she felt some of the tension fading as her beloved forests and the neighbouring farms came into view. She leaned out of the window and took deep breaths of the sweet country air.

It was cold, but lovely. They drove on, winding uphill, until they reached the snowbound grassy plateau set amongst the forests that framed Boubin Manor.

Leaving Andrea in the safe hands of the housekeeper, Marietta hurried out to find Miki, their groom and gardener, in his cottage hidden amongst the trees. Work was obviously forgotten and Miki was unshaven and dirty, his hands were shaking and he looked like a man in the depths of despair.

'Sit down and share some wine with me,' Miki said, with unusual affection, slurring his words. 'Come! You are a grown woman now, and you can take a drink with me for old time's sake. D'you remember when I used to take you into the forest to gather cranberries and mushrooms and teach you about the birds and the wild creatures?'

He was maudlin and sentimental. Marietta felt embarrassed. She sipped some wine and tried to pretend that she was enjoying the conversation, but Miki's fear permeated her soul. She had seen him facing wild boars and bears, or rescuing snarling foxes out of poachers' traps, but she had never seen him so afraid.

'What is it? Why are you afraid?' she asked him gently.

'He's a gypsy. Isn't that enough?'

She jumped as Jan limped in, smiling sadly. 'There was a gypsy settlement in the forest. I don't have to tell you that, you knew them well. Last week the troops came and took them all, destroyed the wagons, shot the dogs, set light to the caravans and sent the gypsies to a camp ... women, babies-in-arms ... everyone! God knows if any of them are still alive.'

'On my land?' She was white with anger.

'Your land!' his eyes mocked her. 'Did you think you were some sort of protector? Like a magic charm. Whatever they see is theirs. Anyway, Boubin is about to be expropriated for the troops, which means von Hesse wants it for himself and his buddies. Didn't you know?'

'No! But who are you, Jan?'

He ignored her question. 'Pastor Perwe asked me to keep an eye on you and Andrea. I am his friend. Remember this, Countess ... for the duration of the occupation we're on the same side. You ... the Pastor ... and I. You can rely on me to fight the Nazis until my last breath. When it's over, we shall be on opposite sides.'

'What do you mean, opposite sides?'

'I am a Communist.'

The implications made Marietta feel sick. Had he been planted in their home, because Father was the Minister of Austrian Affairs, and had he spied on Father for all those years? How cold he seemed now that the familiar servant's respect had been put aside.

'You'll have to learn to do without this stuff, Miki.' Jan said. He picked up the stone jar and poured the wine down the sink. 'You don't need Dutch courage.'

'Countess, I shall be staying on in Czechoslovakia, but I will no longer be your servant. I've been transferred, but I can help you with your escape chain.'

'Transferred by whom, what do you mean, Jan?'

'I'm not free, Countess ... I obey orders. If you need me, you will be able to contact me through Herr Zweig. He works for you, by the way, although you've never taken the trouble to meet him. Here's a list of contacts for your escape chain. Tell the Pastor you can rely on these people, but they're only human. God knows what they'd reveal under interrogation. I suggest you spend a part of your holiday meeting them, but be careful. It's important that you are seen to be having fun, too. Remember that.'

She frowned, realising she had been given an order and that she was at a loss to know how to deal with it.

Why am I such a child? she wondered, blinking back her tears as she hurried back to the house. It was absurd to feel so let down, but someone she'd always thought she'd known no longer existed.

A car was just pulling up in front of the house and when she saw who the driver was her heart lifted. 'Oh, Bill,' she cried. 'Thank goodness you've come.'

The Count arrived in time for dinner. He sat at the head of the table, listening to the children and feeling old. Louis was a man, at last. He had shown determination over his engagement to Andrea that the Count had never guessed he possessed. Tonight they were lost in each other and clutching hands under the table. And Marietta and Bill were in love.

The children were watching him expectantly, so he stood up and said: 'Here we are together and I thank God for it. I want to propose a toast in these troubled times. Let the family be our refuge from the madness the Nazis are thrusting on the world. In our home and our hearts we shall preserve all that is moral and sane and decent. To the family!'

At that moment, the maid brought the soup and the family waited in silence for her to leave.

'Furthermore, I want to propose a toast to the gallant Edelweiss students. To your bravery and your morality. With youth like you, I know that Austria will be saved eventually.' He smiled, lifted his glass and drank.

'I'm proud, too, that our brave little tigress, Ingrid, has joined you in taking on the Nazis. Well done, Ingrid. Your bravery has thrilled me, my dear.'

Ingrid flushed.

'All of you have proved yourself to be thinking, caring persons,' the Count went on. 'Nevertheless, I'd like to convince you that there's no morality in being foolhardy. Be careful, or you may leave yourselves open to savage reprisals.'

'I know you mean well, dear Uncle,' Ingrid said, smiling sweetly. 'But I will not give in.'

'I'm not asking any of you to give in to the Nazis. We have reached a terrible period in the history of our country. Evil is abroad, contaminating everything it touches. I would never ask my family to sup with the devil. As Christians we must all believe that goodness, justice and love will triumph eventually.

'At the same time, I implore you all to be careful. Go underground! You can be sure that the SS has a spy in your group. They have their spies in every house. It will be someone you trust. Find out who it is before it's too late . . .' He broke off as an unwelcome thought thrust into his mind. Involuntarily his eyes turned to Ingrid. With a lurch in his stomach he remembered her regrettable affection and vulnerability to Hugo as a young girl, for which he had always blamed himself. But no! Surely he was being unreasonable. He turned to all of them. Was he contaminated, too . . . suspecting everyone, even his own niece? He decided not to burden Marietta with his fears.

'Be careful. That's my message to you.' He gazed at them each in turn and sighed.

Chapter 32

AFTER DINNER LOUIS INSISTED ON DANCING, but Marietta excused herself as being exhausted by the journey and retired. After a few minutes' hesitation Bill followed her and heard muffled sobs as she closed her door. Without a second thought he entered the room behind her.

'Oh Marie, sweetheart, what's wrong? Don't cry. Tell me what's wrong,' he said, stroking her neck and her hair.

'Oh Bill ... Bill ... hold me,' she sobbed. 'I'm so tired of being strong. I can't stand it. I thought here, at least, there would always be security and stability, but no one is secure. Miki was so afraid ... everyone's becoming "categorised". The people are trapped here and no one is who they were. Jan is not my friend and servant, but a Communist and he's been spying on us for years, and the kind German Czechs are rabid and marching and my dear brother, Hugo, is going to expropriate Boubin Manor. Oh God! Where will it all end?'

'Shh! Don't cry, darling. Don't give in now.'

She pushed her face in the pillow. After a while her shoulders stopped shaking, but Bill sat stroking her neck and back. She spoke again. 'The truth is, I'm frightened. Today I realised that we can't win. I never believed my countrymen would accept such evil, now I've seen that all the power is with the Nazis. We can only fail.'

'No. That's not true. Before long, Germany will be at war with the rest of the world. It could take years, but the Nazis will be beaten eventually. When war breaks out I shall join the army. You will come with me, we will fight them together.'

'I won't run away,' she said softly, while every instinct told her that running away might be her salvation.

Aware of her vulnerability and her need for reassurance, Bill gently pressed her against the pillows, his fingers shakingly undoing the buttons of her blouse.

Her longing for him, which she had buried so deeply for so long, was now surging out of her. She pushed herself hard against him and they seemed to lie there for an eternity, lips on lips, bodies hard against each other, her heart thumping against his.

'I want you . . .' she gasped. 'I must be part of you. Oh Bill, love me!'

He leaned over her and kissed her damp hair which was falling over her face and smoothed it back. His lips lingered over her long eyelashes and her beautiful eyelids. Her lips usually so firm and brave were pouting, trembling moist to his touch. With delicacy and reverence he removed her clothes, stroking her silken skin, whispering words of love and passion, until they both lay naked on the vast bed.

He kissed her breasts and her navel, and her soft pubic hair and threaded his fingers through it, feeling, kneading, longing for her. He bent over her swiftly, his tongue licking her dusk rose nipples, his forefinger stroking; she was moaning, pleading, and writhing with pent-up passion. He moved her legs apart and lowered himself gently on to her body, feeling her quivering naked flesh against his, and her breasts, like luscious cushions under him, and her firm belly shuddering. She was open and wanting him, clamouring for more.

'Are you sure . . . ?' He gasped.

'Yes, yes . . . oh, yes.'

Tenderness flooded through him as he gently thrust into her.

He heard her moan, and felt the exquisite flesh pulsating and writhing around him. 'Oh Marie, my dearest, dearest love . . .'

Why did I come? Ingrid wondered, lying in bed feeling tormented and rejected. The answer to her question was easy: she had sensed something suspicious in Marietta's sudden urge to take a break in Bohemia, so she had accepted the invitation in order to spy on the girls. Now she was suffering as she heard obvious sounds of love-making coming from Marietta's room next door. She could hear the bed creaking amidst giggles and sighs.

She wanted to run away, but instead she found herself creeping towards the wall and listening intently. At last their sex was over. Ingrid slumped to the floor, quivering and crying, imagining Marietta, replete and joyous, lying on Bill's shoulder, just as she had once imagined she would. She heard Bill moving around. Glasses clinked.

'Okay Marie, what's this all about . . .?' The rest of Bill's question was inaudible. Ingrid pressed her ear against the wall. Then she clearly heard Marietta say: 'An escape route to Austria . . . over the hills to the border . . . a chain of safe houses and contacts . . .'

Only snatches of their conversation were distinguishable, but what she heard Ingrid wrote down carefully. Shortly afterwards she heard the bed creak and Ingrid crept back to her lonely mattress. She lay awake for hours and heard them make love again just before dawn, then the door creaked and she heard the sound of Bill's footsteps returning to his own bedroom down the passage.

It was eight o'clock when Bill was wakened by Marie creeping into his room. 'I haven't had enough sleep,' he complained.

'Come on, Bill. Get dressed,' she said, pulling his blankets off. 'Andrea and Louis left before dawn for Vimperk. They're going to see the local priest. He's a friend of the Pastor's.' Marie's dedication was intimidating, particularly at this time of the morning. Bill left his warm bed with a sigh.

'I'm going,' he told her sternly. 'You're staying here. I have the safety of my American passport and my job to protect me. You have nothing.'

'That's not going to work, Bill.' She stood there, her hair tousled, a taut, lop-sided smile on her lips, frowning at him.

'Marie. Give me the addresses. You're not going and that's final.'

'I can go without you, Bill,' she said softly. 'I came to do this and you can't do it for me. These people won't trust you ... you're a stranger to them. Besides, the addresses are in my head and there's no way you can get them out of me.' She smiled softly. 'I'm touched that you want to protect me, Bill, but you don't own me.'

He got dressed in a hurry, feeling scared.

At the station, they took the train to Volary and then hiked uphill through the trees for half an hour. At last they reached the sawmill at Lobkowitz, run by Herr Zweig. He was an old man, but with a young man's eyes of fierce, penetrating crystal blue, which contrasted strangely with his iron grey hair and lined skin. There were deep bags under his eyes, and the stubble of two days' beard was a darker grey than his hair. His eyes were hooded, his nose hooked, his hands wrinkled, but he excuded strength and vitality.

He said: 'Well, well, Countess Marietta von Burgheim in person. I have worked for you and your grandmother for forty-five years, but this is the first time I have set eyes on you. It must be an important occasion.'

'I can't think of anything more important than combining our resources to fight the Nazis,' Marietta said, unaffected by his sarcasm, and ignoring Bill's horrified expression.

She looked around. This was an isolated place, little known, and often cut off by bad weather for weeks at a time. Herr Zweig used a horse-drawn cart for that very reason.

'My contact told me you would be sympathetic. I need a safe house for fugitives. This is an ideal place for a halfway house,' she said earnestly. 'It's isolated, and you can't be easily surprised. The only access road zig-zags up this steep slope in full view of your sawmill.'

Bill was squirming. Zweig could be an informer, or even a Nazi, for all she knew, and here she was blabbing her head off. She had guts all right, but she was a child when it came to guile.

'How would people get here?' she was asking.

'There's a bus and a train twice a day in week days. After that they walk, as you did, unless I know they're coming.'

'You are prepared to offer sanctuary to so-called enemies of the Reich?'

'That goes without saying, Countess.'

'You will need horses and mules, extra supplies, but we will pay you . . . somehow.'

'Why did you come here, why are you dirtying your soft hands with this? Who sent you?' The penetrating blue eyes scanned her face carefully as he asked.

'I can't tell you that,' she smiled at him, 'but my hands are already dirty.'

Something in her stance and her voice convinced the old man of her sincerity. He gravely shook her hand.

After coffee and half an hour of small talk, they had a long walk back to the car and Bill ranted most of the way. She was too trusting, naive, gullible and far too talkative, he said, ice-cold with anger.

'The person who gave me these names is someone whom I trust,' she said eventually. 'I know this country, Bill, it is you who is naive.'

They reached Strakonice at one. The proprietor, who was also the waiter, suggested they might prefer to sit outside. Despite the cold, he was so insistent that they agreed. 'Go back now,' he said urgently, when they were seated. 'There are several Nazis in this town and they're always watching. There was a party of Jews here two days ago. They were sent to the priest in the church up there on the hill. A pretty place as you can see,' he said pointing up the hill. 'Father Diederichs gave them shelter in the church. He thought he had the villagers in his pocket, but he forgot the younger generation and their

Hitler Youth cult and their weird ideas on how Czechoslovakia should be run. We've two garage mechanics, sons of the local garage proprietor, who are practically running the Hitler Youth in this area. Most folks think it was them who informed on the priest and his refugees.'

'What happened?' Marietta whispered.

'Yesterday the Gestapo came, but there was plenty of warning, because you can see for miles from up there. The fugitives ran off into the forests, but the SS had brought dogs. They were all shot, except one young boy who was alive and taken for questioning. He couldn't have been more than fifteen, if that. This morning they took the priest outside and shot him in front of his church. You wouldn't want them to notice you two. Don't worry. I'm always here and I can help you. You can contact me through our mutual friend, but don't linger now. Finish your coffee and go.'

'Let's get the hell out of here,' Bill said, when he was out of earshot. 'It's time to go home.'

'Pilsen,' Marie said obstinately. 'That's our next stop. We'll take a train.'

Walking around Pilsen's town square, Bill was amazed at the outdated equipment being used by the German army. It was lucky for Hitler that he'd managed to annex the Sudetenland without a shot being fired, he reckoned, since his troops were so badly-equipped. The men had the strangest selection of fighting machines Bill had seen. Most of them were on bicycles. Some had carrier pigeons in cages strapped to their backs. Horses and carts were tethered among the tanks and the few pieces of modern artillery.

It was nearly dusk, and they were both tired when they reached the city. They walked into the next bar on their list and ordered some red claret and a pie each. A sign in the window said: *Under new management*, and the weasel-faced proprietor had the wrong name altogether. They both felt depressed as they sat by the bar counter making small talk.

'Someone got here before us,' Bill said, feeling uneasy. 'How many more on your list?'

'That's it. Andrea's doing the rest. I hope she's all right. Let's go home.'

'I couldn't be more thankful.'

They reached Boubin Manor at midnight. Andrea and Louis were waiting for them. Ingrid had spent the day with them, but she was in bed, Andrea told them. They sat sprawled on the carpet, in front of the fire in the family room and swopped news. The day had scared all of them more than they cared to admit.

'Horrible, horrible,' Marie kept muttering. 'To think that these things can happen to perfectly innocent people. They were only trying to escape. They hadn't committed a crime.'

At one, they were still talking when Jan came in with a bundle of logs for the fire.

'There'll be a heavy snowfall tonight,' he said, looking grim. 'You must stay here and ski. Have fun and make it obvious – remember you're on holiday. You might have attracted attention at Pilsen. I'm sorry about that contact. The owner was arrested recently, but I didn't know. All of you did well today.'

Marietta watched him gravely. She wasn't sure exactly how to react to his changed status. After he'd left, she stood up, white-faced and tense. 'We'd be well advised to take his advice. Four days of fun is the minimum we can get away with. We'd best get on with it.'

She made it sound like a punishment, Bill thought, watching her gravely. She shot a glance of blank despair at him and went to bed. Bill waited a decent interval and then followed.

Chapter  33

ANDREA WOKE THE NEXT MORNING feeling dismal. She didn't fit in with the family; it was madness to imagine that she ever would. She was at a loss as to how to behave.

Sharp at eight, there was a knock on her door. The maid entered with a tray of milky coffee and freshly baked pastries. 'Everyone's waiting for you, Madam,' she said. 'The skiing party is due to leave in half an hour.'

'I'm not skiing today,' Andrea replied. Nor any other day, she told herself miserably. She allowed the maid's disapproval to waft over her.

She heard the skiers' happy voices calling to one another as they assembled outside the door under her window. At last they left and Andrea went to sit by the window. It was a beautiful scene. The lodge was perched on the edge of a mountain slope. Below her was the broad sweep of a snow-covered slope falling to a valley far below with a calm lake nestling in the valley. She decided to dress and enjoy the solitude of the house while everyone was out, but when she reached the morning-room she realised she was not alone after all. The Count was sitting by a blazing fire behind his newspaper. He folded it, stood up and ambled towards her. 'Come and sit with me,' he said. 'Why aren't you skiing with the others?'

She sighed. 'I can't ski,' she said flatly. The Count looked surprised. Then he grinned and suddenly he looked years younger. 'I taught my first wife to ski. Go to the ski room, Jan will fit you up. I'll get you started.'

Andrea had never felt more uncomfortable in her life as she hobbled along the path in borrowed ski boots. It was like learning to walk with artificial legs. The Count helped her into the trap and soon two white ponies were racing off uphill, bells jingling, into the misty whiteness. There, Andrea discovered, was a world of incredible grandeur, with wide, sweeping views over the valley and long sloping runs which, the Count explained, were ideal for beginners.

Two hours later Andrea could stop, start, stay upright downhill and plod uphill, and she felt a little less vulnerable. The Count convinced her that she had gained enough skill to ski down the more advanced slope leading to the restaurant. Besides, he pointed out, there was no other way to get there. He was famished. Wasn't she? They had all arranged to meet there for lunch.

She was far too nervous to be hungry.

'This slope's a bit steep,' he warned her, 'and you can't negotiate the bends as yet, so we shall circle to the front of the restaurant. That's the beginners' way. Follow me carefully?'

'Fine,' she said.

They set off, with the Count slightly ahead, calling encouraging comments. Surely they were getting near? Andrea raised her head to look, and without meaning to, altered the course of her skis. In a split-second she was zooming down a steep embankment that led to the back of the restaurant.

Faster and faster she raced. She saw an elderly couple walking their dog in front of her. How had they got there?

'Look out!' she screamed. 'I can't stop.'

They flattened themselves against the wall as she raced by.

The dog leaped at her, caught her pants and hung on. She was sure they would collide with the wall, but miraculously her skis followed the ruts in the snow.

She had only time to scream: 'Aaaah!' as she went sailing over a small rise and into the air, still gripping her ski sticks, with the dog hanging on.

She caught a glimpse of startled faces. Some of the skiers dived for cover.

Her legs crumpled in shock as she landed. She skidded across the patio spread-eagled on her stomach in a flurry of snow. She felt her pants ripping as the dog tugged harder.

Louis ran towards her, followed by the girls. He scooped her in his arms and wrapped his jersey round her waist. After that he took off her goggles, and kissed the tip of her nose.

'Idiot!' he said.

Andrea tested her limbs. They all seemed to be connected to her, which was a miracle.

At that moment, the Count arrived. 'You should have stayed with me,' he said mildly. 'You might have hurt yourself.'

'Any bones broken?' Bill said, trying to keep a straight face.

'I've never seen anything so funny,' Marietta said, laughing.

'That's a very tough dog,' Louis said. 'It didn't let go, but its feet never touched the ground.'

'Neither did Andrea's,' Marie said between gales of laughter.

'What an entrance!' Even Ingrid was smiling.

The Count led Andrea back to a table and poured her a glass of brandy.

'Of course,' Marie said, making room for Andrea on the bench. 'You must go straight back out there after lunch. It's important to do that, or you might lose your nerve. I remember my first horse show. I was so nervous I jumped clean over the horse and landed on my head on the other side. The audience laughed at me. Grandmother was furious.'

They all had painful memories of their first skiing lessons which they told each other, with hoots of laughter, until Andrea couldn't help smiling herself.

It was 6 p.m. Louis and Andrea were in the sauna. Louis had coaxed Andrea there by promising that she would recover from her many bruises. She was wrapped in a large white towel, her hair was wet with perspiration, her skin was gleaming and her face was swollen and red. To Louis she had never looked more desirable.

Louis wrapped his hand around Andrea's ankle. He moved his head and pressed his lips around her big toe, sucked it, and wiggled his tongue between her toes. Then he ran his fingers up the inside of her leg to her thighs.

There's something wrong with me, Andrea thought, feeling uncomfortable. I'm engaged, but I'm a virgin ... at eighteen ... that makes me a freak. It's just something about my make-up. I don't believe that sex is wrong, but I can't stand all this propaganda about being told to do it for Hitler ... to produce another little Nazi. The Führer has made me frigid. Poor Louis. She drew away from him and pushed his hand down.

He smiled lazily. 'I didn't bring you here to seduce you.'

She frowned and glanced down at him, peering from under her long lashes.

'What did you bring me here for?'

'For you to seduce me.'

She laughed. 'Well, I'm not going to. I'm stiff and aching all over.'

'Then I'll go to sleep.'

He stretched out full-length on the slatted wood. Andrea leaned forward and spooned some water on to the coals. The steam hissed and a strong smell of eucalyptus filled the small room. The resin was oozing from the wood; the steam was fragrant. Andrea smelled fragrant, too. Louis grabbed her foot again and ran his tongue under her sole.

He said: 'I'm too lazy to do more than seduce your foot.'

She laughed and wiggled her toes. 'Go ahead! My foot feels passionate.'

'Dear Fräulein Foot,' he whispered. 'What delicate toes, what sensuous bunions ...'

She jerked her foot away. 'I don't have bunions and you're tickling.'

Louis watched the dim light shining on her skin as she moved. Her hair fell forward over her shoulders, her eyes were smouldering; one breast was almost revealed as her towel slipped.

He said: 'If you think that sex is all I want from you, then you're mistaken, Miss Soltys. I want all you can give . . . and quickly. We must be married very soon. God knows how long we'll have together.'

She lay very still. Did he mean . . .?

'If there was a war, would you be called up?'

'Of course.'

Andrea pondered over this new, unwelcome threat. How strange that she had never thought about it . . . perhaps because she hadn't wanted to think about it.

She sat up abruptly and then groaned. 'Oh, oh, I can hardly move. I'm so bruised and stiff,' she wailed.

'I'll call the masseur,' Louis said.

'Is the masseur a man?'

'Oh, Andrea, drop your silly modesty. It's old-fashioned and petty. A masseur is a masseur is a masseur . . .'

She gazed at her feet. 'Look! They're turning black. It's those ghastly boots.'

'I'll buy you new ones.'

'No, you won't.'

'Don't speak for Fräulein Foot. She and I have an understanding.'

Louis took Andrea around the waist and hoisted her over his shoulder. He pushed open the door and staggered into the landing.

'Put me down! For goodness' sake,' she whispered. 'Someone might see us.' Louis dumped her on the bed and slammed the door shut. 'Turn on your stomach,' he commanded. 'Luckily for you, I'm extremely good at this.'

Apprehensively she obeyed him, shuddering as she loosened the towel from her back and folded the end of it over her buttocks.

His firm fingers began to knead her shoulder muscles and slowly, languorously, she abandoned herself to Louis' sure touch. He worked swiftly, pummelling the stiffness out of her muscle, and, now totally relaxed, she turned over, letting the towel slip away. Louis gasped when he saw her breasts, and her delicate throat, and the angle of her square shoulders, and the vulnerable armpits, covered with soft down. Her hips flared from a narrow waist and her skin was flawless.

'You're beautiful,' he gasped. He could not look away from her rampant nipples thrusting up from their circle of brown skin.

'Louis,' she said softly. She gazed trustingly into Louis' eyes, which were suffused with tenderness.

'How did a fool like me get a girl like you? Dearest, dearest Andrea.' He traced one finger over her mouth, then he nuzzled her neck and her chin with his mouth, smoothed his hand over her hair, lifted it, stroked it, until she felt her scalp tingling. 'Oh,' she sighed. 'Don't stop.' She reached up longingly and touched his chest. He was taut and sinewy. 'You're like a coil of steel,' she said wonderingly. 'You've always seemed so sensitive and soft.'

'Just muscles acquired in the Military Academy,' he said.

Her body shivered. Then she turned to him and pressed her mouth on his. Her arms coiled round his neck, and her legs wound round his thighs. 'I love you,' she said. 'Every day I love you more.'

'I never doubted that, my love,' Louis said, brushing his lips over hers.

Andrea looked up at Louis and saw his eyes, brooding and solemn. There was something strange and new. Not tenderness, not love, a fierce predatory look. She shuddered and turned her head away, but his strong, firm hand moved her head back until she faced him. 'Look at me,' he said urgently. 'Don't look away. Look at me.'

She wanted to close her eyes and blot out the sight of him. Part of her wanted to push him away, but she felt a strange acquiescence growing inside her, a need to be dominated. She was giving way to his will.

He pushed her legs aside and stroked her pubic hair. The sensation was shocking. Too shocking to bear, but again this strange languid sense of giving up her will prevented her from moving.

He looked haunted, as if he were in agony. He knelt between her thighs and took off his towel robe. His penis was rampant and rearing up between them, huge and glistening, as if it had a life and will of its own.

He laughed. 'You look so shocked.'

'I never saw ...' She broke off, not wishing to look so unsophisticated.

'It's your first time,' he said dreamily. He bent over swiftly and thrust his mouth against her sex, and his tongue gently wooed her. New, strange, exquisite sensations tore at her ... unbearable, yet wonderful, a series of ripplings of exquisite sensations, moving through her body to her stomach and her breasts, and then consuming all of her, so that she was only a mass of sensuous ripples. Nothing else! She hardly heard her sharp little cries and her tears, as wave after wave assaulted her psyche.

She was only dimly aware of his flesh inside hers, and his fingers massaging some magic place that had stored all these feelings, for all these years, which were now pouring out, like flood waters from a burst dam, at his coaxing.

She clung to him, her nails piercing his shoulder, her eyes half-closed with passion and her body drenched with sweat. They were together on a roller-coaster, plunging and rising, up and up, until that one brief vital moment in time when they both cried out and clutched each other and fell back, breathless and filled with wonder at their shared joy.

She felt his body slowly relax and then he eased off her and lay on his back, staring at the ceiling. Her body craved for him. She wanted him back there inside her forever, but he had slipped away, mentally and physically, and she pined for him.

She moved towards him, unwilling to let go. She wanted them to be joined forever by some mystical umbilical cord that took the essence of him into her. She pushed his arm up, and nuzzled her head on his shoulder, then she flung one leg over his thighs. Now she could feel his warm thigh hard up against her crotch, which felt strangely empty and abandoned. She pushed harder.

He turned and gazed at her, half-tender, half-teasing. 'Greedy-guts,' he said. 'You can't have more. There's nothing left. I gave my all.'

'Mmmm,' she sighed. 'I have it all. I feel it still vibrating inside me.'

For the next few days the family threw themselves in to the serious business of having fun, but to Ingrid, it seemed as if God had singled her out for special punishment as she listened to their silly shouts and hysterical laughter echoing from the mountains. What pigs they were. They never gave her a thought. Later came the thumps and bumps and giggles from Marietta's room. She had to put her head under the pillow to muffle the sounds.

They were like moths dashing themselves against a lamp. Surely they knew that their world was over forever, that they would soon have to face their destinies. It seemed to Ingrid that there was something crazy about their joy, those last few days in Bohemia.

Chapter  34

MARIE WAS HIS, yet she was not his. She loved him, but she would not marry him. In bed, she was his passionate slave, out of it, she was a wilful, obstinate, headstrong woman. Bill loved her with all his heart, but she drove him crazy because he had no hold over her and he could not influence her. As the weeks passed, their relationship ripened into a strong, abiding love, untainted by emotional or physical dependence. They were together because they loved each other. They had to make the most of the present because there was no future.

Bill took all the spare time he could off work. Most weekends he arrived at Marie's apartment on Friday evening. He would leave for Berlin late on Sunday afternoon and drive through the night. Whenever possible, he found Bavarian news stories so that he could stay longer.

One morning, early in February, Bill arrived unannounced at the girls' apartment having driven overnight, to find a strange young woman sitting at the dining-room table sipping coffee. For a moment she was frozen into stillness, her shocked brown eyes stared at him over the coffee cup. He noticed the prison pallor of her skin, how her reddish brown hair was cropped closely, how her hands shook and her eyes were red-rimmed as if she had not slept well for a long time.

'Oh, hello! That is, good-morning,' he said gently. 'I'm sorry to burst in on you. Where're the girls? I'm Bill, Marietta's friend. Who are you?'

The woman turned even whiter. She struggled to place her cup in the saucer, using two hands. She stood up with a jerk and fled down the passage, slamming the door of the servant's quarters.

'She's a fellow-student temporarily without digs,' Marietta said, without even blushing.

'She's studying music,' Andrea volunteered.

Bill had come to Munich, he explained, because the Minister of Propaganda, Josef Göbbels, was to lecture students at the University later that day and he intended to cover the event. The truth was, Bill had reckoned that Göbbels' appearance on the campus would be as tempting to Edelweiss students as honey to a bear, and they would get into trouble, so he had come to prevent any such foolishness on their part. But Marietta seemed disinterested in Göbbels' visit. She had decided to take the day off, she told him. He could go without her.

By noon, the streets were full of Brownshirts and Gestapo, and the buildings were decked out with swastikas, while the campus was crowded with armed SS guards. Bill had to present his Reuters' card to get into the main lecture room, where he was shown to the press table at the back of the hall.

There was a continuous murmur of approval from the students. The seats had been packed for half an hour, but the students kept surging in: a clapping, cheering, stamping mass of exuberant youths. The adulation rose to a roar as Göbbels mounted the rostrum. Delirious with enthusiasm, the students yelled their 'Heil Hitlers' in unison until the hall was rocking with the sound. The sheer impact of so many voices raised in salute was terrifying. Bill felt oppressed. Then Göbbels, a slight, ineffectual figure, began to speak. Bill shuddered as he acknowledged the man's genius for swaying the masses.

'Life in National Socialist Germany has become more beautiful,' he said softly into the microphone. 'Adolf Hitler's Germany is great and powerful as never before. Our immortal people become nobler and better from day to day.'

Göbbels waited for the applause to die down. Then his soft, insidious voice began again. 'Soon, Aryans all over Europe will unite with us to create a wonderful new world. They will realise that we are blood brothers. We shall show them the way to a better, more moral, uplifting world . . .'

Bill felt sick, and he was still afraid that Marie might be planning something foolish. All at once Bill caught on to her plans. Marie was unconcerned at Göbbels' visit because she had more important things to do. He left in the middle of the lecture, pushing his way through the crowds.

Back at the flat Marietta, harassed, bolt-eyed and with her hair in a mess, was about to leave. She had never looked more vulnerable to Bill as she loaded the boot with a collection of paper bags. There were five young women clustered around her; all were scared, thin, with newly shorn hair and scarves tied over their heads. They piled into Louis' car and Marietta got into the driving seat.

'Let me drive,' Bill said, feeling furious with her.

Sullen eyes, downturned lips. 'Don't spy on me,' she hissed. The car sped forward and moved out of sight.

Bill spent an anxious day until Marie returned at seven that evening. 'Marie, what you're doing is dangerous . . . terribly dangerous,' he said. 'Eric has no right to ask you to do this for him.' He folded his arms around her and held her tightly, despite her struggles.

'Let me go.' She brought her elbows up hard, trying to push him away. Then she stood very still, as if shrinking away from his touch. 'This is not your concern. You're not German, or Austrian . . . you don't have to feel responsible. Why can't you understand what it means to be a part of this wicked maelstrom?'

'I love you. That makes it my business. If you fell foul of the Gestapo I don't know what I would do. That makes you my concern.'

'Then let's stop seeing each other. Love should never be used as a form of control.'

'Is that what I'm doing?'

'You know you are.'

'Maybe ... Oh, Marie, dearest, I'm so scared for you. What are we going to do?'

Suddenly she relented. She was like that. One minute furiously angry and then, like a balloon pricked by a pin, all her fury would be spent.

'Bill, you must understand that Andrea and I are part of the Pastor's chain of escape, but only a very small part. Just one stop overnight and on to the next place of safety. There are so many of us, but we only know the house ahead. It's safer that way. While they are in our area, these fugitives are our responsibility. Andrea and I take turns in driving them on. Sometimes Ingrid helps. Sometimes they are Jewish, sometimes children, or perhaps maimed or mentally retarded and therefore destined for euthanasia. We shelter them and pass them on. They are merely passing through. That's why we had to let Frau Tross go. It wasn't fair to involve her in this and besides, we needed her rooms. We're a link in the Pastor's chain. That's all! A chain that you and Taube were all too glad to call upon.'

'Oh God, don't torture me. What's happened to Taube?'

'You'll hear in due course.'

'Can't you understand I'm worried about you? Worried sick ... that's all. Anyway, how do you cope with them all? How do you feed them?'

'We share our rations, or we buy on the black market. They have no ration cards, they are non-people. To the Nazis they don't exist and have no right to any food. To send them away ... well, I might as well shoot them, or turn them in. The result would be ...'

'I know ... I know ...' Bill couldn't dispel the lump in his throat. 'I'm not exactly without feelings, but you ... and Andrea ... Oh God!'

The next time Bill arrived unexpectedly was on Valentine's

Day, a Tuesday, but he'd managed to find a local story to cover. He'd brought a hand painted scarf, and a card, plus tickets for Walt Disney's *Snow White*, which was showing at a local cinema. He tried not to notice the obsequious old man who crept down the apartment passage to the bathroom every hour.

They held hands in the cinema. Bill couldn't take his eyes off Marie. At nineteen, she had blossomed into a lovely, mature woman. She was wearing a plain blue shirt and bluish tweed skirt. She'd taken off her coat and rolled up her sleeves, but despite her rough clothes, she stood out as something altogether special. She was gazing at the screen with almost childlike attention, her eyes mirroring the sadness and the humour of the story. Her lips were slightly parted, white teeth glistening.

She turned suddenly. 'Stop staring at me,' she said, and squeezed his hand.

He looked back at the screen, without really watching. He'd taken enough photographs of her over the past two years to know her face by heart. He'd noticed the strange difference between the two sides of her face. Once he'd cut two pictures in half and made two images of her. In one she looked lost and appealing, lips slightly downturned, eyes sad. A lost child. In the other, she looked serene, her eyes shone with confidence, her mouth curled into a smile, a jaunty, devil-may-care expression that made him smile.

To Bill's surprise, when the lights went up at the movie, Marie's cheeks were wet with tears. 'I love happy endings,' she sobbed, clutching his hand tightly as she stumbled out of the cinema.

'Will we have a happy ending?' he asked that night, as she lay in his arms after making love. 'I, too, have dreams. My favourite is of you in the paddock, breaking in a horse, with two or three kids hanging over the corral fence. They all look just like you. And you look just as you did tonight in the cinema, engrossed, happy, involved. Please, Marie, if you've got any heart at all, you'll marry me and leave Germany. For God's sake, Marie, you owe it to our future kids.'

'Oh, but now you're playing dirty, Bill. That's not like you.

I've told you before, you can't set love and duty on either side of a pair of scales and say which one is the heaviest. Love is a gift. Duty is something you live by. That's all there is to it.'

Bill cursed her blue-blooded roots and her damned aristocratic upbringing. Why couldn't she be normal and selfish, and put her own happiness first, instead of this God-awful dedication to duty and tradition that was ruining both their lives?

Bill didn't see Marie for the next few weeks. His bureau sent him to Czechoslovakia, where he covered Hitler's triumphant entry into Prague. He wrote about the people crying as they saluted and the hissing and jeering when there were no SS troops to hear. He wrote about the deportations, about the Czechs being turned off the land and the Germans and *Volksdeutsche* moving into the lush farms. He wrote about the dismantling of the factories to be shipped back to the Third Reich, the arrests of the intellectuals and the starvation rations that were imposed, and the wholesale looting of anything that was moveable. Eventually he went home, feeling more despondent than he had felt in his life.

The next few weeks were busy ones for Bill. Germany was getting its house in order and preparing for war. On May 22, Italy and Germany signed the Pact of Steel, agreeing to support each other with full military resources. With the threat of war looming, Britain was enrolling its first military conscripts, and planning for the mass evacuation of two and a half million children from south-east England.

Bill snatched whatever time he could to see Marie, but they usually quarrelled, for he was frantic with fear for her.

His next assignment was the launch of Germany's new *Heinkel He-178*, the very first fighter aircraft powered by a jet engine. Germany's technological advance was frightening the hell out of Bill. He managed to get some first-class photographs to send over to the States.

By mid-July, it began to look as though the Baltic port of Danzig could provide the spark that would set off the long-expected European war. Bill was sent there by his bureau.

He sent back an eye-witness account about the arms and military instructors who had been smuggled into the free city. He wrote about the local Nazis who were acting as though Danzig was already German territory. He was on the spot to describe several Nazi attacks on Poles. By this time, Bill was being followed wherever he went and regularly pulled in by the Gestapo and questioned. Then he had a scoop following a tip-off. He managed to smuggle out photographs of Poles, employed in the shipyards, being arrested and deported to concentration camps inside Germany. On July 20, two thousand Nazi troops arrived from Germany and Bill was at the station to photograph them leaving the train.

The Germans were ready to fight for Danzig, which was predominantly a German-populated city. The Poles, too, were mobilised to fight for the protection of their corridor to this Baltic port, their only access to the sea. Danzig must remain a Free City under League of Nations mandate, the British government stated. They, too, were mobilising, for if Poland was forced to take up arms to maintain the status quo in Danzig, Britain was bound by a treaty to go to their assistance. As Bill returned to Berlin, Europe was trembling on the lip of war.

Chapter  35

THE MOMENT MARIETTA SAW TAUBE, fear and shame flooded through her. It was the strangest feeling: butterflies fluttered in her stomach, there was a gurgling in her bowels, and her mouth felt as dry as a desert. Why? Why should the sight of Taube leaning against the doorframe hit her so badly? Over fifty fugitives had passed through her home recently. But Taube wasn't a fugitive. She was a friend of Bill's.

'You,' they both whispered, as one.

'Come in,' Marietta said. 'Are you alone?'

'Yes,' she said simply.

Marietta shut the door. 'I'll warm up the soup,' she said, filled with a sense of unreality.

Taube sat in the kitchen on a stool and gazed at the table fixedly. There were streaks of white in her hair, Marietta noticed. Taut lines had appeared around her lips and her eyes were bloodshot and swollen. She looked old, and tired and very shocked. She was so pale that Marietta guessed that most of her time had been spent hiding in attics and cupboards.

'I wish I could say something cheerful, like only another four stops along the way, but I don't know anything about the chain, only my small part.'

Taube stared at her, all her fear and the longing shining from her eyes. 'Is Bill still in Germany?'

'Yes. He always asks if you've been through yet, but of course we know there must be other chains.'

'There's a job waiting for me in America with Bill's uncle,' Taube said. 'A good salary, an apartment, a new life . . . I have a letter of appointment with my papers.'

She looked so wistful. She might have been a child talking about fairyland. Intuitively, Marietta realised that Taube did not expect to reach America.

'I'm sure it won't be long,' she said as forcibly as she could.

Ingrid came in and stopped short. 'Taube,' she exclaimed. She made a big fuss of her, and went to fetch a scarf and gloves for her to wear. Taube was looking awkward, so Marietta shot Ingrid a warning glance.

Ingrid flashed them a smile. 'I'm just going out to buy some cigarettes,' she said.

'I wish you would stop smoking. It's so common,' Marietta grumbled as she passed a plate of soup to Taube.

'Oh, don't lecture me all the time.' Ingrid flounced out of the room, closing the door loudly behind her.

Once outside, Ingrid shuddered and stopped short. She turned abruptly and retraced her footsteps. Then she turned back to the road. Eventually she broke into a run. Reaching the café, she asked to use the telephone and dialled Hugo's private number.

'Now,' she said when she heard his voice. 'It's now. She's there.'

Leaving the café, she walked rapidly away from the area. She would wait until the girls were asleep before returning to the flat.

Marietta woke with a sense of urgency. Had the alarm gone off? She flicked her torch at the clock and saw that it was only 3.45 a.m. The alarm was set for 4 a.m. She might as well get up, but she lay for a few minutes huddled in the security of her warm bed. There seemed to be an icy hand clutching at her heart. She tried to ignore her fears and summon her courage. 'Marietta, you're being ridiculous,' she murmured. During the past six months she had sheltered so many people on the run and delivered them safely to the next link in the escape chain. They had all been kind, helpful and courteous, despite their fears. Now she was hostess to someone she liked so much ... 'That's all it is,' she murmured. 'I'm feeling over-protective and responsible to Bill.'

When the telephone rang, she reached out with a sense of fatalism, almost as if she had been expecting the call, the sense of doom she had been fighting off for so long folded implacably around her.

'Hello ...'

'They're here ... save yourself ... no time ...' The line went dead. Marietta sat in shock, clutching the receiver. 'Hello ... Hello ...' she said. Then she realised how stupid she was being and replaced the receiver. Whose voice was it? That hoarse whisper had revealed nothing of the caller's identity. She shivered and climbed out of bed. There was a soft knock on her bedroom door.

'Yes.'

It was Andrea. 'I heard the 'phone,' she said.

'Something's wrong. Someone said: "They're here ... save yourself." I don't know who it could be. One of the students perhaps ... or the next link in the chain. Get dressed quickly. We'll leave in five minutes. It was a warning ... from someone.'

Pulling on her blouse and skirt and grabbing a jersey, Marietta ran down the corridor to Taube's room. 'Taube, hurry. I had a call warning us ... it might have been one of the students. I don't know. I'm taking you to the next stop on the chain, if it's safe. Please ... hurry ... Andrea,' she called out. 'Make sure Ingrid is safe.'

Andrea was already dressed. She looked calm and reassuring. 'Let me go instead of you, or better still, we'll stick together.'

'No. It's my turn. We must keep to our routine. We've already decided that it's stupid to go together.'

'Then hurry. I'll call Louis ... just in case.'

Marietta raced to the car with Taube close behind. What

could she do if the wholesaler had been arrested? She had the address of another safe house for an emergency. She would go there. If only she had someone to turn to for help, but Pastor Perwe had been recalled to Sweden for two weeks. Moments later they were speeding towards the city.

The wholesaler lived in a semi-industrial area of central Munich in a flat above his store. There were no street lights and in the pitch darkness she almost drove slap-bang into three black cars drawn along the curb.

'Oh my God . . .' she croaked, recognising the Gestapo livery. She swerved and sped past. In her rear-view mirror she saw the wholesaler being dragged into his car by two plain-clothes agents, his feet trailing uselessly behind him. His wife stood at the door in a state of shock, her children clutched around her. Marietta turned her head for a better view.

'Look out,' Taube called. Marietta wrenched the wheel round, avoiding a lamppost by inches. She struggled to pull herself together. 'Which way . . . which way . . . ,' she muttered.

Andrea was falling into a state of fatalistic calm. No one had answered the telephone at Louis' house, although Andrea had let it ring for over five minutes. She knew without any doubt that Louis had been arrested. Despite her anguish, she was thinking clearly. She must get Ingrid to safety. She must get out into the park so that she could hide, and somehow warn Marietta not to come back here.

Ingrid was taking forever. 'For God's sake, come now.' Andrea stalked into Ingrid's room. Unbelievably, Ingrid was applying mascara.

'Oh, for heaven's sake!' She grabbed Ingrid's arm and pulled her along the passage, only to stop, rooted to the floor, at the sound of screeching brakes as cars screeched to a halt outside. They were too late. But there was the window . . .

Everything seemed to be happening at once. She heard running footsteps as she forced her bedroom window wide open. Batons were beating against the door. 'Open up,' voices bellowed.

Andrea caught hold of Ingrid and heaved her through the window. 'Get out. Be quick. Run for the trees.'

Ingrid was shaking and ashen-faced. 'Oh, Andrea! Dearest Andrea! I'm so sorry.'

'Save your breath! Run!' Ingrid was in shock, Andrea decided as she scrambled after her. She could hear the Gestapo trying to break down the door. It was a strong door and it was resisting them. Andrea mumbled a prayer of thanks. The two girls scrambled out of the window and up the bank of flowers as they heard the door burst open.

'Run for it.'

Ingrid sat on a stone and watched Andrea race across the grass towards the trees. She wouldn't follow. What was the point since the park was surrounded? What would they do to Andrea and Marietta, and poor Louis? She walked around to the front door and went inside. She wondered why she was crying as a Gestapo agent took her arm.

'Get in the car please, Princess Ingrid,' he said.

The drive was long and nerve-racking. Twice Marietta thought she recognised the same car following them, but afterwards she decided that it was just nerves. The emergency safe house was the presbytery of the Church of St Annes, in a pleasant village halfway to Ebersberg. She passed a row of small cottages and leafy gardens behind low wooden fences. Reaching the church at last, she drove past it to the end of the road, then back again. There were no suspicious cars, no lights, no barking dogs. It all seemed normal.

'Someone might have talked, Taube,' she said. 'They might be in there waiting for us. There's no point in both of us walking into a trap. You have money. If I don't return within twenty minutes, try and get to the Cardinal at Munich and ask for shelter until the Pastor returns from Sweden. Tell him what happened.' They were passing a small park with swings and a roundabout. 'Hide somewhere near here,' she said, trying to keep her voice calm. 'I'll come back and sit on a swing and wait for you to find me . . . do you understand?'

Taube caught hold of her as she left the car, her eyes glittering feverishly. 'Don't go,' she begged. 'I'll go. Please . . .'

'I have my instructions, Taube. I must follow the plan.' She pulled her arm away. Taube closed the car door. She turned and waved and tried to smile, but she looked completely lost. 'Good luck,' she called softly.

Marietta drove on and parked outside the church. It was very still and quiet. Well, that was natural, wasn't it? It was only 6 a.m. and still dark. Her footsteps echoed loudly as she walked up the crazy paving. She picked up the knocker . . . it was poised to descend when the door swung open swiftly. She looked into eyes of blue, like pools, she thought, in an albino face. A fist slammed into her jaw. As she crumpled at the knees she felt someone dragging her inside, but she was too dazed to feel much fear. 'Where is she? Where did you leave her? Talk, bitch!' A blast of pain hit her knee cap and then her elbow. Electric shocks? She gazed at the stick. Yes, she could see the cord. They were wrenching off her clothes. 'Run, Taube, run . . . I don't know how long I will be able to stand this.' She heard a shot ring out in the street outside. Mercifully, she passed out seconds later.

It was 9 a.m. the following morning when the Count walked into Gestapo headquarters in Berlin. He demanded to see Colonel von Hesse, but the Colonel was out of town, he was told. The Count had to fill in a form, making an application in triplicate, stating his reason for wanting to see Hugo. He wrote: 'Personal . . . family affairs.'

'Leave your address,' they said. 'You will be contacted if he wants to see you.'

Defeated by the system, the Count spent his time pacing his office, filled with foreboding and despair.

For the next few days, Bill and the Count tried every possible source for news of the girls and Louis, who had also disappeared. No one could help them. People disappeared without a trace, it was a nightly occurrence. At the end of the week the Count returned to Vienna and Bill continued his lonely vigil, contacting the Courts, the police, the concentration camps and prison officers for news of Marie.

In Vienna, the Count's days passed in a blur of misery. He was tense and tired all day, but he lay sleepless at night. He would take a sleeping pill and drop off for an hour, only to dream of interrogation chambers and hear Marietta screaming ... or Andrea ... or Ingrid ... or Louis. Nightly, he wandered around the empty corridors of the palace, wondering where his children were. Were they hurting badly? How much were they suffering? Were they still alive?

On the morning of July 13, the Count received a terse note from Gestapo headquarters in Vienna, ordering him to be there at ten the following morning. He had hardly entered the intimidating building when he came face to face with Hugo.

'Dear Father! We meet again. Could it be that you want something?' He hustled his stepfather into his office and slammed the door.

'I've come to ask for help. Let them out, Hugo,' the Count said softly. 'Louis is your brother, and Andrea is his fiancée. As for Ingrid ... you were always fond of her. Marietta is a fine person. You never really knew her, she was so young when....'

'When you turned me out.'

'Hugo, I'm at the end of my resources. I just don't know what to do. Help them, for God's sake.' The Count leaned forward, his elbows on the desk, too exhausted to plead any further. Looking up at his stepson, the Count saw a quick smile play over his lips and realised that he was enjoying the scene. He wanted to see him beg. Very well, he would beg. He forced himself upright.

'You're big enough to do this, Hugo. Only you can get them freed.'

Hugo raised one hand for silence. 'I'm doing my best for the family. We were ordered to arrest all the Edelweiss students. A special People's Court was convened and they were all sentenced to ten years each.'

'No!' The Count felt dizzy and sick.

'I think I've managed to get Louis released. He's to be transferred to a punishment battalion in the German army. He'll be an ordinary private, but later, if he joins the Party, he'll be able to take a commission.'

'And Andrea?' Count Frederick whispered.

'She's been deported. Tell Louis he owes me a favour or two ... if you ever see him. I put her down as *Volksdeutsche*. They're much in favour with the Führer right now.'

The Count's mouth was dry with apprehension. 'Ingrid?'

'Bad news, I'm afraid ... there's no trace of her ... some foul-up with the paperwork. Perhaps she didn't give her right name. When I find her I'll try to get her deported, too. That's about the best I can promise.'

'You mean Ingrid is lost somewhere inside one of your terrible camps? She might be dead?'

'She knew the risks she was taking. They all knew.'

The sight of stepfather brought to his knees by the plight of his family went a long way towards soothing Hugo's ego.

'And Marietta?'

'Ah, so you've left your little pet until the last.' Hugo licked his lips in pleasurable anticipation. 'She's in prison in Munich awaiting trial. Apart from her activities in the subversive Edelweiss movement, she was also caught red-handed, helping Jews to escape from the country. She was with Taube Bloomberg, who used to be Roth's secretary. Miss Bloomberg was shot and killed while trying to evade arrest. There's nothing I can do to help Marietta, it's out of my hands. I'll keep a close eye on her case and let you know what her sentence is.' His final sentence sounded like an afterthought.

The Count went white. He stood up shakily, ignoring Hugo's outstretched hand as he left the room.

Hugo watched the broken figure shuffle away. 'I did warn you,' he thought. 'I told you where the power would be. But you were too bloody arrogant to believe me.'

Chapter  36

INGRID GAZED ANXIOUSLY INTO THE MIRROR. She looked pale and emaciated. She smoothed her hair back with a trembling hand. Lately her stomach was always churning with anxiety. What was going on? Abruptly, she crumpled on her bed and burst into tears. She could ring the bell. If she did that her so-called companion would come rushing in, full of false sentiment and soothing words. 'Don't cause us trouble, dear,' the woman would say, as she always did. 'We are all obeying orders, as you must. Colonel von Hesse will be here soon. He will explain everything. Be patient. It's part of his plan.'

'His Machiavellian plan,' Ingrid thought. She had been hidden away here for three months, and Hugo seemed intent on starving her to death. Ingrid knew that she was in prison. Her guards, who insisted that they were not her guards, but her friends, kept explaining that she was being confined for her own safety. Her meagre diet was for a very good reason. 'Why? What's going on?' she asked repeatedly. It was mid-summer and she longed to go out in the sun, but this was not allowed. She sighed and took a book to read in the library. Gazing through the window she watched the clouds chasing each other across the azure sky, birds were flying free and happy in the garden. Lucky birds.

Dusk came, another day lost, and Ingrid felt a deep depression sinking into her. Then she heard footsteps coming along the passage. She didn't have to turn to know whose firm tread it was. Hugo had come at last.

He was out of uniform. In his white shirt, and grey flannel trousers, he looked a picture of health and virility. His skin was glowing with well-being, and his eyes were wide and lustrous. 'You've been fencing.' she said. 'And you won.'

'You're very observant,' he said. 'That's good.'

'Why are you keeping me here? I want to go home.'

'Home?' he queried. 'Why do you think you have a home?'

She shrugged, sullen and uneasy.

'Have you kept out of the sun? Yes, you look a little pale. And you're thinner. Excellent!'

'I'm a prisoner here. You have no right to do this.' She turned on him with a flash of her old fire.

'I'm saving your life.'

She gulped and flushed. 'What are you talking about, Hugo? I'm not in any danger.'

He cocked one eyebrow. 'Go if you like. You'd be dead before nightfall. People suspect that you informed on them. A great many have suffered and some have died.

'Marietta has appeared in court, but her trial was postponed. She faces a charge of spying, and *you set her up*. Bill is about to be deported. Louis is in a punishment battalion. Many of the students have been sent to the camps for life. Did you think you could get away with what you've done? We had to arrest you to save your selfish little skin.'

Ingrid was invaded by a physical self-loathing. It seemed to fill each part of her until she was shuddering with disgust, and sick with fear.

'Perhaps you're not aware of just how successful you have been,' Hugo continued smoothly. 'Single-handedly, you have revealed the identity of all the Edelweiss students. They are either dead or in camps. You've informed on several prominent anti-Nazi politicians. You've shown us which professors are against us. You've also helped us to set up Bill as an enemy agent. Congratulations, my dear. You've been invaluable.'

Ingrid could not speak. Her mouth was opening and shutting, but no sound came. Her eyes began to burn.

Eventually she managed to speak through frozen lips: 'I only passed on information for your research.'

'Research which was needed for their interrogations and some of them died under that interrogation, Ingrid.'

'I am not a spy,' she burst out. 'I didn't betray anyone. No one will think so. I want to go back.'

'It's not that easy. You were arrested while helping Jews to escape. Are you one of them or one of us? I can't protect you if they think you are a traitor, which they will if you return.'

How did I ever get into this trap, Ingrid thought. If this is what he'll do to me when I'm on his side, just what will he do if I turn against him?

'I'm turning you into a martyr,' Hugo said patiently. 'It's the only solution. You'll be officially deported. It's the only way for you to be safe.' He stared at her strangely and she shivered. 'You do understand that you're either with me or against me, don't you? You can't have it both ways. Some martyrs suffer and die horribly. Others become rich and powerful.'

Ingrid covered her face with her hands. I want to stay alive and I want my family's wealth returned to me. I have the right to what is mine. Her thoughts had become her mantra. She took a deep breath. 'I'm a dedicated Nazi,' she said firmly. 'It's just that I'm tired and no one tells me what is going on.'

'The next month will not be easy for you, but it's the only way,' Hugo explained. 'Make one mistake and you could be killed. It's a risk we'll have to take.' He made it sound as if he were sharing the risk, she noticed. 'This is what you must do.'

She listened, her heart thumping, her palms sweating. 'Swear that you'll give me back my parents' property. Swear it,' she cried out, when Hugo had finished.

'I swear it, to the nearest field or two.' He turned away from her when he answered.

It was midnight. The Count was sitting in his office trying to concentrate on his work, but his fears for his family prevented him from thinking straight. It was four months since they had been arrested.

The sudden, shrill ring of the telephone shocked him. What new horrors were to be heaped upon them all? He lifted the receiver reluctantly. 'Yes?' he whispered.

'Father. Listen carefully.' Hugo's deep, resonant voice was throbbing with urgency. 'I've found Ingrid at last. She's been in Sachsenhausen, a concentration camp outside Berlin. I've not only found her, but I've managed to get permission to have her released, but only if she leaves Germany immediately. Can you get to Berlin by the day after tomorrow? I've had to pull strings. You must hurry.'

The Count sat bolt upright. He hardly knew what to say. He'd given up all hope of Hugo's intervention.

'Is Ingrid well? Have they harmed her?'

Hugo's voice reassured him. 'She seems thin, but healthy.'

'And Louis? Have you any news of Louis?'

'He'll be transferred any day now. You'll be able to see him briefly at the station.'

'And Andrea?'

'On her way to Prague.'

'Hugo, I am deeply in your debt, you have proved to be a good son. But what about Marietta? Have you managed to see her ... or help her?'

'I can only advise you, Father. There's very little hope for her, unless you join the Nazi Party. If you were to do that, and perhaps take on some task for the benefit of the New Order, they would probably commute her sentence from death to life imprisonment. But I cannot guarantee it.'

'Then I have no choice, even if there is no guarantee that her life will be saved,' the Count said brokenly. 'Thank you, Hugo.'

'They're my family as well as yours. Now listen, you must bring some cash for Ingrid and some clothes, travelling things, bring a hat or a scarf ... whatever you think she'll need and put her on the train for Paris. From there she can make her own way.'

*

The count was waiting well before the appointed time. His housekeeper had packed most of Ingrid's possessions. There were six suitcases in the boot of the car.

At noon exactly, a small door within the gates of Sachsenhausen swung open and a thin, pale, figure stumbled through. She seemed to be bewildered, as if she did not know where to go. She took a few steps forward, looking dazed and suspicious.

The Count stared in shock. He had been propelled back in time to the station in Vienna. There stood the hungry, shaven, wretched waif, except that this time she was taller and older.

'Oh my God!' he murmured as he rushed forward. 'Ingrid . . . Dear little Ingrid . . . Thank God . . . Thank God . . .' He noticed how Ingrid's clothes were hanging on her, and he felt how thin she felt as he folded her in his arms. 'You're safe. My poor, poor little Ingrid.'

'Hurry,' his driver whispered nervously.

'Here, put this coat on, darling,' the Count said. He had brought his late wife's best sable, which Ingrid had always coveted. But why was she so quiet? Was she ill?

He wrapped the long sable coat around his niece, while she sat silent and hostile, gazing out of the window. Watching her, the Count felt quite inadequate, and he tried not to stare at the large tattooed number on her wrist.

At the station, Count Frederick showed Ingrid the special locked compartment in her briefcase, where she would find all the private papers: a letter of credit to their bank in France where his lawyer had started an account for her with a large deposit, share certificates, all the dollar bills the Count had been able to get together at short notice, letters of introduction to influential friends, the address of their Swiss lawyer, where more funds could be obtained if necessary, plus her passport.

When the train began to move, Ingrid stared sullenly at him. 'Forget about me, uncle,' she said. 'Just forget I ever existed.'

'No, never, darling. I never stopped searching for you, but it was Hugo who found you.'

Ingrid's expression confounded him, a veiled, hostile look which pierced his soul.

'What is it? Tell me, tell me. What have I done wrong?'

Ingrid turned away and climbed into the compartment, her head averted as the train began to move, but the Count stood on the platform long after it was out of sight, the tears streaming down his cheeks.

Chapter  37

LOUIS WAS CROUCHED ON THE GROUND in front of the tent he shared with four other footsloggers in the punishment battalion, hungrily spooning his soup out of a tin. Two divisions were camped along the Polish border, waiting for orders and as far as the eye could see were rows of tents. Everyone knew they were going into Poland, but no one knew when.

Very little of the former Louis was recognisable in this wiry, lean, tanned soldier in camouflage grey. In his three months of training in the notorious Brandenburg Battalion, BB 505, reserved for political undesirables and criminals, Louis no longer had any illusions as to the depths of degradation which the Nazi system had created for its opponents.

He heard his name being called. It was Wegener, their lieutenant's driver. Wegener was an old man by army standards, he was short and stocky with enormous breadth of shoulders. Six months ago, he'd been the owner of a garage and workshop, but he and his wife had sheltered a Jewish family in their loft and the neighbours had informed on them.

'Captain Smiedt has arrived back from headquarters,' he told Louis. 'He wants to see you in fifteen minutes.'

Now what? Louis thought. He stood up reluctantly. Louis

and the Captain had been in the same class at the Vienna Military Academy. Although Louis had nearly always beaten him in theory and in practice, they'd been good friends. Smiedt had pursued the girls relentlessly and Louis had rescued him time and again from getting caught AWOL.

'I'd smarten up, if I were you,' Wegener warned him.

Fourteen minutes later, Louis entered the staff office to find Smiedt standing in front of a blackboard. He had drawn a large wavy line over the left-hand side of the board. In the bottom right-hand corner was a square with Warsaw written inside it.

He said: 'Shut the door behind you, von Burgheim. At ease. There's a meeting here in five minutes, but I want to talk you first . . . off the record.' He frowned. 'You saved my skin often enough, so I want to help you. I don't know what the hell you did to find yourself footslogging in this division . . .'

There was a pause and Louis felt obliged to explain: 'I was a member of the Edelweiss student organisation at Munich University, a protest group. We brought out a newspaper listing irregularities in the Nazi hierarchy . . . helped refugees . . . that sort of thing. I was studying music . . .' It was still too painful to talk about. He knew that Andrea was safe in Czechoslovakia, but Marietta was still in prison awaiting her trial and he was tormented by the fear that she would be executed.

Smiedt made no acknowledgement of Louis' terse explanation. 'Do you know the purpose of this battalion?'

'Who doesn't? We provide blotting paper for bullets and mortars at the front line, thereby saving some of the Germany's right-thinking Aryans.'

'That's it. And for my sins I've been put in charge of you.'

Louis wondered what his sins were.

'Well, Sergeant Major Schneider gave you top marks,' Smiedt glanced into his file, 'for resilience, for bravery, and for intelligence. It seems he wasn't sure about obedience. There's a question mark here. I reckoned that with your background you'd be pretty self-confident when it comes to dishing out orders, so I applied for your transfer to an officers' training college. My application did the rounds and landed up on the desk of a certain von Hesse, SS. He turned you down and put this sticker on your file.' Smiedt slid a sheet of paper across the desk and Louis saw the red star on the top.

'You know what that star means?'

Louis shook his head.

'A Communist, someone who would be better off dead. It's my duty to see you get killed. Understand? Schneider hasn't seen this and we'll make sure that he doesn't.' Smiedt took his cigarette lighter and held the sheet as it erupted in flames.

'I decided that someone as rich and as highborn as you would be damn crazy to be a Communist. Besides I remembered what we used to talk about, and I started thinking . . . von Hesse was your stepbrother. Right?'

Louis nodded, feeling too shocked to speak.

'I guess it's a family affair. I just thought you ought to know. Strange how money . . . your sort of money that is . . . brings out the worst side of people.

'Anyway, I'm making you a corporal with immediate effect. I'm going to give you the opportunity to redeem yourself. I expect you know that if you earn the Iron Cross First Class, and have a good service report from your superior officer, you can be transferred to another battalion. Here's your chance. You will choose a squad of twenty men and be prepared to undertake special missions. This will be dangerous, sometimes suicidal, but some people have a knack of surviving. Pick twenty men for your squad, men you can trust.'

'For suicide missions?' Louis lifted one eyebrow and stared hostilely at the Captain.

'On these tasks you can use your brains and initiative to stay alive. In the front line it's a matter of luck. Sometimes luck runs out. I reckon you stand a better chance this way.

'I'm going to call in Schneider and my section heads now, so stand to attention. You will be here at this and future briefings because you will need to know why your missions are so vital.' He grinned and clapped Louis on the back. 'I don't forget old times.'

Schneider came in, followed by Doctor Johann de Horn, a

man who shared Louis' deep love of music. The remaining section heads followed.

'All right, at ease, men. Let's begin.' Smiedt picked up the chalk. 'At dawn our armies will attack from all along the Polish border.' He pointed to the wavy line. 'From the northern areas will come Army Group North, including the 3rd, 11th and 8th armies.' He drew three chalk streaks from the German border across Poland to Warsaw.

'Advancing from the north-west we'll see the Fourth Army moving south-east towards Warsaw along the Vistula River.' The chalk slashed down again. 'From the west comes Army Group Centre, which includes the 8th, 4th and 10th armies. It also includes us and we'll come this way.' Another streak scored the board. 'Mobile units will follow through the gaps the tanks have made. Our tanks outnumber the Polish by ten to one. Our Luftwaffe is five times larger than the Polish airforce and supremely trained. Our army of tanks and mobile units is unprecedented in the history of war for size, concentration, mobility and striking power. My friends, it will be an easy victory.'

Smiedt took hold of the eraser and obliterated Warsaw. 'As easy as that,' he said. He wiped his hands on a piece of cloth.

'There are a few pitfalls, but nothing we can't handle.' To Louis' surprise, Smiedt produced a bottle of brandy from his desk drawer. Moments later they were celebrating their coming victory.

Twenty men! Whom should he pick? He began with his closest friend, Private Hans Konrad. They had gone through the gruelling punishment training together and given each other moral and physical support. Konrad had also fallen foul of the Nazis. Like Louis, he was highborn and was the closest to Hitler's ideal of the Aryan man, with his magnificent six foot two physique, his ash blond hair, clear, pale blue eyes and noble features.

Wegener was also a man he could trust. Then Josef Meyer, a tall, gangly youth of eighteen who had not long left school, but, despite his ungainly big feet, hands and ears and his clumsy appearance, he was a genius with mechanics, and a first class shot. Louis chose him, not because of his qualities, but because he had no family. Slowly he composed his list. Eventually he handed it to Smiedt.

At daybreak on September 1, German troops poured across the Polish border. By 8 a.m. Louis's battalion had advanced five miles along the road to Posen. Louis was trembling with nerves, but his anger was stronger. He was part of a mighty carnivorous beast that was slowly, inexorably moving into foreign territory, killing everything in its path. For the first time Louis felt that he truly understood the beast that was the Nazis' New Order.

Behind him, a three-column-deep file stretched far back into Germany. Overhead, wave after wave of Stuka divebombers hurled themselves over the front line, softening up the Polish defensive positions. The beast moved forward, toppling trees that had stood for hundreds of years, flattening towns and villages, destroying crops and killing everything that moved. It was unearthly and terrible.

As they passed the small villages and farms, Louis watched in despair. *Blitzkrieg* had created a terror which was destined to become the scourge of Europe. Polish soldiers and civilians were being killed on a scale never before experienced, as tanks and aircraft roared towards their targets, destroying troops, ammunition dumps, bridges, railways, cities, towns and villages. Within a few hours of the attack, not only was the enemy's front line annihilated, but their back-up supplies were totally dislocated. Only then came the main advance of German troops.

He saw frightened refugees scurrying away to safety, carcasses of dead animals, blitzed homes, burnt-out tanks, streams of hopeless, defeated Polish civilians and long columns of prisoners en route to labour camps in Germany. He cringed as he saw a peasant woman hurl herself into in a ditch with her four small children and try to cover them with her body as the tanks raked them with their guns. Long after they had passed, her cries echoed in his ears.

Chapter  38

IT WAS DUSK at the end of their first day inside Poland, a day which seemed to have lasted a century. They were marching along a peaceful country road that cut through forest glades and fields of sunflowers shining golden-red. As if from nowhere, the earth began exploding around them, followed by the deafening din of mortars and the chatter of machine-guns. There were shouts and shrieks as the men hurled themselves off the half-tracks and into the ditches beside the road.

Suddenly the fields were full of Polish infantry. Unbelievably, they were singing. Wave after wave of troops burst out of the trees beyond the fields and raced through the stubble towards them. To Louis, it was macabre and unreal ... the screams ... the cries ... the curses, the high-pitched hysterical rattle of the massed machine-guns and the deeper chatter of enemy automatic weapons and the sight of these men racing towards them, intent on killing.

A split-second later, they were firing into the running men. Louis tried to snap out of the awed daze that had fallen on him at the sight of the appalling carnage of writhing, dying Poles everywhere. Louis clutched his sub-machine gun and tried to bring himself to pull the trigger.

'Watch your flank,' Schneider screamed at him. He was right.

The Poles had set light to some haystacks and they were winding their way towards them, half obscured by tall sunflowers and curling smoke. As if in slow motion, Louis brought his weapon to his right hip and pressed the trigger. It started to chatter at his side. 9mm slugs hissed flatly through the haze. The leading Pole went down and then others and he heard the thwack-thwack of his bullets striking flesh. More Poles came rushing clumsily through the smoke screen.

Louis crouched there, legs spread, his body slightly tensed, spraying lead from left to right in a frenzy of fear as more and still more Poles came rushing towards him. Wegener spun round, a dazed, bewildered look on his face and crumpled on to his shoulder. Louis shoved him to the ground. He was dead. A neat purple hole in his forehead was oozing blood. As he crouched over him, a ricochet zipped against Louis' helmet. Louis shook his head to ward off his dizziness.

He raised himself on one knee, rammed in another magazine and rejoined the firing. On his left, a soldier groaned softly and keeled over. Louis kept firing. I'm next, he thought.

His gun chattered to a stop. Louis fumbled for another magazine. The Poles gave a wild cry of triumph. They were only fifty metres away and coming on fast.

'For fuck's sake fire,' Schneider screamed. They were thirty metres away and gaining speed. He rammed home the magazine and his gun erupted into vicious action. Screaming obscenely and mad with fear, Louis obeyed. The Poles seemed to vanish. One minute they were there, and now they were gone. Louis stood up and stared in horror at the writhing men, their faces contorted with agony.

A blinding pain shot up Louis' arm, as a scream pierced his eardrums. Mud and blood showered around him, blinding him. He blinked his eyes and wiped his hand over his face. Now he could see the gunner on his right. Blood was streaming from the man's scorched, tattered sleeve, a piece of shrapnel had torn off his arm to the elbow. He stared at the ragged gory stump as if he could not believe it had happened to him, and he began to howl.

Louis looked down at his own arm. It was numbed by a blow from the shrapnel. Nothing more.

'Keep firing,' Schneider yelled.

A shell fell nearby and the blast knocked Louis headlong against a tree. Now Louis could hardly see through the black and yellow dots dancing in front of his eyes. He blinked, but couldn't clear his vision. He had the impression that there was a large black shape before him and he crouched behind it. Leaning his sub-machine gun on the shape, he began firing. After a while, he saw that he was sheltering behind the corpse of a comrade. His helmet had been driven into his skull, his mouth was half-open, his eyes staring.

Louis crouched lower and closer. A huge shell screamed past. With a hellish crump it exploded a hundred metres away. Flames spurted high, the earth belched mud and branches and the sky rained pebbles on them. Nearby trees caught alight and the smoked drifted over Louis, choking him. He kept firing, although he couldn't see the enemy.

After a while he became aware of whistles blowing. 'Stop firing!' The cry went from tree to tree. 'Advance!'

Like packs of wild animals, the troops surged forward behind Schneider, screaming in triumph. They slammed into the retreating Poles and flung themselves on them. Bayonets flashed, tools came cleaving down on skulls, blood spurted over them. Pole after Pole were hacked to death amongst the sunflowers. Suddenly the field was a mass of mutilated bodies and there was no one left to kill.

The silence that followed seemed like a pulsating roar. Wearily the troops stared at each other, noting their bloodshot eyes, blood spattered tunics, faces grimy with smoke, lips cracked and bleeding. Louis' head ached intolerably. He could hear the blood pounding in his ears. His chest felt ready to burst and he could taste the smoke and blood.

The weary men stumbled into the forest to sleep, but Louis was detailed for guard duty. He stood in the forest, watching the moon rise over the tree tops. Suddenly he remembered the evening when he first saw Andrea. The moonlight had been shining through the open window. Even now he could picture the scene so clearly. Her image was so real, he felt he could reach out and touch her, smell her perfume and the aroma of her skin and hair. 'Oh God, Andrea, I love you,' he whispered. Tears rolled unchecked down his cheeks, hidden by the night.

It was September 3, 1939. The Count paced his study, unable to sit at his desk he was so fired with tension. He was sick with worry for Marietta, and frantic with anxiety for his son. He also feared for the Fatherland, for this morning, Britain, France, New Zealand and Australia had declared war on Germany.

Looking back, he thought how badly he had failed in his ambitions. After the invasion of Czechoslovakia, he and the Mayor had battled to keep the conspiracy alive as the generals dropped out one by one. Hitler had proved to be a master strategist, not a madman. First the Rhineland, then Austria, Sudetenland, followed by the rump of Czechoslovakia, had fallen to the Germans without bloodshed.

Shortly afterwards the Count heard the door open and the Mayor was shown in. He looked haggard, clearly the declaration of war had hit him hard. 'It's not for nothing that I'm late,' he said. 'We have a new and distinguished member, the Chief of the General Staff.'

The Count gasped with pleasure. Then he clapped his friend on the back. 'Well done, Doctor.'

'He's strictly an army man and he feels that Hitler is pushing the army into certain defeat. He's bringing the new army Commander-in-Chief with him.

The Count could hardly believe the good news. With these men how could they fail? All those who had dropped out would return to help devise Hitler's destruction.

The generals arrived at last. After the introductions, the four men sat down to discuss their strategy. After five hours of discussion, they decided on a way to arrest Hitler before he could order his armies to attack Western Europe. They would then force him to sign a truce with Britain and France.

*

Three weeks after the invasion of Poland, the German High Command claimed that the Polish Campaign was over. Half a million prisoners were in German hands and had been sent as slave labour to Germany. In a battle of extermination, the Polish army had been annihilated. Warsaw was blitzed to ruins.

Louis' relief at the battle's end and his promised leave, was dampened by the horrors inflicted on the Poles. Guilt gnawed at his soul as he saw the scorched earth and flattened homes; the starving women digging amongst the refuse, the orphans crying by the roadside as they begged for bread, and the Polish men, their eyes filled with hatred, being herded on to slave trains for transportation to the Third Reich.

The train ride was terrible. There were corpses hanging from gibbets at every station, the Polish countryside was destroyed, crops burned, entire towns obliterated. It was a relief to cross the border into Czechoslovakia, until he saw the gangs of slave labour in the fields, the armed troops guarding them, the old chateaux commandeered as hospitals for German soldiers, and the pitiful stretcher cases being loaded off the trains into waiting ambulances.

Prague looked the same as ever, despite the multitude of German troops and the hostility of the Czechs. Louis was granted leave from Friday afternoon until early Monday morning. Two and a half days – with luck he would find Andrea.

At dawn on Friday morning, Konrad and Louis were summoned to Schneider's office. Schneider wanted them to help round up Czech labour for the camps.

'You two know the districts here. You'll direct us to the places where we're most likely to find the youths hanging around. I've just heard from headquarters that if we don't fulfil our quota, all leave will be cancelled. Heil Hitler!'

Louis returned the salute automatically, rebellion in his heart. 'Wipe that look off your face,' Konrad said when they were outside. 'We're soldiers. We obey orders. That's all.'

Chapter  39

IT WAS 3 P.M. Louis was sitting in the back of a half-truck, behind Schneider and Konrad. They had been partially successful in rounding up youths from the beerhalls, the streets, the stations and the bus shelters.

So far, one hundred and fifty Czechs had been sent back to headquarters, en route to Germany's labour camps, but this was not enough. Konrad suggested they should move towards the poorer, older areas. They began a systematic search, starting in Slovenskra Street. Slowly they moved eastwards. There was a sudden, unexpected burst of shots from the end of Moravska Street. Seconds later the house was surrounded. Shortly afterwards the troops were manhandling the occupants as they dragged them on to the pavement. One youth had barricaded himself into the attic and was firing wildly from the door. A smoke bomb, lobbed through the window by Schneider, soon settled his defiance. The youth stumbled out with his hands on his head, his eyes streaming. His mother, an old grey-haired lady, stood trembling in the doorway. In her eyes was mirrored all the sorrow of the war. Louis cringed inwardly as he stood guard over her. Her husband was openly crying, the tears taking a zig-zag course down his leathery cheeks, while the family spaniel whimpered and shook between the old man's legs.

As two young brothers were pushed towards the truck, one of them made a break for it. Schneider lifted his handgun and took aim. 'Get him or I'll shoot,' Schneider said. Louis lunged forward and grabbed the youth, knocking him hard against the wall. He hit his head and fell unconscious. Konrad picked him up and shouldered him into the truck, but without warning the dog flung itself at Louis' ankles and hung on hard. Louis tried to kick it away, but failed. The pain was agonising. He called to the old man, but he was rooted with shock. He could not move, nor speak, but only stand and cry.

The scene was pitiful. Louis knew that it would be imprinted on his mind forever. The moaning of the mother, the squeals of the two daughters locked in a front room, the spaniel's frenzied snarling, the blood on his trouser leg. Louis took out his gun and shot the dog through the head.

'I'm sorry,' Louis tried to say. He swallowed, but there was no saliva and the words came out as a croak that no one heard. Louis thanked God for that. He backed away painfully and stumbled against the railings that led down to the basement.

Turning his back on the family in their grief, he climbed into the half-truck.

'Let's go back,' Schneider snarled. 'That's enough punishment for one day.'

They were all sweating, although it was almost freezing.

Louis kept his foot hard on the accelerator as he sped northward. He was determined to put as much space between himself and Prague as he could. He was going home to Andrea.

After a five-hour journey, he turned off the main highway and saw Lidhaky nestling amongst the hop fields and the orchards. There was a cluster of houses, a river and a church. Andrea had written to tell him that she had moved to the country for safety's sake and was living in her late aunt's house which she had inherited. He prayed that she would still be there.

It was dark when he drove into the cobbled courtyard and parked under an oak tree. He could see Andrea faintly silhouetted against the lamp in an upstairs room. He sighed with relief and climbed wearily out of the car.

Andrea pushed up the sash window and leaned out. He heard a sudden wail of joy. Seconds later she rushed out of the door and flung herself into his arms.

'Oh ... Louis ... darling ... thank God you're safe ...'

She burst into tears of happiness and relief. 'All my prayers are answered,' she sobbed. She hugged him and kissed him, laughing and crying at the same time, dragging him into the warmth of the house.

'I've been so scared ... listening to the news, worrying ...' She clutched him tightly against her and then pushed him away and examined him carefully. 'You look so different, older, tougher, but your eyes are the same ... they'll never change. Oh my love, I thought this day would never come.'

They held each other for a long time. Louis tasted the salty tears as he kissed her cheeks and eyes and lips. Then, overcome with desire, they collapsed on to the floor, lips on lips, arms around each other.

'I won't make love to you in this uniform. No, never.'

Louis was amazed at Andrea's strength as she hauled his tunic off him. His cap was flung across the room, she tugged at his boots. She looked like a wild woman with her hair hanging over her face, her skin damp with perspiration, her brow creased with frowns. When she had hurled every piece of his uniform across the room, she threw herself over him, spread one leg over his hips, nuzzled her head on his shoulder and burst into tears again.

'Darling. Don't cry darling. We're together now. I love you, darling. Please don't cry.'

They clung to each other and made love feverishly, trying to blot out the past and the future.

After a while, Louis picked her up and carried her to the bedroom. They made love fiercely again and later more tenderly, for Louis had a deep need to lose himself in Andrea.

In the early hours of the morning, as Andrea lay on his shoulder, they talked about Marietta and their fears for her.

Then he told her what it was like in the punishment squad. The words came pouring out of him . . . all his shock, his despair, his degradation and all the time his fight for survival and the terrible knowledge of the fact that he would kill to survive. It seemed to Louis that Andrea alone could purify him with her forgiveness. When she cried, he tried to quell the flood of words by making love again.

At noon, Louis got out of bed, showered, and dressed in his army uniform, since he had nothing else. He sat at the table and watched Andrea moving round the kitchen in calm, sensuous movements. She slid a cup over the table towards him, and began to butter some bread.

Watching her, he felt soiled and contaminated with evil. She cared for beauty, for honesty, for music, for love and, miraculously, for him. She hated cruelty and pain and war and soldiers, yet she still loved him, although he had killed and maimed and experienced the sickening thrill of battle.

He caught hold of her hand. 'We're going into Kladno to get a special licence from the registry office, and tomorrow morning we'll be married. We'll have to pay extra, but I have some cash with me. In future you must always keep your marriage papers with you. Whatever happens while I'm away, you will be the Countess Andrea von Burgheim, and you will have a right to claim German protection. You must take your marriage papers to headquarters and apply for permission to return to Austria. Then you can go to Father and look after him until I return.'

Andrea slowly put down the knife she was using. 'Louis, we can't marry. When Hugo released me from the camp and had me sent back to Prague, he re-classified me as a German-speaking Czech. My German passport was revoked and I can't return to Austria. My papers state that I'm of mixed blood, part Slav because my mother was Czech, and quarter gypsy from my grandmother.'

Louis looked shocked. Then he laughed. 'Maybe not according to Nazi law, but I know a priest who will marry us as Catholics. He's an old friend, retired now, but once he was the parish priest at Sokol Castle We'll go there this afternoon.' He stood up, caught hold of her and hugged her tightly. 'It's not the sort of wedding we had planned, but we may never get another chance. Unfortunately, the marriage won't protect you because we'll be breaking the law.'

Andrea began to laugh through her tears.

'We have two days, Andrea. Two good days. We'll see the priest, and I'll buy some different clothes. God forbid you should marry a German soldier. I'll take you out to dinner, in some romantic place, with candles and music. You'd like that. We can dance if you like. I have to be back at base first thing Monday morning, but we have all Sunday. We'll make enough love to last us for the next year or so. Cheer up, darling. Keep your tears for after I'm gone.'

She put one finger over his mouth. 'You must survive for us, Louis,' she pleaded urgently. 'Not just physically, but mentally and emotionally. Don't let them brutalise you. Find the strength to stay as you are. Come back to me, Louis.'

She persisted until he promised.

Chapter  40

STADELHEIM PRISON WAS A GRIM PLACE where enemies of the
Third Reich were held prior to their trials and despatch to the
camps, the gallows, the firing squad or the gas chambers. There
were many ways to die, Marietta had discovered, but for the
living, conditions were identical, deprived of companionship,
adequate food, fresh air and hope, the inmates slowly but
inevitably succumbed to despair and sickness.

As far as she could work out she had been alone in the cell
for two hundred and forty-eight days and nights. It was,
therefore, March 6. From the fading light coming from behind
the small pane, she gathered that it was close to 6 p.m. Sure
enough a few minutes later she heard the rumble of a trolley and
the rattle of a key in the lock. Her door opened and Toadie came
in, so named for her muddy, blotched complexion and hanging
jowls.

'Hold your bowl,' she croaked.

Marietta held out the cracked enamel bowl and the woman
half-filled it with brown liquid. She thrust one slice of black
bread towards Marietta and went out. Slowly the trolley
squeaked its way along the corridor.

There were twelve women in this block. From their whispered nightly communication, Marietta knew all their tragic

stories and their names. She wondered if she would ever see any of their faces. Her cell was darkening, she had chewed every morsel of bread and drunk her soup, and now came the hours Marietta dreaded the most . . . the long and lonely night.

A new woman had come into the adjacent cell early that morning. Using her shoe, Marietta began to tap against the wall. 'Hello! Hello,' she whispered. 'Can you hear me?' She could hear coughing and sobbing, but nothing else. 'Please answer.'

It took a long time before the woman replied by tapping in return. Marietta pulled her chair to the wall, rolled up her blanket and put it on the chair. In this way she was almost able to reach the air vents. 'I am Marie,' she whispered. 'What is your name?'

'Greta Brecht,' she sobbed.

'Welcome to Stadelheim,' Marietta called softly. 'We pass information to each other . . . we are all afraid, but it helps to talk to each other. Try to be brave,' she whispered.

The woman could not stop crying. Marietta listened sympathetically, as she had done so often in the past months, to yet another sad story. Greta had owned a small nightclub in Munich. She had fallen foul of her Nazi boyfriend over the cash takings he had stolen. After an argument, he had denounced her as a prostitute and social deviant. Now he owned the nightclub.

'I'm sorry, but take courage. Prostitution is not a very serious crime.'

'What will happen to me here?' Greta asked, coughing again.

'Nothing much, unless you break the rules. You don't get enough to eat, that's all. You wait here until your trial. After that you move on. The warders are stupid, but they only obey orders. Try to be calm. It helps.'

Why don't I take my own advice, she thought bitterly. Lately she had hardly slept. Her stomach felt knotted. She would break out in a cold sweat each time she heard footsteps approaching. Were they coming to get her? Was this the end? Her fear of dying was her main preoccupation. Would they shoot her, or garotte her, or hang her? There was also her longing for Bill, her anxiety for her father, and her loneliness to contend with. A howl, rising from the cells below, brought goosepimples to her skin.

'Shut up, pig,' she heard the wardress yell.

As the howls changed to whimpers of pain, Marietta put her hands over her ears. She could bear her own anguish, but not that of others. Here was a place where evil flourished, but she would never become debased. Never, she vowed. 'Don't give in to them,' she whispered to Greta. 'We are not like them. We know how to love.' She closed her eyes and thought about Bill and the love they had shared. She did not sleep.

Princess Ingrid Mignon von Graetz lay between her silk sheets and idly contemplated the painting she had bought. It was called Spanish Dancers, and it depicted a dancing troupe being led away in chains, the blood from their wounds as crimson as the women's dresses. It had been painted by Ricardo Cortes, a young Spanish refugee painter who was living on his wits in Paris. The main value of Ricordo's painting, and so many others like it, which she now owned, was that she had become established in the right circles. Nowadays she was known as a generous patron of the arts, a vehement anti-Nazi campaigner and moderately wealthy, and she mixed with a very sophisticated crowd.

Life had become enchanting. At weekends, she and her new friends would race down to Monaco for gambling at the casino, and spend their days in stately chateaux belonging to one or the other of the right set. Ingrid was also gaining the reputation of being one of the prettiest and best-dressed women in Paris and she was proud of this. War had been declared, but in her circles, no one seemed to care. Only at night her fears surfaced. Would Hugo force her to spy again? Where was he? Why hadn't he called? What would he make her do?

Unbelievably, Hugo had not asked her to do anything for him when he arranged her departure from Germany. She simply squandered the large sums deposited in her bank account and had fun. She occasionally believed that Hugo had forgotten about her, but usually she waited for word from him in trepidation and meanwhile threw herself into a whirl of social events, like a moth dashing itself against a lamp.

She stretched, sat up and studied her bedroom. There was only one word to describe it ... divine! She had engaged the services of the leading interior decorator in Paris, a quaint homosexual, known as Quince. Everything was pink except the ceiling which was covered with murals of cute little bare-bottomed seraphs flitting among the clouds.

Beyond the bedroom was her salon where she could comfortably entertain fifty guests or more, which she did, every Thursday evening. At first it had been difficult to achieve the right mix: hot-headed, left-wing politicians, empty pocketed artists, powerful ministers of state, rich industrialists and impoverished, titled exiles, but eventually she had succeeded brilliantly. The women must be saucy, pretty and fun, the men must be interesting at the very least, rich and powerful was an added bonus. Life had become like a firework display – one glorious happening after the next.

Ingrid climbed out of bed and went to the bathroom where she ran a bath of deep hot water into which she poured her scented bath oil. She leaned back and enjoyed the fragrant water. She found her thoughts wandering to Fernando, the Spanish dancer, who had recently joined her circle of friends. He excited her tremendously. He was divinely handsome with jet-black straight hair, tanned skin, small turned-up nose and slanting black eyes, which flashed fiercely with passion or temper, depending on his mood. He had a lithe, virile dancer's body and endless energy. She had vaguely thought of taking him as her lover.

She ran her hands over her breasts and her thighs and felt ready for love. She knew she looked good. Even her cropped hair was superbly styled. Quite without meaning to, she had started a new look in Paris. Everyone wanted to look as if they'd been shorn and starved recently.

Ingrid dressed and set out on her pilgrimage of self-gratification. She returned at one to find the maid had set the table for lunch, smoked salmon and caviar, with salad and champagne, Ingrid's favourite diet.

She had almost finished lunch when the telephone rang. It would probably be Lisa Fonssagrives, Ingrid thought, as she hurried to pick up the receiver. Lisa, a fashion photographer, wanted to photograph Ingrid in her latest gown of shimmering blue-green voile, for a special supplement to Paris *Vogue* entitled: 'What the Rich are Wearing'. She had decided to say yes. She picked up the receiver. 'Princess Ingrid von Graetz,' she murmured.

'Congratulations, my dear. You've gate-crashed the right set, just as I predicted. I knew I could count on you.'

Hugo's oily purring voice gripped Ingrid with ice-cold apprehension. She had to hold on to the desk-top to save herself from falling on to the Afghan rug, her knees turned to rubber. She wanted to throw down the receiver, deny his existence, order him from her life, but she did not have that kind of courage. And always was the persistent belief that only Hugo could restore her rightful possessions.

'Ingrid, are you there? Speak!' Hugo's voice demanded.

'I'm here,' she croaked, clearing her throat. 'I wasn't expecting to hear from you.'

'Good!' He chuckled. 'Well, my dear, now that you've established yourself so effectively, it is time for you to get to work.'

She swallowed, desperately trying to pull herself together.

'You are to meet your controller, Ingrid. When we've finished this conversation, put down the receiver, walk outside your apartment block and turn left towards the Champs-Elysées. Hesitate at the corner. You will be contacted.'

A click terminated the conversation. Ingrid was left holding the receiver. She let it fall from her fingers and bounce on to the floor. She felt dazed and apprehensive. To steel herself she thought about her family's stolen fortune in land and buildings ... it would all be hers. She only had to obey Hugo for a little while longer. The war would soon be over. She automatically checked her make-up, retouched her lips and, picking up her bag and a silk wrap, let herself out of her apartment.

When she reached the pavement, she realised how cold it was. A fur stole would have been more sensible than silk, she thought. She walked to the corner of the street and stood around feeling lost. Unexpectedly, Fernando appeared at her side. He took her arm. 'Let me escort you across the road,' he said.

'Oh God! No! Not now!' she whispered to him. 'I don't have time to talk to you.'

He was amazingly persistent. He caught hold of her arm and led her to the kerb. They crossed the street while she made feeble efforts to push him away.

'Not now, I tell you. I must wait at the corner,' she hissed.

'For me. Do you not understand? You were waiting for me.'

Ingrid stopped in amazement. Good God! What a mad world. Fernando ...? A Nazi agent ...? She laughed shakily as she accompanied him to the nearest café and allowed him to guide her to a seat.

'Don't look so surprised.' He was laughing at her. He ordered her a glass of Pernod without asking what she wanted.

'Come,' he said, leaning towards her. 'Be daring! Kiss me!'

She raised her mouth in a futile, resigned gesture and allowed herself to be briefly fondled as his lips touched hers. Leaving his hand on her shoulder, his fingers began to dig into her flesh. She flinched and tried to pull away.

'What a luscious little thing you are.' He leaned over her, reeking of garlic, and for the first time she noticed his pitted skin. 'It's a pity,' he sighed theatrically, 'but I must make the supreme sacrifice. From now on, Ingrid, your sexual favours must be used exclusively for the glory of the Third Reich.' He laughed cruelly at the expression on her face.

'Yes, it's time to get to work. Our mutual friend wants to know the precise political leanings of the men in the government who visit your salon. It's a simple beginner's task for you, Ingrid,' he said. 'By the way, my dear, our friend said you must stop spending quite so much money, but as long as he has information about ...'

An hour later Ingrid stumbled back to her apartment in a daze. Her head was full of jumbling questions. Too many questions! Which politicians could be persuaded to work for the Nazis when Germany conquered France? Who would cause the most trouble? Who slept with whom? Who had influence, who did not? Hugo was demanding his price and Ingrid knew it was time to pay.

By the time Ingrid reached her apartment, she was filled with nausea. She staggered to the bathroom. Flinging her bag on the floor, she threw up in the toilet, then fumbled on the shelves for two aspirins, which she swallowed with a glass of water. Her mind was racing around, looking for an escape. How could she get this information without having to sleep with these ugly, flabby men? She glanced in the mirror and flinched as her haggard eyes stared back. She must look beautiful. Feverishly she began to brush rouge on to her cheeks. She would wear her new blue voile tonight, she decided. It made her look young and appealing. She had just four hours to pull herself together.

Chapter  41

IN HIS BERLIN OFFICE, the Count stood staring out at the square below, deep in thought, trying to think of any detail that he might have overlooked. It was January, 1940, and Western Europe was sweating out the phony war. Everyone knew it was only a matter of time before Hitler sent his goose-stepping troops out to impose their New Order on the west, but no one knew just where and when the attack would come. The generals felt that in the long-term Germany must be defeated, and so the Conspiracy had sprung into action again.

Since Marietta had been arrested the Count had aged twenty years. His hair had turned white and his flesh shrunk until the loose skin hung in folds. His eyes were bleak and his lips permanently folded into a thin line of despair. The smart ceremonial Nazi uniform he was wearing stressed his ravaged features. Since joining the Nazi Party, the Count had moved his headquarters to his apartment in Berlin where it was easier to meet members of the Conspiracy. At the same time he was able to ingratiate himself with Hitler's close associates.

Hearing his manservant's footsteps, the Count turned from the window, expecting to see one of the conspirators, but found himself staring into the startling blue eyes of Bill Roth.

'I've tried everything and failed,' Bill said. 'The Embassy

tried. I went right to the top . . .' he broke off as the implications of the Count's uniform sunk in . . . the stiff black tunic, the steel swastika at the neck fastening, the epaulettes denoting the honorary rank of lieutenant-general. His misery turned to shock and then contempt.

'You bastard,' Bill whispered. 'You put her where she is. Yes, you! You trained her . . . you gave her that awful dedication to duty that ruined our lives . . . you taught her to fear no one and to speak her mind. Now you've joined the Nazi Party to save your own precious skin.'

Bill sunk into a chair and buried his face in his hands. 'How much did it take to make you a traitor?' he muttered.

'Marietta's life,' the Count said simply.

Bill looked incredulous. 'They're going to free her?'

'I said her life, not her freedom. They're not going to shoot her, or hang her or garotte her. That was the deal.'

As he watched Bill's expression changed from anger to shame and humility, the Count was filled with compassion for this young American who would give his life for Marietta, just as he would. With his rough, uncombed hair, his hunched shoulders and deeply-lined face, he looked like a man enduring the very worst that life could throw at him. He poured Bill a brandy and handed it to him. 'A life sentence lasts only as long as the Nazis last.'

Bill gulped the brandy. 'Life?' he muttered. 'I was hoping she'd be freed.'

'That was naive of you,' the Count said. 'My daughter is the victim of a trumped-up charge of espionage. She is accused of handing over secrets of German rearmament . . . maybe to you. Who knows? Ingrid was also accused, but fortunately for her she had already been deported.'

Bill looked shattered. 'You mean . . . Why yes . . . Ingrid brought me some statistics once. I thought at the time she should never have had them. She told the source . . .' He broke off and stared at the floor for a while. 'Strange!'

The Count shrugged. 'You weren't the one they were after. I don't suppose the information was all that important. I think they wanted to trap the Edelweiss students ... and they succeeded. Now Bill, you must leave. Don't come again.'

'I helped trap her,' Bill said softly. That agonising thought stayed with him long after he had said goodbye.

It was just before dawn the following morning when the Gestapo came for Bill. After a restless night spent worrying about Marie, Bill had fallen into a deep, exhausted sleep and he did not hear them. He woke, blurry-eyed and dazed, to hear his door being broken open and footsteps rushing down the passage to his bedroom.

He switched on the light and groaned aloud. The Gestapo were wrecking his flat. One of them pointed a pistol at his head. 'Get dressed at once,' he said. He remained close to Bill.

That was unusual, Bill thought, resigned to the worst. They usually dragged off their victims in their nightclothes.

As he dressed he watched the Gestapo systematically search and destroy the contents of his flat. Bill shrugged and looked the other way. There was nothing he could do about it right now. There would be little worth salvaging when they'd finished, and if there was it would be stolen.

He was pushed out to the inevitable black car and thrust inside. It had all been so quick. Bill felt scared, despite his firm intention not to be. Andy Johnson would call from the Embassy in the morning, as he always did. That was a small comfort. He would know that Bill had been arrested and there would be an official protest. There wasn't much they could do to him, Bill reckoned. War had been declared a month ago, but America was neutral and the Bill knew that the Nazis would be happy to keep the status quo. They had enough on their plates.

Reason began to wane in the face of his fear. How would he cope with the interrogation? Was he about to find out just how much of a man he really was? Just how bad would the beatings be?

To his surprise, he saw that they were driving towards the station. Bill was thrust out of the car and marched to a platform. The destination board read Düsseldorf, which was near the

Dutch border. Was he going to be deported? The idea appalled him. How could he leave Germany when Marie was imprisoned there? He'd never stopped hoping that somehow he'd get her out. 'You can't do this,' he said, but his guards ignored him.

It was midnight when the train reached Düsseldorf. The station was deserted. Handcuffed to one of the guards, Bill was driven rapidly north. It was 1 a.m. when he was bundled out of the car. Ahead was the German border post. His handcuffs were unlocked. Then an unexpected kick propelled him past the barriers. Looking round cautiously he saw that he was in a narrow strip of road between two heavily armed border posts of two countries at war with each other. On either side, he was looking into the sights of half a dozen rifles. He reached into his pocket for his white handkerchief and flapped it towards the Dutch. 'I'm American,' he yelled. 'Neutral ... Deported ... Call the American Embassy ... I'm a journalist ... They took my passport ...'

There was no reply. The rifles moved fractionally as he scrambled to his feet. Damn! He'd sprained his ankle in the fall. Cursing heavily, he limped towards the Dutch post.

At dawn, on the morning of April 30, Marietta woke to the usual heavy footsteps and the squealing of the trolley being propelled down the corridor. Her door was flung open. She held out her bowl. The beady-eyed wardress looked triumphant. 'Your trial is today,' she was told abruptly. 'Be ready after breakfast.'

Shortly afterwards, the warder returned with the clothes Marietta had been wearing when she was arrested. She stroked the fabric lovingly. When she put on her skirt and blouse she discovered how much weight she had lost.

She heard more footsteps and her cell door was thrown open. Unbelievably, Toadie was carrying handcuffs. The steel bands were snapped around her wrists. Another guard waited at the door, fingering her baton.

The sombre procession started along the corridor. 'Good luck, good luck,' she heard the calls from the cells as she walked past. She squared her shoulders and held her head high, but, despite her efforts, she was quaking by the time she reached the Tribunal. She recognised the three judges, and there was Hugo, sitting in the well of the court, looking triumphant.

She faced the bench. 'You are Countess Marietta von Burgheim? Is that correct?'

'I should like to sit down,' Marietta said in a clear voice. 'If you would ask one of your men to bring me a chair, I would be prepared to answer your questions.'

One judge, wearing the uniform of a colonel, looked at her in surprise, then motioned for a chair to be brought. Marietta sat down, crossed her legs, and tried to hang on to her pride.

'I am Countess Marietta von Burgheim,' she said.

'Countess, you are accused of the gravest possible charges: spying against the Third Reich. A secondary charge against you is of treason. Both charges carry the death penalty.'

'But you can only kill me once,' she said, smiling sweetly.

'Silence, Countess. The court has sentenced you to life imprisonment. You will be sent to a labour camp where your energy can be put to good use. Heil Hitler!'

Life! She was going to *live*. She wasn't going to hang, or be garotted or beheaded . . . She began to shake uncontrollably and suck in great gasps of air. She wanted to laugh and cry at the same time. It had all been so quick.

Trembling, she was led out into the prison yard. Blessed sunlight washed over her for the first time in months. She looked up into the branches of a sycamore tree and prayed her thanks that she could live and hear the birds sing and feel the sun's warmth. At this very moment she might have been standing before a firing squad.

She was pushed to the back of a queue of women. Many of them had only recently been arrested, it seemed, for they were not as gaunt as she and their skins glowed in comparison, although they looked dazed and frightened.

One of them was beautiful. Her features were delicate, her nose tilted, her eyes deep blue and her honey blonde hair was spread over her shoulders. She was wearing a black velvet suit and high-heeled patent leather court shoes. How frightened she looked. She began to cough and Marietta realised that this lovely woman was Greta Brecht. 'I'm Marie,' she whispered.

She was startled by a hand on her shoulder. Looking round she saw Hugo standing behind her. He seemed to have grown larger and even more menacing. Hugo was her enemy, she knew that now. She frowned and stepped away, but he kept his heavy hand on her.

'Father saved you from death, but the result will be the same, make no mistake about that. You are going to Lichtenberg concentration camp *and you will die there, Marietta, I promise you.*'

She was too shocked to reply.

'But first you will learn humility and suffering and just what it's like to be a person of no account. You are going to learn how low you really are before you die. Those are my orders. Goodbye, *sister*. We won't meet again.'

Chapter  42

AT DUSK THEY ARRIVED at the Lichtenberg women's concentration camp. Bruised and dizzy, they staggered from the railcars and were herded into the prison yard where they stood for hours, shuffling forward at a snail's pace. Marietta took great gulps of the fragrant evening air. Fresh air was becoming a luxury.

The line of women moved slowly towards a low, wooden hut. Eventually Marietta wearily took her turn in front of a table where her wrist was roughly tattooed with a number: 798484. The needle pricked and burned. Marietta rubbed her wrist in shock and tried to tell herself that it didn't matter. They had violated her flesh as well as her mind. She had been branded, as cattle were, and now she was merely a number in a long row of slave labour units, owned by the Third Reich. This was the first step in the dehumanisation process, she knew. Looking around, she saw how all the women were suffering and ashamed.

After being tattooed, the women were sent to another hut where a sergeant sat at a desk. By the look of his pointed nose, his bulbous blue eyes, and his large red hands, Marie guessed that he had recently been a farmhand.

'You are . . . ?' he flicked over a page of a heavy ledger.

'Countess von Burg—'

A wardress standing beside her struck Marietta hard over the ear with her stubby rubber baton, called a *schlag*. 'You're a number. You no longer have a name,' she shrieked. Wearily Marietta read off her number. 'Can you sew . . .?'

'I can work in the fields. I was studying agriculture.'

The sergeant's eyes lit up as he stared at her breasts. She felt naked.

He turned to the wardress and spoke rapidly in the local dialect. 'She's ideal for working in my house. She must bypass the barber. Take her over there after delousing.'

In the next hut, prisoners in striped pyjamas were shaving the women's hair off. Many of the women were crying.

'Not you,' the wardress said, pushing her aside. 'Go to the next room.' She stuck a green sticker on Marietta's coat.

'Go in there and strip. Wait.'

If hair was required for working on her back for that oafish sergeant, then she would be shorn now, Marietta decided. She pushed back into the queue of women. Shortly afterwards her long hair fall to the ground in large handfuls. Her scalp felt raw. She ran her hands over her head, feeling the ugly stubble.

The wardress returned and flinched when she saw Marietta. She lashed out with her *schlag*, hitting Marietta in the face. With the taste of blood in her mouth Marietta shuffled forward in the queue to the showers. The water was cold, but she managed to open her mouth and drink her fill. The disinfectant burned her skin and her eyes, she emerged pink all over to find that she must walk naked across the yard. A group of leering soldiers laughed derisively. Some of them were taking photographs. Marietta wondered wearily how many men and women would peer at her nakedness before the day was through. She refused to be ashamed of her body, nor would she be intimidated by these men.

God, it was endless! She tried not to think of what was happening to her. She was back in Bohemia with grandmother, walking over the fields, examining the crops. She tried to ignore the fingers poking into her hidden places in the medical examination. Naked, she moved on and on, until bundles of prison uniform and clogs were thrust into her arms. She put on her striped straight smock and pants and tied a white head-square over her head. A tin bowl and a mug and a spoon was thrust at her and soon they were shuffling past a mobile soup unit. Supper was a slice of black bread and half a bowl of thin soup. Some things never change, she thought.

The wardress returned, followed by the sergeant. 'I ordered her to move out of the barber's hut, but she disobeyed me.' She looked frightened.

The sergeant stared at Marietta, undecided. She stared back scornfully. 'Ten lashes,' he said. 'She must learn to obey.'

Another supervisor followed, checking their wrists. 'You are 798484?'

'Yes,' Marietta said weakly.

'You are to go to the punishment cell.'

The punishment block was half a mile away and Marietta was marched there at high speed, her calves lashed whenever she faltered. In her weakened, semi-starved state, she almost collapsed. It was a long, low bunker. As Marietta and her escort approached the handful of guards disbanded their card game.

'Ten lashes for this one.'

One of the guards stood up. He pushed Marietta into a cell and forced her to bend forward over a table. The wardress flicked her overall up. Ten lashes were given rapidly, without malice or any real thought. To Marietta it was the most humiliating experience of her life. She bit her lip grimly and hung on to her pride. By the time she had stood up and pulled down her skirt, the guard was back playing cards.

She was marched back to her place on the parade ground where she stood for another hour. Eventually they were all delivered to their various bunkhouses.

Marietta heard the door slam shut behind her. It was dark and stuffy and smelled of sweat, urine and misery. When her eyes adjusted, she saw that she and six others – all newcomers – were replacements for the empty bunks for which they had to search. With growing horror she saw that the bunks were four deep, in rows down each side of the room, with only two foot of space between them. In the manner of the living dead, two hundred women were lying in this hut.

She wandered down the aisle, found a space on top, and climbed up carefully, trying not to stand on the others who were lying prone. She knew she would be verminous by morning.

She lay on her back and tried to ignore the pain from her beating, her sore lip and cheek, and the prickles from the straw and hessian mattress. The moon rose and in its light she was able to see the simple design of the bunkhouse.

Attic-like, the roof slanted down on either side from a peak in the middle, so that her feet were almost touching the lowest section of the roof. The centre of the ceiling was of glass, reinforced with steel bars. All the light came from this glassed section. The only ventilation, however, was through two air vents at each end of the hut. It was nowhere near enough for two hundred women.

She turned to the women below her. 'Don't they ever open the windows?'

The woman replied in a stream of unintelligible sounds. Polish! Marietta realised that she was amongst some of the thousands of Polish women who had been dragged from their homes and families to work in Hitler's slave camps.

Marietta stood on her bunk and felt towards the roof. It was ordinary glass. 'Is there a broom anywhere here?' she whispered. 'I'll have a look,' someone whispered in German. Shortly afterwards a figure materialised below her bunk. She saw the huge eyes of Greta looking up at her from under her shaved scalp. How strange she looked. Marietta realised that she must look as odd. 'Here's a broom,' Greta said. 'You could die for this,' she added in a whisper.

'What could be worse than suffocating?' Marietta replied as she poked the broom through the glass over the passageway at the end of her bunk. There was a loud crack and the sound of falling glass. They listened fearfully, but no one came.

'Pass me the broom,' Greta said. 'We'll die together, but tonight we'll breathe.' She, too, made a hole through the glass near her bunk.

Soon the pressure of the heat abated and cool night air began to penetrate the bunkhouse. Fresh air is worth dying for, Marietta told herself.

As they breathed the soft air, the two women began to talk and Greta's self-disgust dominated. 'What sickens me is that I thought I loved him,' Greta whispered. 'And he did this to me. For money!' She broke off in a fit of coughing.

'I should never have fought him, knowing how highly-placed he is in the Party,' she said. The fact that her lover had been false and betrayed her, seemed to matter more than the loss of her freedom.

'You have a lovely voice. Were you ever on the stage?' Marietta said, trying to comfort her.

'Yes,' Greta said. She sounded pathetically grateful for the compliment. 'I studied drama and singing. I had some good parts, but then I found I didn't have the stamina.' She coughed again. 'I have tuberculosis.'

'I'm sorry,' Marietta said inadequately.

'When my father died I put my inheritance into a small restaurant. I built a bar, very discreet and very sophisticated. I used to help with the cooking sometimes, serve at the tables and afterwards sing. I only employed three other people. That's why it was so profitable. It became a fashionable place. Now he has it all, and I've been sentenced to forty months' hard labour.'

Later, Marietta lay staring at a star that she could see in her own circle of private night sky. It twinkled and winked and comforted her until it passed out of sight. The moon set, the sky darkened and she lay listening to the heavy breathing of too many women in close confinement. A few snored and cried out in their sleep, some sobbed silently, but most of them lay awake, engrossed in their private misery. 'Dear God, help me,' she prayed. 'Am I to be absolutely abandoned and forgotten in this terrible place?'

She experienced a strange feeling that she was a leaf drifting in the wind, cut off from the mother tree, abandoned, useless and forgotten, fit only for compost. 'Dear God,' she prayed again. 'Send me a sign that you have not forgotten me. Send me something to hang on to in the days ahead.'

There was a sigh of breeze and a soft scraping sound as a leaf was blown across the roof. It fell through the hole and fluttered on to her.

Marietta smoothed it carefully. Even a leaf can be used by God, she thought wonderingly. It's a sign. I, too, can be God's messenger. She clutched the leaf against her breast. It was the most precious gift she had ever received.

Chapter  43

INGRID WAS SITTING ON HER BED, wrapped in a blanket, for the tenth time that morning reading a letter from Uncle Frederick. She shuddered violently as she again absorbed the truth behind his words, that Marietta had been sentenced to life imprisonment and was in a concentration camp. What shocked her more than Marietta's punishment, was the fact that the von Burgheims had fallen so low and were powerless to change the sentence. Uncle had written to warn her to get out of France before it fell, as she, too, was implicated in the charge of spying. Well, Paris could fall at anytime, she knew. Most of France was under German occupation, but still she sat, waiting for her orders from the elusive Hugo or his minions.

He had been right, after all. He *did* have all the power. Despite her guilt about Marietta's fate, she couldn't help congratulating herself for choosing the right side.

When the telephone rang, the noise echoed alarmingly in this new, silent Paris. Ingrid snatched at the receiver. It was Fernando. She shivered.

'I have received our orders,' he said. 'We are to flee to Britain as refugees, leaving at the last possible minute. You will apply for political asylum and find work in a strategic industry near London. When you are established, go to this address . . .'

His voice droned on and on ... endless instructions. Ingrid struggled to concentrate on his words, her mind in a turmoil. No, she wanted to shout. No, I won't do that. I refuse. I love my apartment ... how can I leave it? And they shoot spies in wartime. When Fernando rang off she was frozen with shock and terror of the unknown.

'No ...' She pummelled her fist against the wall and tried not to cry out in hysteria. How could they expect her to do this terrible thing? Why should she go? Why not refuse?

The answer to that question was simple. She wanted her family estates. And she was afraid of Hugo.

Gripped by panic, she threw some clothes and toiletries into a suitcase and raced downstairs, only to find that the exit was locked and barred and the concierge absent. She managed to force the folding gate aside enough to squeeze through. Weighed down by her case, with no cabs or public transport, she walked to the station and learned that the last train to the coast had left hours before. She heard the sound of heavy engines in the street, and leaving the station, discovered only military traffic was abroad. Checking that the markings on the vehicles were British, she let one shoulder of her jacket slip provocatively and raised a hand as though hailing a taxi.

Armentieres, at dusk, resembled an army garrison. Trucks and artillery jammed the square. Civilians added to the confusion; the streets were full of cars, people pushing wheel barrows, bicycles, horses and carts ... anything and everything that could carry a few possessions. The French were moving away from the coast towards the interior, while the British were pushing on towards Dunkirk.

Ingrid had never seen anything like it. Her hands were wet with sweat and slipping on the metal rail of the lorry she was travelling in. As they began to clear the chaos of the town the first German divebombers strafed the convoy and the vehicles slammed to a halt. The men scrambled out and raced for the ditches.

Ingrid sat petrified as the bombs fell around her like skittles.

The noise had sent her into shock. A plane dived low, shooting at fleeing civilians, but she was unable to move. The dive-bomber circled and returned from behind, spraying bullets. A soldier raced across the road, hurled her into the ditch and flung himself over her.

A lorry exploded, igniting three others behind it and the blast hit her like a physical blow. She heard the line of tracer-bullets whining through the ditch. Ingrid clapped her hands over her ears. When at last the planes were gone and the troops called the 'all clear', Ingrid scrambled up the bank to find her transport was a smoking ruin and was being pushed off the road. Tears of despair rolled down her cheeks. She was finished. Everything she owned was gone. She stood in the middle of the road and watched the pathetic civilians gather around their dead and wounded relatives.

She looked up at the soldiers who were climbing into their lorry. 'Can you give me a lift?' she pleaded again. One of the soldiers winked and held out a hand. 'All right. Scramble up. We can't guarantee we'll reach the coast, but you'll be better off than walking on your own.'

She climbed into the back of the lorry and huddled between two Tommies, only too grateful for their warm presence.

As dawn broke, Ingrid heard a dull roar in the distance. Soon the sound became fragmented. Ingrid could pick out the scream of shells, the drone of the Stukas and Messerschmitts circling overhead, the shrill whine of bombs falling, the deafening blast as they exploded, the repetitive shriek of shells zooming overhead and the aftershocks as they hit their targets. The lorry kept inching forward towards what sounded like certain death.

Eventually she fell into an exhausted sleep and only woke when someone began pulling her out of the truck into the smoke and uproar that was Dunkirk. She watched the troops march away and had never felt more lonely, or more afraid.

Feeling stiff and thirsty and very hungry, she climbed to the top of a low cliff. Now she could see that the town was razed. As far as the eye could see were men waiting. Hundreds of thousands of soldiers were clustered on the beaches and in the ruined town. A mile out to sea, behind the breakers, was a row of waiting British destroyers and steamers.

She watched as if mesmerised as a line of planes shot out through low-lying clouds at tremendous speed, splattering bombs and bullets over the beach. The soldiers threw themselves down. The movement was like corn on a windy day. The khaki wave rippled up again. Most of the blast was lost in the sand, but she knew there must be many casualties.

Ingrid plucked up the courage to go down into the town and push her way through the waiting queues of men towards where she thought the harbour lay.

'Can't go to the harbour, Miss . . . bombed to ruins,' a soldier told her. 'The Huns took care of that. Our boats can't get into shallow water to pick us up. We're trapped.'

Ingrid turned away hopelessly.

There was nowhere to go. No escape. She wanted to dig a hole in the sand and crawl into it like a small animal to await either deliverance or death. What was she supposed to do? Did Hugo think she could swim the Channel?

Instinctively she followed the soldiers down on to the beach, her knees trembling with every step, for it was taking the brunt of the Luftwaffe's attack. The Messerschmitts never left them alone. They came in low, wave after relentless wave. Ingrid dodged from one dug-out shelter to the next, clawing her way towards the sea.

She felt dizzy and tired, she was reaching the end of her strength. Faint with hunger, she at first thought the roar in her ears was her imagination. Shaking her head to try and clear it, she looked up and realised the sound was from hundreds upon hundreds of men cheering their lungs out.

Out to sea, Ingrid saw that the English Channel was covered with tiny black specks on the grey water, like mosquitoes, and they were moving towards the shore. She rubbed her eyes and looked again. The black dots were small craft bobbing on the ocean, and they were advancing steadily. As they neared the shore, she could see that there were yachts, tugs, barges, motor boats, fishing vessels, pleasure steamers ... forming a great tide of private craft advancing steadily through the hailstorm of bombs and bullets.

The Stukas saw them, too, and began to dive-bomb the armada of mosquitoes, but it was unsinkable. It's like swatting at flies, Ingrid thought, and just as ineffective. There were far too many of them. As the first line of boats reached the surf, the cheering soldiers began to surge forward.

Ignoring the shells and the dive-bombers and the bombs falling on every side, the men began to advance into the sea until they were standing chest-deep in water, buffeted by waves. The first boats hauled the men aboard until they were perilously laden, then turned back into the cauldron of milky foam, churned by bullets and exploding bombs, and sped towards the waiting ships lying at anchor. The next wave of boats came bobbing and wobbling to the beach.

Ingrid saw with astonishment that queues were forming and she hastily got to the back of one and stood there, hoping that they would take her with the soldiers. Every time a small boat put to sea, the men walked forward a few yards. She calculated it would take this day and the night before she would reach the sea. To her surprise, the Tommy in front of her turned and spoke to her.

'I reckon we're going to make it, Miss. We're going to cheat Jerry out of his spoils. He thought we was trapped here like rats in a cage, ready to be shipped into one of his damned camps. I suppose you've heard what happens there.'

'I've been in one,' Ingrid said, feeling desperate. 'Look.' She held up her wrist displaying the tattoo with her number on it.

The soldier's eyes filled with incomprehension and pity. 'You look all in,' the man said. 'Here!' He called to the others. 'Are you going to let this little lady, who's escaped from one of them concentration camps, stand here until she drops from exhaustion? Come on mates, let's push her up front.'

A small wooden boat was approaching. She stared at it pleadingly. It would take thirty, perhaps, but more than fifty were ahead of her. The next minute strong arms pushed her out towards the boat. She was chest-deep in the waves. Choking and half-drowned in the foaming spray, she was picked up and pushed towards the front. She felt herself being lifted and shoved from behind, and for a moment she was poised, spread-eagled, half-in and half-out. The soldier behind her gave her legs a mighty shove. Someone in the boat grasped her armpits and she found herself sprawling on the deck.

It was a private fishing boat, she discovered, with two outboard engines. An old weather-beaten man of about seventy was sitting by the tiller, his face impassive as the soldiers were loaded on board. Two youngsters, not more than sixteen, were helping the troops. She guessed the old man was their grandfather. The boys were counting: 'Twenty-eight, twenty-nine, thirty. That's enough,' one said. The last soldier hung on sobbing, and tried to haul himself aboard, but he was pushed back. 'We'll be back soon, mate, don't you worry,' the other boy called out.

The old man twisted the throttle and they were speeding off towards the waiting convoy of ships.

Ten minutes later, Ingrid was helped up a rope ladder. She reached the deck and gratefully felt the weight of a blanket across her shoulders.

'Safe at last, Miss,' one of the soldiers called to her. Ingrid burst into tears. Safe? Oh God, she would never be safe again.

Chapter  44

THE FOLLOWING MORNING AT DAWN, Ingrid filed down the gangway at Dover harbour, amongst the exhausted British troops. The stretcher cases were lying side-by-side, filling the roads and pavements all around the docks. What seemed like the entire local population were moving amongst the bedraggled survivors, handing out hot drinks and blankets. Someone handed Ingrid a cup of tea. Her sex and lack of uniform soon attracted an official. 'Are you a French citizen?' he asked.

'I'm not sure where I should go . . .' she began.

He gave her a quick, hard glance. 'Come this way, Miss,' he said. Shortly afterwards she was in a hastily converted school, awaiting an interview with the 'appropriate authorities' along-side a collection of Frenchmen, who looked in an even worse state than she.

The first time she was questioned she was terrified and she didn't have to act the part of a shell-shocked refugee. She regressed into the lost waif who had been dumped on the von Burgheim family. It was weeks and several more interviews before she was sent to London and passed to a volunteer welfare worker, who issued her with a ration book, an identity card and a temporary permit, establishing her right to live and work in the area, until she gained more permanent status. She was given some secondhand clothes and a room in Camden Town.

Her welfare officer was middle-aged, overweight and smelt of gin. 'You will have to earn your own living, er, Princess Ingrid.' She hesitated in awe over the title.

Ingrid nodded.

'Have you earned your living before?'

Ingrid shook her head. 'I had a private income,' she stammered. 'I think the capital was held in Switzerland. The money used to come into my French bank every month. I can give you the account number.'

This seemed to disconcert her questioner. 'I'll ask someone to look into that. Meantime, we must find you a job.'

Ingrid held out her wrist. 'I nearly died ... most of my family have perished ...' The tears were rolling down her cheeks. 'Please ... you must understand ... I long to do something worthwhile. I want to help defeat the Nazis.'

An expression of relief swamped the woman's fat features, this attitude she could understand. 'Then that's exactly what you will do. I can't think of anything more important than helping to build Spitfires. Can you?'

Three days later, Ingrid arrived at a series of large asbestos-roofed buildings covered in camouflage netting, beside a field where cows grazed. She was shown how to clock in by the foreman, a short, myopic balding man with an apologetic manner, whom she dismissed at once as a fool.

She was directed to a long white-washed shed, housing rows of work benches. A canteen, toilets and a sick bay were situated in an adjacent shed, while a more sturdy two-storey brick building housed the manager's planning office with a window overlooking the plant. She was introduced to 'the girls' and given an overall and a scarf to wear.

Within half an hour she was standing at a bench being taught how to do her small, but essential job, which although repetitive required a good deal of skill, she discovered.

She was faced by a clamp into which she fixed part of the nose cone of a Spitfire. On her right was a lathe and her task was to cut a groove into the inside edge of the cone. Her soft fingers soon grew raw from the metal filings and her hands were ingrained with the oily lubricating fluid.

When she had finished cutting, the cone passed on to an attractive young brunette, with rosy cheeks and glowing brown eyes, who manned the workbench next to hers, and she polished it.

Above the continuous hum of the machinery, her neighbour introduced herself as Gwen who, despite her aristocratic background and her private income, was one of the two million British women who had volunteered to work in munitions factories.

On Saturday morning, Ingrid visited the bank and found herself richer by five hundred pounds from cash transferred from Switzerland. Her morale immediately boosted by the amount, she decided to look for better accommodation and after some searching she found a delightful mews cottage in Knights-bridge, whose owners had departed to Canada as war was declared. Their agent took her minimal deposit in relief, and she was able to move in straightaway.

The time had come to contact Fernando and that same afternoon she set off by tube, found the newsagents and walked in smiling nervously.

The man behind the counter had his back turned. 'I'm looking for Czech newspapers . . .' she began nervously.

'You're Ingrid, I assume.' When he turned she tried to hide her surprise. With his side whiskers, his droopy moustache and his dark, curly hair, the newsagent looked as if he had walked out of a Dickens novel. He was very pale, with shadows under his eyes. He had large, soft brown eyes, his nose was bulbous, his ears large and sticking out, and there was a dark shadow of beard on his cheeks. She sensed a veiled menace behind his soft manner and involuntarily shivered. He introduced himself as Paddy O'Connor, proprietor of the shop. 'Call me Paddy. Welcome to London, Ingrid. The freak is back there.' He gestured over his shoulder.

The freak ...? She pondered over that as she walked to the back and found Fernando on his knees, undoing bales of newspapers. At first she hardly recognised him, for his face was thinner and more sallow, his hair greasy and unwashed and he looked tense and haggard. 'It took you long enough to get here,' he snarled when he saw her.

'I've only just got my papers. I was lucky to get out so soon.'

'Don't let the pimp shove you around. If you have any trouble, just remember, I'm his boss.' Paddy had followed her into the backroom. 'Get those bloody papers on the van,' he snapped at Fernando.

Fernando cringed, leapt to his feet and hauled two bundles out of the door.

'Queer bastard,' Paddy said. 'Now, *Princess* let's get to work. It'll be lessons every night for you, for a month at least, depending on how fast you learn.'

He took her upstairs to a door in the loft, hidden behind some boxes. She walked through it, into a neat, functional room containing a photographic laboratory, a darkroom, and a well-stocked workshop.

'Now, concentrate,' Paddy said. 'I don't like saying things twice. You ever taken photographs?'

She nodded.

'Well this little beauty will be your best friend. I'll show you how to use it,' he said, handing her a small, complicated camera with a flash attachment. She began to enjoy herself.

There were so many new skills she had to acquire, she discovered during the next few weeks, but she was an attentive pupil and Paddy liked teaching her. He never made a pass at her and she was thankful for that.

'A good-looking girl like you should be able to get her hands on all sorts of information,' Paddy said at the end of her training. 'You've got to use your title and your connections to infiltrate the British establishment. That way you'll reach the kind of men who know what's going on. Be careful not to get emotionally involved with any of them. That would be suicide for you, and besides, you'd miss out on the others.'

He seemed not to notice her expression of fury.

The air-raid siren sounded as she walked slowly home that evening. German bombers were pulverising London every night. The invasion must come soon, thank God. Ingrid felt sick with loathing for the life she had been forced to lead. But at the end of it was wealth ... unimaginable wealth ... Not long now, she reassured herself.

Paddy began nagging Ingrid for results. His first demand was for her to photograph drawings on Spitfire design from the manager's office.

Impossible, surely? Ingrid became tense with fear as the days passed. There was only one vague possibility and that was tea break, that unbreakable British tradition, when the manager joined the girls in the canteen. But he always locked his papers away so carefully when he left his office.

Her chance came unexpectedly when the plant had a sudden, unwelcome inspection by three men from the Air Ministry. They left at last and fired with relief the manager rushed to his cold tea and buns, leaving the papers out.

Trembling, Ingrid hurried to fetch her camera which she hid in her overalls. Her hands were shaking, her breath coming in short pants, her heart beating loud enough to be heard in the canteen. Oh God! Anyone could come in. She would be dragged out, arrested and shot as a spy. 'Oh God help me,' she prayed.

It took only minutes, but it seemed like hours. She thrust the camera out of sight and rushed out. She could still hear their loud voices in the canteen as she hurried there. Someone was telling a joke and she joined in their laughter, a sense of euphoria making her giggle loudly, although she hadn't heard the punchline. It was pure relief. How foolish the British were, how careless! No wonder they were losing the war. With Western Europe occupied by the Nazis, Britain was fighting on alone, and everyone expected the invasion at any time. Civilians and troops were working frenziedly to put up cement blocks and rolls of barbed wire along every beach and cliff. Nightly, London was pulverised by bombs and each morning the BBC news broadcast told of more ships lost at sea. Rationing tightened, for food could not reach the British ports. Britain was being bombed and starved to death. Even the King was learning to shoot. He had publicly said that if necessary he would die fighting, and the Queen had refused to leave him, but was staying at his side, with their daughters. Britons from all walks of life were pulling together to survive.

Ingrid had deliberately set out to become friends with her well-connected workmate and, at the beginning of August, Gwen invited her home. 'My parents have a place in the country and you must be lonely away from your family. Come for the weekend, there'll be plenty of people to meet. We usually have a party on Saturday night ... for the boys, of course. They deserve some fun.'

Ingrid's eyes glistened, and her face brightened. She'd missed the good life bitterly.

Chapter  45

CLASPED IN THE ARMS of a young naval captain, Ingrid danced barefooted on the lawn to the distant strains of 'Moonlight Becomes You'. This weekend she had become close to feeling relaxed. The weather was hot, the sky cloudless, the evenings long and filled with dancing and drinking on the terrace and just fooling around. She had drunk too much, but so had almost everyone at the house party. Entertaining 'our boys' on leave was a patriotic duty, she had discovered. She had played tennis that morning, attracting compliments on her athleticism and collecting enough invitations to last her the season.

Her partner interrupted her reverie. 'I say, look at Stephen. He's really letting his hair down. You'd never guess that a rapier mind lurks behind that fuddy-duddy exterior, would you?'

'Does it?' she asked, feeling bored.

'He's in some intelligence outfit ... brilliant fellow ... bit of an odd-ball. Works all hours in a seedy office in Baker Street pretending to be an importer, but everyone knows he's one of the richest men in England.'

A plum had fallen into Ingrid's lap. It didn't take much guile to lose the naval captain and make her way towards her quarry, her eyes glinting with zeal.

He was quite old, easy game, she guessed, as she smoothly

introduced herself, flirting, probing and teasing.

By midnight she had got nowhere. In desperation, she allowed herself to be seduced. Surprisingly, Stephen proved to be a considerate and skilled lover and Ingrid enjoyed herself, but she didn't extract a single item of interest for Paddy.

Ingrid woke to the first light of dawn seeping through the curtains. Next to her, Stephen Schofield was still asleep, gently snoring. What a wasted night. She sat up and studied him. He was old . . . at least fifty-five, she could see. He had receding grey hair and a furrowed brow, but his face looked kind and caring. He's sort of craggy, she thought, but in an attractive way.

His eyes opened. They were large, grey eyes and they scanned her. It was a disconcerting feeling. 'Good-morning,' he said. 'I'm Stephen Schofield. Who are you?'

'If you can't remember, then you don't deserve to know,' she snapped, feeling humiliated.

'Is this your bedroom or mine?'

'Mine!' She laughed lightly, but in truth she was seething with rage.

He was naked and when he got out of bed she was surprised at how fit he looked. He was almost six foot tall and slender, but wiry. He began to get dressed with cool self-confidence which annoyed her. Obviously he was used to this. He paused at the door. 'How was I?'

'Terrible,' she lied.

'I can do better, I promise you.'

'No second chances.'

He shrugged. 'If you say so.' The door closed softly behind him.

At Sunday lunch she sat next to a naval commander who immediately began chatting her up. He was flying to Scotland that evening, he told her. Already well-oiled by aperitifs, the wine loosened his tongue further and he regaled her with a rambling account about a convoy of submarines hidden away in Cromarty Firth, which were being fitted with a new type of radar.

'Of course, I shouldn't tell you this,' he added belatedly. 'But

I know how hard you're working for the war effort. Gwen told me about you. You're the bravest girl I've ever come across, and quite the loveliest. Let me have your address in London, I'll be back as soon as I can.'

The party dispersed after lunch, and Ingrid returned to London well pleased with herself. Paddy ceased to nag her so much and she began to enjoy burning the candle at both ends. From the initial batch of invitations she'd received at Gwen's Ingrid rapidly expanded her network of acquaintances. Each weekend brought a new wave of men home on leave and they all had something in common: they were desperate for love and feminine companionship. They were often in a state of shock despite their bravado. It was just before dawn when they were at their lowest ebb. Invariably they talked, sometimes without any prodding on her part. It was all reported back to Fernando or Paddy.

For Ingrid, this casual no-promises and no-ties love was ideal. She wanted a warm male body next to hers to while away the lonely, terrifying nights and she preferred not to get to know them.

Then Gwen brought her an invitation to dinner at her father's London home one Saturday. 'Lord Schofield is very keen to be formally introduced to you, but I believe you've already met.'

Ingrid suppressed a smile. She was going to be introduced to the man she had spent the night with. How very British.

Once properly introduced, the invitations and flowers came daily. Stephen, as he wanted to be called, monopolised her time. His rank ensured that no other men came near her. In London he wined and dined her night after night. At weekends they went riding together or tramped for miles through the country-side.

Ingrid's information gathering was hampered by Stephen's attentions and she never learned anything useful from him. One evening Fernando tackled her in the back of Paddy's shop. He caught her arm and twisted it viciously. 'Drop Schofield!

You've got nothing out of him so far. Concentrate on the officers home on leave or else.'

'Or else what?' she sneered, pulling her arm free and hastily leaving the room. Paddy was leaning over the counter as she rushed out. 'Hey, wait a minute, Princess.' He examined her arm. 'You're going to have a bruise,' he said softly. 'The man's a thug.' He gave her a soft, crafty smile that repelled her. 'Let's have a cup of tea, I want to talk to you.' Paddy lived over the shop. Beside the store room was a kitchenette, with a dirty sink and a kettle on a hob. He made some tea and led her to his back garden where he bred rabbits.

'Let's sit on the bench,' he said. 'It's a fine evening. I like to sit here and watch the rabbits. D'you know anything about rabbits?'

She shook her head. Paddy irritated her. He was common and he had dirty fingernails. Her cup was dirty, too, and she was waiting for a chance to tip the tea on the flowers. She longed for a cup of good Viennese coffee.

'Those are Flemish Giants,' he said, pointing to some big grey rabbits with floppy ears. 'This little beauty is a White Dutch. She's my favourite.' He opened the hutch and took hold of the rabbit gently. She seemed afraid as he put her on his knees and stroked her head.

'We're all in this war for something. No one does this sort of work for nothing. I'm in it for Eire. Germany has promised us independence. Not that I set much store by German promises, but it's some sort of a target.

'You're in it for yourself. You've been promised your family's fortune back, I hear. Well, there's all sorts of ways girls can get fortunes. They can get them in bed,' he winked slyly. 'I expect Lord Schofield will propose. When he does, shoot him a line that will keep him hanging around, but not monopolising you. He's useful, but not to the exclusivity of your other contacts.'

There was a long silence while Paddy slurped his tea.

Then he said: 'A beautiful girl like you might think there was a way out of the mess you're in, like marrying Schofield, just as this little rabbit might think she could escape – I call her Ingrid because she's a real beauty. Just like you.'

The rabbit was a glossy white doe-eyed creature and she sat deadly still as he took his hands away. For a second she trembled on his knee. Then she jumped.

Paddy's hand moved in a swift, powerful chop that broke the rabbit's back in mid-air. She fell to the ground with a high-pitched screech of anguish. Ingrid was speechless with horror. The rabbit was trying to get away, using its front legs to drag its paralysed hindquarters behind it.

'Of course, one can never escape,' Paddy said. He smiled at her and turned to watch the rabbit's efforts. 'I think I'll put Ingrid out of her misery.' He bent over, picked up the rabbit and with a quick snap, twisted its neck. Its head lolled over at an impossible angle.

He sighed. 'The fact is, she was only ever supper.'

Ingrid felt sick. She put down her cup and stood up. 'You revolt me.'

He smiled. It was a tender, knowing smile. A lover might smile at one that way, Ingrid thought.

Ingrid avoided Stephen for a few days and took up with a young Polish airman who told her about his night-bombing training. She took the details to Fernando, trying not to speak to Paddy.

The following week, a heatwave settled over Europe. On Friday evening, Stephen took Ingrid for a walk along the Embankment. He seemed nervous as they stood side by side, leaning over the railings, watching the boats pass.

'Darling, will you marry me?' he said, out of the blue. Then, without waiting for her answer, he went on: 'My dear, I want you to take time off to see my lawyer. He can arrange settlements, that sort of thing. You do have a London lawyer, I assume. If not, I can give you some names. You'll find that I'm highly eligible . . .' He laughed, looking embarrassed. 'Enough to ensure that the pre-war standards you were accustomed to are maintained.' *Eligible.* The word struck a deep chord in her memory and she remembered Hugo and his list of eligible men, pilfered from Princess Lobkowitz's study. Lord Stephen Schofield had been on that list. She almost laughed aloud. She could hear Paddy's warning echoing in her mind. She had to say 'no'. Anyway, she consoled herself, just how eligible would Lord Schofield be after Britain was conquered?

'I'm not free,' she said. 'There's someone waiting for me in Austria. Someone in a camp,' she ad-libbed. 'Until such time as he dies or is released, I cannot be free. Perhaps . . . one day . . . Who knows . . . ?'

Stephen looked shocked and bewildered, then terribly hurt. 'I'll wait,' he said. 'Just don't cut me out of your life.'

Chapter  46

IN THE CAMP WORKSHOP, where Marietta had been sewing army uniforms for the past six months, the summer heatwave made life unbearable. It was midday and their brief lunchbreak had not yet been called. The soup was late and Marietta was weak from hunger. Her sewing machine began to waver in and out of focus. In front of her, Greta was nodding forward and Marietta looked around to see if the supervisor, known as Pig-eyes, was watching.

'Greta, wake up,' she whispered. Greta lurched forward and the needle zipped right across the trouser leg she was making.

Greta was grabbed by her collar and hauled into the aisle. As the supervisor laid into her with her *schlag*, Marietta leapt forward and touched the woman's arm. 'Leave her alone,' she pleaded. 'She's tired. Our food's late and she's not well.'

Pig-eyes swivelled towards her new victim. Greta was forgotten as Marietta was marched out into the parade ground.

She was beaten with the *schlag* until she fell, but the supervisor kicked her until she got back on her feet. Painfully she stumbled back to work and tried her best to complete a seam every thirty seconds as the garments landed on her bench. She could hardly see for black spots dancing in front of her eyes and every movement hurt. The supervisor had another punishment for her, she was to miss her soup and bread.

Marietta bent over her machine, not by word or expression would she show this sadist how devastated she was by this casual decree. She tried to make sense of what had happened to her, but there was little energy for thinking in Lichtenberg.

Acutely aware of her bruised back and shoulders, Marietta dragged herself through the rest of the day. At 10 p.m. she threw herself on to her bunk with a sigh of relief, but she had difficulty finding a position to lie in that didn't hurt too much. She was shifting restlessly when she heard Greta groaning. Her friend sat bolt upright, stared around as if in a trance, and fell unconscious on to the floor.

Marietta scrambled out of her bunk and bent over Greta. She had fallen badly and her cheek was bruised and grazed. She tried to lift her, but didn't have the strength. Soon several Polish women gathered round and together they managed to get Greta to her bunk. After that, Marietta sat for an hour beside her, bathing her face with cool water, but Greta remained unconscious, twitching with delirium.

She wouldn't last the night without medical attention, Marietta thought, but access to the medical block was only in daylight hours, accompanied by their supervisor.

Greta mustn't die, Marietta thought fiercely, she was the only one of them who had a good chance of being released. She had to live to be free. 'I have to get her to the doctor,' she said aloud, and went to the door.

The guard stationed outside their bunkhouse was young and impressionable. He saw Marietta's frightened eyes peering through the ventilation slats and he felt sorry for her.

'Stay inside,' he said urgently. 'Be careful. You'll be beaten if you come out.'

'I don't care. Shoot me! Do what you like. My friend is dying.' Somehow she was going to get Greta to the hospital block. She had never felt so determined in her life.

'No one comes out after lights out. Go to sleep and stop making a disturbance.'

She looked over his shoulder and in the lingering summer

dusk saw a wheelbarrow parked by a pile of bricks.

'You're Austrian, aren't you?' she said.

'Yes.'

'I can tell from your accent. So am I. I used to be a person of some consequence before I came here. Nowadays, I'm known as number 798484. My crime was to help some unfortunate people flee the country. I'm coming out to get that wheelbarrow. I'm sorry, I have no choice.'

'Stay inside,' the guard begged her. 'I'm not the only guard here.

Ignoring his threats, she stepped over the threshold.

'I'll shoot,' the guard whispered desperately.

'Then shoot. I'm nearly dead and my friend certainly will be dead by morning unless I get her to a doctor.'

Unnerved by her determination, the guard let her pass. It seemed to take a very long time to walk across the darkening yard and wheel the barrow back.

The women helped her to lift Greta into the barrow. She gave a strange moan, but didn't wake.

Shaking with the effort of balancing the deadweight of her cargo, Marietta set out across the yard, the eyes of the guard and the barrel of his rifle seeming to bore into her back like hot pokers.

She searched for courage. What was it Father had taught her? 'The greatest man is he who chooses right with invincible determination ...' Now who had said that ... ? One of the ancient Greeks ...

The hospital block was three hundred yards away and it took her five minutes to get there. Greta remained unconscious and Marietta was worried that her friend might be dead. The doctor, a German Catholic, was appalled to see them. 'What's the point of this heroism?' he railed at her. 'Do you know what will happen to you? And for what? She has tuberculosis. She's going to die anyway.'

'Save her,' Marietta said. 'She's not a political prisoner. In three years she'll be free. She must live for all of us.'

Early next morning, Pig-eyes meted out Marietta's punishment. 'You are being sent to solitary confinement,' she said triumphantly.

'For how long?'

'Maybe forever.' She replied, smiling to herself, enjoying Marietta's fear. 'Most prisoners die there,' she added viciously.

Marietta followed Pig-eyes to the cells. A barred gate before some stone steps led to an underground passage. She shuddered as a wardress, with mean eyes and a pale, pimply skin, snatched at her hand to read the number on her wrist.

'She's in solitary . . . until further orders,' Pig-eyes said. The wardress laboriously made an entry into a heavy ledger, then Marietta followed the woman down another flight of stairs. She couldn't stop shivering as she walked behind the woman, along an underground passage dimly lit with electric light. It smelled damp and stale. The wardress unlocked a thick door and motioned Marietta to enter. She slid her foot forward into total blackness, fearing that she would fall into a bottomless pit. A sharp push sent her sprawling into the dark unknown.

She screamed with terror as she fell on to coarse concrete, hardly registering as the door clanged shut behind her. It seemed that the darkness was suffocating her. She curled foetus-like, sobbing and beating the ground with her fists. Soon she was too exhausted to cry, and lapsed into silent despair.

Later she realised that she had missed several meals. She had no way of knowing how much time had passed, but she felt dizzy and light-headed. Were they going to deprive her of food as well as light? She tried to stand up, but lost her balance and fell. She would crawl, she decided. She fumbled her way around the floor. Her cell was constructed of rough cement and brick, it was dusty with a faint odour of vomit and human sweat all around. She crept forward, feeling her way like a blind creature.

After what felt like hours on her knees she'd worked out that her room was small, about nine feet by twelve. There was a toilet, a tap and a bucket, a bed, a coir mattress and one blanket. After a while she relocated the prickly mattress and lay on it, aware of her bruises and smarting from the knowledge that they were self-inflicted. She strained to hear sounds from outside, but no noise penetrated; she suspected her cell was sound-proofed. She tried to count to check the passage of time, but the silence was so numbing, her brain seemed incapable of working.

'I must survive!' She spoke aloud to try to shatter the stifling atmosphere, but burst into tears again. 'Dear God, help me to survive,' she chanted to herself. 'Give me courage. Surely I can cope. Others have. One day these evil people will be brought to justice, and I will be there to see it happen.' She tried to believe her own words, but felt completely defeated.

Chapter  47

THE WARDRESS SAVED MARIETTA'S LIFE.

She had lain in a daze for hours or days or weeks, she had no way of knowing how long it was since she had been there when a sudden blaze of light pierced her stygian depths. She hid her face in her mattress and put her hands over her head.

'She'll be dead soon. They go quickly once they give up,' a female voice said. 'I've seen it happen so often. She hasn't eaten for days . . . there's no point in bringing her food. Some of them are fighters, but she isn't. I prefer the ones that go quickly. They're less trouble.'

They left, and Marietta lay shivering with horror. Was she going to do them a favour and die? White hot hatred shot through her, warming her.

She sat up cautiously. Waves of dizziness made her long to give in and lie back on her bed to wait for death. *But that's what they want*.

She tried again. I must be strong. How else can I defeat them. Strong . . . strong . . . She dragged herself around her cell and found the meagre food left for her. She gagged on the stale bread, but forced down every crumb. She prayed and she meditated. She imagined herself free, walking out through the camp gates, plotting her destruction of Hugo and all his kind.

273

'Yes,' she muttered. 'I will survive.'

Her anger gave her strength. She began to keep track of the days by scratching on the wall with her spoon. Never again would she give up, she vowed.

'I will accept this period of my life as your will ... a time to grow strong. I will gain control of my mind. I will tackle this task by concentrating on the present. In this way I shall only face one small step at a time. God, give me strength,' she prayed.

She counted the days by the arrival of her food. She created a pattern out of nothingness, ringing bells in her mind for the end of one period and the start of the next, making sure that she walked a mile a day by pacing her small cell, meditating three times a day. She set herself mental exercises, reciting poetry, alphabetical lists of rivers, geographical features, artists – anything to stop her remembering happy times. She forced herself not to think of what might be happening to her family and friends, especially Bill.

She had to keep her mind busy, for all the time she was fighting off the beast that came out of the darkness to prey on her. It would snuffle at her side and she would fend it off with deep breathing, or exercises, or putting her mind to work making a poem ... anything! The beast was called despair and she knew that it could kill her. 'Go away,' she would say aloud. 'I will survive, for Father, for Bill, for myself, but most of all, for damn Hugo.'

Dark day followed dark night. She was like a mole, confined to the bowels of the earth. Moles survived, didn't they? So would she.

After three months in solitary confinement in pitch darkness, Marietta was unexpectedly released at 3 o'clock one afternoon. Disorientated and blinded by daylight, she was marched back to her bunkhouse.

The women's warm welcome touched her. They welcomed her with hugs and sang a carol in her honour. They wanted to show their appreciation of her courage. Many of them tried to press some small gift in her hands: a half slice of bread, some rags stolen from the laundry.

Marietta searched for Greta and found her asleep on her bunk. She sat quietly beside the bed waiting for her to wake. When she opened her eyes she smiled.

'Dearest Marie, it's you,' she muttered, her husky voice pitched even lower. 'You're alive. Thank God. I've been praying for you. Now I shall die happy.' Her expressive blue eyes looked even larger against the pallor of her skin. There were two burning red spots on either cheek, her lips were red and she was dreadfully emaciated.

'Don't talk about dying,' Marietta said sharply. 'Talk about living. You'll be free. Hang on, Greta.'

'Brave words, my friend.' Greta coughed, her thin frame racked by the spasm. 'There is no cure for me. You'll have to survive for us both.'

'You should be in hospital,' Marietta said.

Greta grasped Marietta's hand. 'No. There's nothing they can do. Besides, they take the incurables for medical experiments. I don't want that. Promise me, Marie.'

Marietta squeezed the skeletal hand, unable to speak.

As she bent over her friend to hug her, she silently vowed to put aside part of her rations for Greta.

At seven, when the women were called to roll-call before supper, Marietta had to support Greta. Afterwards, she carried Greta's bread back to the bunkhouse and soaked it in the acorn water they called coffee to try to make her eat. Weakly she managed to swallow a couple of mouthfuls, but it was with surprising strength that she gripped Marietta's wrist.

'If we were to exchange numbers when I die, you could become me.' She hissed. 'My number could so easily be changed. Look.' She turned up her wrist and pointed to her number. 'The three could be changed to an eight and the one to a four.'

'You're not going to die.'

'No one knows who we really are,' Greta said, ignoring her remark. 'No one cares. We're just numbers. This was meant to

be, Marie. You will change my number with this,' Greta
fumbled under her mattress and produced an indelible laundry
marking pen.

Marie frowned. 'How did you get this?'

'I bribed one of the laundry girls to steal it for me.'

'With what?'

'My bread for a week.'

'Oh, Greta, no wonder you're so weak. Oh, my dear, how
could you ...' Marietta could hardly speak. Emotions were
flooding through her, gratitude, guilt, a surge of hope, quickly
dampened with more guilt.

'Don't let my life be wasted. Promise me.'

'It won't work, Greta.' She spoke sadly. 'Now eat your food
and try harder to get better.' She smiled softly at her.

'When you were in the punishment bunker someone burnt
their arm badly. Her number was obliterated, so they tattooed
her again higher up her arm. That's what gave me the idea.'

It could work. The swift shaft of hope unsettled her. 'Please
don't die,' she cried out.

Greta persisted. 'Now listen. I'm going to tell you about my
home, they might ask you questions.'

The following morning, Marietta was sent to work in the
laundry. It was back-breaking toil to bend over the steaming
vats of bubbling foamy water and scrub mud out of the
uniforms.

Her day began at five when the warmth of the dismal shed
was welcome, but as the day wore on, the heat and the steam
made the atmosphere unbearable and almost unbreathable.

At midday they were fed some watery potato soup and a slice
of black bread. At 7 p.m. the women were sent out into the
freezing night air, and they would shiver and cough as they
stood in the open until roll-call was over, and were given their
evening rations.

Later that night, Marietta pulled her blanket around her and
sat shivering next to Greta's bunk. Greta's temperature was

high, and she was half-delirious. 'Change the number,' Greta whispered.

'You have a fever, but you'll be better in the morning. Just stay calm.'

'You promised.' She lay back exhausted.

Marietta held her friend's hand and stayed beside her. She mumbled all the prayers she could remember. Her body was wracked with shivering for she, too, had a fever and it was icy in the hut. As the room grew quiet, Marietta dozed. When she woke in the early hours, Greta was dead.

A shaft of light from the full moon was shining on Greta's face. She looked very peaceful and ethereal. Marietta fumbled under the mattress and found the pen. 'Thank you, my friend. I will use your gift well.'

Taking Greta's cold wrist, she carefully changed the one to a four, and the three to an eight. She was shaking so much she was sure she would spoil the number. This was madness. It would never work. They would kill her. Would it matter? Creeping back to her own bunk, she lay awake for the rest of the night aching with fear.

At 5 a.m. the doors were flung open and Pig-eyes entered, striking bunks with her *schlag*, hauling the blankets off the women as she strode, gnome-like, through the hut. When she returned, any women still in their bunks would be badly beaten. She stopped where Greta lay prone and calm.

Pig-eyes brought her *schlag* down hard on Greta's feet. Marietta tried not to look. She made a note of the number on Greta's arm and detailed two prisoners to take the corpse away for cremation.

At roll-call, Marietta only just remembered to respond to Greta's number. She suddenly panicked. She had not thought about their fellow prisoners. She would be taking on Greta's tasks in the laundry, not her own. And her wrist still bore her own number.

Would her fellow prisoners betray her? Informers were given more bread and easier work, and she'd seen herself that many succumbed to bribery.

She looked around nervously. The Polish women seemed to be watching her all the time. The day passed with agonising slowness. Why were they watching her so intently? Were they going to betray her?

Just before the midday break for soup, when Pig-eyes was at the other end of the shed out of sight in the dense steam, Marietta was pushed towards the steam presses. One of the women grabbed her arm and thrust it into the press, the other brought down the lid. Marietta screamed in agony and shock. She tried to fight them off. The pain was agonising and endless. Her last conscious thought was for her father. He would think that she was dead.

Chapter  48

SEVEN MEN WERE GATHERED in Count Frederick's office in Plechy Palace. At the head of the table the Count sat looking wretched and old; he had lost weight, his skin sagged and there were etched shadows under his eyes. For Count Frederick, each day dawned at four when his tormented mind surfaced from its amphetamine fog to face the reality of his daughter's imprisonment. The Conspiracy had become his lifeline, knowing it was also Marietta's, for only when the Nazis were overthrown, would she be freed. Often he came close to despair.

In turn Denmark, Norway, the Low countries, France and Belgium had been occupied by Hitler. Italian troops were invading Egypt and Greece, and only Britain held fast. Consequently, The Führer was considered less like a madman and more like a master strategist and the Conspiracy were finding it hard to recruit allies. Those that remained true to their ideal were not in command of the regiments they needed to overthrow the Nazis. Their hearts were in the right places, the Count mused, looking round at the surviving six, but they had no power and he could practically feel the air of failure.

'Gentlemen,' the Major interrupted his thoughts. 'Unless the generals in command turn to our way of thinking there's little we can do. We don't have the power to organise a *putsch*, we can only bide our time and wait for the tide of war to alter course.'

The Count's heart was heavy. Disappointment made him
weary. The victories of Hitler's armies would keep him in
power for years, while Marietta could succumb to disease or
death in that terrible camp. He desperately wanted to make
them fight on, but he knew in his soul they were a powerless,
ineffectual cabal of ageing men.

He was jerked out of his self-pity by the entry of his butler.

'Excuse me, Sir. I know you asked not to be disturbed, but
this letter has just arrived and it's marked extremely urgent,' the
manservant said, pale-faced. 'It's from Gestapo headquarters.'

The postmark was Lichtenberg. The Count excused himself,
hurried to his desk at the corner of the room and tore at the
letter with fumbling fingers.

... *your daughter Countess Marietta von Burgheim died of
tuberculosis on January 5 1941. Her ashes will be forwarded for
burial.*

The stark words seemed to rise up and hit him in the face.

A red hot sword pierced his chest. He couldn't breathe. He
fell heavily to the floor.

Count Frederick regained consciousness at midnight. After
several moments of confusion he realised that he was in hospital
and he remembered the letter that had brought on his attack.
Then anger and sorrow drowned every other sensation.

The ward was quiet and the night light was on. The Count
wondered how much damage had been done to his body. He
needed his health, his strength and his mind. He was thirsty,
but when he tried to reach the carafe, it was too much of an
effort. He managed to locate the bell and a nurse appeared
almost immediately. 'Good, you are awake. How do you feel?'

'What happened?' His voice was a weak croak.

'You had a mild heart attack yesterday. The doctor has left,
but he'll be back in the morning. In the meantime, please try to
be calm.'

Calm! He turned his face from her to hide his bitterness and
despair.

Part Two

October 1942 – June 1945

Chapter  49

ON FRIDAY, OCTOBER 1, 1942, Marietta was summoned to the camp commandant's office. Her legs were leaden and she was numb with despair as she waited to hear what new torment was awaiting her. He said: 'Well, Greta Brecht, you have earned six months off your sentence for good behaviour. You are to be released today.'

She stared at his teutonic features in disbelief, and in a trance found herself taking possession of Greta's papers, only half-listening to his instructions.

'You'll be given transport to the station and a train ticket to your home town.'

Dazed and confused, she was marched to the showers, handed a bundle of clothes and pushed inside. 'Be quick,' the wardress snarled.

In amazement she realised the ever-efficient Nazis had preserved the clothes Greta had been arrested in, but that had been in May – now it was cold and Greta's clothes were pitifully inadequate. Nevertheless, she wore them proudly and lovingly. Marietta blinked back her tears as she smoothed the creased skirt and blouse. Her legs were clad in black silk stockings, and the high-heeled shoes, hand-stitched of patent leather, pinched horribly, her feet being so much bigger than Greta's. Marietta picked up Greta's purse and opened it. There was no money, but a small embroidered handkerchief, a penknife, a hand mirror and lipstick had survived. Marietta held up the mirror with a shaking hand. She saw a gaunt, ugly face with haggard, haunted eyes and sallow skin. She gasped. Her hair was a little over an inch long and her features seemed those of a stranger. Horrified, she pushed the mirror back into the bag.

After the years of imprisonment, her guards now couldn't get rid of her quickly enough. Compared to her entry to the camp, her exit was marked by bureaucratic lightning, and still dazed by events she found herself on the right side of the gate.

As the walls of the camp faded from sight, Marietta began to shudder with guilt for those left behind. In the past year, conditions had become progressively worse as the camp was crammed to overflowing with women from every occupied country. Hanging, flogging, decapitation, shooting and gassing became commonplace. The humiliation and pain of the inmates were secondary to the thousands of deaths from disease and starvation. And always more and still more helpless victims flooded through the gates to take the place of the dead.

Full of shame, Marietta turned her back on Lichtenburg.

At the station, travellers kept their eyes averted, as if she had leprosy, or worse. She stood shivering on the platform, avoiding the crowds in the waiting-room. When the train arrived she scuttled into the corner of the nearest carriage.

It was heated, thank goodness, but as the train started she began shaking uncontrollably . . . weird memories flashed before her eyes. One moment she was walking over the fields with her grandmother, then with Greta in the camp. Her brain was a kaleidoscope of fragmented bits and pieces shaken out of context and presented in rapid succession as if real and happening now. A bolt of sheer joy ripped through her. *Free!* That magic word was resuscitating her starved body and her battered ego. A spasm of fierce energy thrust through her, giving her warmth and strength. She'd made it!

The train rattled on and Marietta swayed with the rhythm, her eyes closed, but her mind in a fever of planning. There was so much to do. She must get strong and fit. She couldn't fight until she'd overcome the physical effects of her long incarceration.

Thank you for my life, Greta, my friend. I won't forget my pledge to you, she whispered.

It was 8 a.m. and Bill was briskly walking towards Regent's Park, when a news poster caught his eye. *Stalingrad defended house by house.* He stopped and fumbled in his pocket for some change.

'You look as fit as a fiddle, mate,' the paperseller said, pointedly looking at Bill's civilian clothes. 'Got a cushy billet, 'ave you?'

'You look pretty fit yourself,' Bill countered as he picked up a paper.

He walked on, oddly disturbed by the innocuous exchange. The truth was, he *had* joined up and for three months he had trained in a hand-picked commando unit stationed at Aldershot. He'd drilled and learned unarmed combat and at least a dozen methods of killing and he'd loved every minute of it and had looked forward with relish to active service.

Then he'd made the mistake of showing off his fluent command of German in front of some visiting staff officers. Shortly afterwards, British Military Intelligence hauled him up to London, put him through a series of vigorous interviews and transfered him to SOE (Special Operations Executive), that very British intelligence organisation which controlled most of the covert activity in enemy territory.

They'd given him a commission and put him in charge of a propaganda campaign aimed at coaxing America into the war. When Pearl Harbor made his job redundant, they had promoted him to Captain and found a new job for him, assisting the man who co-ordinated and controlled the various Eastern European intelligence departments, which were mainly staffed by escaped nationals from those countries.

Bill's boss was Stephen Schofield, a strangely introverted man with a rapier mind who pretended to be a tea and coffee importer. Gradually, the two men had become friends, but Bill continued to rail against being a paper soldier.

At the office, Schofield was as usual elbow deep in empty coffee cups and overflowing ashtrays. His office was over-heated and stank. Bill couldn't get used to the British aversion to fresh air.

Looking at his boss, Bill could only guess at the stress he was under. The bags under his eyes were larger than ever, his face was puffy and grey. Clearly he had worked all night, a circumstance which had occurred frequently in the last few weeks.

'Sit down, Roth,' he said now. 'As you know we've been getting in a lot of not very conclusive intelligence that the Nazis are developing a long range missile. On top of those snippets we are certain they are also working on a nuclear bomb.' Schofield stood up and paced the room.

'Last night,' he went on, 'I had a call from a colleague in Stockholm. He'd been at some function at the Foreign Office along with a General von Haupt — he's a desk man and he's spent the last three years in Prague under Heydrich. The general took exception to some snide remarks about their V-3 and claimed he'd seen it with his own eyes. He was recalled to Berlin immediately.'

Bill raised his eyebrows as he absorbed the information.

'And another interesting piece of the jigsaw,' Schofield paused to light another cigarette. 'The Nobel prize for Physics was to have been awarded to the German chemist Otto Hahn, in recognition of his pioneering work in nuclear fission. However, the Germans have declined to allow him to accept the honour. It appears they don't want a lot of attention paid to his work. All this adds weight to the already convincing argument that there is a research facility somewhere near Prague.' He turned to face Bill, his eyes bleak. 'We cannot let the Germans progress with this research. If they reach a stage where they can successfully detonate such a terrible weapon they will have the world in the palm of their hands.'

'Where do I come into this, sir?' Bill asked quietly.

'You know Czechoslovakia. Your task is to get in touch with the Resistance there and charge them to pinpoint the location of this plant. We can't get anywhere without knowing where we need to strike.'

For the next hour they pored over papers and maps, a secretary quietly supplying them with coffee. Eventually Schofield called a halt to their meeting. 'Off you go, Roth, report to me daily, even if there seems nothing to say.'

Bill gathered his papers and retrieved his coat. As he was about to leave, he said tentatively. 'Sir. Could I draw your attention to my application for a transfer to active forces, which I left on your desk on Friday?'

'You're a persistent sod. The answer's "no", as usual. Particularly now. For God's sake stop littering my desk.'

Bill went back to his office and sat deep in thought, remembering Prague and pre-war Bohemia. He didn't have any idea where to begin this investigation. Did he have any contacts?

Off-hand, he couldn't think of one. Then he remembered Pastor Perwe. He might be able to reach him through the Church of Sweden. The recollection of the Pastor brought memories of Marietta flooding back, despite the many months he'd spent exorcising them. She was dead he admonished himself, recalling the moment her father's letter, smuggled through Switzerland, had caught up with him. The pain was as intense now as it had been then.

It had taken Marietta a considerable amount of time and guile to change Greta Brecht's ticket to Berlin for one to Austria, and after numerous changes and delays, Marietta reached Vienna hungry and exhausted. With no money for a tram fare, never mind a taxi, she set off to walk home. The pavements bucked and rolled under her feet. Black spots danced in front of her eyes and she was shivery cold and burning hot in rapid succession. She felt confused and disorientated, but instinct kept her going in the right direction. 'Home,' she muttered. 'I'm going home.'

When she saw Plechy Palace she wanted to call out with joy, but she knew she had to be cautious. She stumbled towards the staff entrance in the back courtyard. Their old housekeeper timidly responded to her knock, but there was no sign of recognition in her eyes.

'Is Count Frederick at home?' Marietta, swaying on her feet, clutched the doorpost.

The woman hesitated. 'Why d'you want to see the Count?'

'I used to work for him. I have a message for him. Please!'

'Do you have an appointment? The Count is a very busy man.'

'Please,' she whispered. 'Give me a pen. You can take a message to the Count.' When the woman brought pen and paper she wrote: *Greta Brecht, Edelweiss*, shakily across the page, then in Greek: *Help me*.

Count Frederick was conferring with three generals in his office when his housekeeper came in. 'I must speak to you urgently, sir.'

The Count excused himself. His housekeeper had never before interrupted his meetings.

'There's a young woman downstairs. She's like a skeleton.' The woman crossed herself. 'I wouldn't have disturbed you, but she insists I give you this.' She passed him the slip of paper.

When the Count saw Edelweiss scrawled across the page and the message, he turned white. It must be one of Marietta's friends, perhaps on the run . . . or even someone who had known his daughter in the camp.

He hurried through the corridors and then broke into a run, his heart hammering. When he reached the kitchen, he nearly cried out in horror. The woman was a bag of bones. She was slumped in a chair, apparently unaware of his entrance.

'Leave us,' he said hoarsely to the housekeeper, and slowly approached the gaunt figure.

He did not recognise her face, but those cornflower blue, Szapary eyes were unmistakeable.

The Count shouted 'No . . . My God . . .' he fell on his knees and peered at her. 'Oh, my poor Marietta. What have they done to you? My dearest little daughter.'

He clasped Marietta in his arms, rocked her backwards and forwards, as the tears streamed down his cheks. 'I thought . . . I was told . . .' His voice cracked and he lapsed into silence. 'But you're alive,' he whispered eventually. 'You survived that hell-hole. Thank God!'

Chapter 50

PROFESSOR LUDWIG ALESH was the antithesis of all that Hugo expected in a man. With his long limbs, his huge eyes, his white, moist skin, and bulbous forehead, he looked more like a primaeval, subterranean insect than a human being.

Blinking nervously, his brown eyes enlarged by thick lenses, and twitching with tension though he was, Alesh still defied him, Hugo noticed the subtle sneer of contempt as he argued. 'You will obey the Reichsführer Himmler,' he said, trying to control his fury. 'Your orders are that every prisoner will be executed after six months in the mine.'

'My life would be simpler if our orders were not so contradictory,' Alesh said softly, making no effort to hide his antagonism. 'Murdering our workers as soon as they are trained is madness. Don't you realise that it takes us months to get any degree of efficiency out of these wretches?'

'Security is of overall importance,' Hugo retorted.

'And morality? What happened to morality?' the man muttered. 'How can I meet your ludicrous timetable if I'm forever training workers?'

'The slaves are unskilled labourers, they do not merit training,' Hugo pointed out.

'You do not build these weapons with muscle alone. I have a

first class goldsmith, a dozen excellent draughtsmen, yet you want me to shoot those whose experience is irreplaceable.'

The two men glared at each other. 'Show me around the plant, Herr Professor,' Hugo demanded.

Alesh was the world's leading expert on aerodynamics and physics, apart from being the assistant head of the missile team. He was immune to Hugo's fury, and Hugo knew it.

Grudgingly escorted by Alesh, Hugo looked around for something he could criticise, but off-hand he could not see anything. The plant was spotless and superbly run. Dozens of technicians were bent over their benches in the main hall. He could have been in any plant, he thought, examining the sheer walls and panelled ceiling for flaws. There was no indication that this circular hall, six stories high, was built in the main crater of an extinct volcano. The ceiling was unique, in which hydraulically operated panels could fold back on to each other at the touch of a button, opening the building to the sky. Around the sides of the central hall were six levels of circular corridors connected by several metal staircases and four lifts. On the outer side of the corridor were offices and accommodation for the German staff. The labourers slept below this floor, where the air conditioning was at its weakest.

A prototype of the V-3 rocket standing on a platform in the centre of the hall reassured Hugo that progress was taking place. Hitler's secret weapon was a guided missile, designed to carry a nuclear warhead. One such weapon would destroy a city. Ten would destroy all resistance. Let the Allies crow about their petty gains in the Middle East and the Pacific. Here was the real guardian of the Third Reich, a tribute to German inventiveness and efficiency. Hugo inspected the prototype with pride.

Preceded by Alesh, Hugo passed through a series of security doors until he reached the underground railway line. He did not miss the expression of relief that flitted over the scientist's face as the train drew away from the platform. Ten minutes later Hugo was in Theresienstadt concentration camp.

While waiting for his driver, Hugo observed how over-crowded Theresienstadt was: Jews, Catholics, Czechs, Slavs,

Poles and Russians of both sexes, were standing in well-guarded queues, waiting for classification and despatch. Teutonic thoroughness would soon have this lot on their way to their work places in the Reich.

Hugo dismissed his driver, and, taking the wheel, sped along the highway towards Prague. Chestnut trees were turning to glorious shades of red and gold on either side of the road. Beyond them, fertile farms flashed by. He raced past the little village of Nove Dvory, on the banks of the River Ohre, having to brake violently as a file of schoolchildren crossed the road. The sight of their blond hair gleaming in the sunlight gave him a sense of intense satisfaction. All the farms in this neighbourhood had been resettled with good Germanic stock.

On impulse he parked by the roadside and gazed back at the distinctive shape of the mountain known as Richard's Mine, where the V-3 project was hidden. Legend had it that in those volcanic hills Rip and Czech, two nomadic shepherds, had made their home, the first men to settle in Czechoslovakia. Throughout the centuries, local inhabitants had mined the rich vein of tin concealed there, and consequently the interior of the mountain was a warren of tunnels and chambers.

Adapting the defunct tin mine for its present military purpose had been Hugo's idea. The site was ideal, being impregnable to bomb attack, and of containable access. Entry was from either a small airfield, situated on top of the mountain, or by underground train from Theresienstadt.

This was the advantage of the site. Any enemy agents watching the movement of supplies and guards, would imagine that all this traffic was merely connected to the concentration camp.

Hugo resumed his journey suffused with the heady glow of personal success. Since he had taken over economic development and internal security of Czechoslovakia, brutality and cruelty had become a way of life. The Czechs had learned a bitter lesson, they could collaborate and live, or resist and die. Production figures were up in all industries. Ruthlessness had won through.

Hugo, however, was still a worried man. Germany could not hope to fight the entire world and win. They were now facing the full brunt of America's technological might. Even the Russians were beginning to churn out tanks and guns in the Siberian wastes. It was October, 1942, and the latest news showed the signs of the turning of the war tide. US troops had routed the Japanese in the Battle of Midway, the German advance in the desert had been halted at El Alamein. Axis shipping was being sunk, and consequently the Afrika Korps was desperately short of supplies, particularly petrol. Even the heart of the Fatherland was affected, only last night had seen a 1,000-bomber raid on Cologne where 600 acres of the city had been devastated.

Hugo was a realist. This was the first glimmer of the retribution coming their way. It would take a miracle to win the war now. But they had that miracle – the V-3. It was his own special responsibility.

Pushing aside thoughts of his special project, Hugo turned his attention to more personal matters. That morning he had received interesting news: his stepfather had been regularly meeting certain generals he suspected of being engaged in a conspiracy against the Führer. Father was without doubt a traitor, but if he were to be executed for treason, the State would claim his estate. And Hugo had been assiduously protecting his stepfather for years, for this very reason. Marietta had died in the camp. Louis would never get out of Russia alive. Ingrid would be killed when her usefulness ended. Only Andrea remained a problem. Hugo had only just learned that she was about to become the mother of Louis's bastard, and he didn't want any claims on the estate plaguing his rightful inheritance.

Approaching Sokol, he felt saturated with satisfaction: it was all his – or as good as his – this wealth, this land, this marvellous castle, just as he had promised himself all those years ago when he had been flung out. He was singing *lieder* at the top of his voice as he crossed the bridge over the Vltava and drove into Sokol's courtyard.

As soon as he walked inside, he remembered that it was

Freda's birthday. Servants were rushing around with vases of flowers, boxes of provisions, plants, lights, drinks and glasses. Freda, clad in slacks and an off-the-shoulder blouse, was directing operations.

Watching her, Hugo approved of her change of image. She had lost fifteen pounds, improved her hairstyle and her make-up and now wore sophisticated clothes. Catching sight of him, she ran towards him and he saw her eyes searching for a present. He smiled as her face fell. He kissed her on the cheek and put his arm around her waist. 'What colour dress are you wearing tonight?'

'Green,' she said, puzzled. 'Why?'

'You'll see,' he said, deliberately brushing a hand against her breast, and hurried to the vaults, where he unlocked the heavy combination safe door he'd installed across the underground passage. Hugo switched on the light. There lay the priceless Lobkowitz collection of jewellery. Part of it had been despatched to a private auction in Switzerland, some to Spain. With the proceeds Hugo was buying land in South America. If Germany were to lose the war, he would exile himself for a few years in comfort, until it was safe to return. He selected an emerald bracelet and put it carelessly in his pocket.

The champagne was flowing, the ballroom was blazing with lights, and the band was playing a waltz. Freda wandered from group to group in a happy daze, her avaricious fingers continually fondling the bracelet, radiant in a green chiffon dress created by Lartigue.

The party was a tremendous success. Long after midnight it was still in full swing. By 3 a.m. the guests were only just beginning to leave, with many diehards prepared to greet the dawn still drinking.

'I don't think anyone will miss us. Why don't you go on up.' Hugo whispered to Freda.

By the time Hugo reached their bedroom, Freda was naked, perfumed and lying between the sheets. Hugo stripped off his clothes and placed them carefully on the dumb valet. He was a fastidious man, he'd been outcast for too long to take the trappings of wealth for granted.

He glanced at himself in the mirror. Still a magnificent physique, he thought. He threw himself on the bed. 'I'm exhausted. I haven't danced so much in years,' he said, slurring his words. 'Suck my cock,' he demanded.

She shivered slightly, but dutifully bent over him and rounded her mouth so that his penis could slide between her lips without touching her teeth. Soon her jaw began to ache from holding her mouth open so wide for so long. She relaxed slightly.

'Ouch! Hey! Careful there. I've told you before, you should have those front teeth removed. You could wear a plate. If you loved me, you would.'

She tried harder, using her fingers and her mouth to stimulate him, but he had drunk too much and she knew that nothing would work tonight. Eventually his penis shrivelled in her mouth and his breathing became deep and even. She opened her mouth and moved cautiously away.

He stirred. 'Don't stop,' he murmured.

Freda sighed. She stroked his belly, moving in slow, sensuous movements and at last she was rewarded by his snores.

Chapter  51

MARIETTA HAD BEEN HOME for two weeks. Physically she was improving steadily. Although she was still emaciated, her flesh was slowly fattening, her skin improving, and her eyes were not so haunted. But mentally she seemed worse. Restless and depressed, she was like a wounded bird who would not recover in captivity. The Count, who was a truthful man, had to admit that all the love and all the ideas for amusing her, and books and paraphernalia that he had dragged up to the attic at dead of night, could not heal her. If only she would be content to hide, at least a few months longer, but that was not her way.

He stood staring at Marietta moodily. Sadness was always with her, like the clinging scent of a wreath after the lilies had shrivelled. It seemed there was no escape from it, not in this attic, for her refuge had become her prison. His daughter was tortured by the lucid emptiness of her days, crucified by images. She screamed in her sleep and woke sweating with fright. All day she paced her narrow rooms. She wanted to leave, but was too frightened to.

'What am I to do?' he asked her one morning with his customary frankness. 'I see my own daughter languishing in my care and all the chicken broths and apple strudels in the world cannot mend her.'

She smiled, and this made him feel better. Smiles were rare nowadays. Standing by the attic fan light, the sunbeams catching her hair, it seemed as though she was wearing a halo but she was so thin and pale, she looked like a tragic sprite, not an angel.

'Marietta,' he said. 'Pastor Perwe can get you to Switzerland. You can join the Red Cross. You have first-hand knowledge of conditions in the camps, and you can alert the world to what's going on in those hellholes. It is your duty to go. Besides, you could see Bill again.'

Marietta looked away, hiding her face. Did Father guess how tormented she was, or how much she longed for Bill? Father was playing on her emotions. She scowled at him.

'Lately I've been thinking so much about duty and responsibility, and the promises I have made ... to Grandmother, to my friends, probably most of all to Greta ... I intend to fight the Nazis. My mind is firm, but my silly body is taking so long to mend.'

The Count turned to the door, unable to look at his daughter. 'I will tell the Pastor your wishes,' he said brokenly.

At midday on 24 March, 1943, Hugo was called to the telephone. Czech partisans had attempted to raid the granary outside Prague, but they had been surprised by five SS guards. The guards were dead, except for Lieutenant Kosimer, who was seriously wounded and in Prague Military Hospital.

An hour later the hospital informed him that the Lieutenant had died of his wounds.

That night, the command came from Berlin headquarters. He must select and destroy an entire village and its male population. The women would go to a concentration camp. His actions would stand as an object lesson to the Czechs not to oppose the Third Reich.

Fate was playing into Hugo's hands. It didn't take him long to choose a village.

Andrea and three friends were sitting in her front room

rehearsing for a show they were organising for the children. It
was *Peter and the Wolf* and it gave every village child a chance
to participate. The activity had helped Andrea overcome her
depression at Louis being sent to Stalingrad. For her baby's
sake she was trying to stifle her fear and remain optimistic, for
she was eight months pregnant and brimful of motherly
feelings.

It was 9.30 p.m. on a beautiful summer evening and still light
when they stopped. Andrea strolled to the garden gate to wave
goodbye to her friends, enjoying the scent of the honeysuckle
and new-mown grass, and the sound of birds twittering as they
gathered in the branches of oaks and elms. She felt a physical
spasm of well-being surge through her body. This was the
perfect place to rear their baby until Louis returned. He would
come back. She never allowed herself to doubt that one day they
would be together again.

She heard a rumble coming from the direction of the main
road. She saw a convoy of military vehicles turn into the lane
towards her. A shiver of apprehension touched her heart, then
she went inside and muttered a prayer, 'God, just let them roll
on past Lidhaky.'

The lorries swung into the village and stopped in a row in the
square. Peering through the curtains she saw soldiers pouring
out, guns cocked as they ran towards the houses. Andrea was
paralysed with fright. Moments later rifle butts were hammering on her front door, but before she could move it burst open
and soldiers raced down the narrow passage. One of them
blocked the doorway and pointed his gun straight at her.
Instinctively, she spread her hands over her stomach to protect
her unborn child.

'Outside! Line up in the square.'

Three other soldiers begain smashing furniture. She stood in
a daze as they trampled over china and pictures and sent the
piano crashing to the floor. She stumbled outside and heard her
neighbours' possessions being destroyed. Crockery was flying,
sheets and blankets were being hurled from top windows, smoke
began to curl out of every home.

She was herded sheep-like to the square and lined up with the village women, many of whom were in their nightclothes. Everyone was trembling, their faces white and their eyes dull with shock. Mass reprisals had become a way of life and they were all terrified.

A young boy darted back towards his mother. A soldier lifted his sub-machine gun, bullets razed the cobbles, the boy fell in a pool of blood. His mother cried out, ran forward, hesitated as the machine guns swung towards her, then collapsed.

'They're going to kill us all,' a voice screamed. One woman made a sudden dash towards the trees, again the rattle of a machine gun and she fell groaning.

Why? Andrea screamed silently, the question hammering at her head, even while her heart beat against her chest. Her hands were sweating and her breath was coming in swift, shallow gasps. Oh God, what will happen to us? I must be calm. I must protect my child, she thought, my baby must live.

The soldiers began to question the boys. Those who had turned fifteen were put with the men, the remainder were pushed across the square to the women's side.

Andrea grasped her neighbour's hand. Her back was aching, her stomach felt heavy and her throat was raw from thirst. I'm going to die, she thought sadly, and all I can think about are my aching back and my thirst.

The soldiers herded the women to the schoolhouse. As if in a nightmare, Andrea moved with the terrified women. As soon as they were locked in they heard the rat-a-tat-tat of machine guns and shrill screams from the square. The sound went on and on, and the grieving women abandoned hope for they knew their men were being murdered.

In the schoolhouse the soldiers forced the women to hand over their watches, earrings, wedding rings, wallets and anything else they had of any value. When they left, the women listened to the destruction of their village, and smelled the smoke.

At dawn the women and children were marched to the station.

No one resisted, they had lost their husbands and their children, their homes, there was nothing else for them to live for. But Andrea had her child in her belly . . .

As the women were pushed into cattle trucks, Andrea and three other pregnant women were marched to a waiting lorry. Why had they been singled out? Andrea leaned back and tried to cushion the shocks as they bumped over the rough road.

'Marietta has hardly begun to recover from her terrible experiences, Pastor,' the Count said.

It was midnight and the two men were trudging through the streets of Vienna towards Plechy Palace. It was a cold November night and both men were wearing heavy overcoats, fur-lined boots and hats. The Pastor's skin was glowing and his eyes sparkling, he revelled in the cold, but the Count looked pale and old.

'Forgive me for dragging you out at such an terrible hour, and on such a cold night,' the Count said. 'The palace staff work until eleven and this is the only safe time.'

'My friend, I work all hours,' the Pastor said. 'Besides, I'm longing to see the Countess. When you told me she was alive . . . well . . . words fail me. I can't tell you what it meant to me.'

'I want you to convince Marietta to join the Red Cross in Geneva. Tell her how much good she could do by publicising her terrible experiences. How could she survive in the Resistance in her condition?'

Ten minutes later the two men were with Marietta in an attic of Plechy Palace. The Pastor tried to hide his shock when he looked at Marietta. She was unrecognisable. The girl he remembered was gone. In her place was a hard-faced, determined woman, emaciated, old before her time, with short stubbly hair and bleak, determined eyes. There was very little point in trying to persuade this woman to do anything she didn't want to do, the Pastor thought, watching her carefully. She had been shaped and tempered on an anvil of pain and suffering. She seemed to be indestructible.

As if reading his thoughts, she said: 'It's no good listening to

Father. I know my own destiny. Nothing will stop me. I have too many good friends to avenge. Can you help me to join the local Resistance?'

The Pastor frowned. 'You'll have to be patient,' he said. 'You need to be fit, but if you're still as determined in a month's time, then I think you should return to Czechoslovakia and work with Jan. In the meantime, please, stay here and build up your strength. You will need all the stamina you can muster.'

He turned to the Count. 'These are dangerous times. Some matters are more important than individual lives. Marietta knows this. She has suffered bitterly. She would be the first one to understand what happens to ordinary people when morality and goodness are forgotten. I believe that God saved her for a special mission.'

The Count gazed helplessly at Marietta for several moments then, with a gesture of defeat, he left the room.

Chapter  52

JAN STOOD BEHIND THE NURSE, sensing her inner panic and her self-loathing. Her voice trembled when she spoke to her patient. 'We need to contact your family, Lara,' she whispered to the *Volksdeutsche* woman dying on the bed.

There was no answer.

'Lara,' she persisted. 'Where is your mother?'

'Dead,' the girl muttered eventually.

Jan sighed with relief.

'And your father?' the nurse asked.

'On the Eastern Front.'

'I'm sorry. What about a sister, or a brother?'

'No one . . . there's no one.' She began to moan softly.

'I'm sorry, Lara. Don't excite yourself. I just thought it would be nice for you to see your family.' The nurse gently helped her to sip some water.

Poor Lara Zimmerman. She had no chance of survival, Jan knew. That was why he was here. She had been caught in the crossfire between Nazi guards and fugitives from a labour gang. She had been shot in the chest and stomach.

The nurse looked over her shoulder and said to Jan. 'Soon . . . I don't think she's a fighter.'

'Is there no chance that she might live?'

The nurse shook her head.

'Then you must ensure that she dies at night, otherwise her death will be wasted.'

The nurse sighed and stared unseeingly at the young woman. 'Wait outside,' she said eventually. Shortly afterwards she called the male orderly to wheel Lara Zimmerman's corpse to the mortuary. 'She's to be cremated tonight,' she said. 'Send her ashes to reception. I'll get them to her relatives myself.'

Leaving the orderly to perform his task, she hurried to Registry. 'Give me the file of Lara Zimmerman,' she said. 'The doctor wants to go through her papers. She's to be discharged in the morning.'

Feigning an air of tired resignation rather than the extreme nervousness she felt, she waited for the girl to retrieve the papers and walked quietly back to her nursing station. She made careful notes of every detail, Lara Zimmerman's admittance papers, her discharge on medical grounds, her hospital report, her birth certificate, details of the shooting and of her 'release'. She handed all this to Jan, together with the papers of five young men who had died of their wounds in the past twenty-four hours.

It was almost time to go home, but she felt tired and strangely drained. After the war, I shall feel better about all this, she thought. I'll remember how I helped so many patriots to live, and forget how I forced the dying to die.

It was Monday morning and as usual Max Amman, household manager for Sokol Castle for the past nineteen years, was at the wholesalers haggling over the price of groceries. Armed with permits, ration cards, SS buying orders and pockets full of documents and authorisations, he was able to make large purchases and bargain the wholesalers' profit away. The merchants guessed that some of the discounts went into his pocket, for he always made a part-payment in cash, but Amman was a powerful man and they did not dare challenge him.

It was a lovely May day and on the way back, Max decided to park his lorry and walk along the embankment beside the

Vltava near the Charles Bridge. Like all Czechs, he had a special love of the river. He was never happier than when walking beside it, watching the river traffic and admiring the Palace up on the hill. Today, he had another reason for his walk. All morning he had gained the impression that he was being watched. He was almost certain that he had been followed by an old van. Now he wanted to be in the open and to see if they would approach him, whoever they were. After some minutes, he became aware of limping footsteps behind him. Max sat on a bench. Sure enough, a man approached and sat beside him.

'Hello Max. Fancy seeing you.'

'Hardly a surprise, Jan. You've been following me for hours. What d'you want?'

'You're a strange man, Max,' Jan mused aloud. 'I can't work out whose side you're on.'

'My side. The only side one can be sure of. I used to be on the side of Princess Lobkowitz and her family, but since they're all gone and there's a cuckoo in the nest, I'm taking care of Max Amman.'

'D'you know what would happen to you if General von Hesse found out you were robbing him?'

Max laughed contemptuously. 'I learnt it all from him.'

'He's protected. You're not.'

'If you're trying to blackmail me, why don't you come to the point?' Max said. He scowled at Jan. He had never liked him, not even in the beginning, when Jan had been the von Burgheim's chauffeur. Later, he'd realised his suspicions had been correct. All that false humbleness was a cover for Jan to infiltrate himself as a trusted servant in the household of the Austrian Minister of Foreign Affairs. The truth was, he was a member of the Communist Party.

As always, Jan was struck by the incongruity between Max's expressive eyes and the wreckage of his face. His skin was pallid and yellow-tinged, caused by some liver ailment he'd picked up in his youth. His eyelids drooped, and with his hanging jowls, he looked like a long-suffering bloodhound, yet his eyes were shrewd, tough and alert.

'I want you to help a young *Volksdeutsche* Czech woman, Lara Zimmerman. She was accidently wounded by gunfire when the Nazis were rounding up some poor sods. She's of farming stock, hardworking, shy and she wants to get out of the city. I happen to know you're looking for someone to run the dairy at Sokol.'

'A woman . . .? Running a dairy? Are you mad?'

'There aren't many men available, are there? And she's worth helping. Her father's fighting on the Eastern Front. He won the Iron Cross. I'm sure that would influence von Hesse.'

'Huh. Hardly a qualification for coping with cows. And she wouldn't be strong enough, you said she's been wounded.'

'She was brought up on a dairy farm. Two peasant women would be enough to help her. I've never asked you for a favour before, Max. I'm asking now. Give her the job, and all the work and travel permits she will need. Von Hesse will accept your recommendation. If you do this, I will forget about certain entries for cash payments made to you by the wholesalers. Otherwise . . .'

The two men sat in silence for long seconds. Then Amman said softly. 'Don't try this too often, Jan, I'm not so easy to push around as you think. But this time, I'll go along with your request. But if she tries to involve me in any underground activities, it will be you who will suffer. Understand?'

'I knew I could count on you, Max,' Jan said. He stood up and put one hand on the older man's shoulder. 'You and I have something in common . . . we both hate von Hesse.'

Father was looking harassed and upset. Marietta was leaving and he was terrified for her. He took out an envelope from his briefcase and placed it on the table. 'This is for you.'

Marietta opened the envelope and saw a passport with her mother's photograph inside. It was made out in the name of Ruzenka Bilä. There was also a birth certificate, travel permits and an Austrian work permit tucked into the passport.

'Absolutely authentic,' her father said.

'But these are old pictures of mother.'

'Yes, that one came off her passport. I have many more of

them from various documents,' he added simply. 'Remember that.'

'I don't look like Mother.'

'Yes, you do. Sometimes you do very strongly . . .' His voice broke and he almost choked. A moment later she was in his arms. For a long time they held each other. When she stepped back, she examined the papers carefully. 'Heavens, Father, you're a magician.' She smiled at him through her tears.

'Ruzenka Bilä married a Swede and went to live in Stockholm long before the war started,' the Count said. 'So you see, there was such a person. Here is her authentic birth certificate. She was five years older than you. The Swedish Embassy supplied the papers. It might come in handy.' He rubbed his hand wearily over his eyes.

'Don't worry so much. I have to go, but I'll be back. When the war's over, we'll be together again.'

The Count tried to smile, but failed. He had a strong premonition that he was never going to see his daughter again.

Andrea woke to find herself in the maternity ward. A nurse was bending over her. 'Close your eyes,' she whispered. 'Pretend to be unconscious. Don't speak. I'll come back later when it's safe to talk.'

'Water,' she muttered. She didn't really understand what had been said to her.

'Be quick.' Her head was lifted and she sipped a little. 'Not much or you'll be sick again.'

Andrea was afraid to move. Her stomach seemed weighted with lead. She cursed herself for not asking how her baby was, but the nurse had left. She could hear a male voice speaking harshly and she guessed that it was a guard.

She lay back and tried to sort out her muddled sensations and the horrors of the past few hours . . . was it hours . . . or days? She had been taken from the platform with three other pregnant women and driven to Prague. It had been a relief to find herself in the clean white ward. Unbelievable, too. Was it because of Louis? Common sense told her, no. The doctor had come, white-faced and solemn, to tell her that the baby was to be induced. Then came the nightmare of the birth pains until, mercifully, they had given her gas.

So what was she doing here? Why had the nurse asked her to be quiet? Where was her baby? And why had they forced her to give birth two weeks early?

She heard the sound of a child wailing and then another. It seemed that the creche was in a room off the main ward. She longed to see her little Louis, but when she tried to get out of bed she discovered she could hardly move, and was overcome with dizziness. She fell back into a heavy sleep, still drugged by the anaesthetic. The next time she woke it was dark. The night nurse was bending over her. 'Sip this,' she said. After Andrea taken some water, she went on. 'Listen carefully. There are Nazi guards outside. They have orders to take you to prison as soon as you recover sufficiently to walk. We want you to pretend that you are still unconscious. Delay your recovery, please. We would like you to be stronger before you leave hospital.'

'Please can I see my baby?' Andrea caught hold of her hand and looked up at her imploringly. 'Please! Help me! You are a woman. You must understand how much I long to hold him in my arms, if only for a moment. Besides,' she put her hand to her breasts wonderingly, 'I am so painful and swollen here. Is this milk?' She touched the damp patches on her nightdress. 'I must feed him. Isn't that so? He's my first, so I don't really know the procedure.'

The nurse looked grave. 'I am going to help you to ease the swelling. Then I'll bind up your breasts. That will help the pain a little. We have given you something to stop the milk, but it will take a while . . .'

'Stop the milk? Why? You must tell me where my baby is. Give him to me.' She struggled to sit up, panic almost overcoming her physical weakness. 'What's happened? Why won't you tell me?' She caught hold of the nurse's arm and shook her as her voice rose in hysteria. An SS guard appeared at the door. He took a notebook out of his pocket, with it open in his hand he asked, 'You are Fräulein Andrea Soltys?'

'Yes.'

'Tomorrow you leave for Ravensbrück camp to join the other women from Lezhaky. You will be put to work there.'

'My baby can go to relatives,' she whispered.

'On the orders of the Führer,' he began stiffly, 'all males living in Lezhaky were put to death as a reprisal for the murder of Lieutenant Hans Kosimer. Your baby fell into this category. He was executed at birth.'

His words fell like hammer blows on her heart. She screamed. She was still screaming when the doctor rushed in and thrust a needle into her arm. She was falling . . . falling . . . down into the bowls of the earth. 'Executed . . .?' she muttered, her lips hardly able to frame the words. She hung on to the nurse and begged her. 'Tell me he's lying.'

The nurse's face showed sadness and anger.

'Bullies, criminals, madmen,' she sobbed. 'Yes, you're insane. All insane! To kill a little baby. You are not human. To kill an infant fresh out of the womb. Who could do that? Only madmen . . .' As Andrea felt waves of unconsciousness surging through her body, she hung onto the nurse's hand. 'How could you let them?' she mumbled. 'Did he suffer badly?'

'He just fell asleep,' the nurse said. 'They gave him an injection. That's all. He felt nothing.'

The nurse watched Andrea's mouth moving. She bent closer. 'Louis, help me,' she was murmuring. Then she drifted into sleep. The nurse turned to the doctor and mouthed the words: 'Don't tell her the truth,' with her lips. As long as she lived she would never forget that morning when the SS guard had picked up Andrea's baby by its heels and dashed its head against the wall.

Chapter  53

FOR THREE WEEKS, Louis had been advancing through a macabre wasteland: towns, cities, trees and farms were all destroyed, the stench of Russian dead was everywhere, but Louis was no longer affected by the scene. There was no place for compassion in his life. His goal was to stay alive, to be warm and to eat his fill. They were nearing Stalingrad and Louis could hear the rumble of thunder coming from the front mobile – line guns. Every few minutes formations of planes flew overhead, to drop their bombs ten miles ahead and return shortly afterwards. Soon he could pick out the different sounds. One of them struck terror into Louis. It was an ugly wail, like some hideous tortured beast screaming from the battlefield.

'It's the Russians' secret weapon,' Schneider told him. 'We call it Stalin's Organ. It's a large rocket launcher, built on to tracked vehicles. Effective and mobile – we must all watch out for it.'

When darkness fell, the Eastern sky glowed blood red from reflected fires from the burning city. Louis knew that they would be in the thick of the fighting by the next day. As usual, his stomach twisted with cramps in reaction to his fear and he was unable to eat much of the stewed horseflesh he was given.

That night in his tent, Louis tried to make sense out of the rumours he'd heard in the camp. Stalingrad, he remembered from army school, was an important industrial centre set on the River Volga in the Caucasus Mountains. Its factories were churning out a quarter of Russia's tanks and armoured vehicles, and Russia's vital oil wells lay in the mountains just beyond the city. Now, Stalingrad was defended mainly by armed civilians, and many of the women and children had not been evacuated. Two days ago, German troops had crashed through the city's southern defences to reach the river. The rest of Stalingrad had become a raging inferno.

Early next morning, Louis was ordered to take his squad and flush the Russian workers out of a tractor factory. He did not expect much trouble and opened the operation with a massive barrage. After two hours, when the factory was a mess of fire, smoke, tangled steel girders and blackened walls. Konrad, who spoke some Russian, hailed the workers through a loudspeaker.

'Surrender. We will spare your lives. Come out with your hands raised.'

The answer was a hail of bullets. Louis flung himself down, feeling nothing but hatred for the Russians. Couldn't they see that there was no hope?

From the firing, he guessed there were about thirty armed workers. He gave the signal for storming the factory and watched his squad run for cover. Seconds later they were moving in.

It was like going into hell, Louis thought. He gagged on the smoke and heat. His eyes were streaming, his throat burning. He heard footsteps, but whose were they? He couldn't risk firing ... panic gripped him.

Out of the gloom, a gaunt man with staring eyes, black hair, and a fixed bayonet sprang towards him. Louis froze in a split-second of incredulity. Then he kicked at the bayonet, and they fell in a heap on the floor, tearing at each other's faces. The end came abruptly as Konrad thrust his bayonet into the Russian's back.

'Thanks,' Louis croaked. He signalled to Konrad and they

threw a grenade into the next office. When they charged in, the room was wrecked, but deserted. Some sixth sense made Louis yell, 'Get down!' A split-second later, shots came from the room they had just left. They were being circled.

With a sinking heart, Louis realised that each square foot would have to be fought for time and again, against civilians who were mad with rage and determined to die rather than retreat. He was filled with savage anger for the Russians and their inhuman heroism.

By dawn on their second morning, Louis was on the point of collapse. His hair was blackened stubble and he could scarcely see. He felt weak from lack of sleep and his hands were blistered with burns.

There were four surviving Russians and they had barricaded themselves into the stairwell, between the first and second floors. From their impregnable vantage position they could snipe at the Germans for as long as their ammunition lasted.

'Bring in a flame thrower,' Louis ordered grimly. 'Set it up there. Now! Get ready. Fire!'

As the flame shot up, a horrible scream echoed around the shaft.

'Burn the bastards,' Louis shouted. Despite their cries, he kept the flame thrower spurting up the stairwell. Soon the agony stopped and the bodies fell, charred and unrecognisable.

Bastards! he thought as he surveyed the corpses pitilessly. Two days lost and four of his men dead. For what? A ruined factory.

As winter set in, a final attempt was made to clear the city of Russians. It failed and German casualties were excessive. Louis and his squad were still fighting along the Tsaritsa River, trying to reach the Volga. Day after day, Louis was up to his thighs in thick, cloying, freezing mud. When their equipment was bogged down, he and his men put ropes around their shoulders and hauled their anti-tank guns through the mire. They sweated and cursed and fell, until they dropped with exhaustion.

It rained heavily for weeks, a churning mass of water that turned the roads to swamps, reduced vision to a few yards and bogged down their motorised vehicles. Only horse-drawn wagons were able to keep moving. At the beginning of November the rain stopped and the cold set in. Now they were able to fight again on solid ground, but soon the temperature began to plummet. It began snowing and by dusk on December 1, a blizzard raged mercilessly around them.

The troops had not been issued with winter clothing, so Louis padded his clothes with sheets of newspaper and strips of his blanket. To stop the wind blowing up his sleeves, he bound his wrists with string. This was only the beginning, Louis knew. They were fighting in unknown conditions, in temperatures that they had never before experienced, made worse by the icy wind. Every day, convoys of ambulances moved toward the west, filled with wounded, frost-bitten soldiers. The streets were full of German casualties, freezing to death as they lay on their stretchers. Many more kept arriving. They would lie there until the ambulances returned on the next relay to take them westwards. Louis felt sick with anger and grief.

Louis had a mild case of frost-bite in his fingers and toes. If it worsened, his limbs would have to be amputated. After agonising over it, Louis decided that they must raid the prisoner-of-war cages being sent to Germany across the snow. He stole the overcoat, fleecy-lined trousers, pullover, felt-lined boots, gloves and helmet from a Mongolian lieutenant who was about his size. He ignored the slit-eyed grimace of ferocious despair, as the Mongolian was left clad in his underwear for the long journey to the slave camps of Germany in sub-zero temperatures.

That night Louis and his squad found shelter in a dugout under a burnt out railway carriage. He ordered the men to light fires and keep their guns warm for instant firing. He fell asleep smiling. He was no longer freezing.

He dreamed that he was retreating at the end of the column of men when he heard a low moan coming from behind him. Something about the sound made his skin tingle with horror. He stared over his shoulder and in the twilight gloom, he saw the ghost of the Mongolian lieutenant gliding over the snow, barefooted and clad in his underwear, moving as silently as a shadow. 'You will join me in this icy hell,' he screamed.

Louis woke, sweating with fright.

By Christmas, Louis and his men were freezing and starving. They fought until their strength was spent, in temperatures of fifty degrees below zero in howling icy winds. Then the blizzard stopped and the sun hung poised over them in a steel grey sky. But now it was colder still. It seemed that the entire earth had frozen into a gigantic ball of ice crystal.

Only stone rubble and ruined walls remained in Stalingrad, but the city could not be taken. Below the rubble were the cellars and underground tunnels, linking the Russian's defensive positions, some stretching to the gullies and ravines that ran along the outskirts of the city and even to the river, providing marvellous cover for the defenders. Armed civilians and soldiers emerged in unexpected places from unseen holes, to inflict grave casualties.

At the end of the year, Louis received mail from home, his first for months. He crouched between a half-ruined wall and a burnt-out tank and opened the envelope with trembling fingers. He could hardly read from the smoke in his eyes, he'd been deaf for days from blast, and he was shaking so badly that he had to lie the letter on the the broken wall and crouch over it, to read the words.

My dearest Louis, I love you and I am praying for your safe return all the time. Try hard to stay fit and well and come back to me, my darling, because I have special need of you. Our loving produced a wonderful result. I am pregnant . . . a warrior child, I feel sure, although I shall do my best to persuade him otherwise. Yes, I am sure it is a 'him'. I can picture him exactly. I have never felt more contented. I spend my days decorating a nursery in what was the guest room. Oh, how I love you, and now I have a part of you with me, growing larger each day, and beginning to kick . . . Louis' tears were spattering the paper, smudging the precious ink. He wiped his eyes with the back of his hand.

There was much more, but the sudden horrendous wail of a rocket sent him diving under the tank. Moments later there was an explosion that knocked him out momentarily. He recovered to find himself lying on a heap of stinking corpses. They had been piling their dead in ghastly heaps, because there was no time or energy to bury them and the ground was frozen.

The following day, the long-expected Russian counter-offensive began. The Soviets fell on the Germans' Rumanian army back-up with a barrage from 3,500 guns attacking from the north and the south. The Rumanians broke and fled leaving a quarter of a million German soldiers surrounded and trapped without supplies. Louis was one of them. He was called to a meeting under a ruined railway bridge.

'Bad news, men,' Schneider told them. He looked twenty years older, his face was haggard, sunken eyes stared from folds of grey skin and his hair had turned white. 'We're trapped here. Five hundred tons of food a day are needed to feed us. The *Luftwaffe* is going to do its best to fly in our provisions and ammunition.'

Over five hundred supply planes had been shot down by the Russians, and it was only a matter of time before their stocks dwindled to nothing. Louis ached with compassion as he watched his fellow troops suffering. They had come to realise that Hitler's dream of *Lebensraum* had become a nightmare. God was not on their side ... yet they fought on with untold heroism against impossible odds, and without hope.

By January, the troops had eaten what was left of the Rumanians' horses. Rations were reduced to a few ounces of bread. General von Paulus was forced to make the terrible decision to feed only those men fit enough to fight. Those who could not fight sat around waiting to die of starvation and the cold.

Then the moment Louis had dreaded came upon them ... the Volga froze. Earth met sky in a blank canvas that seemed to stretch to eternity. Out of the misty whiteness, Louis saw his worst fears materialise. Siberian soldiers, clad in white, were pouring across the ice into Stalingrad, with dogs, staunch little horses, skis and guns that functioned in these icy temperatures.

Supplies to the beleaguered Germans had ceased completely. Louis was weak from hunger and exhaustion, and so were his men. He had no ammunition or fuel left. Smiedt gave orders that they should destroy their guns. Truck drivers were ordered to set fire to their vehicles. All around him, the wounded lay untended, their faces exhausted and expressionless, blood and pus seeping through the torn rags of their bandages, dying of their wounds, or starvation, or exposure, whichever took them first.

The Soviets began to move around them freely, knowing that they had no ammunition. Many of the troops tried to surrender, but the Russians did not want to be burdened with prisoners of war. They were going to die, Louis knew.

On January 22, Louis was called to the radio by Smiedt. He listened to von Paulus explaining that without ammunition, he was forced to capitulate, together with his remaining 94,000 men. The radio switched off for the last time. Louis could see that Smiedt could not grasp the awful reality of their helpless position. 'Old friend, take your men and join the rest of the Sixth Army,' Louis told him. Smiedt nodded wearily and slowly walked to the back of the tent. Seconds later Louis heard the sound of a gunshot.

Louis decided there was no point in trying to go anywhere. He sat on a broken axle outside Smiedt's tent and gazed around. Shells and bombs were pounding the ground. He wished that a bomb would shatter his anguish.

At 10 p.m. all sounds of war ceased. Apart from the howling wind, an eerie, painful silence descended on the dead city. Louis stared around, filled with horror. Dead soldiers, frozen stiff, seemed to glare at him accusingly. All around him lay the snow-covered debris of a ravaged city. Louis stood up and stumbled forward. In the pale moonlight his shadow stretched out huge and menacing.

What was he? Man or beast? A beast . . . he knew that now. He looked up and howled. It was a harsh, resentful mourning for his fallen comrades and the enemy he had killed. Black despair clutched his heart . . . for the deeds he had done, for his Catholic soul that was damned forever, and for the suffering he had wreaked on the human psyche and most of all for Andrea.

A ghastly apparition loomed out of the snowscape. It was his Mongolian lieutenant, once more clothed and armed. Had he come to lead the way down to his terrible, ice-bound hell? The Mongolian beckoned and Louis stood shocked and staring. He beckoned again, and, as if mesmerised, Louis followed him.

Chapter 54

IT WAS ALMOST DAWN when Marietta and Jan climbed down through the forest keeping close to the rushing river to muffle their footsteps. In the distance, she could hear dogs barking. The unwelcome sound brought a vivid recall of the camp, the smell of unwashed bodies and the prisoners' sickness and fear, the sound of marching feet and shouting ... always shouting. The scream of pain as someone was struck. 'No,' she muttered. 'I must never remember. Never again.' She realised Jan was staring at her and cursed herself for her lapse of concentration. She was wearing a nurse's uniform and it was crumpled and damp. The navy cape was inadequate against the cold mountain air, and she could feel a sore throat and cough begin to form. She had dyed her hair black and plucked her eyebrows to a thin line. This, plus a pair of spectacles, completed her disguise. It was absurd, she felt, anyone would recognise her. But if her real identity was discovered she would be lost. Hugo would look for her until he found her and would return her to the camp and this time she would be executed ... She huddled into herself and searched for courage.

They had travelled by train from Vienna to the border town of Gmünd, a hazardous, frightening journey, with uniformed guards checking their papers at every station. At Gmünd they simply walked to the outskirts of the town and hiked through the forest. Later came a gruelling climb through the snowy, forested mountain slopes to cross the border into Czechoslovakia. Jan had chosen an inaccessible area through the frozen bogs, where he knew there would be no fences or guards. Afterwards, the going was easier as they descended towards the Upper Vltava Valley. Jan knew the way intimately and she tried to remember it in case she had to flee this way.

Out of the pit of her agony and her fear grew a small resolve. I have come here of my own free will to help to destroy Hugo and his kind. Despite the dangers, this is what I must do. Whatever I am going into, I must put my fears aside.

Nevertheless, she could not stifle the last remnants of fear and they remained with her like a tiny sick feeling in the pit of her stomach as they walked.

'I have arranged for you to run a dairy,' Jan told her. 'You know the work, and it will ensure that you are fed adequately, and give you freedom to move around, as well as the use of some sort of vehicle. You'll have to deliver milk to the troops and collect butter from the farms. You will be able to talk with the soldiers and make friends. You'll pick up all kinds of useful tips. Remember you're a *Volksdeutsche*, one of them … the reason why Hitler went to war, you don't have to be scared.'

So he had noticed. She tried harder to pull herself together.

'If the British are correct and the V-3 is in Czechoslovakia, then it's my guess that von Hesse inspects the place often. You might make friends with his driver.'

And if Hugo catches sight of me? she thought, keeping her mouth closed.

'While you're doing this, I may ask you to run messages, or help to transport people. You will also be in charge of the radio. Communications are our lifeblood. Our groups are scattered and they seldom meet. Only proper liaison can mould them into a unit. Then we report regularly to the Free Czechs in London … it takes hours to get through. That will take up much of your nights.'

She began to wonder if Jan was talking so much to keep her

mind off her fears as they descended into the Upper Vltava Valley. He had changed, she realised as she listened to him. He was an equal, not a servant.

'I assume you know that Hugo has been appointed a Brigadier-General and that he has expropriated Sokol Castle for the Nazi party. That means for his own use.'

'Father told me,' she answered softly.

'I'll try to draw you a broader picture of how we operate . . .' Jan said.

The temperature slowly rose as they tramped downhill. As she listened, Marietta began to understand that Jan was the overall chief of the various groups in Bohemia, while George Kolar, who used to manage her Sokol estates, ran the Resistance group around Prague. She tried to memorise all she was learning, but time and again memories intruded, for they were approaching mist-covered lakes and they could see the forest in the dim morning light. Her lakes! Her home! She caught her breath, and then put foolish memories away. That happy, carefree countess belonged to another lifetime before Edelweiss, before the war, before the camp.

She shuddered, remembering that it was Hugo who had supervised the destruction of Lidhaky and sent Andrea to a camp. When she had heard the news she had been physically ill.

'Wait,' Jan said, holding her by her shoulders and swinging her round to face him.

'What's wrong?' she said in surprised alarm.

'Your eyes! They burn too fiercely. You are not cowed, nor beaten and you have learned to hate. Don't ever look at the Bosch as you're looking now, if you can't control it always avert your eyes, pretend to be demure. That look, more than anything else, gives you away.'

There was a horsedrawn cart full of cabbages waiting at the edge of the forest. Herr Zweig was smoking a pipe while his horse grazed on the grass. 'You made good time,' he said, by way of greeting.

Jan indicated Marietta. 'This is Lara Zimmerman, a nurse,

who is joining my group in the forest. She has returned
voluntarily to help our fight.'

The old man's eyes watered and a large drop dangled from
his nose. He pulled out a dirty rag and wiped it away. 'You are
a brave woman. Welcome,' he said.

Marietta sighed deeply. He hadn't recognised her. 'Let's get
going,' Jan said anxiously. They climbed under the tarpaulin,
and settled themselves amongst the cabbages.

'This is the plan,' Jan muttered as they bumped uncomfort-
ably over the rutted road. 'We're going to split up soon. You
have enough money to get food at the station. Buy a ticket to
Sokol, then walk to the castle ...'

'Sokol ... ?' she gasped.

'Ask for Max Amman. He's expecting you, by the way. Be
careful. Keep out of sight as much as possible ...'

'Max knows me well ... and he's German. This is madness.'

Jan glared at her. 'I have my reasons for sending you there.
Amman will give you the job we need and you will live in the
farmhouse up the river. The one over the old cellars. Remember? I shall contact you later. Don't worry, it's all arranged, but
you must go for the interview alone. You need a pass and a
permit to drive, to draw petrol and to move around. All this will
be invaluable to us. Amman will organise fingerprints ... a
photograph ... that sort of thing. They're very organised at the
garrison.' He laughed curtly.

Marietta lay amongst the cabbages in a state of confusion.
What if she came face-to-face with Hugo? Spasms of fear were
thrusting through her bowels. How could she manage to get
away with this?

Half an hour later the old man gave a curt command to his
horses, and, as the cart slowed, Jan helped her over the side.
Within seconds the cart had rumbled away and Marietta found
herself alone.

It was like a journey into the past. As if in a dream, she left the
station and walked down the country road towards the castle. It
was achingly familiar and dear. So many memories! Tears

pricked in her eyes. Gazing up, she saw the swastika fluttering from the tallest spire. Then anger surged, momentarily blotting out her fear. That dreaded symbol had hounded her for six years, and it was squatting on her home like a malevolent bird of prey.

Steeling her nerves, she walked the final distance and entered the courtyard. She was startled by a sharp clatter of hooves as a horse galloped up from the river. The rider, statuesque and haughty, dismounted, flung her whip to the ground and hurried to a parked limousine.

'Call the groom,' she called over her shoulder to a corporal who had hastily left his sentry box and who was making a bad job of straightening his uniform. 'I'm late. Take a message to the kitchens,' she snapped. She glanced at the sky and Marie looked up, too. Not a cloud was in sight. It was a perfect July afternoon.

'Cocktails on the balcony. Dinner in the Persian room. Cook's special onion soup, poached fish, wildfowl in burgundy, red cabbage with apples, new potatoes, and red wine sauce.'

Marietta gulped with hunger and envy.

'Who the hell are you?' she frowned as she caught sight of Marietta.

Marietta curtseyed. 'Zimmerman, Ma'am,' she said. 'I'm here about a job as a dairymaid. I have an appointment with Herr Amman.'

'Get along then. Don't stand there gaping.'

She started the engine, reversed and swung round, tyres squealing. Marietta guessed she had just had her first sight of Hugo's whore.

She found she was shaking with fright as she mounted the old stone steps. She heard a shout and cringed.

A corporal was racing towards her. He caught hold of her shoulder and pushed her down the steps. She landed in a heap, bruising her ankle. This was it, she thought. She'd been recognised.

'What do you think you're doing going up to the main door?' he fumed. 'Take the servants' entrance.'

What a blunder! She hurried to the side door. Otto the cook was gone, she realised, peering into the kitchen. In his place was a huge woman, with bulging biceps and big red hands. She was carving a side of beef with gritty determination. There was no shortage of food here. The kitchen had been refurbished to look like a hospital canteen, gleaming with stainless steel.

Max's office had always been along the passage and third on the right, but after the bright sunlight, she couldn't see down the gloomy corridor. Half-blinded, she stumbled forward into the light room ahead. She found herself staring up at a portrait of her mother hanging beside the window. Tears stung her eyes for the walls were covered with photographs: Louis and her as children, Ingrid sitting with grandmother's dog, and there she was with Trudi, her horse, at a gymkhana. Dozens and dozens of family pictures had been rescued and hung in Max's study, a permanent reminder to everyone of her face. She struggled to stay calm. Then she heard a voice behind her and spun round.

'Touching, aren't they?'

Marietta was startled. She gave the Nazi salute.

'Oh, you don't have to do that in here, Nurse Zimmerman,' Max said. He hurried to lock the door. 'I don't know who you really are and I don't want to know. I was ... let us say ... "persuaded" to give you this job. I'm not in the Resistance and I'm not a Nazi either. I'm just a servant.'

Max walked behind his desk and sat there staring at her. 'Hm! Well ... it has all been arranged. The general is anxious to help relatives of soldiers at the Eastern Front, so it didn't take long to talk him into taking you on. You don't even have to see him. Jan was anxious that you should not.'

'Thank you.'

'Just remember ... the less I see of you, the happier I shall be. I don't want to be involved in anything you Resistance might be up to. Got it?'

She nodded.

'Now ...' He drummed his fingers on the desk. 'Something about you worries me.' For several frozen moments he studied her intently. He stood up abruptly. 'We must attend to dozens

of details. Soon you'll be so bound in red tape you'll find it hard
to move.'

'Yes,' she said, trying to fight off a feeling of unreality.

'Remember to say "Sir". I can see you're not used to that.'

'Yes, Sir.'

'I've been trying to work out why you people want one of
your own in this position. You seem a nice woman. I feel sorry
for you. Your so-called Freedom Fighters are a tough bunch of
power-mad, pseudo-politicians, jockeying each other to get into
power at the end of the war. Jan is the leader of the Czech
Communist Party.' He watched for her reaction. 'I can see that
doesn't surprise you. I know a thing or two about Jan. You can
tell him that if he puts pressure on me again I shall do likewise.
And don't think a knife in my back would solve the problem,
because I have documents hidden that will come to light if I
die.'

'And if you die by accident, Sir?'

'Nurse Zimmerman, my role as your protector lasts only as
long as I live. Now . . . let's get going.'

An hour later Marietta was driving a van towards the dairy,
half a mile upstream from the castle. She parked in the
courtyard and gazed around wistfully. This was one of the
oldest properties on her estates, built in the fifteenth century.
Once it had been the castle winemaker's house. Beneath were
the cellars, connected to the river by a downhill passage, where
wine barrels had been rolled to waiting river steamers. She had
played here as a child with Louis and Ingrid. In those days, it
had been occupied by one of the Kolar family, now the door was
swinging on one hinge and several windows were broken.

Marietta unloaded the provisions and cleaning materials Max
had given her. As she walked inside, she felt sad to see the old
place so neglected, but thrilled to be in her own home. She
should start cleaning, but she was exhausted. The bed was
rickety, rats were racing in the loft, the rooms were filthy, but
she flung herself on the bed, pulled the blankets over her and
briefly allowed herself to think of Bill before falling asleep.

Chapter  55

A LONG AND SCARY MONTH PASSED before Marietta had her first piece of information about the mine. A *Volksdeutsche* caterer, whose business was exclusively for Nazi gatherings, asked her for more eggs, chicken and cream than she had. He had the permits to buy another forty chickens, he told her, but no supplies were available.

'I'll try my best,' she said. 'The farms are almost barren nowadays. I don't know what's going to happen. D'you have to have forty? And what's the absolute latest deadline for them?'

'I told you ... tomorrow at noon. Von Hesse will have my licence if I let him down. Thirty bigwigs from Berlin are flying in tomorrow night. I have to supply a light lunch inside Richard's Mine, and a big supper later at the castle.'

'You mean, inside the camp?'

'No, I mean the mine. It's not the first time, either. They fly the delicacies to the runway on top of the volcano ... it's a new arrangement ever since they got melted icecream. The train takes too long, you see. It's the the top brass coming this time. I know because he's having Russian caviar. Danish does for the rank and file.'

'Messy business eating inside that old tin mine, I should think,' she asked.

'Can't be messy everywhere. Somewhere they've got a place for table napkins, cut glass decanters, silver cutlery . . . nothing but the best for this lot. Best cigars, too.'

She began to make inquiries.

From Max Amman, Marietta learned that Hugo went into Theresienstadt Camp at least twice a week. Lately, he had rushed out there at midnight, after some emergency telephone calls.

Marietta went off to search for forty chickens in a thoughtful mood.

Shortly before dusk, Marietta steered her wheezing old lorry down towards Helen Kranzler's farm, for she had always bred the finest chicken. The farm road wound under tall elms, past hawthorne hedges and clumps of sweet-williams, buttercups and daisies in the hedgerows.

It was past 7 p.m. but the slave gangs of broken, starving men were still toiling in the fields and two armed guards were lolling against the trees smoking as they watched the labourers working.

The farmhouse was in a sad state with hanging shutters, peeling paint and a damaged roof. Broken farming implements lay scattered around the yard. Two small children stood biting their nails, staring distrustfully at Marietta, while she spoke to their mother.

'You vulture,' the woman snarled, before Marietta was inside the door. 'Preying on poor people. My children are starving. Look at them! Their father is in a concentration camp and we are robbed of all we have.'

She crumpled in a chair and burst into tears. 'I can't fulfil my quota,' she sobbed. 'Now they'll take the cattle away. Can I help it if the cows dry up before their time? I don't get enough fodder for them. It's the same with the chickens. So you want me to slaughter good fowls for the pot.'

Marietta felt helpless in the face of the woman's anguish. 'Everything was stolen from us,' Hella sobbed. 'Our poultry and pigs were sent to Germany. I have one sow left, but her piglets are registered at birth and taken away at four months and God help us if one of them has died ... I have ten fowls and the bastards expect forty eggs a week from me.'

'Hush, don't cry.' Marietta crouched beside Hella and held her hand. 'Everyone is suffering. I'll contact the Resistance and see if they can do anything to help you. Be brave ... You must find a way to hide some of your livestock,' Marietta pleaded. 'Please, listen to me. The Germans are going to lose the war. The Allies are winning in North Africa, English bombers are destroying German cities, two thousand German factories have been destroyed so far. Eventually the Germans will be beaten. You must hang on for your children and for when your husband comes home. Try to be strong. Don't give up. Be brave, for the sake of your children.'

It was always the same, she thought bitterly. The people were starving and devoid of hope. They no longer had the courage to fight back. There and then, she decided to make it her mission to persuade the suffering farm wives to support the Resistance and to help each other.

She missed her deadline for the chickens and the cream, arriving two hours late, but with a promise to help out with the preparations. Despite four hours hard work in the caterer's kitchen, she could not glean any more information. It was Jan who made the big breakthrough. He had plied a train driver with some rare schnapps and after some of the fiery spirit had been drunk, learned that prisoners who had worked within the mine were regularly sent east to the Polish death camps. They were due to pick up another consignment, the driver explained. He was so befuddled by drink he never remembered he had told Jan the date planned for the next shipment.

Marietta was armed with a British-made sub-machine gun loaded with thirty rounds and she was standing alone in the dark, guarding her lorry and shivering with fright. She felt ashamed that her stomach was clenched into painful knots and her hands were wet and slipping on the barrel.

A minute later the train came into view. It was clanking loudly as it slowed. The heavy, darkened wagons seemed to pass in slow motion. Minutes later an orange flare seared her eyeballs. Then came the sound of the explosion. Silhouetted against the flare she saw the shape of the first engines rear up, stand on end, and tumble slowly over.

She heard the rattle of the guards' machine guns as Jan's squad opened fire. The noise of the carriages smashing against each other almost drowned the screams of agony.

Out of the darkness the bulky shape of a man loomed towards her. Who was it? She aimed her gun and hesitated. The figure was almost upon her and still she was searching for some identification. Almost too late she saw a swastika glittering at his throat. As his gun swung towards her she tugged at her trigger. Her gun shot up in a massive recoil. When she opened her eyes she saw the German soldier lying still on the ground. She gagged at the sight of the tearing hole in his chest and the blood gushing into the earth.

A terrifying silence had settled around her. What did it mean? Were the Resistance all dead?

It seemed like hours before a line of men came stumbling towards her. Were they men? They were shambling, broken figures who could hardly force one leg in front of the next. Seeing those skeletal faces and sunken eyes and smelling their fear and their unwashed bodies, Marietta was propelled into the past. Unable to move, she stood transfixed, hearing again the camp dogs, the guards and their *schlags*, the frightened eyes of the new intakes.

Jan was shaking her. 'Get them into the lorry,' he was screaming. 'Move, damn you! What's got into you?'

Shame washed through her as she moved to the truck. Within minutes the prisoners were loaded and Marietta drove slowly towards the river, trying to get a grip on her shaking hands and panting breath. Would she never get there? She was trembling so violently she could hardly drive. At last she reached the rendezvous where Kolar and his men were waiting.

'What's wrong?' Kolar demanded.

'Nothing. It went off as planned. Jan's coming.'

'You look sick. Take it easy.'

Within five minutes the prisoners had been loaded on to the waiting boats. They would be hidden by the peasants. Marietta was left alone to watch the dawn break and overcome her fears as best she could. It was the sight and smell of the prisoners that had propelled her back to those nightmare years in the camp. Next time, she vowed, she would be more prepared.

Jan came by way of the river at midnight. 'We're in luck,' he told her with a smile. 'God smiles on you. Listen to this. Two of the prisoners we rescued from the train were working inside Richard's Mine. The mine has been converted into a massive research station. It's heavily guarded, with access only from the railway station inside Theresienstadt. The train goes underground most of the way. The prisoners think that they're building some kind of rocket. It's so secret that every six months the slave labour is replaced for security reasons. Rumour has it that the old batch are always executed. These two were en-route to the gas ovens. I've left them both down there.' He gestured towards the cellars. 'Don't feed them too much all at once. Little and often is the best way, or they might die on you.'

Marietta found the two men completely exhausted, but after a while they began to tell her about themselves. Willi Maeier had been a goldsmith and Hans Schwerin a banker. Maeier was a dark haired, sorrowful man, with large, hooded brown eyes, long delicate fingers and an olive complexion. He was so weak, he kept falling asleep as he talked to Marietta. Schwerin was more robust. She guessed that he had once been an athlete. He had red frizzy hair and blue eyes and freckles on his cheeks, but his eyes were haunted and he coughed continually.

Schwerin was agitated. 'They'll come looking for us,' he said. 'We know too much. We shouldn't be here. It's not fair on you.' He broke off into another fit of coughing. 'I must tell you about the mine . . .'

'Please don't tire yourself,' Marietta said gently. 'An expert is coming to debrief you.'

She broke off as she heard a shot in the distance. The sound of the searching troops and dogs was close. Maeier's frightened eyes sent thrusts of painful fear through Marietta's stomach. The Germans had launched a massive manhunt for the lost prisoners and the terrorists who had wrecked the train. All day the forests had been echoing with shots, shouts and barking dogs. The three spent a sleepless night huddled in the cellars, but at dawn the troops moved further south.

Hugo's rage was uncontrollable. The Camp Commandant, the train driver and the guards were court martialled and punished. During the interrogations, it was learned that one of the guards had sighted a young woman with the terrorists, but that fact was of no interest to Hugo.

Losing the men who had worked inside the research plant was the very thing that he had feared the most. That was why he had ordered that the slave workers should be executed on-site. The Camp Commandant had disobeyed his orders in sending them to Auschwitz.

For two weeks, SS troops combed the forests and the hills and searched every house for miles. Hugo managed to conceal the fact that some workers from the mine had been among the escapees. His career was at stake. Would the Czechs be clever enough to interrogate the prisoners and find out about the V-3? he wondered. And if so, would this leak reach the Allies? Hugo had one way of finding out. He sat down and thought about Ingrid for a while. Eventually he picked up the telephone and put a call through to his SS agent in Berlin who controlled Paddy, the Irishman.

Chapter  56

THE FIVE MONTHS SINCE MARIETTA LEFT were the worst the Count had ever experienced, for he had no way of knowing whether or not she was alive. Likewise, there had been no news of Louis since Stalingrad fell and the Count feared that his son was dead. Through his powerful contacts, he had discovered that Andrea and the surviving Lidhaky women were being held in Ravensbrück concentration camp where medical experiments took place, Polish and Ukranian women were worked until they dropped like flies, and twelve thousand prisoners were cramped into quarters designed for half that amount. The Count moved to his Berlin apartment and spent weeks trying to obtain Andrea's release. He lobbied powerful friends, he pleaded, argued and finally bribed, but without success.

Apart from his sorrow for his family, the Count was grieving for his compatriots, too. The past six months had seen a major reversal in the war. German troops were retreating in Italy and Russia and daily the enemy moved closer to the Fatherland. Allied retribution was terrible. RAF bombers at night and American bombers by day were pulverising Germany's main cities and industrial areas. Thousands were dying in the raids ... many more were homeless. Ten thousand tons of bombs had been dropped on Hamburg alone during the past eight days.

Seven square miles of the city had been reduced to rubble.
Shipyards and factories had been flattened. U-boats had been
destroyed in their pens and the Elbe tunnel was totally
demolished. Civilians also faced the terror of the Allies' new
weapon, a phosphorus incendiary bomb that created such
intense heat the asphalt-paved streets turned into rivers of fire.
Casualties were horrifying . . . a ghastly preview of what was in
store for them.

Yet it was not too late to save Germany and Austria from
Hitler's madness and Allied retribution, the Count reasoned. If
Hitler were to be assassinated, a new German government could
petition the Allies for a ceasefire while peace was negotiated.

The Count had never been superstitious, never believed in
the devil, but lately he was wondering if a force of evil really did
exist. Time and again pure chance saved Hitler from the
Conspirators' plans. Eventually the Count realised that he must
take the responsibility of assassinating Hitler upon himself,
even if this meant sacrificing his own life. Could he succeed
when so many attempts had failed? Was the devil looking after
his own? The Count put his fears aside and made his plans.

An exhibition of the new army greatcoats had been arranged in
the infantry school outside Berlin for 11 a.m on Wednesday,
August 11, 1943. The Count's driver pulled up in the VIP
entrance at exactly 10.30 and opened the car door. The Count
tried to smile reassuringly as he stepped on to the pavement, but
failed. Overhead, wave after wave of Allied bombers were flying
in close V-formation.

'Bastards,' his driver muttered, scowling as he watched them.
'Will you be here long, Sir?'

'An eternity!' The Count shuddered. 'Perhaps an hour. Who
knows?'

By 10.50 the hall was crowded, which bothered him greatly.
He had hoped to avoid killing innocent young men. Once again
he ran through his plan. When the Nazi entourage came in
sight, he would prime the bomb and keep a careful minute
count. It was a ten-minute fuse, which was all the time he would

have to manoeuvre himself close to Hitler's side. Time passed agonisingly slowly.

It was two minutes past eleven, but still there was no sign of Hitler. Then a message was relayed to them over the loud-speakers. The Führer had been delayed by the chaos caused by the bombing raid. The official cars had been forced to take a detour. Glancing at his watch, the Count was horrified to see how badly and visibly his hand was shaking.

By 11.20 the Count had himself back under control. At 11.25, a shout came from the door. 'Here comes the Führer!' The junior officers cheered.

Looking through the window, the Count saw a train of five black cars coming into the car-park with a motorcycle escort. He put down his glass and fumbled with the fuse. It was a simple matter of pressing a switch, but in his state of suppressed excitement, he could hardly manage. At last it was done. He glanced at his watch again. The bomb was set to explode at twenty minutes to twelve.

A voice over the loudspeakers boomed: 'The Führer and his entourage are leaving their cars. Start the band. Form the guard of honour.'

The music was deafening, but over and above it came an even louder roar, drowning the band completely. A bomber was flying low overhead, pursued by three German fighter aircraft. It was dropping its bomb load in an attempt to gain height. He heard the sound of whistling as the bombs fell. A split-second later the first explosion rocked the building. The floor heaved, the walls trembled. The next explosion was closer. Plaster fell around them. Everyone dived under tables and chairs.

Seconds later, a third explosion tossed him headlong against the wall. A bomb had exploded in the yard behind the school. Smoke poured through the windows. Something was burning inside the room.

The Count picked himself up shakily. Feeling his way through the smoke and dust from the blast, he staggered across broken glass to the window in time to see the convoy of cars speeding away. The Führer had fled.

He looked anxiously at his watch. Eleven-thirty! What had happened to the past five minutes? Had he been knocked out? He shuddered. He had exactly five minutes before he blew these innocent bystanders into oblivion. It was impossible to defuse the bomb, but where could he dump it? His mind was racing. The hall was thick with SS guards, all zealous Nazis.

He walked outside. He had three minutes. 'Oh God,' he muttered. He ran headlong into the smouldering wreckage, scorching his shoes and feeling the heat and smelling the burnt rubber as he ran faster. Dumping the bomb, he turned and fled. A split-second later, a massive explosion threw him against the wall and he slumped on to the ground. His last conscious thought was the hope that he had not been seen. 'God protect my children,' he prayed.

Two days later, Hugo received the news of his stepfather's death with mixed feelings of pleasure and regret. 'You old bastard,' he muttered to himself. 'Have you any idea how many times I've protected you from your foolish, treasonable actions? Too many times. D'you know why? Because Father, I have done everything to make sure I am your only living heir. And I am not going to allow my inheritance to be expropriated for treason.'

Hugo was quick to travel to the scene of the explosion and make a public show of grief. A young officer eager for promotion was only too happy to state that he had seen the Count discover a bomb hidden under a table and flee with it outside. A hero's funeral was organised.

Standing at the graveside, Hugo peered at the casket of the Count's remains and threw some flowers over it. He muttered his last words to his stepfather.

'Marietta died in the camp. Louis is missing, presumed dead. Either way he'll never get out of Russia alive. Andrea's out of harm's way and her baby is dead. So there's only me left, Father. You never appreciated my worth, you always over-looked me, but I promise you, I'll make better use of your estates than the others would have.'

Hugo took up residence at Plechy Palace later that week and called in an interior designer to change the study and the main bedroom to suit his taste. Then to his chagrin Hugo discovered that he could not take up his inheritance as easily as he had assumed. The lawyers needed proof of Louis' death, otherwise years would need to pass before he could be legally presumed dead. Hugo had never been a patient man and he returned to Prague determined to find the answer to his problem. 'The will, allied to brutality, conquers all,' he murmured. The SS motto gave him confidence that fate would send the documentation he needed.

Marietta was in the loft of the dairy, hidden behind bales of straw, tapping out a radio message in code, when Jan broke the news of her father's death to her.

'Louis ... and Andrea's baby, and Andrea in the camp, and all the *Edelweiss* students dead or gone. So many of our comrades. So now it's Father ... and I can't even mourn him properly. I feel numb. Too many people ... too much to grieve. Maybe later I will feel something. Oh God! Where will it all end?' she muttered, more to herself than to Jan.

Jan felt a surge of compassion as he saw her eyes fill with tears and her tragic face turn paler. She was a brave woman and he grudgingly admired her, despite her title and wealth.

'I'm sorry, Marietta,' Jan said softly and saw her glance at him in surprise.

'You never call me that,' she said.

'I admired your father very much,' Jan said stiffly. 'Despite my job I always respected him.'

Now her eyes had become bleak and hard again. She turned away to hide her pain. She was carrying too much on her shoulders. 'Oh Jan,' he heard her whisper. 'I wish he could have lived. I needed to see him again.'

'The time to mourn will come later.'

Jan was right, Marietta thought with a deep sigh, she would put her personal feelings aside. With a heavy heart, she went back to the radio. When she had finished she hurried down to the kitchen to prepare some food for the freedom fighters who were meeting in the cellar tonight.

They were great talkers while the wine lasted, Marietta thought treacherously. So many men came to these meetings in the wine cellar. Most of them were strangers to her, but she had known some of them in pre-war days. For instance, Georg Kolar's third son, Klaus, was one of them. Klaus was a huge man, with bright ginger hair and a freckled skin and, like his father, Klaus had worked on the Sokol estate, taking a degree in forestry at Charles University. Before the war, he'd been full of ambitious plans for the future of the woods and game within them. Another Resistance member, Wolf Erhardt, leader of N-Group and based north of Prague, was handsome in a gypsy way, with sultry lips, sensual eyes and regular features. His tanned skin contrasted with his white, even teeth. In pre-war Czechoslovakia, Erhardt had been the owner of a textile factory, now taken by the Nazis. He was a pest for he was always hanging around her. Not that it mattered, she thought. They didn't see him that often.

One man she knew particularly well was Alex Jablonec, who had once skied for Czechoslovakia. She had skied with him sometimes and they had been friends and she was surprised that he had never recognised her.

Milan Holub was an ex-merchant banker, a tall, distinguished-looking man with thinning hair, grey eyes, and a pronounced stoop. She was amazed how he had survived the rough outdoor living, for he was old and his wealth had cocooned him with easy living. She remembered his beautiful home and his passion for collecting Dresden china.

Ludvik Kalish had run the local supply store, buying and selling pigs, chickens, harvesters, eggs, pumps and even an entire sawmill at times. He had been a rich man until the Germans came. Like the rest of them, Ludvik had a price on his head. He kept his squad on the move and imposed the maximum punishment on the Bosch.

Miki, her gypsy groom from Boubin Manor, was still with Jan. He was a shy, diffident man, who kept to himself, but his knowledge of the forest and the animals was invaluable. He taught the freedom fighters how to survive in the forest and to live off the land.

They, and hundreds of others who came and went, formed a loosely woven, shifting mass of men that made up the Czech Resistance. Their only common bond was their hatred of the Nazis. Most of the time they were prepared to work together under the leadership of Jan or Kolar, but sometimes they went their own way, raiding Nazi garrisons or trains for personal gain. They were like modern-day highwaymen and, apart from the Communists, Jan detested all of them for their lack of discipline and their carelessness, but he needed them and he tried to wield them into a unit.

A scruffy mob, she thought, watching them wonderingly, but amazingly efficient. Half-starved, ragged, unshaven and dirty, they lived from day to day, constantly shifting through the forests, relying on their wits and local peasants to feed them.

Tonight she had managed to scavenge bread and cheese to go with the wine and the men wolfed it down in no time. The talk went round in circles. They were all waiting for Jan, no one knew why he was so late and the room was full of fearful expectation.

It was after midnight when Marietta heard footsteps overhead. Jan came down, followed by Schwerin and Maeier, with a third man she did not know, but whom Jan introduced to them as Dr Marius Dietrich, a physicist. He was a tall, beanpole of a man, skinny and tough, despite his delicate hands and features. His story was typical of many former Czech intellectuals. Once he had been a professor of physics at Charles University. He had been dismissed and sent to a camp in the very early days of the occupation. Eventually he had managed to escape and join Kolar's group.

Dr Dietrich had questioned the escaped prisoners and come to the conclusion that the Germans were producing a new type of long-range missile. Other top-secret research was taking place in other parts of the mine, but none of the ex-workers had been able to give any details.

'It must be vital since it's so well guarded. I need to get into the mine and see for myself,' Dietrich told them.

'The problem is, it's impossible to get inside,' Ehrhardt argued, 'except via the railway line that links the mine with Theresienstadt concentration camp.'

For an hour they argued over how to breach the fortifications. Eventually, Marietta decided to join in. 'We must accept that Maeier and Schwerin got into the mine. Involuntarily, as it happens, but the point is, they got in. If there truly is no other way, we may be forced to get ourselves arrested.'

There was a long silence while the implications sank in . . . they would get in, but not out.

'It would be suicide,' Jan said. 'But you're right. If there's no other way . . .'

The arguments became even more heated, but it was finally decided that three men should be arrested on minor infringe-ments of the occupation laws, in the hope that they would be sent into Richard's Mine rather than straight to one of the death camps. There was little chance of escaping, so they would have to devise a way to send messages out. Jan would have to find someone who had access to the mine and would be prepared to act as a courier.

Dr Dietrich insisted on being one of the three and they drew lots to choose the other two men. Milan Holub and Alex Jablonec were chosen.

The following afternoon, Marietta parked her lorry untidily at the kerbside. Braking too suddenly, she and Milan Holub were thrown forward in their seats.

'Ouch! Sorry,' she said. 'I think I'm a bit nervous.' What an understatement, she thought wryly, trying to ignore her shaking hands and dry lips. The truth was, she was in a state of abject terror. She was driving a man to certain imprisonment and probable death, a man she liked and admired. With fumbling

fingers she pulled on the brake and switched off the motor.
Milan put one hand over hers.

'Don't upset yourself, Lara. I knew what I was in for when
I volunteered to come back from France. Remember that.'

'I didn't know . . .'

'In 1937, I left the bank and started an export business, based
in Paris, mainly Czech-made instruments. I flew back just
before Prague fell to the Germans and joined the Resistance. I
was captured later, but I escaped. I knew the score. Just as you
did when you joined the Resistance.' He tilted his cap over one
eye, and opened the door. Then he looked over his shoulder and
winked. His face creased into a grin of pure affection. 'Come on
. . . smile,' he said.

Smile! She was quaking. It was more difficult to endure other
people's suffering than one's own, she thought. She watched
him give the thumbs up sign and stride along the pavement.

'Thanks for the lift,' he called loudly.

It was Marietta's job to report back exactly what happened,
but she had hours to kill. It would be better to drive away and
come back later, she decided. Milan, carrying the papers of a
Free Czech labourer, was going to the Spova café round the
corner. There he would complain loudly about his unfaithful
girlfriend who had spurned him in favour of a German corporal.
He would curse all Germans and pull down the poster of the
Führer, which the proprietor had hung behind the bar hoping
to curry favour with his German masters. The proprietor would
call in the troops and they would be just in time to arrest poor
Milan when he staggered out drunk after curfew. That was the
plan, but would it work?

'Milan was superb,' Marietta reported to Jan that evening. They
were sitting around the table in her kitchen, eating stale bread
and cheese. 'He should have been an actor. He rolled out on to
the pavement exactly ten minutes after curfew. The pigs were
late pitching up, so he obligingly passed out under a lamppost.

'Naturally, the Bosch kicked him until he came to, threw him
into the van and drove off at high speed,' she said. 'He was taken

to Petsechek House.' She shuddered. This had been the banking headquarters of friends of hers, all of whom had perished in a camp. The building had been chosen for Gestapo headquarters because of the huge underground vaults ... ideal for interrogations. She shuddered, suddenly overcome with depression. 'Oh God!' She burst into tears. 'I drove off and left him.'

Jan put one arm around her shoulders and hugged her against him. 'Hush, stop blaming yourself. Milan knew the odds. He volunteered.'

Marietta blew her nose noisily and pushed Jan away. There was a long, awkward silence.

'I've got to get tougher,' she said, 'it's just that ...' She broke off. How could she explain how much she loved all of them, for their bravery, their ability to put up with terrible conditions and keep smiling, for their sense of humour in the face of danger, their compassion for each other and the downtrodden Czechs. Each one of them was special.

Later that night, Marietta liaised by radio with the various Resistance groups. At dawn she learned from Georg Kolar, operating the Prague squad, that Dr Dietrich had been sent to Gestapo headquarters for interrogation, Milan Holub had been despatched to Theresienstadt, while Alex Jablonec had been arrested for breaking curfew, but no one knew where he was being held. She could only pray that all three of them would be sent into the mine.

Chapter

57

THE CANTEEN IN THE EAST END where Ingrid worked was dark
and decorated with posters of pretty girls with cheery grins,
scantily clad in bits and pieces of men's uniform. The air was
full of smoke and the strong smell of baked beans, bacon and
beer. In the hot fumes from the stoves, a dim electric lamp
swayed to and fro, lighting the soldiers' faces as they sang.
Ingrid was singing, too. She was leaning over the counter, filling
teacups from the battered urn. Even in a shapeless blue overall,
with a blue scarf tied round her head concealing her hair, she
still managed to look exquisite. Her eyes were shining wistfully,
her lips moving sensuously as she sang, the milky white skin of
her throat glistening in the light. *'There'll be bluebirds over, the
white cliffs of Dover, tomorrow, just you wait and see.'* In a sudden
lull in the singing, her voice rang out clearly.

Someone called out: 'You're as good as Vera Lynn. Carry on,
Miss.'

'Yes, sing some more,' their voices called longingly.

Ingrid began again and heard the men humming a background chorus. The song came to its poignant end and everyone
clapped.

'My goodness,' Ingrid said shakily. 'I've spilt the tea.'

'Who cares. You gave them something more important than

tea.' Ingrid looked into Stephen's eyes and blanched.

'I've missed you,' he said in a growl, as if the words hurt.

How could anyone miss her? He was lying. Perhaps he was trying to trap her. 'I'm always here. At least, most nights.' She broke off as someone switched on the radio for the news.

Several factories had been obliterated by the RAF in a raid on the Ruhr, she heard; 400 acres of Düsseldorf had been laid waste, while in Berlin the RAF were dropping 900 tons of bombs on the city centre each half an hour. Ingrid was filled with despair and she tried to block out the announcer's voice. The next time she looked round, Stephen was nowhere in sight.

When she left the canteen, she found Fernando waiting for her in the dark alley of the side entrance. He smiled grimly as he saw her flinch. 'You haven't brought anything in this week.'

'I've told you before. It's not safe for you to come here. I haven't been able to get any news. People are wary. Looking for spies has become a national phobia.' She wrapped her scarf round her head and scowled at him. 'D'you know who's here? Stephen Schofield! Didn't you tell me how shrewd and clever he is? What if he saw you?'

'This is an emergency,' Fernando muttered. 'Listen carefully. You are to contact a certain officer working for British Intelligence.' His sinister voice as always chilled her to the bone. 'We're not sure what he does, but we know it's important. Your job is to find out, and to photograph whatever documents he brings home. Live with him. That's an order, but continue working at the factory and the canteen.'

'What if he doesn't want to live with me?'

'That would be too bad because your orders come directly from von Hesse.'

Ingrid scowled and lapsed into silence. 'What's the point of all this effort?' she said rebelliously. 'We're losing the war.'

She had uttered the ultimate betrayal. Fernando's face turned ugly. He caught hold of her arm and twisted it. 'There's no way out for you, Ingrid, except in a coffin.' He put pressure on her arm. 'Here's a dossier giving the details you will need to know about this officer. You'll see the places he frequents. Arrange an impromptu meeting. Study the file and destroy it. Is that clear?' With a final sneer, he hurried off into the dark. Ingrid rolled up the envelope and thrust it into her handbag.

Bill Roth could only see the back of the head and the line between the shoulders and the tiny waist of the woman sitting at the bar, yet he could not take his eyes off her. There was something familiar about her long smooth neck, the way she sat, upright and graceful, and her beautiful ash blonde hair.

Feeling unsure but convinced that when he could see her properly he would know her, Bill walked across to the woman and tapped her on the shoulder. She turned her head and Bill found himself gazing into Ingrid's slanting blue-green eyes.

'Ingrid!' He was too stunned to say anything else. 'Dear, dear Ingrid.'

With a look of complete astonishment, she flung her arms around his neck and pressed her cheek against his. 'Bill . . . Bill . . . Oh God . . . It's you . . . Don't say anything. Just don't say anything,' she whispered. 'Please . . . hold me.' Bill put his arms around her shuddering body. He felt how thin she was beneath her expensive gown.

Good natured whistles and catcalls echoed round the bar. They drew apart, laughing with embarrassment, and sat down at a corner table. For Bill, seeing Ingrid was like a blow in the stomach. She brought a vivid recall of the past. Suddenly, he could visualise Marie sitting beside her cousin as clearly as if she were real. The pain was almost unendurable. He tried not to show how moved he felt. He said: 'This calls for a celebration.' He attracted the attention of the barman. There was no champagne and they settled on Scotch to toast their reunion.

Ingrid had changed since he saw her last, Bill observed. Her thinness made her eyes look even larger. With her white face, pointed chin and slanting eyes, she resembled a mythical sprite. Bill felt a surge of compassion for what she had suffered.

'Oh Bill! Thank God we met. I can't tell you what it's like to be alone in a foreign country . . . I long for Vienna, but those days have gone for ever. I mustn't dwell on the past. Now you're here in the present and I'm grateful.'

Feeling obscurely threatened, Bill listened to Ingrid babbling on. He took her proffered hand and squeezed it in his.

'It's not bad. Oh no! Don't get me wrong,' she was saying. 'The girls at the factory are very kind, but I'm a stranger here ... and I'm homesick ...'

So she had work, that was something. He would do whatever he could for her, Bill promised himself. He owed that to Marie.

Ingrid listened to her voice aimlessly rambling on and tried to pull herself together. The shock of seeing Bill had almost caused her to break down. She had an almost irresistible impulse to tell him the mess she was in and beg him to extricate her from the nightmare she lived. She felt the same old attraction and once again it weakened her loins, brought sticky heat between her thighs and an overwhelming need to clutch him close to her.

I can't afford to be a woman, she thought. To her horror she felt tears pouring down her cheeks. 'You remind me of Vienna and Marietta, and our happy past,' she said with a surge of pure inspiration. 'I'm sorry, I'm embarrassing us both.'

Bill put his arm around her frail, trembling body. 'Don't cry ... I miss her, too, you know, dreadfully.' He almost choked on the last word, and with a visible effort shook off his memories. 'This won't do either of us any good, let me get us some food and you can tell me what you're up to.'

While they ate a pub lunch, she told him about her life in London to date. Bill marvelled at the coincidence which had led her to come here of all places.

He gripped her hand and squeezed it. 'I must be back in the office by two-thirty,' he said, 'but how about Sunday? Are you free?'

She nodded and smiled tremulously. Part of her was crowing with triumph. She'd pulled it off! What an actress she was! Bill was as good as hooked. Yet underneath, a small voice was saying, 'You weren't acting, Ingrid. You love him. You always will. And now you must deceive and betray the man you love.'

'I'll pick you up at eleven,' Bill was saying. 'If that's suitable, of course. Write down your address here.' He handed her a pen and pad.

'But Bill.' She became aware of how he was dressed and managed to sound puzzled and slightly disappointed as she gazed at his civilian clothes. 'You always said you were going to join up.'

It was the kind of remark Bill hated. 'I have a cushy job in civvy street instead,' he retorted.

Bill arrived home late that night, but instead of rushing to bath and getting into bed, which was his usual routine, he poured himself a stiff Scotch and sat in his one and only armchair, in his shoddy room, absorbed by the past. He could not banish his memory of Marie, looking lost but determined, as she sat on the train in Vienna, guarding her refugee children. He had always loved her, but on that night he became inextricably bound to her forever. Now she was gone and fate had thrust Ingrid into his life.

Bill drained his glass and stood up. He had a hard day tomorrow and he needed his sleep, but his memories of Marie kept him awake for most of the night.

Lieutenant Anton Klima, of the Free Czech Liberation Movement, stirred restlessly in his poky, Baker Street office. It was a semi-basement, looking up to London's pedestrians, splashing past in galoshes and boots. The rain fell in dirty trickles into the drain outside the window, adding a dismal background dirge to a thoroughly depressing scene. He sighed and longed for the hills and lakes of his native Bohemia.

He frowned as he re-read the message he had just decoded: a research project believed to be for a new type of missile . . . or a new type of missile fuel . . .

He called to his colleague, who was also his cousin. 'Hey, Miro, take a look at this.' Miro was an oddity in their blond-haired, blue-eyed family. He looked like a Turk, and he was different in his ways: introverted, restless, and very clever.

'Have we had messages from this agent before?' Miro asked.

'He's new, but some weeks ago, Jan warned us to expect another radio operator – code name Edelweiss.'

Miro lit a cigarette and perched on the edge of Anton's desk. 'We'd better make sure it's from a genuine source ... contact the Wolf. Yes, and Kolar's group.'

'Will do.'

A day later, Anton asked Bill to drop round to their office. After welcoming the big American into their tiny quarters he handed Bill the decoded message.

'We received this yesterday. Edelweiss is authentic, we've checked. He's some sort of assistant to Jan.'

Bill immediately visualised the enigmatic face of the Count's driver and he physically shook his head to clear away the memories. He scanned the transcribed message: ... *believed to be engaged in research into long-range missiles, an advanced missile fuel ... research plant in a converted mine. ...*

With a shiver of excitement, Bill wondered if they'd hit the jackpot at last. 'Okay. There's not much to go on, but it seems we have something. Send a message back to Edelweiss. Tell him to get more information ... somehow. Ask if they could just find out the names of the. German scientists working in the mine. They must have families nearby. That would help us a good deal. We know what subjects most of them specialised in, and just how good they were, prior to the war. Meantime, I'll pass this info up the line.'

Chapter  58

FOR THE FIRST TIME since Bill had begun working for Schofield, he used some of his petrol ration for pleasure and on the Sunday drove Ingrid to Oxfordshire for a pub lunch. Later they walked along the river bank, enjoying the hot August afternoon, and leaned over the bridge to talk about any old thing except pre-war Vienna. After a while, Ingrid reached out and took his hand. Bill could feel her fingers caressing and kneading his palm and wrist. Unexpectedly, she wound her arms around his neck, brushing his lips with hers.

Bill kissed her gently, trying to keep sex out of the embrace. When he felt her body pressing against his, and her tongue moving against his lips, he pushed her gently away. 'Ingrid, you don't want to start something between us, do you?' He bent forward and stroked her face with his finger, outlining her lips, her nose and the beautiful line of her cheek. 'I'm sure you know what a desirable woman you are. Those appalling experiences you endured haven't spoiled your looks. If anything, you're even lovelier. But even though she's gone, I still love Marie.'

Ingrid pouted. 'I was only flirting. I wasn't proposing marriage. I wanted a little warmth, a little love, perhaps something to tide us both over until the war ends.'

Bill put his arm round her in what he hoped was a brotherly

346

gesture. 'I was thoughtless once,' he began clumsily, feeling the need to clear the air between them. 'You were hurt and I felt a heel for months. Well ... to tell the truth, I still feel bad about it. I don't want to hurt you again, Ingrid.'

'Stop being so serious.'

'Okay. I'm sorry.' He kissed her on her cheek and hugged her tightly against him. Perhaps that was what they both needed, someone to hang on to for a short-term affair. An interval of warmth and happiness. Was that so bad? All over England, men and women were snatching what comfort they could, never knowing how long they would survive, or whether they would see the end of the week, never mind the end of the war.

It began to rain. 'That's England for you,' Bill said, feeling glad of the reprieve. 'One minute you have a fine day, and then it's pouring. Damn!'

They ran back to the car and on the drive back to town chatted easily about nothing important.

Bill left Ingrid sitting in the car outside his block of flats, while he stopped to pick up a raincoat. 'I'm not going to take you inside. It's the shoddiest apartment imaginable and down in the dungeons,' he told her.

By the time he returned the rain had turned torrential, so they settled for the cinema and saw Walt Disney's *Dumbo*.

While Bill was driving Ingrid home, he tried to explain why he was inextricably bound to the past. 'Most of the time I think about my work. I've kept my emotions tucked out of sight for the past two and a half years, but seeing you ... well, it sort of made everything fresh again.' Bill stretched out and gripped her hand. 'I still love Marie.' He cleared his throat. 'Only she's dead. I've got to get over her. When she was arrested I nearly went crazy . . .' He broke off.

'Bill, don't feel alone. I loved her, too. That gives us a bond, doesn't it? Let's be friends, we both need it.'

He parked outside Ingrid's cottage and opened the door for her. She kissed Bill lightly on the cheek and ran inside. As she leant against the door, listening to the sound of the engine fade away, she dropped her mask. There was anger and sadness on her face, but lately she had acquired a new expression: a certain stealthy wariness, like a predatory cat crossing the road on a dark night.

She took a deep breath. 'Oh God. There's no future for failures. Not in my situation,' she whispered to the empty hallway. The thought of what Paddy might do to her if she didn't succeed with Bill made her feel sick, but even stronger was her sense of rejection. 'Damn him! He's in love with a corpse. Why can't he take me. I'm living . . . and I'm longing for him.' With gritty determination, she went to her bedroom and with feminine calculation changed her clothes. Fifteen minutes later she left the house and was lucky enough to find a late taxi.

The driver dropped her outside Bill's flat. She was shaking as she made her way through the dark interior to the basement. She could hear the sound of running water behind the door and she knocked loudly. After a while she heard footsteps. The door swung open and Bill stood there, naked except for a towel wrapped round his lower torso.

'Ingrid!' He swore quietly, pulled her inside and shut the door. Then he pulled down the blackout and switched on the light. 'What is it? What's the matter?'

'Bill, listen to me,' she pleaded urgently. 'I love you. There's no point in trying to stop me from getting hurt. I've always loved you. Let me have a little of you . . . please Bill.'

The words kept tumbling out. She wasn't sure whether this outpouring of emotion was real or whether she was the world's most accomplished actress. And when Bill put his arms around her, her tears and gratitude felt real. When she wrapped her arms around his naked torso, her longing felt real, too.

She looked up and saw pity in Bill's eyes. Damn him! Trying to conceal her desperation, she took off her raincoat and laid it over the chair. She was surprised to find herself trembling. But why? He was only one in a long line of men. Not true, she knew. Bill was special.

Her skin was tingling, her lips felt dry and feverish, her eyes were burning, and she was panting slightly. She took off her blouse and skirt and flung them on the bed. She fumbled with

her bra, and all the while Bill was staring at her with the
strangest expression in his eyes. How dare he feel sorry for her.
She flung the bra on the floor. Suddenly her eyes were
brimming with scalding tears and she couldn't see.

To Bill, the sight of Ingrid's genuine hurt was baffling. What
had he ever done to provoke this adoration? Years back in
Vienna he'd been sure that she was simply after the Roth
fortune. Perhaps he'd been wrong. After all, he'd been wrong
about so many things concerning Ingrid. Her dedication in
fighting the Nazis had been a complete shock.

He watched her moodily as she stripped. He longed for more
than she was offering, both physically and mentally. On the few
occasions when he had bedded British girls, he'd gone for milky
white complexions, full, firm breasts and shapely hips. He liked
to feel soft flesh in his hands. Something substantial! But here
was this wraithlike girl, naked and begging for love. Perhaps he
could forget Marie ... accept second-best ... but Ingrid
deserved more than that. There was no denying her beauty and
her need. He said: 'Dearest Ingrid, please don't cry,' and folded
her shivering body in his arms. 'I'm not running away,' he said
mildly. 'For starters, I've got no pants on. Relax.'

What gave him the right to be so damned patronising? Damn
him and damn Paddy and Fernando and Hugo to hell. All of them!

She burst into angry sobs. 'I hate you,' she whispered.

'Do you? You're confusing me.' He began to draw away. She
ran her hands over his chest and fought for control. She mustn't
give way to the storm of emotions raging inside her. She had a
job to do and she must be calm and fully in control of herself.
When she felt his sensuous lips touching hers, it was like
nothing she had ever experienced. She seemed to lose herself in
Bill. For a while there was no other existence but his moist and
sensual mouth and his tongue probing hers. Then his hand
moved to her breasts and fondled and caressed her. She felt her
body throbbing with desire and Bill was stiffening, growing and
pulsating against her belly.

He picked her up and carried her gently to the bed, and lay
beside her, tracing his forefinger around her cheeks.

'You're a wonderful girl, Ingrid. I admire you so much.'

Admire? Why not love? she shrieked silently. She saw the slow, sullen rise of passion in his eyes as she waited, with bated breath and sweet agonised longing, for him to make this final movement that would join them. She felt utterly abandoned. She was his, the ready partner for his thrusting penis. When he entered her, it was the most poignant moment she had ever experienced. It felt so right, so natural, and her deeply suppressed physical longing for him came bubbling out in wonder.

'It's so beautiful,' she moaned.

Her hands stroked his back, feeling the soft hairs on his firm, wonderful skin, the supple muscles rippling under his smooth flesh, his tight buttocks rising and falling. Sudden flames of feeling seared her stomach and her thighs. In a crescendo of pleasure she screamed, gasped, and lost herself in wonder.

He came soon afterwards, and lay there with his arms around her and his wilting penis still inside her. Now she could feel the slackness of his balls against her inner thighs. All that essence of Bill was inside her.

Eventually he rolled aside and pulled her against his shoulder. He glanced sideways at her, a trace of awkwardness in his gaze.

'Now I know what it's *really* all about,' Ingrid said, with a secret smile. 'Now I know why I have always loved you.' She felt briefly suffused with happiness.

'You're pretty hot stuff yourself.'

No mention of love, she noticed, suppressing a sigh, but maybe with time Bill would learn to love her.

'Scotch?' he was saying, 'or what?'

'Scotch, or anything. Mmm.' She lay back and stretched like a cat, listening to him moving around the kitchen. Then she got out of the bed in a swift, decisive gesture.

She looked around the room and giggled. It was long and shadowy. One wall was covered with a gilt-framed mirror, looking into its green depths made her feel she had been long submerged under the sea. An old and broken chandelier hung from the ceiling, the sofa and armchairs were over-stuffed and full of holes.

'It's too much, too much! I've never seen anything like it. It's a gem. The shoddiest place in the world,' she said as Bill came in with two tumblers of warm whisky.

'But it's home,' he grinned.

They lay on the bed in companionable silence sipping their drinks. In Ingrid's mind was a terrible fear that she had overstepped the limits of her control. How could she withstand real feeling in this macabre world of make-believe she inhabited? She felt more afraid than she had ever been. In an attempt to dispel her morbid thoughts, she turned to him.

'Bill,' she asked. 'Why aren't you in uniform?'

'Heart problem.' Then in a quick decisive gesture, he turned her on to her back and climbed between her thighs.

'Heart problem,' she murmured incredulously, as he made love again. Later, she remembered why she was there and she began to question him as he lay drowsy and replete.

'Where d'you work, Bill? In London?'

'Uh-huh.'

'So what do you do all day in this "cushy" job?'

'Ingrid, stop prying, you know the rules. I may not be on active service, but I'm still with the military.'

'Well, don't you have a rank?'

'Sure, I'm a captain. You mustn't ask about my work.' His hand reached over and fumbled with her breasts. Ingrid abandoned her questioning and gave in to her own desires.

Bill rose early and woke Ingrid with a cup of tasteless coffee. 'You can use the bathroom first, that way you'll get some hot water. It's only for early birds.'

She laughed. Swinging her legs over the bed, she stood up and stretched. 'I'll bath at home. Don't worry, I'll take a taxi. How about dinner tonight?'

'Sorry. I can't.'

'You say when.'

'Maybe Saturday. I'll be in touch.'

She put on her clothes feeling she'd been used.

'Darling, I've got to hurry.' Bill kissed her briefly. 'Goodbye pet. See you soon.' He disappeared into the bathroom and shortly afterwards she heard him whistling over the sound of running water.

Bill's briefcase lay by the door. It was not locked, but her hands were shaking so much she could hardly open it. I'm never this nervous, she cursed under her breath. This was no time for weakness. She was playing for her own survival. She took her camera out of her bag.

Months had passed since Bill first heard about the Richard's Mine research project, but still they had no proof of what was happening there. It had been mooted that they should try and send in some undercover operatives. It was an idea which appealed to Bill, but Schofield believed the risks outweighed the chances of any success. But precious time was passing as they argued the point and Bill resolved to try once more to get his superior to see things his way.

'We've let too many weeks go by, sir. Trouble is, there's so little to go on. Just the hearsay of these two men, both ex-prisoners. Let's face it, the very fact that the mine security is so good means that there must be something worth guarding in there.'

Schofield sighed. 'I'm learning to respect your hunches. What do you think is going on there?'

'It's like this, Sir. Back in 1938, Albert Einstein warned President Roosevelt that the Nazis could develop an atom bomb first. We can't afford to ignore this possibility. Even if the war was virtually won ... if the Germans manage to produce that bomb, together with long range missiles, they would have the Allies over a barrel. Enemy missiles could be launched from Czechoslovakia, or Poland, or the Low Countries. It's not impossible. It will take us over a year, maybe longer to win the war as it is now. That gives them ample time to manufacture the bombs.'

'Hm! I'm inclined to agree with you. So we assume that the warhead being developed in Czechoslovakia, under conditions of the greatest secrecy, could be the much-flaunted V3, which Hitler is hoping will win him the war.'

'Exactly, sir. It's time to get moving.'

'This matter has gone to the very highest level,' Schofield said. 'I don't have the authority to mount the mission you propose, but I am charged with gathering more information, so tell your Czech friends to get us more details.'

'OK,' Bill stood up. 'I'll try and push them harder.'

After he'd gone, Schofield stared at his desk, obsessed with his own personal anxieties, pondering over the cruel games fate liked to play. In the past two years, Bill Roth had proved to be the finest officer in his group. The man had also become his friend, despite their age difference. What he hadn't disclosed to Bill was that he'd been told to suggest a good team for training in case it was decided to drop them into Prague to join the Underground. Their mission was near-impossible ... to delay V-3 production so that the rockets were never fired, but without destroying the plant or the research which had to remain intact for the Allies at the war's end. If the Soviets took Czechoslovakia first, they must be prepared to blow up the mine and themselves with it, rather than let the Soviets take control of the scientists and the research.

On paper it was a certain suicide mission, but how could he send Bill Roth? He had to admit that Roth was the best man to head the team of saboteurs and the mission was important enough to warrant wasting this fine officer, but he didn't want to make the decision.

Chapter  59

THE PUBLIC LIBRARY AT CHALK FARM always depressed Ingrid, although she was never sure why. People stared at her, although she went to some pains to look like them, and that morning she was wearing an old gaberdine raincoat with her hair pushed into a thick net. Nevertheless, they all looked up as she walked in.

She tried not to glance at the posters on the wall, but she never succeeded in ignoring them. *Be like Dad, Keep Mum*, reminded the locals of the danger of spies around them. *Careless talk costs lives* was another. They always jolted her out of her world of make-believe and back into the dangerous, treacherous present. *If she were caught . . .*

If only Fernando and the rotten world she was trapped in would disappear. If only she could be free of it. There was only one escape route . . . If Bill were to marry her and take her back to the States she would be free of them all.

Tearing her glance from the posters, she passed the counter. The librarian, a small woman with rimless glasses, iron-grey hair and a sour expression, sat behind the desk pounding books with her stamp. Her name was Annie Atkinson and Ingrid disliked her. Annie had nothing better to do than poke her nose into other people's business. 'Ah ha! Our one and only celebrity, Princess Pluck,' she said in her unpleasant nasal whine. 'What brings you here so early in the morning? I haven't seen your picture in the papers for a long time. Come to think of it, I haven't seen you here, either.'

'I've been away,' Ingrid lied.

'Lucky you,' Annie said, her eyes glittering with envy. 'There's a new historical romance in. It's all about the Habsburgs. Just up your street. Here it is . . .' She thrust a book at Ingrid.

'No . . . thanks . . . I'll just look around.' Ingrid had been told to leave her films in the Irish literature section, and she needed to take a book from those shelves as part of her cover. 'Please don't bother yourself, Miss Atkinson. I prefer to manage on my own.' She could sense the woman's malice as she hurried down the aisles.

Fernando was hunched over a table reading the morning newspaper. She walked past him without looking at him, made a pretence of selecting a book and thrust her microfilms deep into the shelf, leaving two books slightly extended in the row.

'Yeats?' Annie said, when she returned to the counter, looking at her in amazement. 'Collected Works and an analysis! Oh my! We're an intellectual, are we? I look forward to hearing your views on Yeats.' She sniffed again and stamped the book with extra venom.

Refusing to rise to her sarcasm, Ingrid smiled briefly and briskly made her way out.

Ingrid trudged home feeling tired out. She was overworked, as most people were. On her few free evenings, Bill tried to be with her, but all too often a hasty call cancelled dinner. This evening she had planned something special. She'd managed to buy a bottle of French wine on the black market, which would be marvellous with two small pieces of steak she'd coaxed out of the butcher.

Bill arrived at ten, carrying a briefcase full of work that had to be finished before morning, he told her. Lately he always looked so tired, too. He went into the dining-room and spread his work on the table. After a few moments he shut the door, leaving her alone in the kitchen to warm up the ruined food.

She couldn't help feeling depressed. She'd got nowhere with Bill. She'd been so sure that she could make him fall in love with her, but he had not. He stayed over two or three nights a week, but he'd retained the independence of his own flat. He was not committed. Probably, he never would be.

Dinner was a disaster. His late arrival had ruined her careful plans, the meat was over-cooked, the wine tasted like vinegar and the potatoes brackish and watery, but Bill munched everything distractedly.

'What are you thinking about?'

'Just work. I'm sorry, Ingrid. Please forgive me. Something happened today . . . of course, I can't talk about it, but I think maybe we finally hit the jackpot. I'm sorry, I'm not much company, am I?'

She reached across the table and thrust her hand into his.

'Bill, darling, after the war . . . well, I mean . . . you'll go back to the States, won't you?'

'Uh-huh.'

'Do you think that you and I . . .'

Bill glanced at his watch and leaped up with an exclamation of disgust. 'Goddammit, we nearly missed the news.'

Was he deliberately fobbing her off? Ingrid wondered.

The wireless took its usual interminable time to warm up, but eventually the announcer's voice came through:

'*Good-evening. This is the Home Service of the BBC. It is Thursday, September 16, 1943. Here are the news headlines, read by Alvar Lidell. The Germans are retreating from Salerno as the Allies advance in a continuous line across Southern Italy. Troops in the Soviet Union, are continuing to advance and are on the outskirts of Smolensk. The tide has turned in the Battle of the Atlantic, and the U-boats are on the run . . .*'

'Not much change since yesterday,' Bill said, at the end of the bulletin. 'It's only a matter of time now . . .'

'How can you be so sure?' she blurted out and instantly regretted it. Could they lose the war? Was it possible? Ingrid's stomach contracted in painful twinges. She dared not look at Bill. She was too afraid that he might read her expression of fear and misery. Once again she was drawn to the inescapable conclusion that there was only one way out for her. She gazed at the debris of the meal and tried to rehearse exactly what she should say to Bill.

'Ingrid, you're not concentrating,' she heard.

Looking up, she realised that Bill had been talking to her. He was showing her a map he'd sketched on a message pad. She struggled to concentrate. He was explaining to her exactly why the Germans could never win the war. Oh God! How could he know? She placed her hand over his.

'Make love to me. I want you to love me tonight. I want to feel I belong to you. I love you, Bill.'

Bill sighed. At that moment he wished he were anywhere but there. Was he doomed to repeat the whole Vienna fiasco? How could he let himself fall into the same trap twice over? There must be something wrong with me, he thought, I never learn.

Putting his qualms aside, he held her in his arms and kissed her tenderly. Dear Ingrid, he had so much compassion for her ... and lust. Did lust plus compassion equal love? It was an equation which bothered him whenever he thought about it. Would he ever be able to bury his ghosts? Probably not.

'What are you thinking? You're so far away.'

'No,' he lied. 'I'm not.' He turned his attention to Ingrid, but this evening she was insatiable. She came again and again, and each time she exploded into loud sobs and clung to him.

Desire fled and Bill gave up. He pulled her on to his shoulder. 'I'm bushed,' he said.

'The war is going to end one day. Will you go back to America?' she asked.

'Maybe!'

'Could we go together?' Bill pretended to be asleep, but the next moment, Ingrid leaped out of bed, flinging the blankets on to the floor.

'Forget what I said,' she snarled. 'I must be drunk. I'll make some cocoa.'

He didn't try to stop her, but lay back in exasperation as he listened to her clattering in the kitchen. He felt a heel, but how could he marry her?

'You fool,' Ingrid muttered as she retrieved the sleeping pills from their hiding place. Fernando had given them to her and they worked like a charm, but she hated drugging Bill. Lately he complained of feeling muzzy in the morning and always waking with a headache.

Twenty minutes later Ingrid had Bill's case unlocked and his papers spread over the desk. She photographed each page. After a while, she paused and tiptoed to the bedroom door, but Bill was breathing heavily, so she carried on.

Her eye caught the name Edelweiss on the sheet she was photographing. She paused in her task and began to read the paper ... *believed to be the V-3 ... vital research ... prisoners en-route to the extermination camps ... instructions needed ...* Then, to her surprise, she found a Czech phrase book under the papers. Many of the words were ticked or under-scored and the book was dog-eared. Why was Bill learning Czech?

She was so engrossed that she hadn't registered the air-raid siren and the distant clamour of the ack-ack guns. Suddenly there was a massive explosion and the lights failed. The floor lurched, her stomach jolted up and banged against her ribs. She was flung forward over the table as glass showered across the room. Ingrid lost consciousness.

Was it minutes or hours later when she dragged herself to her feet? Oh God! Her camera was lying on the floor. She grabbed it, thrust it into her dressing-gown pocket and looked around. The window was swinging open crazily, papers were scattered all over the place. She could hear Bill's shuffling footsteps. There was no time to put anything away. The next moment he appeared, dishevelled and half asleep.

'Are you all right?' he said, shining his torch into her face.

She shielded her eyes with her hand and burst into tears.

Bill put his arms around her. 'Sweet Jesus! What happened?'

'I heard the siren,' Ingrid gabbled. 'I came here and . . . I simply don't remember another thing. Look what the blast did. It blew the window open.'

Bill looked in horror at his briefcase. 'I must have forgotten to lock it. Goddammit!' he swore. He began shuffling his papers together, swaying on his feet. She could see how muzzy he felt. 'I must have gotten drunk,' he said, looking apologetic. 'I had no idea I'd had so much. Heck! I'll have to be more careful in future.'

Chapter  60

'SO,' JAN SAID, climbing down the ladder from the radio in the loft. 'I have decoded a message from London. It's all settled at last. The British want us to send them Professor Ludvik Alesh, now all we have to do is to get him to Switzerland.'

'Why not the moon?' As Marietta struggled to load the lorry with empty milk churns, she felt depressed. Last night she had dreamed of Bill. It had been a poignant, fulfilling dream and so real that when she woke she had cried with longing.

'Have faith, little one. If I tell you how we're going to pull it off, will you do as I ask? Now listen . . .'

Frau Mira Alesh was in the garden pruning the roses. She was a tall woman with thick brown eyebrows, a round face with pleasant, regular features and laughing eyes that slanted down at the corners. In her blue woollen jersey and tweed skirt, she looked the perfect helpmate for a man at the top of his career. Her mother-in-law, Erica, was sitting on a garden bench, huddled in a fur coat, with her back turned. Marietta could see her blue-white hair and the blue of her thick stockings.

'I've brought some flowers, Ma'am,' Marietta said, trying to look brisk, as she walked towards the front door. 'They're heavy,' she added as Frau Alesh held out her hands. Her

360

mother-in-law followed, looking curious.

Mira opened the door and led Marietta into the house. 'I wasn't expecting . . .' she began, reaching for the card.

'You were Frau Erica Goldstein, weren't you?' Marietta asked, turning to the older woman. 'I'm a member of the Czech Resistance. I came to warn you . . . please listen to me . . . you're in danger.'

Mira stood up. She looked both angry and bewildered. 'This is ridiculous. Our name is Alesh. Get out . . . I'm going to call the police.'

'Wait a minute.' Mira's mother-in-law looked pale, but from her fierce eyes and calm manner, Marietta guessed she was a fighter. 'Just tell me why you're here and be quick. Mira, please . . . let's listen to her.'

Marietta began to breathe easier as she turned to Mira. 'One of our contacts in the Gestapo informed us that your mother-in-law, Frau Erica Alesh, and her family, including your children, are scheduled for resettlement. Perhaps you didn't know that your husband's family were Jewish. They changed their name when Ludvik was a boy.'

'Ludvik . . . a Jew? I don't believe you.' Clearly, she did, for she suddenly crumpled on to a chair.

Erica was as white as a sheet. 'How did they find out . . . ?'

'Counter checking records in Rumania, Ma'am. You were able to pay for a false entry in Prague parish records registering your birth, but your real records are in the synagogue in your birthplace, Rumania, once Transylvania. Recently the Germans double-checked the records. Your son is on the list, too.'

'Mira,' Erica began with a deep sigh. 'I'm sorry.'

It took ten days for Marie to finalise her plans. A time of tension, for it seemed that Mira was verging on a breakdown. Klaus Kolar had been given the task of following her to keep an eye on her, while also giving her the impression that the Gestapo were on her trail. He reported that she had burst into tears at a restaurant on the second day. On the third day, she had raced to her children's school and brought them home.

Erica was of sterner material. She calmly went about her normal routine as if nothing had happened.

'So what's the plan?' Marietta plagued Jan. 'What are you doing about the Professor?'

'All I can tell you is that Herr Professor is going to collapse at work. He will complain of overwork and strain. The mine's medical staff will do what they have always done and prescribe a week at one of the Nazi's rest camps. Alesh will choose Franzenbad, near Cheb, the Nazis' favourite spa.

'You will concentrate on the rest of the family. We have contacted Pastor Perwe. A member of his chain will take over once you get them over the hills into Austria. Use the route you yourself took. Do you need my help?'

'Yes,' she said firmly. If only she had Jan's attitude to life and war, she thought later. It was midnight. Jan had disappeared via the river and Marietta knew that she might not see him for days. 'You win some, you lose some,' was his creed. For her, failure was inconceivable. She had a sacred trust to get this family to safety. She sat up all night worrying about her mission.

Hugo had been recalled to Berlin for a meeting at Gestapo headquarters, but his plane was delayed and it was nearly midnight when he was shown into an enormous, oak-panelled room with a highly-polished boardroom table and a well-stocked bar beyond. Several high-ranking SS officers were gathered around the table, and at the end of it sat Heinrich Himmler.

Hugo feared Himmler more than any other man, including the Führer. For years, Himmler had been worming himself up the ladder until he was head of the Gestapo and the SS. He personally controlled the Death's Head units that ran the concentration camps. Recently, he had been appointed Military Commander-in-Chief of the Army Reserve. Himmler had reached the pinnacle of Nazi power and Hugo knew that he would ruthlessly crush anyone who opposed him. He never underestimated him.

'Heil Hitler,' Hugo said, giving the Nazi salute.

'Welcome, von Hesse, welcome,' Himmler said in his soft, insidious voice. 'Glad you arrived at last. Travelling is becoming hazardous ...' his voice tailed off as someone handed Hugo a glass of brandy and introduced him to the other officers.

'Whatever is discussed here will not be mentioned again,' Himmler said. 'So we can all feel at ease ...' he fiddled with his glass, his gaze fixed on his small, white hands.

'We called you here, von Hesse, because we have had disquieting news. General Wolf von Doerr, of the Abwehr,' he nodded towards a dour faced man to his right, 'has drawn our attention to some serious indiscretions.'

Hugo watched the General curiously. He knew how much Himmler feared and despised the Abwehr. This organisation, which had always been in charge of German military intelligence, frequently came into conflict with the Gestapo's activities. The two organisations often ran parallel, and both had spies overseas. As a military, rather than a Nazi Party organisation, the Abwehr attracted non-Nazis and opponents of the regime. Hugo hoped his face was not showing the anxiety he felt.

'Before we get to this extraordinary lapse in security, I want to hear your opinion on the war, General von Hesse. Can Germany win the war without the V-3? What do you think?'

Another shiver of apprehension ran down Hugo's spine. Any talk of losing the war was labelled defeatist, even treasonable and severely punished. Himmler seemed to sense his concern.

'Feel free to talk confidentially, but truthfully,' he added.

Hugo was a fast thinker. He decided to speak in guarded, general terms. He stood up slowly.

'I'm sure we all understand the curious phenomenon of war which always puts the aggressor nation at an advantage,' he said. 'It is their ability to mass-produce the most modern of armaments in advance. For instance, a tank has nearly 7,000 assemblies which are made from about 40,000 parts. To build a prototype tank takes highly skilled workmen one to two years. Add another year to get the assembly line in operation. But once the tank is in production, output can leap to thousands a month, but it takes three years to do this. So winning a war is mainly to do with the production of superior arms.

'That explains why there's an overwhelming advantage to the aggressor. Only that country knows when the first blow will be struck. It's up to this nation to win quickly, within three years, before his advantage lapses.'

Hugo glanced round the table and noticed how startled everyone looked. He decided to soft-talk them. 'We have to make our own decision as to whether the German soldier's natural superiority in bravery and intelligence will withstand the coming massive technological advantage the Allies now have.'

He sat down abruptly. Had he said too much? He sensed their antipathy. His mouth was dry as he reached for his brandy.

'And with the V-3?' Himmler asked, his eyes glinting dangerously.

'Ah yes.' Hugo stood up again. This time he was on strong ground. 'The V-3 will win the war without any doubt. Every weapon we know of becomes outdated in the face of nuclear power. This energy is so far beyond anything we've seen, it's hard to grasp. We would only need to drop two or three such bombs to call a halt to the war.'

'And how long will it be before we can use this new weapon?'

'Two years or more for a prototype ... The missiles are ahead of the bombs. We're working round the clock. Two years might be optimistic, but that's my private target.'

Hugo took a deep breath. He had acquitted himself well. They could draw their own obvious conclusions from the picture he had painted.

'An excellent answer, von Hesse.'

Hugo beamed, and strained forward to hear what Himmler was saying.

'Now we come to the question of security at Richard's Mine. Well, von Doerr, let's have your report.' Himmler turned to the Abwehr general.

'It's quite straightforward,' von Doerr said. 'I received this from my London contact.'

Hugo almost gasped as he listened to von Doerr reading from

a photographed paper of the derailed train and the two slave workers who had been freed by the Resistance. He had been so sure no one had known but his immediate staff.

The General reported that a Czech agent, known as Edelweiss, who had been operating in and around Prague for the past six months, had successfully derailed a train taking slave workers to the extermination camps in Poland. The slaves had been debriefed and, consequently, the Allies knew exactly where the Hitler's secret V-3 atomic missile was being developed and built.

Ashen-faced, Hugo glanced around the table. He hoped Himmler hadn't seen how his hand was shaking.

'Did you know about this matter of the escaped slave-workers?'

'Yes,' Hugo said. 'My orders were that the slaves should be executed on-site. I was disobeyed.'

'You must take the necessary action,' Himmler said. 'Identify and arrest that Edelweiss agent without delay. I'm not going to relieve you of your duties at this moment, mainly because you know more about security of the mine than any other man available. Allied agents will try to enter the plant, you can be sure of that, this is not the time to put the mine in the charge of a new man.' Himmler stared at Hugo coldly. ' Of all the losses Germany has sustained this year, I count this as the worst.'

'I agree,' Hugo said hoarsely. 'At the same time, you must know that Richard's Mine is impregnable.' He cleared his throat and hung on to his composure. 'No bomb can penetrate to the research station. The sheer slopes of the mountain make any assault impossible. There are only two entrances, from the small airfield on the roof of the mine, which is heavily guarded, or by underground railway from Theresienstadt concentration camp, which, of course, is out of the question. No one can get in or out of the camp unchallenged. We have hundreds of guards there.'

Hugo turned to von Doerr. 'How did this information come to you?'

'I'm not at liberty to reveal my sources,' von Doerr snarled.

'So there we have it,' Himmler said. 'A dangerous situation. You must ensure the mine is as impregnable as you say. Your career and the Fatherland's security depend upon this. For the time being you may go.'

Scrambling hastily to his feet, Hugo saluted and left. He would arrest Alesh as soon as he reached Prague, he decided. He wondered which of his SS agents were also in the pay of the Abwehr.

Hugo returned directly to Prague and his office in Hradcany Castle, but he had not had time to call a meeting on the mine's security before the news came that Professor Alesh and two SS agents assigned to guard the scientist had gone missing on their way to the spa. There was mist in the mountains and presumably they had wandered off the usual route, but troops were combing the forest.

Half an hour later, the bodies of the two guards were discovered. There was no sign of Professor Alesh.

In pent-up fury Hugo paced his office, longing to get his hands on the terrorists responsible for this outrage, but, other than calling out an entire SS division to guard the border areas and to comb the surrounding forests, which he had done, there wasn't much else he could do, but wait ... and the waiting was killing him.

With sudden inspiration, Hugo called the head of Richard's Mine security. The Alesh family, consisting of Ludwig's wife, mother and two sons, had left that morning to join their father for a week at the spa, he was told, but they had not arrived. Hugo's mouth was dry with fright as he put out a description of the Alesh family to all military and railway personnel in Bohemia.

Hugo poured a drink with shaking hands and tossed it back. This had to be the work of Edelweiss. Somehow he must find and arrest him. Hugo suddenly realised that he was locked in mortal combat with a man he had never seen and would not even recognise. With his third drink, some semblance of calm sunk into his psyche. After all, he had the resources of the Third

Reich at his disposal, while Edelweiss had only his wits and a few half-starved peasants to rely on.

The train was due to leave in half an hour and so far the Alesh family had not arrived. Marietta tried to keep calm as she paced the platform. She was dressed in peasant black, a scarf tied over her head, her boots soiled by the earth. She glanced at her watch.

A bustle of movement made her turn towards the barrier. The Alesh family hurried on to the platform. Marietta stared in dismay. The two women looked as if they were going to a funeral, while the boys, eleven and thirteen, hung around their mother, demanding and spoiled, wearing their Hitler Youth uniforms and gazing contemptuously at everyone who passed.

The family went into the station restaurant and Marietta positioned herself so that she could watch the restaurant entrance as well as the platform. As the train pulled in they emerged from the restaurant and struggling with their luggage, they settled themselves in an empty compartment.

Marietta grabbed her bag and boarded the train. As it started to move, she hurried along the corridor and joined the Aleshes in their compartment. She bent forward and spoke softly. 'Frau Alesh, it's time to take the boys into your confidence. Please tell them what is happening.'

Mira looked as if she would rather die. Tears glistened in her eyes.

'Must we?' Erica asked.

Marietta nodded. 'The boys must be ready to obey orders implicitly. We might run into problems. We'd have to act quickly.' Marietta turned to the eldest boy. 'Karl, thirteen is old enough to act like a man. You must look after your mother and your grandmother.'

'Who are you? I don't need to listen to you.' With pouting lips and sullen eyes, the boy turned his back and kicked his heels against the seat.

Mira closed her eyes and leaned back against the upholstered seat. 'We are forced to leave Czechoslovakia,' she said in a small,

tired voice. 'Your father and grandmother . . .' She broke off
and seemed to come to a decision. 'Your father and I are Jews
and the Nazis have found out. We could be killed if they catch
us. At the very least, we would be put into a camp. Our house
would be taken away. Jews cannot own houses. I'm sure you
know that . . .'

Marietta decided to leave the family on their own while Mira
attempted to explain their new position. When she returned to
the compartment half an hour later, the boys were subdued,
with expressions of shock and fear in their eyes.

At Pilsen they left the train and walked to another platform,
where they sat in a tense, unhappy row.

They waited for hours. Eventually a guard passed by and told
them the train had been diverted. Marietta felt heavy with
dread. It was only a matter of time before a routine check ruined
their plans.

When the next train arrived four hours later they were all
exhausted from the tension of waiting. The family found a
compartment and huddled in their seats. Marietta dug in her
bag and pulled out some bread and sausage which she sliced,
and handed to the boys, but they declined haughtily.

'You won't get another chance to eat for hours,' she said.

Kurt gave in, but Karl looked out of the window as if there
was a foul smell under his nose. Mira was too upset to notice the
boys' behaviour. She stood up abruptly. 'I'll be back soon,' she
said, looking scared. When she returned there was a sheen of
perspiration on her upper lip and her hair was damp at her
temples.

It was 10 p.m. when the ticket inspector flung open their
carriage door. His friendly manner was abruptly terminated
when he gazed at the small party. Suddenly his eyes became
wary, he hesitated, then he hurried off. Marietta's heart sank. It
was lucky that the guard seemed a simpleton. The Gestapo
would be waiting for them at Strakonice. Or perhaps they would
stop the train.

The next hour dragged slowly and, on the edge of the Boubin
Forest, the train halted at a level crossing. Marietta looked out

of the window anxiously. They were only yards from the sheltering forest. There were no waiting guards. They wouldn't get a better chance. 'Quickly . . . Jump . . . Run for the trees . . . Don't make a sound.' She pushed the boys out. 'Jump, Mira.' She took hold of Erica's arm and hustled her off the train. 'Faster,' she whispered. 'Try to run.'

They reached the trees as the train lurched forward. Thank God . . . But how long did they have? Half an hour at the most, and she had an old woman to look after. Soon, the soldiers would come with their guns and their dogs. Blanking her mind to her fears, she pushed the tired family into single file and hurried them deeper into the forest.

Chapter  61

THE NIGHT EXPRESS TO VIENNA was about to leave Prague station. The engine-driver, a short, stocky man with a shock of white hair and a pronounced limp, was shouting at the stoker. The stoker was trying his best. His dyed black hair was singed, his hands were blistered, and he could not see without his glasses.

'I'll help you when we're out of here,' Jan told him. 'Meantime stoke faster or we'll get nowhere.'

'I'm trying,' the stoker said. 'I hope you've found an easier route for Mira. She's not fond of hard work, you know.'

A hundred miles away, Mira was crying from exhaustion and fear. They had walked for five nerve-racking hours through the forest. At last they came in sight of Herr Zweig's sawmill. The old man, who had been watching out for them, hurried to meet them. 'I've been praying for you. Come inside. When I saw the troops brought into Strakonice I thought you were in trouble. Then they began to search the forests around the track, so I came straight home. I guessed you'd come here. Luckily for you the train stopped several times and they don't know where you got off. Right now they're searching further west so we've got a bit of time.'

Minutes later they were sitting on a rough bench in the millhouse, sipping hot tea and eating bread and cheese.

Marietta watched the family guardedly. Erica was calm, but exhausted, but Mira was on the point of collapse. The children were complaining of blisters and they were tired and scared.

'We're going on horseback,' Zweig told them gently. 'It doesn't matter if you can't ride, because you only have to sit tight. The horses know the way. We shall be moving fast, in single file, at first through the river and later through the bogs, so don't fall off. The Bosch don't know the route through the marsh and they wouldn't attempt to try to get through.'

Mira began to protest, but Herr Zweig cut her short. 'With respect, Ma'am, we have no other route open to us, there is no other way.'

Ten minutes later the party set off. Watching Zweig sitting erect on his lead horse, all his senses alert to the sounds of the forest, picking his route with care, calming the horses with strange crowing sounds, she knew they were in safe hands.

Just after dawn, the tired party crossed the border at four thousand feet. There was a thick mist, visibility was down to a few yards, and it was close to freezing. Soon afterwards they approached a woodsman's hut, set in dense bush along the eastern reaches of ɹne Bohmer Wald mountains. Pastor Eric Perwe materialised out of the mist and Marietta slid off her horse and ran to embrace him.

He gripped her hands. 'Well done, my dear,' he said simply.

'Troops are not far behind us. I'm sorry . . .'

'We're well organised . . . have no fear! The two women will join my convent for a few days, the boys are to leave at once. It's safer to separate them for their journey to Switzerland.'

There was a brief, tearful scene between the boys and their mother, but Erica remained calm. 'Who would believe it . . . a Jewish nun?' she muttered, a flicker of humour showing in her exhausted face.

Damn the fog, Bill thought. It was a cold November evening. He stamped his feet and shrugged into his duffle coat in the draughty waiting room at a secret RAF base outside Dover.

The airstrip came to life as the fog lifted enough to make landing possible. Bill went outside to watch as an aircraft came in low from the Channel.

The Dakota made a reasonable landing and the steps were lowered. As the door swung open, a slight figure stepped down, looking bewildered and tired. Watching Alesh, Bill felt overwhelmed with relief. He whispered a private 'thank you' to the Czech Resistance and Edelweiss, whoever he was, for a job exceptionally well done.

Hugo was at his desk at Hradcany Castle when the decoded cable was brought in by his adjutant. Professor Alesh and his family had reportedly arrived in London where they had been accepted as Jewish refugees and offered political asylum.

Hugo's hands began to shake so badly, he dropped the message on to the floor. The stab of pain in his stomach was like a knife wound. He looked up into the shrewd eyes of his assistant. 'Shall I call off the search, Sir?' he asked.

'No ... The female terrorist who accompanied the Alesh family must be caught. How many men are you deploying?'

'A hundred, Sir.'

'Treble it ... house to house searches ... comb the forests and the farms. You have twenty-four hours to find her. See to it.'

'Yes Sir!' His adjutant saluted smartly and left.

Still shaking, Hugo poured himself a brandy. He wouldn't give much for his chances when the Führer discovered that Alesh was in enemy hands.

At dawn the next morning, Hugo was wakened by a telephone call. His stomach clenched as he reached for the receiver, but it was not Berlin, as he had feared, but the security chief at the mine. There had been an explosion. The air ventilator and the electrical wiring in the rocket firing station were badly damaged. All work would have to halt for at least two weeks.

Five minutes after receiving the call, Hugo was racing

towards Theresienstadt. A massive jolt of acid to his ulcers had left him in agony. This latest disaster would undoubtedly ensure that he would be the scapegoat for the failure of the project, and he knew the sort of fate which probably awaited him.

As soon as Hugo got to Richard's Mine he was hurried to the conference room beyond the cobbled parade ground. Several worried technicians were gathered around the long table. Someone had drawn a diagram on the blackboard.

Despite their verbose explanations, their verdict came down to two words – human error. Hugo was a good listener. His eyelids lowered until he seemed to be asleep, but he was listening for a hint of nervousness or subterfuge. There was none.

Hugo took the Commandant aside and issued his orders. Even if there was no evidence of sabotage, all the unskilled slave labour from that area of the mine were to be interrogated and afterwards shot. Never again must they be sent to the death camps, it was too dangerous. All executions must be on-site.

Hugo was also worried that Edelweiss was deliberately getting his Freedom Fighters arrested in the hope that some of them would be sent to work in the mine. Well, he would outwit him and he would trap him. Eventually, the terrorist must fall into his hands.

Marietta parked outside Kladno abattoir and sat gazing at the entrance, unwilling to go inside. Her sixth sense told her that Miroslav Kova, recently recruited as their messenger, was unreliable. He was extravagantly paid to smuggle messages into the mine in carcasses and bring them out hidden in empty crates. She had met Kova once only and, as well as his shifty attitude, he had been unwashed and stank of his bloody trade, his long ginger hair unkempt, his clothes stained. With a shudder of repugnance, she forced herself to go inside.

Kova came hurrying in from the yard. He was a massive man, his hands and arms were covered in bristly ginger hairs and his pig-like eyes shone greedily at her.

'Do you have anything for me?' she said, more sharply than she had intended. Something about the veiled violence of the man frightened her. He dealt in death and he had no sensitivity to pain or suffering. She would not like to be his enemy.

'Yes.' He produced a roll of bloodstained paper.

Marietta smoothed out the crumpled sheet with shaking hands. It read: *I have been chosen. A is joining the farm labour gangs. D. has been executed, H.*

Forcing herself to be civil, Marietta thanked Kova and left the abattoir feeling sick. The death of Dietrich would devastate everyone. He was one of the first three volunteers to go into the mine and he had lasted for eight weeks. Now they would have to send more men in. And for what? Production had been held up for a week or two. Was that worth a life? That night she radioed London, asking for trained saboteurs to be dropped in to take over the mission.

'Well Roth! How's it going?'

Schofield looked tired, Bill thought. It was late in January, 1944, and Britain was fast turning into a gigantic off-loading ramp. Shiploads of American troops and equipment were pouring into Britain daily. There was so much to be done and the Major had to run most of the SOE Eastern European departments single-handed. He had his key men, but he carried all the responsibility and it showed.

The war was being won. It was only a matter of time. Last night, thousands of British and American troops had stormed ashore at Anzio, just thirty miles south of Rome and were thrusting swiftly eastwards to cut the supply lines of the 100,000 German troops at the front. The RAF were blasting Berlin nightly. Over 17,000 tons of bombs had fallen on the German capital during the past two months. Bill knew how desperate the Nazis must be to get their V-3 into operation. He said: 'I had to let Alesh go, Sir. He's flying to the States tonight. Back home they're really squealing. They want him as of yesterday.'

'I have your report here,' Schofield said. 'It'll take me a week to read it.' He wrapped it with his knuckles. 'Give me the gist of it – what the hell is going on over there?'

'We don't know whether or not they're ahead of us in atomic research, because that's not Alesh's field. The bad news is they're definitely ahead of us in missile development. According to the brains who've been debriefing Alesh, this advance could prove disastrous. The German V-3 is a missile carrying a warhead whose true power and side effects are quite unknown,' Bill went on. 'The damn thing is housed in one of the safest locations in the world. It's totally impervious to conventional bombing. Professor Alesh has confirmed the suspicions of the Resistance, that this is Hitler's much publicised V-3 weapon.

'Now, Sir, according to Edelweiss's latest report, two Czech Freedom Fighters have managed to penetrate the research plant by getting themselves arrested and incorporated into the slave labour gangs taken to the mine. The first one trained some of the inmates and they managed to set off an explosion which held up research for two weeks. Unfortunately, he was executed. Another has taken his place. Edelweiss wants us to drop in saboteurs and equipment and take over the entire mission.'

'The PM's office has taken a personal interest in this mission, Roth, and we're waiting on their decision. They're liaising with the White House.' Schofield frowned and fumbled with a file on his desk.

'I have here the dozens of applications you've made to be transferred to active duty. Still feel that way inclined, Roth?'

'Yes, Sir,' Bill said.

'Your wishes may yet be granted. Meantime, you're going to Scotland to be trained. One of those secret establishments for people who are to be dropped into enemy territory. In your case we'll have to make it from Friday afternoon until Monday morning, since I can't spare you during the week. Make up some story for Ingrid to explain your absence.'

Ingrid? Bill mused. How the hell did Schofield know about her? Or did he keep tabs on all his staff?

He walked out feeling more cheerful than he had for months. Things were moving at last. As he drove home he desperately tried to think of a convincing story to satisfy Ingrid, but his mind kept dwelling on the mystery of how Schofield knew about their relationship.

Chapter  62

INGRID WAITED IN A QUEUE at the library while Annie gossiped with an elderly customer. Every few seconds she rapped her fingers on the counter to show her impatience, but Annie took no notice. Having dealt with the pensioner, she was now quizzing the woman ahead about her children. They had been evacuated to Wales, Ingrid heard, but Mum had brought them home when she found they were being neglected. The children coughed and sniffed and hung around their mother's skirt. It was damp and nearly freezing, the yellow fog was curling in from cracks around the window. Ingrid felt heavy with depression.

It was her turn at last. She handed in her book, frowning with annoyance.

'Ah,' Annie said. 'One of my favourite authors. So you're a fan of Wodehouse, too?'

'No . . . yes.' Ingrid scowled at her.

Annie was not going to be put off like that. She grimaced, showing teeth as false as her smile. 'Not every foreigner can understand British humour,' she needled.

'Perhaps it's too slapstick for foreigners,' Ingrid retorted.

'Slapstick indeed!' Annie snapped. 'You might have missed

the subtlety of it.' She thumbed through the book. 'What part did you like best?'

Ingrid gaped at her. 'Why . . . I didn't read much of it . . .'

'My word! Perhaps Yeats is more to your taste. Which is your favourite poem?'

'Yeats?' What was the woman talking about?

'You never read these books you take out, do you?' Annie's expression was malevolent.

Worried by the direction the conversation was taking, Ingrid took her tickets in silence and hurried to the back of the library. She grabbed a book, pushed her envelope into the shelves and returned to the counter. She couldn't avoid the expression of amazement in Annie's eyes as she stamped Zola's *Rome*.

It was a week before Annie plucked up courage to take her suspicions about 'Princess Pluck' to the local police station. This was not the first time she had reported alleged enemy agents, so when Sergeant Hodgekiss saw her coming, he heaved a sigh and nudged his assistant, Constable Penny. ''Ere! You take over, mate. I'm going to have a cuppa.'

'She's been in the newspapers,' Annie explained excitedly. 'She's supposed to be a Habsburg princess. I have my suspicions.'

The Constable let her run on. He had never heard of the Habsburgs, but Annie was a well-read woman.

'I'll swear she never reads the books she takes out,' Annie went on. 'Besides, she behaves strangely. Everyone else browses around, but *she* rushes to a particular shelf, grabs any book and rushes out again. There's this man . . . he's either waiting around, or else he comes in shortly afterwards. A Spaniard! Dead eyes and big hands.'

'Go on,' Constable Penny said patiently.

'Well, last Friday . . .' Annie's eyes were glinting as she reached the best bit. 'I saw him take an envelope out of the shelves she'd been looking at and put it in his pocket. Now, I ask you, what would a hoity-toity Habsburg Princess want with Wodehouse?'

'I like them Jeeves books,' the Constable said. He laughed and patiently took down the details.

'Okay,' he said. 'You don't have to wait any longer.' He patted her on the shoulder. 'That's the stuff, Annie. The Fifth Column's everywhere. I'll see this gets to the right people.'

'Come in. Sit down, Roth. We've received this report, dated February 4, from the police. I want you to read it.'

The Major slid the official report of Annie's complaint across the desk. 'Unfortunately it took three weeks to reach us.'

Bill picked it up and read it. He wanted to laugh out loud. Ingrid . . . a spy! It was ludicrous. The smile died on his lips, but Ingrid had never read a book in her life. Looking up from the papers, he said: 'There must be some explanation. Perhaps she gets them for a friend.'

'Perhaps. That's what you and I must discover. How about telling me how you met her.'

'How *did* you know about me and Ingrid?' Bill asked.

'As soon as I read this report I had her background checked. I was extremely worried when I heard about your connection with her.'

Bill described Ingrid as he saw her – penniless, brave, pitting her wits against the Nazis and winning through. Somehow he couldn't get it over the right way, and Schofield remained unconvinced.

'So you're saying her political conscience came to the fore just about the same time as she was told about her inheritance. Furthermore, of all the Edelweiss students who were arrested, she alone was released from the camp and deported.'

'She was Hugo's step-sister. I believe they were quite close once.' Bill closed his eyes. He seemed to be condemning Ingrid with every sentence. 'Let me think,' he said angrily. His mind turned back . . . back to Berlin, back to Munich. Ingrid had been vivacious and lovely, but uncaring. Then she had changed. When? When dammit? The tattoo mark on her wrist? Didn't that prove something? *The mark of a martyr or the perfect cover?*

Suddenly he couldn't stop remembering the time Ingrid had

brought him those statistics about German rearmament. She had asked for the cheque to be made out to Marie, because she was in debt to her ... or so she had said. But if she had been working for Hugo ... Think! He could only remember the Edelweiss students and their terrible sentences. Had Ingrid betrayed Marietta? If he could only concentrate, but that terrible thought had addled his brains. Past images tumbled through his mind and each one of them condemned Ingrid.

'Roth!' Schofield's voice broke in on his torment. 'I know you're doing two or three jobs at once. So, how d'you fit in the work? At night? At home?'

'Of course. I stay over at her place about three nights a week. I've kept my own apartment. Never wanted to burn my bridges,' Bill mumbled. Why did Ingrid get up in the night and make him cocoa? No, but that's impossible. Crazy! He suddenly remembered the night the bomb had shattered the window. It had seemed strange that his briefcase had blown open, scattering his papers. And the safe had been open, too. How many deaths had she caused, this beautiful girl, whom he bedded night after night? Guilt surged like bile in his throat. He had helped her, unwittingly, but nevertheless he had helped her. A wave of nausea struck him and he excused himself and threw up in Schofield's private toilet.

'Steady on, Bill. Here. Have some brandy. No drink it ... I insist,' Schofield said. 'I might as well tell you that you're not the only one who fell for Ingrid's charms.'

Bill looked at his superior in astonishment. 'You ...'

'Yes. I proposed to her just before you and she ... Don't look so shocked. She's a lovely girl ...'

Bill put his head in his hands and closed his eyes. He was remembering the day she'd come to him and asked him to teach her to be a journalist. She'd wanted a list of his contacts. Jesus! Even then she'd been a spy. Six years ago. It was beginning to fit together. She was Hugo's agent. Hugo had recruited her, trained her and put her in the camp to give her an alibi and a suitable record for the future.

Feeling disgusted with himself, Bill got up and paced the

office trying to make sense of a kaleidoscope of unbearable memories. He was living with a murderess. She had cold-bloodedly shopped her friends in Germany. Hundreds of innocents. They would never know half of it, Bill thought. Most of all, he grieved for Marietta. Suddenly Bill hated Ingrid with a passion he had never known he possessed.

And he was equally to blame. Why had he been so careless? How had he been taken in by the little actress playing the martyr, a victim of Hitler's death camps? Poor little Ingrid. Ingrid the patriot. Jesus, when he got home, he would choke the life out of her.

He wondered dully why she did it. For gain? Or was she a fanatical Nazi?

'Now listen to me, Roth,' Schofield said. 'I know this is a shock, but you have got to play along and this is what you're going to do . . .'

It was 9 p.m. Bill was late. He'd had two drinks at the pub on the corner before plucking up courage to go to Ingrid's cottage. He rang the bell and heard light footsteps in the passage. The front door was flung open and she pulled him inside.

'Bill, darling.' She threw herself into his arms and smothered him with kisses. She stepped back. 'You're so late. I thought you weren't coming. You always 'phone. Bill, what's wrong? Something's wrong!'

Bill smiled wearily. Not a very good start, if she can already see that something's wrong, he thought. 'I'm damn tired, Ingrid, and I missed you like hell.' That was the first lie. It didn't hurt all that much.

'Why are you late?' she asked.

'You know I can't tell you that, Ingrid. I'm cold and hungry.' That was the second lie. He didn't care if he never ate again.

She smiled. 'I'll feed you and warm you in bed.'

'Promise?'

She nodded. 'I've been keeping something special for you, I've got a bottle of champagne. You'll never guess where I got it.'

She gabbled on and on about her friends in the establishment set, and so-and-so's rich cousin who had received a case of champagne from a rich friend. Bill wasn't listening. He was thinking what hell it was going to be, to have to live with Ingrid now that he hated her. But she's been forced to live with me. Does she hate me? She had prostituted herself on orders from her controller. He felt sick with embarrassment when he thought back to their London reunion. What a sucker he'd been. How she must have laughed at him.

Then there was the day she had come to him and admitted that she loved him, and begged him to give her a chance. He'd been surprised at the time. It was unlike her to beg, but his male ego had encouraged him to believe that she spoke the truth. He looked up, realising that she was watching him curiously. 'I wish this training were over. It's exhausting,' he said. Then he swore. 'I shouldn't have said that. Please forget that I did.'

'Bill. Don't think I didn't guess. I'm worried sick. Just tell me that you're not going to be involved i 1 any sort of fighting.'

'You know I can't talk about my work, Ingrid.'

'Of course. But I'm so worried for you.'

'Listen, Ingrid. I'll be gone for about six months, maybe seven. If it were anyone but you, I wouldn't say a word, but you deserve my trust. You've fought the Nazis right from the very beginning.' Jesus! he thought, watching her. She can still flush. 'I'm going into occupied territory and you know why. The invasion is only months away. The Resistance must be trained. All sorts of preparations are needed. I'll be all right and I won't be far away. In fact, if I look hard enough I'll see the cliffs of Dover. If it gets rough I could even swim home. People do quite often. I shouldn't tell you this, but if you need help, you must go to my office. Here's the telephone number of someone who can help you, if you have a problem.' He gave her Schofield's number, as they had arranged.

When Bill went to bed later, he muttered that he was tired, but instantly her nubile, clinging, treacherous body was writhing against his. It was as every bit as bad as Bill had imagined it would be.

God, she was a whore! A Nazi whore! He gritted his teeth and said: 'I'm tired. I have a headache.'

To Bill's horror, he discovered he was impotent. And the more he worried about it, the worse it got. But if he did not succeed, she would suspect. She would realise that something was wrong. She was not a fool. He mustn't give her the slightest reason to distrust him. This was his atonement and that, together with his determination that she would pay for her crimes, gave him the necessary willpower.

Eventually he was able to turn his back and feign sleep. Ingrid waited for a while before creeping out of bed and going to the study, to rifle his briefcase.

'Go on, photograph every goddamned page, you Nazi whore.' He whispered into his pillow. 'Don't leave anything out. Every single document has been selected especially for you, Ingrid. You must think it's your lucky night.'

Chapter  63

BILL'S FIRST 'SCHOOL' was like nothing Bill could ever have imagined: a place staffed by cranky adventurers who were paid and housed in order to further their craziness. One afternoon, late in March, Bill saw their instructor go down and nearly drown in a midget submarine in the ornamental pond, with golden carp and water reeds. He was dragged up, in the nick of time, fronds of weeds trailing over his shoulder and several litres of murky water pouring from his blue lips. 'Not quite watertight yet,' he gasped, when he could speak.

The unarmed combat instructor, who lived on brown rice and sat cross-legged in the corner of the floor to eat, could be seen most midnights, weather permitting, making weird movements on the lawn. 'Drawing power from the universe,' he told them mysteriously. These were two amongst so many strange men. They taught him to shoot, and to fight dirty, and how to live off the land, and a variety of ways to turn ordinary items like cutlery, ballpoint pens and garden spades into lethal weapons.

Bill was training with four Czechs, all crazed with ambition to get home and kill every German they saw. Anton and Miro Klima were from his Czech office. Then there was Karol Hemzo, once a historian, now a bull of a man with a pointed black beard and shrewd, ice-blue eyes, who collected lovesick females wherever he went, and Franz Kussi, who had gained his doctorate in physics at Oxford before the war started, but had thrown up his career to join the forces. He was very thin and could be mistaken for a weak man, but he was as strong as a coil of steel wire. His dark frizzy hair, smoothed and shiny with cream, cocker spaniel eyes and olive skin made him look romantic, according to the girls working at the school. Perhaps he was in peacetime, Bill thought, but he knew him as a dedicated fighter. They had all been well-picked. Later, Bill knew, there would be many more, but these were the men who would parachute in with him. They had all volunteered to penetrate Theresienstadt concentration camp.

At the school, Bill found himself the target for hostility from many of the instructors, who seemed to think that all Americans needed pulling down a peg or two. His American accent was going to bring about his undoing within hours of dropping in, they told him contemptuously. It might even kill his comrades.

Bill tried to keep his sense of humour. He knew that Britain was full of Yankee soldiers, beaming New World charm and optimism, able to jive and hand out coffee and booze, their pockets stuffed full of cash and bars of chocolate and their evenings free, after a hard day of mock battles, gearing up for the invasion. British boys were losing out with local girls and feeling bitter about it.

After eight weekends at the combat camp came the demolition school, located in a large house near Inverness. Amongst the mature early spring flowers, on stately lawns, Bill exploded mock-ups of railway lines, bridges, interior machinery and stable walls a foot thick.

Then it was time to move on to the parachute course, which was more complicated than it should have been, mainly because of the abnormal amount of gear he would be carrying.

Bill was becoming fitter and tougher than he had been in his life and he found he enjoyed the training. Only the waiting was worrying him. Hitler's so-called first *Vergeltungswaffe* or reprisal weapon, known as the V-1, was menacing Southern

England. This pilotless, jet-propelled aircraft, known to Londoners as the doodle-bug, was capable of 400 mph and carried nearly a ton of high explosive. The bombs flew at low altitudes, powered by petrol and compressed air. So far, anti-aircraft guns were proving useless against the V-1. Production of the V-2 had been disrupted by expert RAF bombing, but it was only a matter of months before this improved rocket terrorised London.

It was the V-3 that kept Bill awake at night. Thank God hardly anyone knew about it. Would they be in time? he wondered. The training was dragging on and the SOE seemed to be in no hurry to start their mission.

'My dear fellow, you'll be there until the war ends, so what's your hurry?' Schofield countered when he complained. 'The later you go, the more chance of survival you'll have. We'll let you know when the time's ripe.'

There was nothing to do but wait, and the tension was beginning to affect Bill. Lately, Southern England was chaotic. Britain had become one huge armed camp. All coastal areas were banned to visitors, and US troops were camped on every pavement and corner of spare land. Military exercises were taking place in every second village, fake concentrations of troops and dummy ships were being moved around coastal areas to keep the enemy guessing as to where and when the strike would come. Railway timetables were being reorganised to allow hundreds of thousands of British, American and Commonwealth troops to be moved to invasion assembly points swiftly and efficiently when the time came. Villagers became used to hundreds of parachutists dropping all around them and heavily-laden gliders swooping low overhead, as the troops practised and practised again for the big day.

Bill sweated it out, wishing he could do his bit.

Then, on the morning of May 10, 1944, Bill was summoned to Schofield's office. 'Good news, Roth,' he greeted Bill, 'You've been promoted. Let me be the first one to congratulate you, Major. Secondly, I have the okay for your planned mission into

Czechoslovakia. Sorry it took so long. The decision was made right at the top. That's where we're going now, Bill, to see the Prime Minister.'

Half an hour later, they were shown into Number Ten, Downing Street, and asked to wait in a comfortable, homely sitting-room. Sharp at nine Bill Roth and Stephen Schofield were escorted to Churchill's study. Bill peered through the fog of tobacco smoke, across the dark oak-panelled room with the heavily curtained bay windows, at the man who was sitting behind his desk. Churchill seemed older than he appeared in the newspaper photographs. He had huge bags under his eyes and his chin and his heavy jowls shivered and shook as he spoke. But his blue eyes were alert and penetrating. After listening to him for a few moments, Bill realised that he was in the presence of an incredible mind and a formidable power. 'I've been keeping track of you, Roth,' he said. 'I've read most of your pre-war articles. As one ex-journalist to another, you did a good job back in '38. Appeasement was the name of the game then. The more's the pity. We were voices in the wilderness, Roth.' Bill started to murmur something, but soon realised that he had been summoned to listen, not to talk.

'It was a considerable feat to get Alesh out. Well done, my boy.'

'Sir, with respect, I merely liaised . . .'

Churchill ignored him. 'This mission you've volunteered for might call for the greatest sacrifice, Roth. I want to wish you luck and tell you that we'll all be with you, in our hearts and minds.'

Bill, swept away by the force of Churchill's rhetoric, was still trying to work out why he was there.

'There's a group of scientists known as the Berkeley Group, working at the University of California,' Churchill told him. 'They put in a classified report in May 1941, which I have here.' He tapped a folder with his finger. 'It states that a nuclear explosive cannot be made available before mid-1945, that a chain reaction in natural uranium is probably eighteen months off, and that it will take another year to produce enough plutonium for a bomb.

'Late in June, 1941, President Roosevelt personally established the Office of Scientific Research and Development,
under the direction of a top physicist. Just a few days ago, the
decision was made to go ahead and make the A-bomb.

'Now, you're going into enemy territory, Roth, and for
obvious reasons I'm not going to continue this story. Suffice it
to say that it's possible Germany and America are running neck-
and-neck in the research and development of this new and
terrible weapon. The enemy might even be ahead of us.

'That's where you come in, Roth. We don't want their plant
destroyed. We need their research, particularly in guided
missiles. Furthermore, when that area can be taken, it will be
essential that we reach the mine before the Russians do. We
don't want to capture a ruin, Roth. Remember that! We want
all their research and know-how, with their scientists alive and
kicking. You see what I mean?

'At the same time, it's essential that their development is
delayed by a series of "accidents". The Czechs must understand
that their sabotage must be limited yet effective. The Bosch
must never produce that bomb, nor fire that missile of theirs.'

Churchill paused. He began shuffling the papers on his desk.
It seemed that his mind was concentrating on something else.
But he added: 'That's a very important point. No doubt you'll
appreciate the fine line of decisions that will be required. That's
your job, Roth. A delicate job. A sensitive job.

'We'll be hard at work on our side of the project, which is
making sure British or American troops get there first, not the
Russians. You of all people will understand that such a weapon
in Russian hands might prove as disastrous as in German
hands.'

He picked up another file and began leafing through it. 'You
get over there, my boy, and stay there. We'll get to you just as
soon as we can.'

Bill and Stephen stood up and shook hands. Churchill was
was smiling at them, as his aide was showing them out of the
door, but his mind was on the next problem.

Bill drove back with Stephen feeling dazed. He guessed he'd

better do what he had been ordered to do, but it was turning out
to be more complicated than he had expected. Bill went on to
Miro's office to tell them the news.

'Send this coded message to Edelweiss,' he said. 'Your
request has been approved. Restrict all activities for approximately thirty days, and build up supplies. As from now, this
operation is under SOE control.'

He looked up at his two colleagues, who were also his friends.
'I assume you two are volunteering to come along,' he said.

Bill shooks hands solemnly with Anton and Miro and they,
in turn, clasped him in their arms and hugged him, Czech style.
Miro produced a bottle of good brandy and they toasted
themselves and the mission until the bottle was empty.

Chapter  64

BILL HAD NOTHING LEFT TO DO at the office. He had passed on his work to others, completed his filing, put his affairs in order and cleaned out his desk. Tomorrow, on June 4, 1944, he would be taking off for Czechoslovakia.

He wanted to get back to his own rooms and get to sleep early, but he knew he must say goodbye to Ingrid and he was dreading the scene she was bound to create. As a delaying tactic, he decided to catch up on some reading. Finally, around ten, when he couldn't think of another damn reason to stop him from going, Schofield's secretary came looking for him. Her boss wanted to see him.

Schofield rubbed his palms together. 'Aha! Here comes the man with the hot line straight to Hitler. What will you have to drink? Brandy? Scotch?'

'Scotch.' Bill sank into the chair.

'You look all in, my boy. Well, they say a change is as good as a rest. You won't have to be in Czechoslovakia for too long. Maybe a year. Not much more. I don't mind telling you that our Nazi Princess has been extremely successful. U-Boats are being misdirected, dummy airfields are being bombed nightly. Of course, it's only a matter of time before they latch on to Ingrid passing false information. When they do, I'm afraid it's curtains

for her, unless we bail her out. They'll think she's a double
agent. But she's been very useful and done her bit for the Allied
war effort.' Bill leaned back and thought about Ingrid and her
plight. It was the first time he had really thought of what would
happen to her, since he'd found out that she was a spy.

'Right now we want you to enhance the myth that the
anticipated Allied landing on the European mainland will be at
Calais.'

'I've already done that. Anyway, I'm leaving tomorrow.'

'Exactly. Be nostalgic. Say goodbye. Be a little indiscreet.
Think you can do that?'

Bill nodded, feeling depressed.

As Schofield went on planning, talking and giving him advice
on running the Czechs, Bill had only half a mind on his
instructions. Part of him was thinking about Ingrid.

Recently her manner had become affectionate to the point of
hysteria. Occasionally, he caught a glimpse of the agony she was
enduring. He'd felt pretty awful, too, just having to be with her,
but this was the first time he had wondered what it must be like
to be Ingrid. He shuddered. Lately, he had lost much of his
anger. Ingrid was a victim, he decided. Hugo's pawn. One day,
he thought. I'm going to get close enough to Hugo to settle the
score.

Bill reached Ingrid's home just after midnight and let himself
through the front door quietly in case she had gone to sleep.

He frowned when he saw her, pursed his lips and for the first
time in weeks felt compassion. Ingrid was sprawled across the
table, her face in her hands and she was fast asleep. Beside her
stood a half-empty bottle of French wine and one used glass.
The table was set romantically, but the candles had spluttered
to pools of wax.

Bill walked softly through to the kitchen and saw the food on
the stove, the wine sauce which had clotted, the fish which was
like shoe leather, the tiny potatoes covered in butter and parsley,
the peas with a sprig of mint over the top, wilted and brown. He
pursed his lips and whistled softly. He replaced the candles and

lit them, took a bottle of French claret from the cupboard and opened it. He could see from Ingrid's puffy face that she had sobbed herself to sleep. He hoped she hadn't taken a sleeping pill, since he'd brought home a batch of documents to be copied. Ingrid stirred. She pushed herself off the table and rubbed her red cheek. She gazed suspiciously at Bill as he retrieved the ruined food from the kitchen and carried it to the table. She blinked, bleary-eyed and depressed.

Bill tried to summon up his hatred, but it was entirely missing. He felt only sadness as he bent over her and kissed her cheek.

'I warned you not to love me, Ingrid,' he said. 'I'm not free. There are too many deaths to be avenged. The war must be won. When it's over, maybe I'll become human again. Sit up, Ingrid. Let's drink to peace. I'm leaving tomorrow. I won't be back until after the war.'

She cried out involuntarily. Real tears glistened in her eyes.

Was she two women inside one body? Sometimes it seemed like that. Ingrid the woman, and Ingrid the spy. Did she know which one was real?

'What's going on? Why were you late?'

That was the spy talking, he decided. 'I can't tell you anything, but I want you to know that it's very big. It's probably the most important thing that's happened since the war began, and I'm in charge of a part of it. I'm leaving tomorrow. I won't see you for some time and I don't want you to think about me.'

'If only feelings could be controlled so easily.'

That was the woman talking, Bill thought. Or was it?

'You'll manage because you have to. Tell you what, Ingrid. When it's over, I'll take you on a day trip and show you where I was and what I was doing. We'll take the overnight ferry. Is that a deal?'

Now her brow was wrinkled and her eyes gleamed suspiciously. He could almost read her mind. Why was he being so garrulous when he'd never told her anything before? She wasn't stupid.

He placed two plates on the table and spooned the clotted sauce over the fish.

'The fish is ruined,' she said. Her voice broke off with a hiccup.

'No, it's not,' he lied. 'Besides, I had a few drinks with the boys, just to say goodbye. I won't notice the difference.' He poured out the wine and chewed the charred remains. 'Mmm, a little tough, but nothing serious. I'm starving,' he added manfully.

Ingrid prodded at hers with her fork and pushed her plate away.

Bill picked up his glass. 'Ingrid, I want to propose a toast: "To the invasion".'

'To the invasion,' she echoed dully. There was doubt in her eyes . . . and fear. She was trying to pull herself together, but she had drunk too much wine. He sensed that she was near breaking point. He wanted to do something to help her . . . longed to cure her of loving him. He knew he would never marry her. That was out of the question after what she'd done.

He put one hand over hers and said: 'Ingrid. Please forget me. Once you asked me to give "us" a chance. D'you remember? Well, I did and it didn't work. At least, not for me. This is goodbye, Ingrid. In any event, the chances of my surviving are virtually nil. But if I do survive, I won't marry you. Not ever. Although you'll always be my friend, if that's acceptable to you.'

A terrible expression appeared in her eyes. Bill had seen a rabbit look like that once when it was caught in a snare.

'Don't you love me at all?' she whispered, dry-lipped.

'No,' he said.

'Don't leave me tonight. Please, Bill. It's your last night. Stay with me. I want you to hold me.'

He picked her up and carried her to the bed. She was ridiculously light. He laid her on the blankets and undid the buttons of her silk dress and ran his fingers over her breasts. 'You're too thin, Ingrid. You must eat properly. You need your strength.'

She turned her head away. Bill gently pulled her on to his shoulder and she snuggled up hard against him.

At midnight she woke him with her clumsy efforts to photograph his documents. He feigned sleep and waited for her to return to bed.

When he woke at dawn she was fast asleep and he managed to creep out without waking her. He wanted to spend his last few hours in his own flat, putting his personal affairs in order.

A friend from the office was moving into his place and Bill was leaving his cartons to be sent on to the States and letters to be posted.

At 1 p.m., Bill swung into the airbase and showed his pass. Shortly afterwards he was enjoying a hearty lunch courtesy of the air force. The Czech cousins arrived, the tall, gregarious blond, Anton Klima, and his small, dark, introverted cousin, Miro.

'Hey! D'you Yanks eat like this every day? No wonder you grow so big. There's enough food here for five men. You're going to starve over there, Major.'

Shortly afterwards, Franz Kussi, the ex-physicist, wandered through the canteen looking for them. He was carrying a tray containing a cup of black coffee.

'God knows when we'll get our next meal,' Bill said. 'Try to eat something.'

Franz grimaced. 'I never eat much before evening and even then it's an effort. Right now my stomach's in knots. Nothing could get through.'

Franz was skinny, almost emaciated, but his strong features and hands gave the impression of a big man. Bill knew from the training sessions that Franz was as strong and wiry as a bear trap. He was a cheerful man, too, always smiling, and he had a quick sense of humour.

'Where's Karol? He's late.' Bill glanced at his watch anxiously.

'Fighting his way out of bed, I guess,' Franz said.

Anton laughed. 'I thought he was boasting, so I checked him out. He shares an apartment with two Australian blondes and he sleeps in a double bed with one on each side . . . fucks them both every night.'

The airmen on the next table were listening in. 'You guys have all the luck,' they said.

Minutes later Karol arrived, beaming happily. His beard hadn't been trimmed for weeks. It merged with the black hairs on his chest and the long curls falling to the back of his neck. His blue eyes were sparkling with fun. The airmen badgered him for the telephone number of his blondes which he handed over good-naturedly. 'Are you strong enough?' he bellowed. 'If not, stay away. It's both or nothing.'

Bill sat quietly listening to them. He hoped their camaraderie would survive in enemy territory.

Bill sat in the cabin, deafened by the noise of the engines.

He felt pangs of fear as the plane took off. Eventually, he pulled himself together. Heaped around the centre of the cabin were the packages of explosives and equipment that was dropping with them. Bill looked down through the hole he had clambered through. With the ladder gone, he could see rooftops rushing by.

A freckle-faced boy, who looked too young to be in uniform, bent forward and fitted the hole with a trap door.

'Scared?' he asked.

'No,' Bill said.

'Sometimes it pays to be frightened.'

'Depends on the circumstances,' Bill answered shortly. How could he explain that at long last he was able to take his place in the front line. He longed to stand up and be counted. He wanted to be worthy of Marietta, who had died for daring to fight the Nazis. This was his chance. How could he be afraid? Yet the sad fact was, he was scared half to death. He leaned back and went over all the details in his mind. Was there anything not done that he should have done?

Chapter  65

IT HAD BECOME DARK. Anton and Miro were caught in a strange somnabulistic reverie, while Karol seemed half-asleep, swaying too and fro to the rhythm of the aircraft, eyes closed, lips moving. It took Bill a while to realise that he was praying. Over Germany the flak began, the aircraft pitched and vibrated. The hours passed and eventually Bill fell into a fitful sleep.

'Hey! Wake up,' the boy was shouting. 'Five minutes to go.' Bill's stomach seemed to lurch up and hit him in the face. The young aircraftsman folded back the trapdoors.

Bill forced himself to look down at the dark night into which he would be falling. Far below, Bill saw a light flashing on and off. Canisters of supplies were being heaved out of the aircraft by two crew members. Bill shuddered as he watched them fall into the black void.

The youngster tapped him on the shoulder. 'This is it, pal. Good luck.'

Bill clambered to the edge of the hole, turned to watch the freckle-faced kid, saw his lips mouthing 'go'. With a final lurch of his stomach, Bill forced himself to step forward into nothingness.

Marietta was huddled in a field, trying to shelter from the wind behind a gnarled old oak tree. It was cold for June, with a strong northerly wind blowing up. Her feet were wet from tramping through dewy grass and she was shivering violently. The half moon was flooding the earth with an eerie light, owls were swooping and calling, and birds, made nervous by human presence, twittered uneasily in the branches above her. Klaus was waiting on the other side of the trees, but she could not see him. Jan and his squad were in the next field.

Eventually she heard a low drone in the distance. A plane was passing too high and too far north. Perhaps it was the British agents, but if so it was slightly off-course. She felt for her torch and sent three brief stabs into the night sky.

The plane droned on, then it circled and came in again, lower and closer. Could this be it? Or was it a German reconnaissance plane on the look out for subversive activity? She signalled again, her heart beating wildly. Then she saw white parachutes floating slowly earthwards, rocking wildly in the wind.

She raced across the field, rolled the first parachute into a ball, saw Klaus reach the second, then came the third. 'Hurry . . . hurry . . .' she mumbled, stumbling through brambles and falling over mole hills. Together, Klaus and she half-dragged, half-rolled the drums towards the river. Their boat was under a willow tree. It took all their strength to load it.

Later Marietta ran back to Jan. 'We've found all the drums. We'll be getting back.'

'The wind's ruined everything,' Jan fumed. 'God knows where they've dropped. Miles off-course. We'll have to split up and search. Send Klaus back to me. You must keep us in radio contact, so get back as soon as you can. Hide the boat under the bushes along the bank.'

She ran back to the river listening to the sounds of engines, barking dogs and shouts in the distance. How far . . .? Two miles . . . ? Or one . . .? They always came so quickly, and with so many dogs. 'Oh God . . . Oh God . . . Let the agents escape ' . . . protect them . . .'

There was a stitch in her side, she couldn't gasp enough air, her legs ached . . . She reached the river, passed on the message to Klaus between gasps, scrambled into the boat, and rowed frantically. Soon she was caught in the current and only had to steer. The sound of shouts and baying dogs faded in the distance. Then all she could hear was the gurgling water, and the sound of her own mumbled supplication.

The next forty-five seconds seemed to last an hour as Bill rocked in the strong wind. He landed in a clearing and was dragged across the ground by his parachute. He began to recite his instructions: 'Get out of sight . . . keep down . . . roll up the parachute . . . bury it . . . hurry!'

There were no lights. No parachutes floating above him, no welcoming committee of the Bosch or the Czech Resistance. He was quite alone and that was better than nothing. He struggled out of his cumbersome gear, rolled it into a ball, slid out of his overalls, transferred his knife and gun to his pocket . . . 'Anything else?' he asked himself, trying to recall every word he'd been taught at the school. Grabbing his trowel, he buried his gear and covered the disturbed earth with leaves.

It was dark, but he could see he was in a forest glade. The wind was bending the trees almost double and he guessed he had been blown far off-course. Where the hell was he? Where was everyone else? He sat on a mound and listened for a while, but heard nothing. Eventually, he decided to walk into the wind and hope he'd meet someone soon.

An hour later he was still walking. He thought perhaps he'd better sit out the rest of the night and have a rethink at dawn. What a fuck up! He felt angry with fate, and with his pilot, and the local Resistance and everyone else he could think of. He'd gone from baking hot to freezing wet and cold, he was shivering violently and his heart was pumping loud enough to be heard half a mile off.

A drizzling dawn came at last and Bill, depressed and hungry, got out his maps and worked out where he was and where to go. In case of emergency, which this was, he reckoned, he had to make for a forest hut, which was situated fifteen miles south-east of Prague, approximately half a mile from the Vltava river bank, near a tall hill. From the lay of the land, he guessed he was about five miles off-course. Not the end of the world. Now which way would the river lie? He set off and walked for over an hour. After a while he heard the sound of dogs baying and he guessed that the parachutes had been seen.

Passing beyond the next clump of dense bushes he heard a shout above him. He was appalled to see Franz hanging from his parachute which was caught in the branches of a tall chestnut tree. He was horribly visible as he swung, kicking aimlessly, unable to reach anything.

'Franz! Hang on!' Bill ran forward, but a hefty blow to his legs sent him sprawling to the ground. He reached for his gun, then stopped. He was surrounded by men, the dirtiest bunch of toughs he'd ever seen, and their guns were pointing at him.

One of them spoke to him in unintelligible Czech.

Bill replied in German. He heard Franz call out in Czech.

'Why the hell are you wasting time? Cut him down,' Bill stormed.

Lights were flashing nearby. A small dark man ran into view. He had a length of rope which he tossed over the lower branch. Moments later he was scrambling up the trunk.

'My name is Klaus,' the man who had kicked him said. 'We found your friend seconds ago. We'll have him down in a moment.'

A party of troops had been lying low. There were shouts, a whistle blew, blasting Bill's ears. Fifty yards ... ? Not much more, he reckoned. Further off, Bill heard dogs again and the sound of gutteral commands.

Jesus! There wasn't time. 'I'll head them off,' Bill said. 'Get him out of there fast and go the other way.'

He began to run forward, breathing heavily, making plenty of noise as he plunged through the undergrowth. Seconds later a doberman burst out of the bushes straight at him. Bill shot the dog and raced on. The troops veered towards him firing as they ran. Now he was running wildly down a slippery slope, sliding, falling ...

A jolt of pain seared his ankle. He sprawled headlong down

a mossy bank, aware of shots lathering the mud around him. He plunged into the river and found himself swiftly carried downstream by the force of the current. His coat became sodden almost at once, its weight dragging him under. The river was deep and rough. Branches, debris and stones, tumbled around him. It was ice cold, murky and black. Bill struggled towards the surface, but couldn't make it.

He knew he must get the coat off, or he'd drown. He was being rolled over the river bed, deep underwater. He guessed that the Germans were gathered along the river bank searching for him. Could they see him? Just how deep was this river? At any moment he expected to feel machine gun bullets ripping through his body. He'd explode if he didn't get air. His lungs were bursting, his head was pounding.

He collided painfully with a rock. Bill hung on to it with all his strength. It felt as if the river was grabbing him with icy fingers ... pulling him down ... trying to drown him ... Bill fought back. Feeling his way carefully, he dragged himself up. When he reached the surface, he gulped huge lungfuls of air, oblivious to the danger. With oxygen, his reason returned. Regretfully, he took one last breath and ducked under again. Looking up, he could see the stars, blurred and large in a crescent-shaped piece of sky, surrounded by blackness. Then he realised that he had pulled himself into a crevice in the rock. He surfaced again. Neither bank was visible, only the rock and the sky and the tumbling water.

Was it fate or luck that had borne him to this place of perfect concealment? Only a boat in mid-stream could see his head and even then it would difficult for he was surrounded with river debris.

His relief at his temporary safety soon evaporated and he wondered how long it would be before he froze to death. His sodden clothes were protecting him to a certain extent. Had they got Franz to safety? And the others? He hoped so. The trapped water beneath his clothes had warmed a little. He felt sure he could survive for a day. He'd just have to stick it out. He could hear the sound of the search as dogs and men scoured the river bank. It would be suicide to move until nightfall. Bill remained in the river all day listening to Nazi troops passing backwards and forwards. As darkness fell the noises ceased, and an hour later he took off his sodden coat and swam downstream towards the deserted river bank. He knew that he would die of exposure if he stayed in the icy water any longer and hauled himself ashore beneath some overhanging branches. He'd lost all sense of direction, but moved off in the direction in which he guessed the emergency lodge lay, but his sprained ankle and lack of energy hampered his progress. He could hardly breathe. It felt as if someone had stuck a knife between his shoulder blades. Waves of heat alternated with shivery cold. It was hard to keep his balance for the earth was whirling around beneath him. He kept moving, trying to keep sufficiently lucid to get his bearings from the map he'd memorised. Eventually, he saw a dark shape ahead. Could this be the woodsman's hut? He stumbled inside, unsure if he'd found the right place. He couldn't see well because black spots were obscuring his vision. Finally he decided to crouch behind the door and hope that the Resistance would find him. By the time the sun rose, Bill was unconsciousness.

June 7. The reports landing on Hugo's desk were portents of doom. The Allies had gained beachheads and could not be repelled from Normandy. In Berlin, Field Marshal von Rundstedt, supreme commander of the German Army in the West, had been ignonimously sacked by Hitler, a chilling reminder of what happened to those who failed the Führer. Nearer home were reports of a large-scale drop. Several parachutes had been sighted, but no one knew if they were dropping men or equipment. Despite a thorough search with dogs, none of the men had been caught, although one was presumed to have drowned.

Chapter  66

WHERE WAS BILL NOW? Was he alive? Had he fallen into a trap? Those were the thoughts that obsessed Ingrid as she worked at her bench. She hardly heard her name being called until Gwen reached over and touched her arm. Looking up, she saw the manager emerge from the canteen carrying three magnums of champagne.

'I believe,' he announced solemnly, as he switched on the radio, 'we are about to hear history being made.'

For a moment there was only the noise of static. He swore and fiddled with the tuning dial.

Gwen whispered to Ingrid: 'It's the invasion! It must be the invasion! It's happened!'

A girl behind them whispered: 'The troops moved out of our area two days ago.'

'And from mine,' another girl said. The fools! Ingrid knew for sure that the invasion wouldn't take place for another ten days.

At last they heard the announcer's voice: ... *this morning, at ten a.m., General Eisenhower's headquarters informed the world that the long-awaited invasion of Europe has begun: Allied naval forces, supported by a strong airforce, began landing our armies on the northern coast of France. No place names were given, but a*

German broadcast, picked up by the BBC, stated that the landings were made in Normandy at about twelve places stretching along more than a hundred miles of coast from West of Cherbourg to Le Havre. Ingrid listened, dazed and shocked, her mind in a turmoil. What was happening? How could this be true? The landings were to be in Calais.

The invasion seems to have caught the Germans unprepared. The strongest German defences are at Calais, and a powerful armoured force in this area has not yet been transferred . . .

When the news broadcast was over, the manager switched off the radio. There was a brief silence, then some of the girls cheered. Another began to sing *Rule Britannia*, others laughed, feeling embarrassed by the force of their emotions. Ingrid stood rooted in shock while she was hugged by her friends.

'This is what we've all been working for,' the manager said. His unexpected smile, seldom seen, revealed discoloured teeth. 'A toast to each and every one of you, and to our brave boys fighting over there.'

Suddenly the bottles popped open, glasses were filled, champagne frothed and the girls were shrieking with excitement.

Ingrid lifted a glass to her frozen lips without tasting the wine. Why had Bill's letters and papers pin-pointed Calais? Even on the map . . . yes, there had definitely been a map and she had photographed it. Think! What exactly had she photographed? Letters, memos, instructions, infallible proof that the invasion would start at Calais on June 13. And what had the announcer said? The Germans were holding their main defences at Calais. Why? Why? Her mind was in a turmoil. She'd been used. Tricked. By Bill. That was the cruellest part of all.

For how long had Bill been fooling her? If she'd been discovered, why hadn't they arrested her . . . because they wanted to use her? And when they had no more use for her, would they arrest and execute her?

An even worse fear struck home, leaving her trembling and faint. Would Hugo and Paddy think she was a double agent? If they did it would save the British a bullet, because Paddy would surely kill her.

She began to feel really ill. Nausea welled up in her throat . . .
her knees turned to rubber. She lurched forward and managed
to reach a chair. She felt strangely light-headed, with buzzing
in her ears and her fingers full of pins and needles.

A heavy submissiveness settled over her like a shroud. She
was not in control of her life. She was only a pawn, moved by
unseen hands in a deadly game. 'God help me,' she muttered.

Louis was wielding an axe against the slender base of a conifer
tree. Each time he struck it the branches shivered and shook and
pine needles spiralled around him. He worked with ferocious
strength. He knew that the Russians thought he was mad
because he worked harder, and for longer hours than he had to,
and God knows the daily target was punishing enough. He
worked to offset the terrible longing for Andrea and the
strength of his despair.

He paused for a moment in his attack on a tree. A Russian,
shaped like an egg, with a face like a moon, tramped past him,
his hand on his rifle. His breath left a scent of cheap wine
drifting provocatively in his wake, his mouth framed the words
of a song.

They were great singers, these Russians. They sang of
romance, of patriotism, of hunger, of their love of the land, and
their tears flowed with the words. They were very simple
people. Louis had learned to like them during his time here. He
liked them in the same way that he might like a pet gorilla, with
caution and respect. Today their behaviour was unlike anything
he had ever seen. Why?

He stepped back and gazed at the deep V-indentation in the
tree. Another two blows and it might fall. He looked around and
saw a group of Russians standing to his left. He went over to
them and mimed that they should look out. He moved back with
them, shooing them like geese. They were half-drunk. One of
them had a hip flask which he pulled out and offered to Louis.

'Your beloved Germans are finished. You joined the wrong
side, my friend. D'you know what we're celebrating today?
D-Day! The Allies have landed in Europe. It's only a matter of

time before we wipe out the Germans,' he laughed.

Louis hung around listening. He heard them say that several Siberian regiments were leaving Ukhta, fifty miles away, to join the front line somewhere in Poland. The guards were longing to go with them. Well, so was he, come to that. He went back to his tree and sent it crashing down.

How long had he been here? Over a year but it seemed more like ten. After the Stalingrad surrender, the Russians had herded the Germans into a vast camp and left them there. Without food, fuel or shelter, and only melted snow to drink, hundreds of thousands of them had died. Eventually, the Russians had sifted out those Czechs and Hungarians still alive and sent them north to Siberia. Louis had claimed he was a *Volksdeutsche* Czech, conscripted into the German punishment corps, and in a way he was. Then followed a nightmare three-week train journey across Siberia. Out of the thousand men who had been herded on to the train at Stalingrad, scarcely two hundred had survived the journey, most of them dead from hypothermia. Louis had been grateful that he was one of the few survivors. Later, when he stood in a frozen line and heard the commandant's sentence – a lifetime in Siberia, separated from the woman he loved, Louis felt that it would have been better if he had died. Since then he had learned to speak some Russian and consequently he had been put in charge of a team of loggers.

The guards were toasting each other, embracing and singing raucously as they became increasingly maudlin. Eventually they were replaced by new guards who staggered from the army camp, even more drunk than their colleagues. It would be easy to escape, but what was the point? Louis asked himself. There was nowhere to go. Only a fool would try. He knew he was separated from the Polish border by two thousand miles of swamps and icy tundra.

But why not go anyway? It would be a long time before the Russians were as drunk as this again. And even longer before a troop train would be leaving this area. In other words, there would never be another chance like this. And if they caught him and shot him? Well, that might be better than a lifetime spent in this hellhole.

In the midnight twilight, when the prisoners were marched back to the camp, Louis simply stood still. That was all. He stood in a pool of shadow under a thick spruce tree with low branches and watched the guards dismiss the prisoners without their customary roll-call. There was no point in waiting. It was not going to get any darker. He had a plan of sorts. He would get into the training camp, where he hoped they were all as drunk as his guards and steal a uniform, and possibly papers, if he was lucky. After that, he would try to board the train to the border. His life was in the lap of the Gods.

Half an hour later, Louis was running westwards through the forest.

Paddy was in the back of the shop making his filthy tea. Ingrid could smell that it was ages since he had cleaned out his rabbit hutches. He turned and stared at her. For a moment she felt paralysed by the menace in his eyes.

'You're a brave girl to come here,' he said. 'You're just in time for a cup of tea.'

She shuddered as she took the dirty cup and drank out of it.

'I don't know what went wrong,' she said softly. 'Help me, please. I was never a double-agent. Is it possible that they suspect me? Or could it be Bill whom they suspect? Bill's been so strange lately, drinking a lot. He seemed to be under tension. He said there was a mole at the office. What d'you think I should do? Can you get me out . . . back to Germany? I'm so afraid . . .'

She went on for a long time . . . pleading, arguing, putting her life in Paddy's hands.

When she'd finished, Paddy put one hand on her shoulder and pressed his fingers into her flesh. 'I believe you,' he said. 'I don't know if Fernando will, but I do. We'll have to find out whether or not they suspect you. You're not the only agent to come up with that Calais story. They were putting it out to everyone, perhaps all of Bill's department. And as for you . . . you'll have to prove yourself to us. Find out where Bill's gone.'

'I have a suspicion . . .'

'Not suspicions, Ingrid. We want the facts. Bring me the proof. Our friend wants to know. When you've done that, I'll try to help you.'

'Thank you,' she whispered, 'I'll do what I can.' She walked out in a daze, her mouth dry, her throat constricted with tension. She felt like a leaf blown aimlessly in the wind. Could she find Bill's phrase book and his notes? She was sure he'd been dropped into Prague. Would that help her to survive? But what about the British? They could pick her up whenever they wished. 'Think, Ingrid . . .' she murmured. 'Think! You've always been a survivor.'

It was one in the morning when Ingrid unlocked the front door of Bill's boarding house quietly and tiptoed downstairs to his basement flat. It was still and empty, yet there was a lingering sense of Bill around. Behind the door were several boxes and a pile of sacks filled with rubbish. A five pound note lay on the table by the door, pinned to a piece of paper: *Dear Mrs Thornton. Please dispose of the contents of the sacks. Someone from the office will fetch the boxes and post the letters. My colleague will move in before the end of the week. Thanks for everything. Sincerely, B. Roth.*

A lump came into her throat at the sight of Bill's familiar handwriting. She was missing him badly. She began to search the rubbish sacks carefully. There was nothing of any interest there other than a well-worn map of Prague and the surrounding area. She laid it over the kitchen table, where the light was better and saw some pencilled marks in places. Then she opened the letters which were waiting to be posted. They were to friends in America, but the last one was addressed to Bill's uncle. Not much of a letter, she thought, skimming through it, for it was mainly instructions to his uncle on how to deal with his estate, in case Bill didn't return. With a jolt she noticed the date – June 4 – and realised that Bill had written the letter after he had said goodbye to her. Then she read: *I've been seeing a great deal of Ingrid Mignon von Graetz. She's a princess, by the*

*way, and a cousin of Marie, whom you've heard about, in fact, they
were brought up as sisters. Ingrid is a sad person and life has dealt
her a raw deal. She's gotten herself involved with a heap of trouble.
Maybe she'll survive the war. I hope so. When this is over would you
please contact Major Stephen Schofield, my boss, and find out where
Ingrid is. She'll need help. Take her into your home and your hearts
and make sure she has a second start. Do this for me. I was once very
fond of her . . .*

Ingrid threw herself on Bill's bed, and burst into tears.
Eventually she fell asleep clutching the letter.

Chapter 67

HOURS LATER INGRID WAS STARTLED by the sound of the door being opened. Her stomach lurched as she pushed Bill's letter into her pocket. She clapped her hand over her mouth and tried to stifle a scream, knowing that it was too late to hide.

In horror she watched Fernando close the door and walk across the room to the bed. When he bent over her she almost passed out, but managed to force herself to sit up and glare at him.

'I hear you went whining round to Paddy. Getting scared, Ingrid?'

At the sound of his high-pitched, insidious voice, her fear diminished and anger gave her the strength to stand up.

'You little fool,' he said. 'Paddy says you're innocent. Well, I'm not so sure.'

She took a deep breath. God, how she hated and feared Fernando. She never took her eyes off him as he turned away and began to rifle the drawers of Bill's desk. It didn't take him long to realise that everything was in the sacks and cartons. To her annoyance, he tipped the first sack on the floor and began to rummage through the papers and discarded items. There was a razor, aftershave, some clothes ... She hated his slug-like fingers touching Bill's possessions.

'Ah-ha. What have we here?'

He was thumbing through the pages of a book. 'Interesting! Our friend was studying the latest developments in missile research and rocket fuel. And look at this . . . Roth was learning Czech. Rather strange . . . for a man about to drop into Calais, wouldn't you say?'

How could Bill have been such a fool as to leave that evidence around? And why hadn't she found it first? 'I came to fetch that for Paddy,' she began sullenly. 'I've seen it before . . . I told him. Then I got tired . . .'

Fernando wasn't listening. He was studying a photograph intently. She walked across the room and peered over his shoulder. He was looking at a snap taken of her and Bill standing arm-in-arm outside a restaurant in Hampstead, wreathed in happy smiles.

Quick as a snake, Fernando spun round and hit her. As she fell back across the bed, she felt his hand in her pocket. Moments later he was smoothing out the crumpled letter to Bill's uncle. 'It's not important,' she said, rubbing her cheek. 'I was taking it to Paddy.'

'You're wrong. It's vital. Bill's on a suicide mission, or so we suspect and this proves it. This letter is one long goodbye. His last will and testament, you might say. And look at this . . . *Look after Ingrid* . . . How touching!' He thrust the letter into his inside pocket.

Her hands were sweating, her lips were cracking, her mouth felt as dry as an oven. What did he mean . . . suicide mission?

What did he know? She must find out without inviting Fernando's suspicions.

'If you told me what we're looking for I might be more helpful,' she said in a brisk voice as she sat up and smoothed her hair.

'We suspect that Roth has parachuted into Prague in order to infiltrate Theresienstadt concentration camp. He's planning to sabotage certain top secret installations, or so we believe. He knows he won't survive, since he's no fool. I wanted some sort of proof. I'm afraid you missed your chance for glory, Ingrid.

Never mind! This picture will identify Bill to the camp authorities. They want him alive. A major in British Intelligence would be worth having, or don't you think so?'

A vivid image of Bill's well-loved body, lying mangled and bloody, flashed through her mind. She thought: I must stop shaking.

'You look pale. Was poor little Ingrid hoping to escape by marrying the millionaire, Roth? Tough luck!'

Poor little Ingrid. Those hateful, well-remembered words hit her on the raw. Her blood began pounding in her chest. She clenched her fists and dug her nails hard into her palms.

'So what else do you want?' she asked curtly.

'A better photograph of Roth ... More letters giving signs that he was putting his affairs in order ... evidence that he was going into Czechoslovakia. This is maybe enough,' he patted his pocket, 'but let's take the place apart.'

Far stronger than her rejection, her anger, and her fear of death, was a voice shrieking in her head: 'Hugo must never get his hands on Bill.' She had to protect Bill with every atom of strength and cunning she possessed.

As Fernando bent over the sacks, she walked into the kitchen. She picked up Bill's razor sharp kitchen knife and thrust it up her sleeve.

'Here's a map of Prague,' she called. 'The drop is clearly marked. I think this calls for a bonus, don't you?'

'Greedy bitch.'

'Come and look.'

Fernando stood in the doorway, one eyebrow cocked, a picture of menace. Ingrid was shuddering, her knees trembling. He turned his back on her as he bent over the kitchen table. She moved closer. 'That cross is near Sokol Castle,' she said, pointing at the map.

He bent to look more closely at the mark. She took a deep breath, pulled back her arm and thrust the knife into his muscled back, using all the strength she could find. It went in easily, right up to the shaft.

Fernando screamed hoarsely and fell forward over the table.

He groaned. Then he pushed his arms under him, levered himself up and turned round. His face drained of colour, his eyes wide with shock and pain, his mouth twisted into a grimace. He took two steps towards her, reaching for her as she backed away.

He gasped something unintelligible, then he fell forward, the knife an exclamation mark on his prone body.

So much blood! Who would have thought a human body contained so much blood? She rushed along the passage to the toilet where she threw up and knelt there retching in dry spasms. Eventually she crept out, wiping her wet forehead on her sleeve. Forcing her feet towards the kitchen, step by terrible step, she reached the doorway and peered round the corner. He was still there, face forward, legs buckled under him, lying in a pool of blood which had congealed around his face and matted in his hair.

She felt sick again. Keeping her eyes averted, she stepped over the corpse and thrust a kitchen towel under the tap. Wringing it out, she pressed the towel over her face.

Was Bill safe? What if Paddy found this evidence when he came looking for Fernando? She stood staring at the corpse for a long time before she found the courage to bend down and retrieve the papers and photographs from his pocket. She burned them in the grate, together with the letter. Then she lay on the bed, overcome with waves of dizziness.

Paddy would come after her. What was she to do? There must be a way out. She hadn't survived so far just to calmly wait for one side or other to find her and kill her. Think, Ingrid, think! She smiled softly as she thought of the one person who could possibly help her and how to ensnare him. She closed her eyes firmly as she pulled the knife out of Fernando's rapidly cooling body. It came free reluctantly and she washed it carefully. She would not contaminate her body with Fernando's foul blood. She went back to the bedroom and sat beside the telephone. She drew the sharp blade over her wrist and saw her blood spurting crimson on to the pillowcase.

Shuddering, she forced herself to repeat the action. Then,

lifting the receiver she dialled the number of Stephen Schofield and after only two rings heard his voice say: 'Schofield.'

'Stephen, dearest Stephen, you must help Bill,' she murmured. 'I've wanted to tell you everything for so long.' She sighed. 'I don't have much time, but I want you to know that I was never free to love you. If things had been different I would have accepted your proposal. Please believe me. I 'phoned to say goodbye. I've decided to end my torment.'

'Where are you, Ingrid?' He sounded frantic. 'Give me your address.'

'At Bill's rooms, but Stephen, it's too late, believe me. I can never forgive myself for what I've done to Marietta.'

'Ingrid, what have you done?'

'Stephen, listen to me, I was forced to be a spy. Do you understand what I'm saying? I've been blackmailed by the Nazis for six years . . . terrible years. They let me out of the camp to spy for them, but they kept Marietta as a hostage for my good behaviour. Now I've betrayed her.'

'Wait! Hold tight. Is that where you are . . . at Bill's place? Stay there.'

'Stephen. Listen to me. They suspect Bill Roth is going to infiltrate a camp near Prague. Something to do with destroying a rocket station. I killed Fernando . . . I had to . . . and burned the evidence. I feel so dizzy, sort of floating. Stephen, I loved you, but I had to obey them . . . for her sake.'

She dropped the receiver with a smile. Now all she had to do was wait.

Stephen Schofield stood over the slim figure of the unconscious girl, her lovely face almost as pale as the sheets of the hospital bed. He scowled. Would he ever be able to sort out his mixed feelings of compassion and anger? How much of her story was lies, how much the truth? He guessed that he might never know, but he knew that he desperately wanted to believe in her.

Soon after he had met Ingrid, he had fallen deeply in love with her. He remembered her working in the canteen, singing to the troops and then going out into the fires of London without a thought of her own safety, and working all night in the midst of a blitz. That took guts.

Had the Nazis really set her up by holding her cousin hostage? Had Bill never told Ingrid that Marietta had died ... or was she still alive?

He thought back to the pain and jealousy which he'd fought to overcome when she'd turned him down and started seeing Roth. Now he understood how the poor girl had been forced into prostitution. Roth had never given a damn about her. He'd simply taken all she had to offer, and given very little in return. For Bill there was only Marietta.

Schofield looked up as his assistant entered the room.

'Sir. Fernando's body was pulled out of the ruins of a blitzed house at 3 a.m. this morning by an ARP warden. The corpse was mangled to shreds and was taken to the nearest mortuary. Fortunately, his identity card was intact and we have sent a man round to his address to notify his landlady, and to tell his employer at the newsagents. Anything else?'

'No. That's good. Just make sure there's no trace left of any intruders in Major Roth's rooms. You cleared out the ashes in the grate, of course?'

'Yes, I've attended to that, Sir.'

'Good man.' Schofield glanced at his watch. It was only 4 a.m. now. Lucky for them that the Nazis had bombed that area. He glanced towards the bed as he heard a soft sigh.

Ingrid stirred and her eyelids flickered. Would he ever trust her? Probably not, he decided, but what the hell. He smiled to himself. Here lay a woman of great resilience, masterly will-power and famous beauty, to say nothing of her royal roots. She would make a fitting mate when the war was won. He was pushing fifty. High time he produced some heirs. Besides, she had proved invaluable in the end. Why waste her talents now? He had much more information he wanted sent to General von Hesse and she was clever enough to hoodwink Paddy.

Yes, he would save her, but she would have to accept his terms. A life sentence, he thought with a grim smile, but possibly not quite the sentence she had expected.

Chapter  68

MARIETTA GAZED OUT of the barn window and watched with anxious eyes as the eastern sky turned pale grey over the forest. It was June 7 and the British agent was still missing. She sighed, stretched and went back to the radio. She had spent an anxious night keeping wireless contact between Jan and the men who were combing the forests for the second night running.

They had learned from the three Free-Czechs who had landed that the missing man was their leader. It would be disastrous if the Bosch were to get hold of him. As far as they knew he was still at large, probably lost and possibly hurt. The entire operation had been a fiasco because of gale force winds and bad visibility. Half an hour later, she received an incoming call from Jan's group. She took down the message, decoded it, and sighed with relief. They had found him. Thank God!

Wrenching off her earphones, she stowed her gear under the straw and hurried downstairs. Have a doctor in the dairy cellars, the message had read. Was he badly hurt, she wondered? Would he live? Or would she have a sick man to nurse for weeks, or months, endangering all their lives?

Dr Klara Mikolash, who acted as the local midwife, was someone she trusted implicitly. She lived in a broken down cottage across the fields and she had a permit allowing her to be out at night. Marietta set off, keeping close to the hedges.

Klara was used to emergencies. She was dressed within seconds and emerged, clutching her bag, tucking her checked blouse into her corduroy trousers, mousy hair awry, blue eyes glinting determinedly.

When they reached the dairy, they heard footsteps coming up from the river. Two of Jan's men were carrying an unconscious man, in the darkness all Marietta could make out was the blur of a pale face with damp dark hair plastered against his skull. They moved swiftly through the dairy and Klara followed them through the trap door. 'I'll need hot water, towels, a cup of soup or hot tea, some brandy . . .' she called over her shoulder.

Marietta decided to stay on guard in the dairy. She busied herself making soup and sending down the things Klara needed.

'Is he conscious?' Marietta asked when Klara emerged through the trap door.

'Just coming round. Give him soup in about half an hour. Small amounts, but often. I think he spent the past thirty-six hours hiding out in the river. God was on his side, that's for sure, but he's a sick man . . . pneumonia, exposure, shock, multiple bruising. He'll need a couple of weeks in bed.'

Jan came up after her. 'It feels as if I've been through every damn thicket in the forest,' he grumbled. His white hair was full of mud and his scratched cheeks were covered in grey stubble. 'We found him in the liaison hut. He'd crawled behind the door before he passed out.'

She glanced at him curiously. There was a strange tone to Jan's voice . . . sullen and apprehensive. She frowned at him.

'It's not his fault he was blown off-course. He saved the life of one of his men. He must be a good leader and a very brave man.'

'If you say so,' Jan sighed. 'Brave or not, he must hide here for a while. There's nowhere else to put him. He'll need plenty of good, nourishing food. Try not to spend *all* your time down there,' he said, pressing his lips together.

'Why ever should I want to?' she asked.

Jan scowled at her. Inexplicably, he took her hands in his. 'Listen to me as a friend. You are my best agent. That's all you are. Everything else belongs to the past or perhaps the future, but not the present. Don't allow yourself to become vulnerable. To long to live ... is to become afraid ... is to die. Please don't become vulnerable.'

She nodded, feeling surprised that Jan understood these things which she had always felt, but never talked about.

'Have I done something foolish? Is that why you are talking to me like this?'

'Not yet,' he said.

Bill knew he had blacked out, but for how long? He lay in a state of shock, feeling scared and tense. He was utterly weary, his body ached in every muscle and bone. There was an intolerable pain in his chest that went right through his shoulder blades. When he moved it was like a knife thrust.

Where was he? He moved his arms cautiously. There were no handcuffs. Then he opened his eyes slowly. No guards ... no prison cell. He was lying in a big underground cellar, down the full length of one side were wine racks. Presumably this had once been the wine cellar of some wealthy farmhouse or even a castle. Bohemia was full of castles.

There was a glass of milk beside his bed, but when he tried to reach it, the pain in his chest brought on a fit of coughing. For a few seconds he couldn't breathe. He thought he would choke to death, then he managed to gasp some air.

A woman raced down the steps and helped him to a sitting position. He looked up and saw Marie standing next to him. The shock of this hallucination brought on another fit of coughing.

'Bill,' he heard. 'Oh my God. Darling ... Darling ... It's you. Oh, Bill. You've come back to me, at last.' Hands grasped his shoulders. Lips were pressed on to his. Tears spattered his face. He opened his eyes and gazed into the deep azure pools he remembered so well.

What a fool he was. Marie was dead. He lay back, sipped at the glass of milk the woman was holding to his lips and kept his eyes tightly closed. The resemblance had been uncanny, despite the short black hair and rough clothes. But what about her voice?

'I know I'm hallucinating,' he muttered, 'but Jesus, I wish it would never stop.'

'Oh Bill, dearest Bill ...' She laughed, that low, thrilling laugh he knew so well and then, suddenly, she was crying, gasping for breath, her body shaking and trembling. 'I'm so happy,' she sobbed. 'So very happy ... Oh God! I never guessed ... never dreamed ...' She flung herself on to the bed and snuggled on to his shoulder.

She felt real enough. So was the pain in his chest, so he couldn't be dead. Was he hallucinating? He was afraid to look away in case she disappeared. 'You see, Bill darling,' she was explaining, 'I escaped from the camp. My poor, dear friend, Greta, had tuberculosis and she was dying ...' Her story tumbled out, but Bill was still snared with a sense of unreality. 'I'm alive and I'm real, I promise you,' she said eventually.

Bill reached forward and ran his fingers through her hair, feeling short soft ends, watching her wonderingly.

He reached out to take her hand, but caught sight of the scars on her arm. 'Oh God,' he whispered, pulling her closer. 'Is this what they did to you?' He ran his fingers over the bumps and ridges of scarred tissue. Then he pulled her arm closer and peered at the tattoo, but his vision was clouded by black dots and she was shimmering in and out of focus. 'Oh Marie. Oh, my poor little Marie,' he muttered. 'I love you. I never stopped loving you.' He pulled her on to his shoulder and wrapped his arms around her.

As he listened to her story, he fell into that strange state of being half-awake and half-asleep, filled with bliss at the nearness of his girl, who had been miraculously restored to him. At last he fell into a deep sleep.

Then next time he surfaced, Marie was gone.

After a while a deep anxiety sunk into him. It all seemed so impossible and even a little unreal. Was it merely the fever, plus wishful thinking that had brought about this hallucination? A torment of grief swept through him, but he struggled to pull himself together. Marie had been dead for a long time. Now was not the time to break down. He had work to do. He had to get better fast.

He pulled himself upright with an effort and tried to get out of bed, but his limbs seemed to have turned to lead. He groaned. Someone moved nearby, a short, swarthy man with curly white hair, who had been sitting at the table writing, but Bill hadn't noticed him. 'Who are you?' Bill asked.

'Jan ... Czech Resistance. We've communicated often enough, Major.'

Bill nodded and looked more closely into Jan's face. 'You were also Marie's chauffeur once. I remember you,' he said. As Jan passed him some water, Bill gripped his arm. He hardly dared to ask. 'Was that the Countess ... ?'

'The Countess died in Lichtenberg concentration camp,' Jan began, and Bill was plunged into despair. 'There are many things it would be wiser to forget,' he went on. 'You saw Lara, a peasant woman who runs the dairy above. Her code name is Edelweiss. To remember anything else would put her in mortal danger.'

It was Marie and Marie was Edelweiss! Bill was too shocked to reply. He lay back, his eyes closed, contemplating the enormity of this information. He'd been in communication with Marie over the past nine months. He swore as he thought of the time wasted and the impossible risks he'd forced her to take. If only he'd known.

'Forget this conversation,' Jan was saying. 'As soon as I saw you in the forest, I knew there'd be trouble ahead. Whatever your private feelings may be, put them aside until the war's over.'

'Jan ... thanks,' Bill muttered. The tears were rolling down his cheeks, his throat had swollen into a lump, he could hardly breathe, but he knew he was the luckiest man who ever lived. Marie was alive. Somehow he'd get her out of Czechoslovakia, he vowed.

Chapter  69

BILL ... HER BILL, was down there, waiting for her and she longed to be with him, but there was so much to do: she had to run the dairy, milk the cows, collect the butter from the farms, deliver food to the Freedom Fighters, cook Bill's food, which she did with extra care and tenderness. When dusk came, she was still busily finding more work, which wasn't difficult.

Miki, who had been looking after Bill all day, came up the cellar steps. He took a deep breath of fresh air.

'It's stuffy down there, I get claustrophobia. I don't know how you can bear to live in these gloomy places. I need a break,' he said. 'Take over.'

'No ... Oh no! I can't ...'

'You must.' Miki walked out, leaving her alone with her doubts and fears.

How could she go down? She gazed in the mirror in despair.

'You are ugly,' she said aloud. 'Yes, truly ugly.' She stepped closer and peered into the mirror. 'Your face is skinny and lined, your skin rough, your hair just black stubble, your shoulders are too large from lifting heavy milk churns ... just look at your muscles! Bill remembers a pretty teenager with a milky complexion and long blonde hair, not this old hag. As for your hands ...' She spread her fingers and gazed at them in despair: roughened skin, short nails, swollen knuckles — a working woman's hands.

She crouched on the bed and allowed herself to wallow in self-disgust. Eventually she pulled herself together. Going back to the mirror, she saw that red eyes and swollen lids were now added to her private catastrophe.

She would have to face Bill. She took the dish of stew she had prepared and carried it down the steps. Bill was lying in bed looking sick and pale, but very definitely himself. He looked older, his shoulders were broader, his hair longer and thicker, his face more crinkled, but if anything he was even more attractive. He was giving her that funny, half-affectionate, half-amused smile she knew so well.

'I thought you'd never come,' he said. 'I've been longing to see you. Marie, come over here. I want to touch you . . . hold you . . . prove to myself you're really here. I could hear you moving around up there. I was tormented.'

'You must eat and you must stop calling me Marie, my name is Lara,' she said. 'It's rather primitive here, but my cooking has improved. If you remember . . .' she broke off, almost choking on the words. Remembering was far too painful. 'You must try to eat, you need your strength,' she said, putting the tray on to his lap.

'I can't eat lying down,' he said, his eyes shining with amusement.

She picked up the tray and put it on the table. When she bent over him to grasp his shoulders, he pulled her down over him. Suddenly she was sprawling over his stomach, his arms wrapped around her waist.

'Let me go.'

'No. Not unless you kiss me.'

Bill burst into a fit of coughing and for a few terrible seconds could not get his breath. He was choking. She pulled him to a sitting position and bent his head over his knees. Eventually he managed to get hoarse, grating breaths, but his face was beetroot red. 'What have I got . . . ? Pneumonia?'

'That, plus bruises, cracked ribs and a sprained ankle.'

He caught hold of her hand. 'Marie, dearest,' he said huskily. 'I never stopped loving you, not for one moment. Don't tell me you've changed.'

'Can't you see that I've changed?' she said sharply. 'You love someone else . . .'

'Don't be absurd. It's you I love.'

He sighed, a sharp forceful breath that brought on another fit of coughing. 'Then?'

'Don't torment me, Bill. The girl you loved is gone. This ugly Lara has replaced her.'

He looked at her questioningly. Then he smiled, a funny, crooked smile and his eyes filled with tears. 'Come here, Marie. Sit on the bed. I don't mind if you turn your back on me, just as long as I can feel you.' He pulled her closely against him. 'Don't interrupt. Promise me?'

'Yes,' she whispered.

'Back in '37, Marie, in the garden at Hallein, I was madly attracted to you. I wanted you more than anyone I'd ever seen. Without doubt you were the loveliest, sexiest, most desirable girl I'd ever set eyes on.' His voice was thick with emotion and he had to clear his throat. 'I'll never forget the way you looked, your blue eyes like pools of water, that perfect profile, those blue clothes you wore and your hair sun-bleached and falling all over the place. You were like a vision. I was obsessed by you.

'Much later, I fell in love with the woman behind the beauty. This time it was real love, Marie. I'll never forget the day it happened, nor the way you looked. You were dirty, scruffy, scared, skinny, your eyes were bloodshot from lack of sleep, you had a funny pinched look about you. Your hair was greasy and scraped back in a bun, and your clothes were crumpled. One of the kids had vomited over you, but I don't think you were aware of that, you were too damned scared to notice. You were sitting in a carriage, trying to calm your little fugitives.

'I found out later from the Pastor, you'd found half of them on your own and hidden them in the attics of Plechy Palace, until he stepped in to help you. You were telling them a fairy story . . . remember? At that moment, the beauty that came surging out of you had nothing to do with your eyes, or your teeth or hair or perfect profile. It had a lot to do with goodness and compassion. It was like an aura, shining around you, an aura of love, transcending your appearance. I fell deeply in love with that beauty and you could as well have been the ugliest woman ever born.

'I love you Marie, and my love has nothing to do with the way you look. Maybe that's why I recognised you at once, because I love the you inside there. I guess one should recognise the woman one loves,' he added shakily.

'Can I turn round yet?' she asked, in a small, strangled voice.

'No. Not yet.' He kissed the top of her head. 'I thought you were dead, but I could never shake free of the past. Although, for a while, I did try. Now Marie, I'm here on a mission and you, too, are in constant danger. There's a long and difficult road ahead for both of us, but we're going to get through it and we're going to make all our dreams come true. I promise you. I'll never lose you again.' She turned abruptly and saw that his eyes were red-rimmed and his face was wet. Wonderingly, she stroked his cheek.

'My love . . . My love . . . ,' she whispered. 'My dearest love.'

Ingrid hesitated outside Paddy's shop, quaking inwardly. She had to face him, but she felt terribly afraid. Yesterday Stephen, or Major Schofield, as he had been on this occasion, had spelt out the facts to her.

'The only way I can save you, is to establish you as a British agent. I can lie – and I will lie, I promise you. I will claim that you were working for me as a double agent throughout the war, but you must re-establish yourself with Paddy. I can't do that for you, and you can only be useful to me if Paddy trusts you.'

'God help me,' she muttered, as she stepped inside.

She could hear Paddy moving around in the back, but she was too frightened to ring the bell. Eventually Paddy emerged, rubbing his hands on a dirty tea towel. His eyes narrowed as he caught sight of her and Ingrid held her breath. Then a customer walked in, and she let out a small sigh of relief.

'The Czech newspapers are out the back, Ingrid.' Paddy jerked his thumb over his shoulder. 'I'll be with you in half a tick.' She sat on an upturned box and saw, to her horror, the big grey Flemish Giant tied by its heels from the ceiling, ripped open from its belly to its neck. She shivered and felt nauseous. 'Death row,' she thought, looking at the hutches.

She heard Paddy's footsteps behind her.

'Where's Fernando?' she cried out. 'He didn't come to the meeting place . . . twice. I don't know what to do.'

'Calm down, Ingrid! We've been busy. I sent him to another area. Best if you bring your news here to me from now on. What have you got for me?'

'Only this.' She produced a dog-eared, pencilled Serbo-Croatian grammar book, which Scofield had given her, plus an aerial map of Sarajevo. He'd also arranged for a forgery of Bill's letter to his uncle, with as many accurate phrases as Ingrid could remember. She crumpled and burst into tears. She didn't have to try too hard because she felt completely helpless.

'Poor Bill,' she sobbed. 'He was trying to help me and I've betrayed him.'

She felt Paddy's hand on her shoulder. 'He didn't marry you, Ingrid, did he? He could have shipped you back to the States. He would have, if he'd cared at all.'

'That's the point,' she sobbed bitterly. 'He didn't care. He's passed me on . . . as if I were an old coat, or a dog, or something . . .'

'Relax, Ingrid. Tell me what happened.'

She pulled out a handkerchief and dabbed at her eyes. 'His boss is Major Stephen Schofield, as you know. Well, three days ago, the Major came round to see if I needed anything. He said Bill won't be back for a long time and that Bill had asked him to look after me. He said . . . he'd promised Bill he'd make sure I was all right.'

'You should be used to that by now. I thought you were tougher.'

'So did I,' she said, feeling safer.

'Maybe you're telling the truth,' he said softly, without

looking at her. 'So we'll play the game Schofield's way and see what we get out of him.'

'Yes,' she said, looking and feeling forlorn. 'There's something else. I copied these plans from the factory. I don't know what they are, but the manager locked them in his safe, which is unusual.'

'Leave them on the table,' he said. 'I'll have a look at them later. I'm having a nice rabbit pie for lunch. Would you like to stay and share some?'

'No,' she said, shuddering. 'I mean, yes, I would like to, but I can't. Schofield asked me out. Well, it's up to you, really. Do you think I should go?'

'Yes, you'd better go. Duty before pleasure, Ingrid. The rabbit pie can wait a while.'

At last she was out of that terrible place.

It was a lovely Sunday morning, a walk would steady her nerves, she decided. She hurried along the pavement thinking about her predicament. Life was getting complicated. She was no longer sure who was doing the manipulation. She had thought she was in control, but perhaps it was Stephen after all. Paddy half-believed in her. Stephen had promised to give her enough good material to convince him, given time. Stephen half-believed in her, too. And Bill? His letter to his uncle showed that he saw her as a victim. Dear Bill. He would never believe that even while she was spying on him, she had also loved him. No, she had lost Bill forever.

The worst of the pneumonia was over by the end of the first week. Bill was off the danger list, Klara told her.

Marie nursed Bill tenderly, bathed him, fed him, shaved him, sat him upright when he lost his breath and massaged his back when he was in pain. Every day she cooked him nourishing broths, she bartered pilfered milk for a piece of mutton or beef – butter for bacon. She kept a few chickens and gave Bill all the eggs. Every night, when her work was done, they ate supper in the cellar and later listened to the BBC news. When the Allies overran Brittany and Normandy they rejoiced together.

After the news, Marietta would snuggle into bed beside Bill and fall asleep instantly, waking from time to time to whisper a prayer of thanks, only to sleep again with a sigh of contentment.

Chapter  70

TWO WEEKS LATER, Jan arrived unexpectedly. He said: 'Major Roth looks fit. Well done! I've come to fetch him. Time's running out.'

There was no point in arguing that Bill was far from strong. She watched worriedly as Bill packed his gear and limped out to Kolar's truck. She stood at the gate for a long time after they left, trying to imagine that she could still hear the sound of the truck's engine.

Two days later Marietta returned from Kova bringing the news that Alex had been caught red-handed carrying a packet of explosives inside Richard's Mine. He had been interrogated, tortured and finally executed, but he had not talked. Later that night, she went to the forest rendezvous where the men were training and broke the news to Jan. The news of Alex's death upset everyone.

Bill was starting the men's training and although he didn't yet know them too well, he felt the weight of their fear and grief. He decided to talk to them about it.

'I want you all to understand exactly why Alex died so horribly, and why some of us may have to die, too,' he began.

Bill explained to the men about the new form of energy which could wipe out a city with one bomb, and the missiles that were being built in Richard's Mine to transport the bomb.

'If we do survive the war,' Marietta thought, 'then what shall I do? Live in the States and have a brood of little Bills? Shall I forget about my vows to Grandmother and Father?' The prospect was inviting and she sat on in happy contemplation. Then guilt set in. Love or duty? It seemed she had been making this choice all her life.

Obsessed by her problems, she was only half-listening to what Bill was saying, but then she heard: 'I'll go in about a month before the Allies arrive, to join those of you left inside.'

At that moment her dreams crashed. There was no future after all. Not for them. He would be caught as soon as he entered the mine ... how could Bill pretend to be a half-starved Czech peasant, with those shoulders ... that self-assured manner, those cool analytical blue eyes. He looked what he was, a well-trained, fit, Allied officer. He would be interrogated, tortured horribly and then executed.

'Any questions?' Bill was asking.

Pale and trembling, Marietta stood up. 'You'll destroy our mission. Surely you realise that you could never hope to survive the scrutiny of the guards. How can a well-fed American pretend to be a Czech? Not one of us has an ounce of fat. You can't even speak Czech. Only German. Even then there's the problem of your American accent. Your whole idea is absurd. You could bring ruin to the entire operation.' She could hear from the men's remarks that they agreed with her.

'I didn't call for a debate,' Bill said, his voice ice-cold. 'Just questions. If you don't have any, then don't interrupt. Right now, Franz is going in. He'll be in charge in there. Franz is a qualified physicist and aeronautical engineer. Now let's get on with the training ...'

She couldn't listen. She stumbled into the forest and sank on to a fallen log. Despite the cool breeze she felt the sweat of fear on her face and stabs of pain in her stomach. *If Bill goes into the mine he'll never return.*

'Thanks for trying to sabotage me.' It was midnight and Bill had arrived unexpectedly, via the river. She had never seen him so angry. Tears burned her eyes. She clenched her fists and bit back a desire to plead and beg him to understan

'You would endanger all our lives. That's what I believe,' she lied stubbornly. She put some bread and cheese on the table with a glass of milk, but Bill refused to eat. He was standing astride, in the centre of the floor, his head lowered, eyes flashing, voice ice-cold.

'Marie, this mission was planned in London by my superiors. I have no freedom of action or thought. I must go in because I'll be needed there and because those are my orders. Listen to me, damn you,' he shouted, as she turned away. 'If all we had to do was destroy the mine, it would be so easy. My orders are specifically not to destroy the mine. It's far more complicated than you realise. I can't tell you anything more. You must believe that I must run the final operation.'

'Karol could . . . or Franz.'

'They have girls who love them, too, Marie.'

His voice, suddenly so soft and understanding, broke through her resistance. She flung herself into his arms and gave in to a storm of tears. For a few moments she let herself go. Then she pushed him away. 'I was so strong,' she said in an explosion of fury, as she backed away from him. 'Inviolate! Nothing could touch me. Now, all I think about is survival for you and me. You have taught me to care again and I know that if you go inside that camp, you'll die.'

'Nevertheless, I'm going in and I must beg you not to sabotage my authority again. How d'you think I feel when you drive to Kladno with a lorry full of explosives? You could be driving into a trap. Sooner or later the Bosch will find and crack Kova.'

She looked away obstinately.

'Come here, Marie. Come close. I want to hold you.'

'No. No more. I will not allow any more emotions to weaken me. Loving you makes me vulnerable. I can't take it . . . not now . . . I must be strong.'

'If that's important for your survival, then I understand,' he said softly. 'Our time will come, Marie, I promise you that. Someone up there has been saving us for each other.'

Marietta must be made of iron, Bill thought, two weeks later.

Once she had made up her mind she never deviated from her path. She had decided to be a fighter, not a woman, and she never betrayed, by a look or a whisper or some slight brush of her hand that she had any feelings. She ran the dairy, liaised with Kova and delivered the explosives. She never failed to bring food each day, even if, as sometimes happened, it was close to midnight. She didn't flag when she missed her sleep, she was never too tired to take over the radio, which nowadays Jan kept in the forest, and when the British made a drop, she was always waiting to help retrieve the supplies.

Bill remained in the forest, training the men. Every week, new men were picked to go into the camp. Some of them died, but some seemed to live a charmed existence, like Franz, for instance, who was still alive and operating brilliantly.

Most days, Marietta brought messages, via Kova ... the generators had blown, the air conditioning had failed, the lighting had fused, grit was found in the fuel, there was an outbreak of food poisoning ... and so on. Franz must be some sort of a genius, Bill decided.

Every night, Bill, Jan and Marietta huddled around the radio to listen to the BBC overseas news. They cheered when, on August 25, French troops led the march into Paris. The Allied armies had advanced fast after the Normandy breakout. General Patton's Third Army had swept through Orleans, Chartres and Dreux to link up with the British advancing on Rouen. On August 31, the Russians, fighting alongside the Rumanians, now their Allies, freed the Ploiesti oilfields, which had been supplying Germany with one third of her military oil. In September, Allied troops swept across Belgium to within twenty miles of the German border.

By mid-September the Germans were on the run right across Europe. In desperate preparation for the coming Allied invasion of Germany, Hitler ordered the call-up of all able-bodied males from sixteen to sixty to form the People's Guard.

Then, in October, came a setback which plunged the Czech freedom fighters into gloom. While Allied troops were concentrating on freeing the Low Countries, German troops made a last effort and penetrated more than thirty miles into Belgium, hoping to recapture Antwerp, in order to cut the Allies' vital supply route to their troops in the north. It was called the Battle of the Bulge, because German forces spearheaded sixty miles behind the Allied lines. By the beginning of December, the 'Bulge' was tying up Allied divisions and holding up the advance.

Bill sweated with fright. Every delay gave the Richard's Mine scientists more time to complete their tests and launch the new missile.

Franz knew the score. The mine must be blown up from within rather than let that missile be fired. Franz had enough explosives hidden away to do the job, but Bill prayed it would not be necessary.

It was Sunday night, December 10, 1944, and Hugo was lying in his huge double bed curled up behind Freda who was asleep. Hugo seldom slept more than four or five hours a night, but he liked to lie in bed and plan. His best ideas came to him this way.

Earlier that evening, Sweden had announced that the German chemist, Otto Hahn was to receive the Nobel prize for his work on nuclear fission. Hahn was a brilliant scientist, but totally impracticable, Hugo considered. After months of pressure, the SS had decided to exclude Hahn from the Richard's Mine team, and leave him to pursue his own theories. Nevertheless, it was Hahn's research which was being put to practical military purposes on the second level of Richard's Mine. Despite Hugo's threats, neither the warhead, nor the new long-range missiles were ready for testing. Hugo's ulcers worsened with the tension of trying to hurry the scientists. Professor Karl Ludwig had given him a date for firing the first prototype ... March next year. Hugo had to be content with that.

Hugo gave a gigantic burp and scalding acid flooded his

mouth. He was plagued with ill-health lately. Last night's war news had been particularly bad: thousands more people were homeless as a result of Allied bombings. There were food riots in Germany, and several women had been killed when they overturned a wagonload of potatoes. The Fatherland was without hope as civilians frantically dug trenches to defend their cities.

The V-3 was their only strength and their belief in the future. No one must be allowed to damage it, there was too much at stake. Hugo was not a fool. Despite their endless interrogations and their frequent executions, the plant was still being sabotaged. He could not believe that the recent spate of disasters were all due to natural accidents. Yet, exhaustive investigations could prove nothing and find no one. He knew he was up against Edelweiss who was always a step ahead, canny and cunning.

Chapter  71

ANDREA STOOD IN THE KINDERGARTEN BARRACK in the camp and tried not to let the children sense her tension. Her mouth was dry, and her heart was beating wildly with anticipation. Would they come? Or would the hours of pleading and planning be in vain?

It was Christmas day and the children had been promised double rations, and something wonderful besides ... so wonderful she could hardly believe it was true. She gazed lovingly at the half-starved mites gathered around her, looking up expectantly ... their eyes locked with hers in absolute trust. She had told them only of the extra slice of bread ... nothing else. She could never trust the promises of the Camp Commandant made to her publicly during a Red Cross visit.

She heard the rumble of the food trolley. Minutes later the half-crazed Russian peasant shuffled along. The children lined up, holding out their mugs and plates, tense with excitement. Two slices of black bread each, two teaspoons of beet marmalade, a cup of unsweetened acorn coffee. The little mites sat cross-legged, as she had taught them, and chewed the food slowly and carefully, extracting the maximum nourishment from each mouthful. All too soon the food was finished, but still their eyes were fixed on hers. In place of their parents and their homes they had only her, and she tried so hard to make their days lighter, but her heart was breaking most of the time.

Andrea went to the door of the camp and stood looking anxiously, but there was no sign of anyone coming their way. 'It was promised,' she muttered.

'Well, children,' she called. 'Put on your coats and line up.'

She had been teaching them Christmas carols, and she had received permission for them to sing to the guards and their families at their homes this morning. She hoped that the women would hand out sweets or presents. Besides, she knew what a treat it would be for the children to get away from their barbed wire enclosure and see grass and trees and perhaps a bird.

They were excited and scared as they left in a long orderly file. She gazed sadly at them, huddled in secondhand coats too large for them, their striped pyjamas flapping around skinny ankles.

Over-awed and silent, they reached the heavily guarded gate leading to the guards' married quarters. It had snowed days ago, and now the slush hung around in gutters. The sky was overcast, but at least it was not raining.

Trudging past the houses, the children oohed and aahed over the trees and grass and flowers. Little Clarissa burst into tears and Andrea swept her up in her arms to comfort her. Clarissa was seven years old, she came from Lidhaky and Andrea loved her dearly and planned to adopt her, if they survived the war, for she knew that both her parents were dead. She had short brown curls, big brown eyes and freckles. Now she was emaciated and pale-faced, but Andrea remembered when she had been a chubby child and always smiling.

They reached the Commandant's house and rang the bell.

'You must wait,' the Polish housemaid told them. Half an hour later the Commandant arrived and they were given permission to go to the back lawn and sing. Several wives were standing on the glass-enclosed balcony. They looked annoyed and embarrassed. The children sang *Silent Night* and *Away In A Manger*, in their sweet, shrill voices. Then the Commandant threw some sweets towards them, as if scattering corn to chicken. The children grovelled in the frozen earth for the sweets and two of them fought. Clarissa burst into tears, for she had not found one. 'Like animals . . .' Andrea heard from one of the wives.

'Only because they are so starved,' she said angrily. Her anger made her bold. Where were the treats she had envisaged?

'Herr Commandant, could we have some more sweets, please. After all, it's Christmas and they are children. "Suffer little children . . ."' she began, quaking inwardly, but nevertheless determined.

The Commandant shot her a glance of grudging respect. They had clashed on many occasions since Andrea took over the kindergarten a year before. She knew how to time her requests when there were witnesses. The Commandant liked to be known as a kind man. He tossed her another bag of sweets.

'And the swings,' she muttered urgently, knowing that she was pushing too hard.

'Yes . . . I gave my orders yesterday. I am a man of my word,' he said loudly.

She walked back feeling hopeful, but not convinced. The wind became colder, soon the children's energy was flagging. They were so frail nowadays, and their lips and cheeks were turning blue. She decided to carry Clarissa. She hugged her closely, smiling at the expression of bliss on the little girl's face as she sucked her second sweet, trying to make it last forever.

'Wonders will never cease,' she muttered as they neared the camp. Prisoners were putting the finishing touches to three swings. Suddenly it really was Christmas. To Andrea, the expressions on the children's faces was molten joy. That night they sung carols, the young voices blending with the tinny notes from the flute one of the prisoners had made for her. Andrea told them the Christmas story and the children took turns to act out the scenes. Their eyes lit up with wonder as the three wise men from the East brought their gifts, which were only pebbles, but in their eyes so real. Later, she tucked them up in bed and kissed each one goodnight.

For the past year and a half, Andrea had been teaching her

charges all she could remember. Hampered by the lack of any
equipment, books or paper, she did her best to teach them in
German, although they came from Russia, Poland, Czechoslovakia, and France.

It was almost the end of 1944. 'Dear God, let these children
live to see the end of the war, and protect Louis. Please let him
be alive and send him back to me. Let us all be free soon,' she
prayed, night after night.

On January 15, Andrea was summoned to the Camp Commandant's office. 'You have been transferred to the medical
block,' he told her, sending her world crashing. 'Report to
medical orderly Schmidt at once.'

'But the children need me,' she stammered, her fear for them
overcoming her terror. 'You said yourself how well I look after
them. You said there was no trouble anymore and that there are
far less illnesses amongst them since I took over the kindergarten. Don't you remember?'

The words tumbled out and the tears poured down her
cheeks. 'Please,' she said, knowing that it was permissible to beg
if it was for the children. 'Please don't send me away from them.
They need me.'

He seemed to have difficulty looking her in the eyes. 'You are
dismissed,' he said sternly. 'I want you to remember that I, too,
only obey orders.'

Why was he apologising to her? This, more than anything
else, set her body in a trauma of fear as she trudged back to the
kindergarten. She had decided to disobey to the extent of saying
goodbye to the children. 'It won't be forever,' she told them.
She tried to blink back her tears and be brave at the sight of
those skinny little faces pressed against the wire. Clawlike hands
clutched towards her and shining eyes, bright with starvation,
watched her walk away from them.

'Be good, be brave,' she called.

Andrea performed her duties in a daze, not really there at all,
but seeing the row of solemn faces watching her walk away. As
the day wore on she became increasingly desperate. Why had

the Camp Commandant apologised? Why had he looked so ashamed? Who was looking after the children? It was dark by 5 p.m. Andrea was changing dressings on the patients when she saw a line of lorries rumbling towards the kindergarten. 'Oh God, no . . . no . . .' she screamed.

Suddenly she was running . . . The soldiers had turned on their searchlights and the kindergarten was as bright as day. She could hear guards shouting, dogs snarling and the terrified screams of the children. She ran faster, almost falling with exhaustion. She arrived as the soldiers dragged the last terrified children out to the lorries. Their anguished cries tore at her heartstrings.

She clawed her way through the soldiers towards Clarissa. A blow from a rifle knocked her senseless to the ground.

One morning early in March, Andrea woke to find herself in the mental block. This was strange. Surely she had been walking in a field with Louis, watching the Vltava flow past. She returned to the present reluctantly. She had no idea what she was doing in hospital. She tried to stand, but it was an effort. Doctor Schmidt found her stumbling around, trying to keep her balance and sent a nurse to help her. She had been there for two months, she learned later that day. Yet the last thing she remembered was little Clarissa standing forlorn in the lorry, calling out to her. It was all over. They were only a memory now . . . those lovely children.

Somehow she obtained permission to speak to the Commandant.

'I see that there are more children in the kindergarten,' she said accusingly.

'Yes, of course.' He stared at his hands, refusing to meet her eyes.

'Will they, too, go to the death camps?'

'Perhaps. Who knows? I told you before, I only obey orders.'

'And in the meantime, who is looking after them?' she demanded.

'Bertha, the Russian.'

'She's half-witted and sadistic,' she burst out.

The Commandant gestured for the guard to leave them. 'Do you know why I am here?' he said, when they were alone.

'No, and I don't want to know.'

'I was invalided from the Eastern front. Shell shock, burns, wounded, unfit for duty, but fit enough to run this camp. Nothing could be as bad as this. Nothing. I always wanted to be a soldier, not a murderer.'

'I'm not interested in your excuses,' she said sternly. 'Others have the courage to disobey orders that are evil.'

He opened her file. 'Your father was the conductor of the Prague orchestra, and you attended Munich university to study music. You play the oboe and the piano and have given several solo performances. It's all here in your file. I can offer you the post of organising a camp orchestra,' he muttered.

'I want to look after the children. At least for the period that they remain here.'

'Very well,' he said, his face impassive. 'But do you think you are strong enough?'

'Yes.'

'You may return to the kindergarten, but if you crack up when the next consignment goes east, I shall not allow you back.'

'*Consignment? Goes east?*' she muttered incredulously. 'Is that you how keep your conscience at bay? With euphemisms? Do you mean when you murder the next batch of children?'

His eyes became very cold as he called to the guard. 'Escort this prisoner to the kindergarten,' he said.

Chapter  72

HUGO WAS STANDING at his office window staring out gloomily. It was cold, even for March, the sky a wintry grey, the wind blustering. A sudden gust sent the curtains billowing and filled the room with the tang of the river.

Hugo's adjutant knocked and came in, saluting smartly before standing to attention. Hugo glanced at him impatiently, saw his fear and understood his agony. He was a fanatical Nazi and he never spoke about the worsening war news. It was treasonable to be a defeatist, but the facts spoke for themselves.

The Allied forces were closing in on Berlin. Cologne had fallen to the Allies only yesterday. Soon the Fatherland would be occupied. Not that there would be much left for them, for 1000-bomber raids were reducing German homes and industries to rubble. It was only a matter of days before the Russians crossed the border into Austria. News had just come through from headquarters that all personnel were being evacuated from the rocket base at Peenemunde because the Russians were only hours away.

That meant Richard's Mine was the only long-range rocket base left. The problem was time and the damned partisans. There had been so many accidents during the past ten days, and this had delayed progress. Did they have long enough to test the missile and know with certainty that the flight plan was accurate? The slightest error could lead to a nuclear bomb exploding on German territory. The scientists wanted to fire three unarmed rockets first, but Hugo was determined that the nuclear warhead be fired just as soon as the rocket was ready for launching.

Could the V-3 win the war for Hitler? Common sense told him that it could not, but it could inflict massive damage, and wipe out several major cities. After the first explosion, the civilian populations of every Allied city would be at risk, and Germany would be in a position to demand favourable peace terms, or even a truce. Yes, definitely a truce. They would hold the world hostage.

'Time is running short,' Hugo muttered, half to himself and half to his adjutant. 'Somehow we must arrest the agent known as Edelweiss. And, for once and for all, we must destroy the Resistance.' He walked to the window and gazed out for a few moments. 'I want you to send for a consignment of Russian prisoners-of-war. When they arrive, we'll execute all the unskilled labour in the mine. Everyone! From now on, we'll stick to Russian workers. Then we'll be safe from infiltration of Czechs disguised as camp inmates.

'Contact the camp commandant. Get me details of all suppliers who have access to the camp.'

'We've investigated every person who liaises with the camp, sir,' his adjutant said. 'Many times . . .'

'We'll start again, and this time, I shall supervise the interrogations.'

Within a day, Hugo had narrowed the list of twenty-five men down to five. One of them was Miroslav Kova, a *Volksdeutsche*. He had been cleared previously because he was a member of the local Nazi party caucus, a relative of the camp commandant, and the owner of a small abattoir in Kladno which was heavily dependant upon Nazi patronage. Why would a man like that turn traitor? Nevertheless, lately Kova had been spending heavily in the local bistro.

*

After two days of non-stop interrogation, Hugo was convinced Kova was guilty although he stuck to his story that he was a drinking buddy of the Commandant and that he was not such a bloody fool as to prejudice his own business. On impulse, Hugo drove to Prague, parked, and shortly afterwards he was hurrying up the black marble stairs into the impressive foyer of Gestapo headquarters at Petsechek House. The guards jumped to attention and saluted as Hugo took the lift down to the old bank vaults. Kova was strapped in a wooden chair, surrounded by floodlights. His belly sagged over his belt, his vest was dark with sweat, his bare feet were grimy. There was something about Kova that stank, apart from his sweating body, Hugo thought with a grim smile, as he watched the man's pathetic efforts to ingratiate himself with his interrogators. Hugo settled down in the corner to study Kova's file. What he saw there gave him an idea.

'Come on, friends,' Kova blustered, 'I'm one of you. All this brutality ... what's it for? You've got the wrong man. I'm innocent, I tell you. I've got a good business going with the camp. They take all my production. Why would I want to double-cross my customers? If anyone asked me to act as go-between, I'd tell them to go to hell.'

'All right, Sergeant,' Hugo said sternly, striding across the floodlit area to sit behind the desk. 'Now! Let me see. Who do we have here?' He glanced at the file. 'Herr Kova looks like an honest *Volksdeutsche* trader to me. Untie him.'

'Have a cigarette, Kova.' Hugo's face creased into a friendly grimace. 'I can see they made a mistake. I'm sorry. Send for coffee,' Hugo called over his shoulder.

Kova was assisted to a chair on the other side of the desk.

'I'll have you sent to the showers. We'll reimburse you for your suit. These SS filth have no understanding of people. They go in like sharks at the smell of blood. You see ...' he rubbed his hands anxiously and shrugged apologetically. 'We have a problem. Some foolish people who oppose the Reich have been pestering every trader who has access to the camp. They're desperate for couriers. Somewhere along the line, someone said

"yes" to their advances.' Hugo gestured towards the interrogators. 'It's their job to find out who that person is.'

Kova shuddered. 'It wasn't me. I said "no".' He was burning
with relief and mopping his brow. When the coffee arrived he
grabbed his cup and began to slurp noisily.

'Ah! So you said "no" . . . emphatically.'

'That's for sure.' Kova thumped his fist on the desk.

'To whom did you say this emphatic "no". In other words,
who asked you?'

'As you said . . . everyone was asked.'

'Did I say that? No, I don't think I said anything of the kind.
We simply imagined that this might have taken place. Now
you've just confirmed our suspicions. Herr Kova, why didn't
you report this conversation to your nearest *Blockwart*? We
could have trapped the filthy spy immediately.'

'Well . . .' Kova was sweating even more heavily now. 'I
wanted to keep out of it. I didn't want to get involved.'

'Obviously you are sympathetic to these subversives, or you
would have reported them at once.' Hugo's friendliness was
replaced with ferocious efficiency.

He fired the next questions like bullets: 'When . . . ? Where . . . ?
By whom . . . ? A full description please . . . On what date . . . ?
How many times have you met them . . . ?'

Kova, by implication, was now involved, in fact, practically
one of them.

'Once,' Kova stammered. 'Only once. It was at night in a dark
alley. I didn't see him.' He cleared his throat noisily. 'I don't
remember when it was.'

'This is very serious for you, Kova. You are the only witness
we have of this traitor. It might be the same man who
assassinated many of our leaders here. You're in big trouble,
Kova. You withheld vital information. The Resistance would
not approach you unless they knew you were sympathetic to
their cause. You've been assisting them, haven't you . . . ? Filthy
swine!'

He stood up and threw the rest of his coffee into Kova's eyes.
Then he hit him hard several times.

Half an hour later, Kova was dragged to the cells. He was so terrified he could not stand. Hugo watched pitilessly as the gross body crumpled.

It took Hugo two weeks to find Kova's fifteen-year-old daughter, who had been hidden with distant relatives in the country. Amazing that Kova could sire such a pretty daughter, Hugo thought, eyeing her. She had long, honey blonde plaits, which looked pretty when they were loosened to hang over her shoulders, and her big blue eyes were swimming with tears. She was led to the interrogation room where Hugo raped her. Her screams mingled with those of her father, who was forced to watch. But he didn't change his story. Then she was raped and sodomised by ten agents until she passed out. They brought her round with buckets of cold water and began fixing electric wires to her body.

By now, Kova was yelling so loudly, it was hard to write down all the information he was revealing. 'Leave my daughter, you fucking monsters. I'll tell you everything ... everything. Just let her go,' he sobbed. 'I liaise with the butcher in the camp. I carry messages for a woman. Her name is Edelweiss ... short black hair ... tall and thin ... I don't know where she lives and I don't know her real name. She's high up in the Resistance, that's all I know. I was recruited by a man with a limp. He never told me his name. Leave my daughter ... I beg you. She's innocent. She knows nothing. I'll tell you all I know, I promise,' he sobbed. 'She's only fifteen. My God!'

Hugo tried to disguise his shock. A woman! Was that possible? Then excitement took over, they were getting close to Edelweiss at last. 'Take the girl away. All right, Kova, you know what she'll get if you give us any more trouble. We have far more imaginative ways of dealing with the daughters of men who betray us.'

'Don't please ... I'm begging you.'

'It's up to you. I want you to describe this agent, this Edelweiss. A woman, you say? That's curious. Think hard. Your daughter's life depends on you.'

Later that day, Kova was patched up and sent back to the

abattoir, while his daughter was kept as a hostage. Hugo drove to Sokol feeling optimistic. The deal with Kova was quite simple: the female traitor in return for his daughter's life and freedom. The trap was set. Edelweiss would be captured within days.

Jan was in the loft liaising with the various groups when Ehrhardt's message came through. Kova had been interrogated and planted back at the abattoir to trap the Resistance. His daughter had been held hostage but, unbeknown to Kova, she had hanged herself in her cell.

'But right now Edelweiss is delivering explosives to Kova.' Jan's finger was shaking as he tapped out his message in morse code. 'Try to intercept Edelweiss.'

'Impossible. We are miles away,' Ehrhardt's message came back before the line went dead.

What could he do? Jan sat tapping out the code number of every group near Prague. Eventually he managed to raise Georg Kolar. 'Tell Kova that his daughter hanged herself. The Nazis don't want him to know this. He must not betray an innocent patriot. He must work with us for revenge. Tell him we're sorry.'

Marietta found Miroslav Kova in the yard. He was skinning a large bullock and she shuddered.

'Kova?' she called out.

'Come over here . . . come quickly.'

When he turned, she gasped in terror. Kova's face was like a yellow pumpkin. Two half-closed, bloodshot eyes gazed at her from a face that was huge and pulpy. *He's been badly beaten. Gestapo!* Too late to run away. Her heart lurched, pain shot through her stomach and her mouth dried. She was doomed. This was it . . . the end. How would Bill cope with a second loss? All these thoughts raced through her mind in a flash.

'Am I trapped?' she gasped.

'Yes. God protect us both. I was waiting for you.' He pushed her into a shed and kicked at a pile of straw. There was a grid with an iron ring set into it.

'Jump down, quickly. The abattoir is surrounded. My daughter is dead, so there's no point in betraying you. I can't let you suffer as she did.' Marietta could hear footsteps running from across the street. A whistle blew. There were shouts from above.

He caught hold of her arm with amazing strength and pushed her into the darkness. The grid slammed back over their heads. 'It's covered in straw, but they'll soon find it,' he muttered.

For a few moments she couldn't stand and all she could hear was her rasping breath. It was pitch dark. 'Pull yourself together. Run for your life. Run,' she heard.

She pushed her hands out in front of her and took her first blundering steps forward. There was a smell of dampness and decay. Rotting flesh collided against her, swaying backwards and forwards, beating against her face and shoulders.

Kova flicked on his torch, flung open the cellar door and thrust her through. She skidded and slipped. The floor sloped away and she was falling ... suddenly she was on her back, sliding down into the mire. She was in the sewers. Rats were scurrying over her, squeaking in panic. There was a sound of water rushing nearby. She climbed to her feet painfully and cautiously, feeling her legs, but Kova grabbed her and pushed her forward.

'Hurry ... hurry ...,' he muttered. 'They'll find the trap door soon. They have lights ... guns ... Move!' They were in the main sewerage channel which was dimly lit from grids set into the road above. They were going downhill. They kept running until she thought her lungs would explode. From time to time she saw trap doors above with stone steps leading up to them.

An hour later, Kova let her rest on a stone block where two tunnels met.

When they could stop panting they listened, straining in the darkness. There was the sound of whistles far off.

'I tried to trap you,' Kova said unexpectedly with a sob in his voice. 'I was going to turn you in. They made a deal. My daughter for you. God forgive me, but I'd do it again, only she's dead. My poor little daughter is dead. Von Hesse raped her ... they all raped her ... and other things. Horrible. She hanged herself. She'd been so well brought up, she was such a quiet little girl. Wouldn't hurt a fly. Can you ever forgive me?'

'I'm so sorry, Herr Kova,' she said. 'Thank you for saving my life. Of course, I don't blame you. I'm so sorry about your daughter.'

'Go that way,' he said. 'Keep to the running water. That'll fox their dogs. I'm going this way, so I'll draw them after me. I know this place like the back of my hand. I deliver meat on the black market, you see. Now listen! Count ten flights of steps and take the eleventh. You'll come out in the outskirts of Slanyl, near the woods. You'll be safe there.'

'Herr Kova,' she said. 'If you survive the war, please come and find me. My name is Marietta. I'm the late Princess Lobkowitz's granddaughter. I would like to ...'

'After the war ... perhaps ... In the meantime, run like hell.'

Chapter  73

BILL WAS DEMONSTRATING a new type of fuse, dropped in from Britain the previous evening. The men were eager to learn, so Bill tried to concentrate and keep his mind away from his fears. Marie had not arrived with their supper. Bill knew she had gone to liaise with Kova, and this had plunged him into a morass of fear and anxiety. Why was she late? What had happened?

So far he had ten men still alive in the mine, apart from Franz, plus enough explosives hidden there to blow the research station sky high. Hopefully he would never have to.

When midnight came and the freedom fighters settled down in the woodsman's hut for the night, and still Marie had not returned from Kladno, Bill began to feel sick with tension.

The men were joking and laughing. An occasional cigarette flared in the dark. 'One of these days,' Bill heard, 'I shall get me a big fat widow and retire to bed for a week. You won't get a peep out of me. I'll sleep the sleep of the damned.'

'And the widow?' one of them called out. 'She won't be very pleased with that.'

'She'll be sleeping too. She'll be too exhausted to do anything else.'

Bill heard a few chuckles in the darkness and he guessed they were remembering better days.

'I shall eat a whole pig to myself,' one of them called. 'I shall start with the trotters and move upwards ... chops, liver, fried with onions and dumplings, roast pork for dinner, with potatoes and pumpkins, masses of vegetables, ham and eggs for breakfast ...'

They were simple men, but honest and brave. They listened, like children to a fairy story, while Bill lay on his back, willing Marie to come.

And I? What shall I do? he mused. I shall build a house high up with a view, so that Marie will feel at home. Perhaps she'll breed horses or run our ranch. Whatever she wants she will have. But what would she want? Plenty of servants ... ? Or a homely lifestyle ... ? He loved her with all his heart, but he had to admit that he had no idea what sort of life she would choose. Would she want one child or many? A ranch style home, or something opulent? Would she be able to settle down as a housewife and mother after all this? He fell asleep dreaming of Marie at home with him, her hair long as it used to be, her face alight with joy, her eyes beaming with love and warmth. Would it ever be like that again? Would their time ever come?

He woke with a start and glanced at his watch. He must not sleep deeply. At 5 a.m. he must be out in the field for the next drop. He hoped they'd remembered the boots this time. His men were reliant on broken and patched footwear and it was very cold.

Bill had another favourite dream, which he indulged in from time to time. It was of going back to London, after the war, and wringing the neck of whoever it was who planned their equipment drops. There was never enough. It was seldom what they had asked for and often it was broken on arrival. Ah well. Perhaps one day all his dreams would come true.

An hour later, Jan woke him and the squad with the news that Marie had been caught. They must move on to new quarters, just in case she broke under interrogation. The dairy was blown and so were the cellars and their radio base, although they had others. The lorry had been towed away. Kova had disappeared.

Bill was shaking with fear and rage as he pushed Jan into the corner. He caught the cripple round the neck and shook him. He would have punched him, had Jan been stronger. 'You little shit. Is that all you can think about ... saving our skins? Goddamn you!' He slammed Jan against the wall. 'We're talking about Marie,' he muttered. 'We're going to rescue her. Where have they taken her? Tell me! Tell me where they've taken her.' He was pulled off Jan by four strong men.

Jan rubbed his neck. 'As far as we know, she's still in the abattoir. Presumably they're interrogating her there to save time. The place is crawling with troops and Gestapo. Von Hesse is there and half his staff. We must move ... at once. She might break. Use your sense, man. There's no way we can rescue her. The whole area is cordoned off. They're taking no chances.

'Two minor explosions have been registered in Richard's Mine by Kolar's group. Franz is doing a fine job. That's what it's all about, isn't it, Roth?' Jan shouted, oblivious to the stares of the men. 'We're here to stop the Bosch from firing the V-3. Or did you think you were here to look after your girl? Now get out of here and supervise the drop.' Sick with fear and grief, Bill forced himself on to his feet. He felt strange: wobbling legs, shaking hands, eyes burning and brimming over. 'Oh God help her,' he prayed.

That night Bill was tortured by his images of Marie in the hands of the SS. He had no illusions. He knew what they did. That night he reached the depths of despair.

The following evening, Marie found Bill in his forest hut, supervising the packing of the explosives dropped by the RAF. He looked exhausted and sick. He was wearing an old, polonecked jersey, and his face was pinched and blue with cold. His cheeks were blotchy and his eyes looked haggard. His breath rose in a white mist above him as he bent over the table, straining to see. It was dusk. The sky was a ruddy glow in the west and the trees were silhouetted black against the deep rose. It was well below freezing and the temperature was still dropping.

'Bill, darling.' She stood in the doorway and Bill was poised halfway between joy and astonishment.

'Oh my God! Oh my dear . . .' He walked towards her looking dazed, his eyes streaming with tears. 'They said you were taken and there was nothing I could do to rescue you. That was the worst part of it, being so helpless, not knowing what was happening to you, not being able to help you . . . Oh, thank God, thank God, my dearest Marie. I've never seen anything as wonderful as you standing there unharmed,' he croaked.

He leaned shakily against the doorpost and caught hold of her. She felt his fingers biting into her shoulder. She could see what an effort it was to hang on to his composure in front of his men. 'Sit down here and tell me what happened.'

They sat side by side on a low wooden bench, Bill's arm around her waist, her head on his shoulder.

Oblivious to the embarrassed stares of the men, Marie poured out her story. 'I feel exhausted, Bill,' she said afterwards. 'And I still smell. Fortunately, I emerged near the Kolars' place and they heated two baths for me, but still I stink like a pigsty. Georg dropped me back here in his delivery lorry.'

Bill shuddered. 'It was so close,' he whispered eventually. 'Too close, Marie. I almost lost you for the second time. I don't want there ever to be a third time. You don't have nine lives like a cat. Please, think of us. Be careful. Keep out of trouble. Stay here in the forest with me.'

'I have to stay here, my darling. I have nowhere else to go. The dairy is blown and so is Lara Zimmerman.'

'You'll never know what it was like for me . . .'

'Oh my love. I was thinking of you. I decided I've been wrong. I should have given you all the love I could, without counting the cost. We may never reach the war's end. I want something to hold on to. Something to live for. My old memories are worn out, I've relived them too many times. I'm going to stay with you tonight and every night while there's still time. I want to love you enough to last a lifetime.'

'Don't say that. Don't talk as if there's no future for us. I'm telling you now, Marie, we're going to win through.'

*

It was a night which seemed to last forever. Moonlight poured through the broken roof and soon the moon crossed their narrow strip of private sky. She clung to him, shuddering with desire.

He unbuttoned her blouse slowly, running his lips over her neck and her small but lovely breasts, sucking the nipples, tugging and caressing.

Marietta felt herself losing control, slipping into a state of uncontrollable passion. Her need was blotting out reason. She forgot the war and the future and their fears and abandoned herself to the present. She had been close to death. This was a reprieve. Who could tell how long they had? She must force a lifetime of loving into these precious days and nights. Nothing counted but the nearness of Bill and her craving to be impaled upon his hard, strong body.

Watching her, Bill had an overwhelming urge to take her somewhere safe and protect her forever. She looked so vulnerable lying there naked on the straw mattress, he loved her brave, straight shoulders, her small waist and rounded hips and the sweet curling blonde hairs on her mound. Her blue eyes were watching him anxiously.

'What is it?' she murmured.

'So frail ... so vulnerable ... but so brave,' he whispered. Passion glowed in her eyes, she was brimming over with it, he could see from the pallor of her face, her swollen lips and moist thighs. 'I love you Marie. You'll never know how I've longed for this.' He pulled her round towards him with an urgent, impulsive movement, pushed her thighs apart and thrusting his tongue into her as she lay on her side, his tongue probing her hidden places, loving the moist, tight feel of her as she lay acquiescent and passive, craving more and still more of him.

She groaned with the anguish and the beauty of it.

'Oh Bill. I love you. If we have nothing else, we'll have this night.'

'Hush, darling ... Don't talk like that. We must both trust that it will work out for us.'

They lay close together, wet body against wet body, clutching each other tightly, until they fell asleep.

In the morning Marietta awoke to birdsong and the knowledge that they were clasped tightly in each other's arms. An onrush of tenderness flooded through her at the sight of that well-loved profile. She put her finger on her lips and touched him gently. He stirred and pulled her close against him without opening his eyes. Strange to love someone so much, she thought. She wanted nothing more from life than to lie beside Bill, holding him. If only she could make time stand still.

Later, she got out of bed, shivering with cold, and pulled on her clothes. She must find some way to wash herself, she thought, looking around. She couldn't help smiling. Bill had tried to make the loft habitable. There was a chair, a primus stove, a radio, a few books, an old blackened kettle, one saucepan with a broken handle, a knife, fork and spoon on a shelf, with half a loaf of stale bread on a rusty plate. 'Oh Bill,' she giggled. 'Is this how American millionaires live?'

'A private place like this, deep in an uninhabited forest, is hard to come by,' Bill said. 'Come and look.'

Through a slit of window in the sloping roof, she saw the new leaf buds on the trees, there were patches of yellow primroses, with violets under the brambles. She could see a hare nibbling new grass and birds were busily gathering twigs for their nests.

'If only . . . ,' she murmured.

From then on, Marie cleaned their hut, cooked their food, washed their clothes and helped Bill to bundle up the tiny packets of explosives that would be smuggled into the mine. Jan had found another courier, the local poultry farmer, whom he had bribed with a substantial cash deposit outside Czechoslovakia.

One day, early in April, Bill confided in Marie.

'After I'm gone . . . I mean into the camp . . . things might look pretty bleak, but it's not as bad as you might think. My main job is not to blow the mine, merely to see that the V-3 is never fired. In fact, if the Bosch try to blow it up, we have to stop them. The Americans are coming across the Bavarian border to dismantle the mine and take the research and scientists back with them. We're not expecting much resistance. The main body of German troops will be guarding their Eastern flanks against the Russians.

'Now Jan, being a Communist, intends that the Soviets will get most of this research. To be honest with you, that's the second reason why I'm here. I have to make sure the Reds don't get it. Blow it up, if the American troops don't make it in time. Hopefully this won't be necessary. Jan must never know what's happening until it's too late for him to do anything about it. As you know, the Yalta Agreement stipulates that Czechoslovakia will be under Russian control. We're expecting that the Germans will try to hold up the Russians for as long as possible on the eastern borders, long enough for the Americans to advance, on the pretence of giving the Russians a helping hand. Once they've freed Theresienstadt and dismantled the mine, they'll retreat, if ordered to do so. So don't count on American troops going further east than the mine. Got that?'

'Marie, there's something else that has to be done and I can't entrust this job to Jan – I'm going to have to ask you. I have here a list of the main scientists we want to swing over to our side. It's possible that some of them might not be in the mine. As you know, they all get alternate weekends off. If any of these eleven men and their families are outside the mine, they must be prevented from fleeing, in the face of the American advance. Held by force, if necessary, until the Americans arrive. There will be agents with the troops, able to talk these guys round to our side. Ultimately they will be given the choice, but their alternative might be a prison camp. Here's the list. Can you do this?'

'Yes,' she said simply. 'The Communists are the best fighters, but I'll have to choose from the others. Fortunately, I know which are which.'

She broke off and watched Bill curiously. 'You're far away, what are you thinking?' she asked.

He was thinking about Ingrid. She, too, had a part to play. 'Too much to think about,' Bill said and lapsed into silence.

Now was not the time to tell Marie about Ingrid, but one day he would do just that. Right now it was up to Ingrid and Schofield to convince the Germans to keep the bulk of their troops on their eastern borders. They must believe that the Americans had no plans to cross the Bavarian border into Czechoslovakia. American troops must be able to move fast. So much depended upon speed. There was a limit to the time he could hold up the mine against a planned attack.

That night, Marietta lay propped on one elbow, studying Bill's face in the moonlight. She wanted to memorise him exactly, so that she could always remember how he had looked. He opened his eyes and smiled at her. 'Everything's going to be all right,' he said, but his pale face belied his words. They clung to each other, and Marie tried not to cry. Time was running out for both of them.

Chapter  74

IT WAS EARLY MORNING in the forest, dew-soaked leaves glittered in the sunlight and there were patches of bluebells under the trees. Marietta was unpacking last night's drop of explosives in the forest hut with the door open, when two shadows blocked the light. Moments later Jan walked in, but she caught a glimpse of a grey uniform outside.

A soldier! Her stomach knotted, but she could see from Jan's manner that there was nothing to worry about. Jan pushed the man away from the doorway. 'Wait,' he said, and his voice was soft. 'It's better if you wait over there.' Something about his tone puzzled her. He was friendly . . . almost gentle . . .

'There's someone here . . .' Jan put his hands on her shoulders, pulling her round to face him. 'Marietta, listen, prepare yourself for a shock. He's not as you remember him . . . What can you expect? He's had a rough time . . . He escaped from a Siberian prisoner-of-war camp. Naturally, he's suffered . . .'

'My God, Jan . . . What are you saying . . . ? Are you telling me . . .?' She pushed him away, ran outside and stopped short, rooted to the ground. The soldier sitting on an old stone bench under the oak tree was white-haired. A tough man, old before his time, and he was crouched forward over his knees as if in great agony, his head in his hands. She searched for something she could recognise, noting the grizzled neck, the strong bony frame, hands that were sinewy, calloused and scarred. Could he be Louis? Could she dare to hope? She crept forward. 'Who are you?' she whispered.

He turned sideways and peered up from under his tousled hair, a familiar gesture that propelled her into the past. Memories too painful to bear flooded in. She burst into tears and rushed towards him, arms outstretched, flung herself at him and then held back. 'Dearest Louis.' She put one hand gently on each cheek and turned his head towards her. His blurred image wavered in and out of focus through her tears. 'Oh Louis,' she murmured again. 'My prayers are answered. You're alive, you came home. Thank you, Louis. And thank God.' She caught hold of his hand and pressed it against her lips. 'You're crying,' she said. 'Why are you crying . . .?'

'Jan didn't tell me . . . He brought me here without warning me. I thought you had died, too. They told me that you had died of tuberculosis in Lichtenstein camp. And now . . . Oh, Marietta, my God, what did they do to you?'

He caught hold of her arm and ran one finger over the burnt tissue, examined her face, ran his forefinger over her cheeks and round her eyes. Then he hugged her so tightly she almost couldn't breathe. She clutched him, feeling the strangely hard, muscled back and the sinewy arms and the massive strength of him. He was like an iron board, his arms like steel girders. 'It was terrible not knowing . . . yes, that was the worst, hoping and often losing hope, and forcing myself to have faith . . .'

He looked at her and smiled. 'I survived. I went to hell, but I'm back.' He tightened his grip, as if scared to lose her.

Marietta tried to stop the tears from trickling down her cheeks. She sniffed loudly and wiped her nose with the back of her hand.

'Steady on,' he said, rocking her gently backwards and forwards. He stroked her neck, and fondled her hair. 'I'd never be fooled by this,' he said, touching her dyed black stubbly locks. 'I don't know why you bother.'

'Because of Hugo. I have so much to tell you, but it can wait for a better time.'

'Are we the only ones left? I can't even say her name. Oh God, it hurts so badly. When I left hospital, I went straight to Lidhazy and then I found ...' He gave a long, shuddering sigh. 'I fought my way back to be with Andrea. The last letter she wrote me was full of happiness because she was pregnant. Oh God, Marietta...'

'Andrea wasn't killed, Louis,' she murmured, still cradled in his arms. 'Your baby died, but Andrea was taken to a concentration camp. The last time we had news, she was still alive.'

She felt Louis shudder. He turned away and covered his face with his hands. All she could see were his shoulders shaking. Eventually, he looked round and smiled wearily. 'Two in one day. The two women I love the most ... both alive. So it was worth it ... all of it was worthwhile. And Father? They said he'd died, too.'

'Yes,' she said gently. 'He died in an explosion. There's so much to tell you, Louis, but not yet. After the war, perhaps. Right now we have work to do. We need you. There's someone here you must meet. You'll be so surprised.'

Andrea struggled to climb out of her bunk, but she felt so weak she could not manage. She had been ill for months. Recurring bouts of bronchitis, enteritis and impetigo had weakened her system until she was hardly able to drag herself around the medical block. There was no joy in her work since the last of the children had been taken away. Physically and mentally she was at a low ebb. Nevertheless, she had forced herself to continue, knowing that the Germans were losing the war and it was only a matter of time before they were freed. Those who became too weak to work were exterminated. That terrible thought had inspired her to use every last ounce of strength she possessed, but now she was finished.

Blows from the *schlag* landed on her body. She pulled her

hands up to protect her head, but even that was an effort. The wretched, half-witted German supervisor, imprisoned for vagrancy, never showed any compassion. A guard was summoned, an entry was made in the prisoner register, and Andrea was half-dragged to the railway siding and pushed on to a cattle train going east. She remained propped against the wall as waves of nausea swept through her. She hardly knew what was happening, only that this was the end. There were fifteen prisoners in the compartment and all of them were very ill. Andrea slipped down on to the floor, grateful that there was enough room to lie straight. She wanted to die before she reached the gas ovens. That was the final humiliation which she had always longed to avoid.

Andrea lay in the compartment, day after painful day, and tried to fill her last hours with memories of the happy times, before she and Louis were arrested. Sometimes she would stare at the stars, and her head would be filled with the most beautiful concertos and symphonies. She felt regret that she would never again play the oboe, never see Louis, or return to Vienna, which she loved so much.

To her surprise, days later, she was still living, still in pain, still starving. If only it would end. How many days had she lain in the compartment? She had no idea, only that it had taken a very long time, with frequent stops for air raids and long waits in sidings for troop trains to take priority.

They were going east, to another camp, the SS sergeant had told them. He seemed to be a compassionate man, for he allowed them to empty their sewage buckets and he ordered the guards to give them fresh water when they needed it. Once a day he made sure they received bread.

On her fifth night in the train, another woman pulled her to her feet and pointed to the eastern horizon which was brilliant with flares and searchlights and vivid flashes of exploding bombs and shells.

The front line! This was unbelievable. She was filled with excitement. She could feel herself flushing, her eyes were burning. Were they so close to rescue? If she could only live for just a little longer. Hope made her feel stronger ... strong enough to stand unaided.

The terrifying thunder of the front line came closer during the night as the train moved slowly eastwards. At dawn they were shunted into a siding for another long wait. One of the prisoners further up the line spoke to a guard and sent back the wonderful news, shouted from one truck to the next: *the death camp was behind the Russians' lines.*

Hope was better than the finest medicines, it surged through her tired body giving her new life. 'Perhaps I shall live after all.'

After a seven-hour wait, the train was shunted on to the tracks. This time they were moving back towards Germany and they were all plunged into a trough of depression. At dawn the train was attacked by Russian planes. They flew so low, she could see the red stars on their wings. The train's engine was hit and the smoke billowed down over the trucks, choking the prisoners. The sergeant ordered his men to unlock the trucks and get the prisoners out. Those who could walk, assisted their sicker comrades. They stood amongst grass and trees feeling bewildered. The SS guarded them, but even they could see the futility of their guns. None of the prisoners were capable of walking more than a few yards.

That night the front line seemed to be only a mile away. The ground reverberated with the blast, so that the noise hurt Andrea's ear drums and battered her meagre body. She thought it was like being beaten by sound. She tried to calm the other prisoners with soothing words. At midnight their guards deserted them. Two of the corporals, who were mechanics, had found an abandoned lorry in a farm, which they had managed to mend. They all piled into it. 'The Russians will come for you,' the sergeant explained, as he left the prisoners cowering in the field.

After that it began to rain and soon they were sodden. Some of the prisoners returned to the carriages for protection, but Andrea sat on a tree stump in the field and drew strength from being free. 'Survive,' she whispered to herself. 'Just survive. Only a few more days. You can make it.'

At dawn, three Russian tanks came rolling towards them. Some of the prisoners held up white rags which fluttered in the breeze. The first Russian driver climbed out of his tank and stared at them long and hard.

Andrea glanced around nervously. She had become so used to the sight of the living dead around her. Now, for the first time, she took in the sunken eyes, the skeletal-like figures from which their striped overalls hung as if from sticks, the shaved scalps. Eyes without hope. Dead eyes! Claws for hands, and they were all so full of sores and blemishes.

The Russians were calling on their radio for ambulances and food. They shared all the food they had and clasped the prisoners' hands, with tears in their eyes and bellowed at them in Russian. Then they left.

Andrea had been given a bar of chocolate. She licked it carefully, not wanting to eat something so precious.

They were free, but destitute, and Andrea was feeling light-headed.

An hour later a Russian army canteen truck came racing over the fields with a Red army doctor who spoke German. He desperately urged them not to eat too much, they could kill themselves by taking in too much food. They were given soup and bread. A feeling of well-being stole through Andrea even from the sparse meal. She could feel every particle of her body seizing joyfully on the food. The doctor dispensed whatever first aid he could. He told them he would wait with them until the troops could locate a suitable hospital for them. Six hours later the ambulances arrived.

'I'm going to live,' Andrea muttered to herself as she lay on a stretcher and was bumped and rocked over the rough road. 'I'm going to survive the war, and I'm going to find Louis.' She began to cry with relief. She felt embarrassed by this absurd reaction to what should be the happiest day of her life, but the tears kept coming and there seemed to be no end to them. She tried to explain to the Russian doctor who was sitting beside her holding her hand. 'I never cried. I fought, and grumbled, and screamed sometimes, and endured as best I could, but I never cried. Now that I'm happy, I can't stop crying.'

'I shall cry for the rest of my life after seeing this,' the doctor said in fluent German.

The hospital was at Sepolno. It had been abandoned by the Germans several weeks before, and hastily restocked and staffed by the Russians. There, Andrea ate three times a day and slept on a clean white bed. Each day she looked better. Despite the cold winds, she spent much of her time on the balcony overlooking the town, huddled in blankets, for this made her feel freer. The hospital staff understood.

From here she witnessed the great Russian army moving westwards and there was always more and still more of it . . . the tank divisions, the columns of guns and trucks, motor cyclists, technical units. There were masses of men, hundreds of thousands of them. There were the columns of marching soldiers: dirty, tired, clad in ragged uniforms, moving over the dusty roads and fields of Poland. They marched slowly in close rank with long even steps. So they came on and on, from the Ukraine, the Ural mountains and the Caucasus, the Baltic countries, Siberia and Mongolia. And there were the columns of women and girls, too, in military grey green uniforms, with high boots and tight blouses and long hair greased with goose fat. At times Andrea would see convoys of administrative staff, in their new German cars, recently taken from the towns they had passed. Behind were more tanks and more marching columns without a beginning, without an end. Andrea wondered how the Germans would enjoy the Russian hordes they had brought on themselves.

Chapter  75

IT WAS APRIL 5. Bill had spent a hard day training the men in a forest clearing, but he was restless. It was two days past the date that Schofield had set to go in, but still he hesitated. He was hoping that luck might show them a better way to penetrate the mine. He walked outside and gazed at the stars. It was 10 p.m. and his hunger was ruining his concentration. He leaned against a tree, listening. He was sure he'd heard footsteps.

It was Louis and he was carrying a sack full of loaves. Louis was fortunate in having a real identity. He could move around as he pleased. He even used his status as a war hero to befriend the local SS, so he was able to bring back useful information.

'Listen to this,' he said to Bill, as his men fell upon the bread. 'Here's the chance we've been waiting for, and this time, Bill, you'll have to take me along. Five hundred Russian prisoners-of-war are arriving at Theresienstadt sometime tomorrow on Hugo's orders. The mine labour is to be changed. You know what that means,' he said grimly. 'They intend to use Russians only in Richard's Mine, to put an end to the sabotage. The camp guards are in an uproar because they don't have the bunks or the food for so many new arrivals. It will be chaotic . . . ideal for us.'

Now Bill knew what he'd been waiting for. He could take more men with him. Louis was right, he would need his

Russian. This stroke of luck would enable him to take Schwerin and Maeier, since they both spoke Russian. The camp guards wouldn't be looking for escaped Jews amongst a bunch of Soviet soldiers. Bill decided to seize the opportunity. He gripped Louis' shoulder. 'Thanks. Let's get moving.'

Ten miles east of Prague, the cattle trucks drew to a halt at a level crossing. There was no moon, which was lucky, as seventeen men, led by Jan, slipped silently out of the forest and levered open the side of the trucks. The noise seemed intense, but the guards were three hundred yards away, engaged in a noisy argument with the signalman who was insisting that the train should not be there at all. The guards were at ease. All the trucks were locked, besides, who would want to rescue the prisoners?

The stench and the heat hit Bill as he climbed inside. He wanted to puke. The Russians were crouched on the floor in rows, packed together so closely there was no room to move. Bill could see their despair and exhaustion. As they looked up, their faces brightened. There was a surge of hope.

Jan spoke rapidly in Russian and the men sat upon their haunches looking respectful.

Bill drew Louis aside. 'What did he say?'

'Jan is a commissar in the Communist Party,' Louis muttered. 'He's asking for volunteers to fight with the Czech Resistance inside the mine and for seventeen of them to change places with us. Naturally they are all volunteering.'

The men were stripping off eagerly. Bill exchanged clothes with one of them who was about his size and took his papers. He was all too aware of the stench of sweat and filth as he put on the Russian uniform. He watched the lucky seventeen running down the grassy bank into the trees to freedom, hard behind Jan.

When Bill crouched on the floor, he began to itch. He could feel the lice on his skin. The train moved forward again and Bill strained to read his identity documents, but could not. Later, when dawn came, he studied them carefully. His name, he discovered with Louis' help, was Yakov Lukich. He was a corporal and a skilled electrician. Prior to the war he'd been attached to a collective farm.

As he rocked backwards and forwards to the rhythm of the train, Bill was gripped by panic. He was trapped and there was no way out. The truck was locked and he'd thrown in his lot with these wretched prisoners, one of whom might betray them all for an extra slice of bread. One slip and they would be lost. He tried not to think of what lay ahead, but his fear was like a living entity that he was forced to play host to. It settled into his solar plexus and spread along his nerve fibres until every organ in his body was affected. Looking round at his men, he noticed they all looked like he felt and most of them were praying.

'Darling, listen to me,' Schofield told Ingrid. 'I want you to record the call I'm about to make. Note my desperation, and suppressed fury, as well as a certain fawning on my part.'

'I've never heard you fawn. I don't think you're capable of fawning.'

'I'm good at it. Just listen!'

Schofield picked up the telephone receiver. Keeping his hand on the rest, he began to speak:

'Schofield here, Sir. I'm sorry to disturb you at this time of night, but I've just heard from American colleagues, that US forces intend to stop their advance at the Czech border, leaving the Soviets *carte blanche* in that country ... That, of course, is not in our best interests ... or their interests either ...

'Agreed, Sir. Future relations with the Russians are of primary consideration ... but we must draw the line somewhere ... to allow them to get their hands on the V–3 is madness ...'

There was a long pause.

'Sir, you don't seem to realise the importance of nuclear research ...

'You think that the Americans are more advanced than the Germans ... ? We have no proof of that, Sir. With respect, Sir, this is a terrible mistake.

'Yes, I have heard of the Yalta Agreement. I'm not shouting,

Sir. Are you telling me that Eisenhower insists that no American lives be lost in Czechoslovakia simply because ultimately the country is to be handed back to the Russians? Yes, I can see his point of view, but surely, in view of this vital research ...'

There was another long pause ... then:

'Sir, I protest. It was impossible to blow up the mine. There's no access except through Theresienstadt. My men were arrested when they tried to penetrate the camp. Yes, all five perished ...'

'Very well, I will drop the matter. Yes, at once, Sir. Good-night.'

Schofield went to the bar and poured two drinks. 'After that conversation, Ingrid dear, I became extremely drunk. While under the influence, I confided in you that Churchill and the Americans were fools who had no idea of the importance of nuclear research and that they'll be sorry. That's all, but be sure to get it to Paddy soonest.'

'Yes, all right. First thing in the morning.'

Ingrid was a dedicated worker. She never shirked her task, however scared she felt. Every day, on the way to the factory, she delivered to Paddy the information that she had supposedly photographed, but which, in fact, Schofield had given her. He gave her genuine news and some research that was not of any vital consequence, just to re-establish her worth to the Germans. He had been building her up, waiting for the time when she would repay all this effort. That time was now. What a uniquely resilient woman she was, Schofield thought, watching her narrowly. She had become a passionate, vivacious companion. Nowadays she looked younger, the shadows had disappeared from under her eyes and her breasts were becoming full and voluptuous. She had always been beautiful, but lately she was sensational. He watched her affectionately and noticed when she gave a long, shuddering sigh. 'Don't look so tired. When the war's won, you'll be free.' He folded his arms around her dainty figure and felt her trembling. 'It's going to be all right,' he said. 'You've survived. We'll get married when we've disposed of Paddy. Soon, my love.'

'Not soon enough,' she said vehemently. 'No, never soon enough. I wish it were now, Stephen.'

Chapter  76

TEN SECONDS! He had exactly ten seconds. Bill waited, tense and anxious for the the train to enter the tunnel. Suddenly they were plunged into darkness. Ten ... nine ... eight ... he counted silently as his fingers fumbled under the seat. He found the small packet of explosives taped there, retrieved it and thrust it into his pocket. As they emerged from the tunnel, he glanced sidelong and noticed that the Russians were gazing ahead impassively. They'd been given their instructions by Louis. They were good men and he was learning to trust them.

It was April 15, and Bill had been inside Theresienstadt for nine frustrating days. This morning, he and Louis had been chosen for the mine squad, but time was running short and there was so much to do.

Bill was jolted back to the present as the train slowed. He saw a gaping hole in the cliffside, and suddenly they were passing through a brilliantly lit, whitewashed tunnel. Seconds later the train slowed to a halt. Guards were yelling at them, dogs snarling ... Bewildered and hostile, they were pushed and beaten into line. They set off at a trot, trying to dodge the blows from the *schlags*.

Bill joined the end of a long queue of shuffling prisoners,

moving towards a trestle table. Five SS officers were interrogating the prisoners in Russian. Fear surged, and Bill's mouth
dried.

'Play dumb,' Louis whispered. 'Stick close to me. I'll say
you're shell-shocked.'

Bill moved forward, overcome with dread. It was taking too
long, Bill heard the Captain say. A curt command sent two
young officers to another trestle table. 'If any of you speak
German, come here,' they yelled. A reprieve! Bill exhaled his
breath as he and Louis moved forward.

'I worked on a co-operative farm,' he said, trying to conceal
his American accent. 'I'm an electrical engineer.' He was given
a pass to pin on his overalls.

'I taught mathematics,' he heard Louis say behind him.

They were given yellow overalls with a large black 'S'
stencilled on the front. Bill was photographed, fingerprinted
and an identity badge was pinned on his overall. He felt
optimistic at last. The *S-squad*, Schwerin had told him,
consisted of men suitable for working in the missile station. Fate
was on his side. Before 9 a.m., Bill was given the job of assisting
Manfred Reiss, the engineer in charge of air-conditioning.
Reiss, a dark-haired, massive Bavarian with bright blue eyes,
despised Russians. He was a perfectionist, Bill soon found out,
which could prove to Bill's advantage, or so he reckoned. On his
first exhausting day, they checked every outlet and duct
meticulously. With Reiss he had access to the maze of chambers
and tunnels that encircled the station, housing the air pipes,
electrical wiring and water conduits.

At three the following afternoon, Bill peered through the
main ventilator shaft into the passage below and saw Franz
wheeling a trolley towards the firing well. He dropped his
spanner which fell with a clatter, just missing the trolley. Reiss
merely swore at him. As Franz passed up the spanner, he
whispered. 'I'm in G dormitory.'

It was past midnight when Bill climbed out of his bunk. The
bars to the air tunnels were locked, but Bill had stolen the key

from Reiss. The dormitories were separated from each other by thick concrete walls, but the air shafts were interconnected and sloped from a main artery down to smaller vein-like shafts leading to each cell. It took him ten claustrophobic minutes to reach the next dormitory where he found Franz.

'You've done well,' Bill whispered through the grill. 'You've hung in here longer than anyone. Keep going, man. There's seventeen of us in here with you, plus the prisoners who are on our side. Can we blow up the plant if we have to?'

'Yes, if necessary,' he whispered. 'Of course, we'd all go with it. Otherwise, there's many ways to delay firing. We can adjust the electronic circuitry, which would hold them up for days, or jam the hydraulic switches to prevent the ceiling from opening, that gives us several hours, we can break the fuel pumps and block the pipes. All easily mended by the Bosch, but causing a delay of hours or maybe days each. Otherwise we could simply blow up the launch pad, but that, too, could be repaired in a matter of days. We can hold them up for a month or more, bit by bit.'

'What about reprisals?.'

Franz looked grim. 'Always bad. Every incident brings too many executions.'

'What if the Soviets get here first. Are we prepared?'

'We have enough explosives stashed away to blow the central well. I've drawn you a sketch of where the fuses are ... in case anything happens to me. It's been worrying the hell out of me. I don't know why I've lasted so long.'

'As a matter of interest, why have you?' .

'Ludwig has very poor vision. The Bosch don't know that. I'm his eyes. He knows about my Physics training, but he thinks it's from a local university. He's hanging on to me. Now listen, the SS have laid enough explosives to blow us all to extinction and they won't hesitate to do that if they suspect the Allies are drawing near. I know where their explosives are and I've dismantled some of them, but I need help.'

'I'll find someone. Schwerin's a good bloke. I guess we'll have to tackle one problem at a time,' Bill said, pocketing the drawing. 'How long d'you reckon it will take them to get ready for firing?'

'The main delay now is weight versus range. They have to complete a lighter version of the electronic wiring and it's taking time. The prisoners are getting clumsy.'

'Tell them to keep on being clumsy,' Bill said as he left. He intended to see most of his men during the night and find out which of the Russians had some knowledge of explosives.

It was April 30. The previous day, Bill had loosened the ducts leading to Ludwig's office so that the air escaped into the tunnel. Ludwig complained, as he'd hoped, and Reiss had given Bill the job of repairing the duct.

It was mid-morning and Bill had spun out this task as long as he could, waiting for the chance to catch the physicist's attention. Through the bars covering the ventilating grating, he could see the professor gazing in despair at his plans. He had attended four meetings that morning and there had been several calls from Berlin. Ludwig was being pressurised into pulling forward the firing date. He was sweating with fright and his spectacles kept misting over. Every few moments, he plucked them off, rubbed them frantically with his handkerchief and gazed round like an anxious owl.

A quick glance assured Bill that the guards were not watching. He unlocked the grid and slid down into Ludwig's office.

'Get out, you dumb Ruskie,' the professor said irritably, not really registering the intrusion.

'No, not Russian. American,' Bill said quietly. 'I'm an Allied agent, Major Bill Roth. I have to talk to you, Professor. Please sit quietly while I fix the grating. We'll say the hinge came loose, shall we?'

Professor Ludwig sat bolt upright, speechless and staring in horror, while his hand hovered over his telephone.

'Don't, Herr Professor. It would cost you a generous research grant and a safe seat in a top American university. Just listen.'

'Are you mad? You'll get us both killed.'

'The war's nearly over. The Nazis have lost, but your brains belong to the world. You must know that.'

Ludwig looked around fearfully. 'Be careful,' he muttered. His eyes glittered through his glasses.

'I have an offer for you from the American government. They promise most favourable terms. How about it? Are you interested?'

The Professor laughed briefly. 'It's too late, my friend. After the V-3 missile is fired, German scientists will become the world's lepers. We'll be hated too much to live anywhere in the West. Don't think I didn't know about the sabotage. I played along because it suited me. I don't want this bomb on my conscience ... it's an unknown quantity ... we can only guess at its power ... as for the rockets they want to fire. They haven't been tested either. The Nazis are desperate men, they'll stop at nothing.' He wiped his perspiring face with a large handkerchief.

'I promise you, the rocket won't be fired. Not from here,' Bill said. 'If the Soviets get here first, my orders are to blow the mine and ourselves with it.'

Ludwig crumpled. He took off his glasses and began wiping them absent-mindedly. 'So if I come over to you people, it will be the same pressure all over again. Different victims, that's all,' Ludwig said. 'You know, I never wanted to be a traitor, but I cannot have the deaths of millions of innocent civilians on my conscience. Give me one good reason why I should change sides ...'

'You'd only be part of the project over there,' Bill said. 'There's a massive research budget, a team of scientists, and only the President of the USA can make the decision to drop the bomb. It wouldn't be on your shoulders alone. There's plenty of other uses for atomic power besides blowing ourselves up. You know that.'

'Very well,' Ludwig said. 'You can count on my co-operation. I pray the Americans get here before I am forced to blow this place apart and us with it.'

*

It was dark by the time Marietta steered her small boat into the shelter of overhanging willows beneath the old east tower of Sokol Castle. Bare-footed, she climbed into the knee-deep muddy water and tied the boat to a branch.

It was a perfect summer evening. Nothing could go wrong . . . not on a night like this . . . balmy, peaceful, fragrant. Her plan was foolproof, wasn't it? She had not reckoned on her own physical symptoms. Her heart was beating loud enough to be heard on the bridge. She was dressed in the green and grey-striped Sokol overall which she had stolen from the washing line when delivering milk a week ago. She was wearing an old blonde wig she had pulled into pigtails and tucked under the compulsory servant's headscarf.

She forced herself to stand still and take several deep breaths, before climbing the grassy bank to the ivy-shrouded river entrance of the tower. Once inside, she stood listening, cloaked in blackness so dense it seemed to press in on her. All at once she was back in the punishment cell. 'No . . .' She gave a low, strangled cry and hung on to her self-control until she was able to continue.

At last she reached the ground level of the castle courtyard. The moonlit cobbles seemed as bright as day and the sound of music came in snatches. Nearer, she heard the call of a night jay and an owl, but no sound of guards. She guessed they were organising cars and parking, for tonight Hugo was having a celebration. Days ago, Max had told her there would be a large party at Sokol and extra staff would be hired. She intended to pass as one of the servants. Smoothing her overall she stepped quietly into the courtyard.

The night was shattered by a piercing siren echoing from all sides. Too late, she realised that the tower exit was wired for intruders. Her body reacted in panic as she fled headlong to the kitchen. There was a large pile of vegetables beside the kitchen sink. Using every ounce of will-power she possessed, she forced herself to pick up a knife and start peeling. The guards burst into the kitchen, guns pointing at the servants.

'Line up . . . over here . . . quickly . . . move,' came the commands. She was pushed into line. All the temporaries were wearing badges, she noticed. She was trembling and dizzy.

'Where's your badge?' one of them snapped at her.

She opened her mouth, but no sound came.

'She's not a temporary. She works here,' a deep voice boomed from the doorway. 'Please don't interfere. We're working to a tight schedule.'

Ignoring the corporal's anger, Max beckoned to her. 'Come,' he said. 'Bring that tray of glasses to my office.'

She took the tray and followed Max to his office. The glasses clinked violently as her hands shook. Surely they would notice? As the door slammed shut, Max took the tray.

'You're mad to come here, Countess . . .'

She gasped and flushed.

'I was a fool not to recognise you in the first place, but you were so thin. Now you're recovering from your terrible experiences. Did you know that it's rumoured the Countess has returned to fight the Nazis and that she's operating under the code name of Edelweiss. You're becoming a living legend. Be careful!'

Marietta leaned against the door and gave a deep sigh that was half a sob. 'Thank you, Max. You saved my life,' she murmured.

'You should have trusted me. What if I hadn't been there? Why are you here?'

'The war is almost over, Max. These murderers will be brought to justice. I need solid evidence of Hugo's crimes. I want to go through his personal files. Has he changed the combination of the safe in Grandmother's study?'

'No. Why should he? D'you remember the number?'

'Yes. Grandmother made me memorise it years ago.'

'Believe me, Countess, you won't get into the general's office as a servant, but you might succeed as a guest . . .'

'Why is he holding this party?'

'There're several top Nazis here from Berlin and they're going to meet local Nazi bigwigs tonight. I don't know why they bother to keep up pretences at this stage of the game. When

Hugo has a party he keeps his office locked, but I have a duplicate key. This is what you must do . . .'

The dust rose in a cloud as Marietta crept across the floor of the castle attic. Rubbing a circle in the grime to see through a window, she saw the guests flocking in. Hugo's mistress, Freda, dressed in a magnificent black silk gown, was greeting them at the top of the steps. The perfect hostess.

Swallowing her hatred, she moved away from the window and began to rifle through the tin trunks for something to wear. All the old garments had been lovingly packed in tissue paper by Max, but what an awful smell of moth balls. That could be her undoing, she thought anxiously. Eventually she found her own discarded clothes. She gasped. 'Oh my,' she whispered and uttered a small half-sob at the sight of so many forgotten dresses, all with their special memories. With a grunt of satisfaction, she uncovered the frilled white dress that she had bought in Paris for her eighteenth birthday ball. Lovingly, she smoothed the folds. The delicate fabric didn't smell so badly. She shook it and hung it over a rafter. She gazed at it for a long time and eventually plucked up courage to put it on. It was a little loose, but passable. Glancing at her watch, she saw that it was past eleven. She began to hunt for shoes and discovered some white summer sandals that fitted.

It was midnight.

Tense, but with a touch of bravado, she hurried down the spiral staircase to the servants' quarters and opened the door to the bedrooms. Seconds later she was descending the main staircase, in full view of groups of guests chattering noisily in the foyer. It was like a journey into the past, for so little had changed except the Nazi uniforms, which were everywhere. As if in a dream, she mingled with the guests, took a glass of champagne and moved slowly towards the study.

'This is not allowed,' a voice bellowed in her ear. A heavy hand was gripping her shoulder. She cringed. Trembling, she peered over her shoulder at an SS officer towering over her.

'Beautiful women cannot remain alone,' he said. 'A house rule. So ... would you care to dance with me?' He introduced himself and offered his arm.

'Perhaps later,' she said, forcing a smile to hide her terror. 'I'm looking for my husband.'

One eyebrow shot up. 'Lucky man,' he whispered.

His clumsy flirting had ruined her calm. Now she was stiff with terror. She was hardly able to force one foot in front of the other as she moved towards the study door.

She had arrived ... a miracle ... but what now? There were far too many people around. What an absurd plan she had hatched. How could she unlock the door and walk inside in front of all these guests? What if Hugo should come in from the garden? She glanced around nervously, but couldn't see him. The sudden loud noise of the dinner gong made her jump, spilling her champagne. Everyone looked towards Max, who was standing at the top of the stairs, smiling nervously.

'Ladies and gentlemen,' he called. 'The buffet supper awaits you in the garden. Oysters, caviar ...' she heard as she slipped inside and locked the door behind her. 'Bless you, Max,' she murmured.

She was ice-cool and efficient as she began to search the files. It didn't take long to discover a letter, signed by Hitler, congratulating Hugo on his efficient destruction of Lidhaky village. She began to shake with fury. So the death of Andrea's little baby was Hugo's evil work.

She tried to move faster, but there was so much more incriminating evidence, including a letter from Heydrich congratulating Hugo for his successful elimination of the Jews and intellectuals from Prague, a letter from Hugo, explaining how the Mayor of Prague had died after three weeks of torture ... more and still more evidence, enough to send Hugo to the gallows when the war ended. Soon this evidence would go to the proper authorities and Hugo would be tried as a looter, a thief and a murderer. She would see him hanged.

She was startled by the door handle rattling. Her heart pounded. Max, perhaps?

Was Hugo still in the garden? It would be suicide to walk into him. Looking out of the open window, she saw Freda scowling. Following her gaze towards the shrubs, she saw Hugo with a woman. He was pulling her off-balance against his chest and laughing down at her. In his other hand he held a glass of champagne and he was giving her sips of it. He looked happy, and carefree and very drunk. The sight of Hugo propelled her back in time to that terrible day when she was pushed into the lorry for transport to the camp. All her old fears began to surge through her body, engulfing her with blind panic. She could hear the dogs barking, the screams, the whistles, the terrible shouting ... and smell the unwashed human flesh and the stench of fear. She had to move away from the window, but she seemed to be rooted there. 'God, help me,' she muttered, her eyes riveted on Hugo.

Almost as if he felt her presence, her stepbrother looked straight up at her. For a moment that seemed forever they gazed into each other's eyes. Then she found the strength to step back from the window. What had she done? She'd gone mad. She fumbled with the latch and fled past Max in blind panic.

Chapter  77

HUGO FROZE. In a split-second that seemed to last forever, he stared straight into Marietta's eyes. His glass shattered on the ground.

'Oh God!' It truly was Marietta. But she was dead! The ghastly apparition moved, but still her eyes bored into his ... they spelled revenge. He had ordered her death, and now she had come back from some infernal depths to haunt him, wearing the same dress that she had worn for her eighteenth birthday ball. Was she a portent of doom?

'No ... ,' he muttered. 'Impossible ... Insane!'

Hugo raced across the lawn, through the hall, to his office, thrusting guests and waiters out of his path with angry mutters.

He tried the door, but it was locked. Fumbling with his key, he flung it open and stepped inside. The room was empty. Icy shivers brought his arms up in goose-bumps.

'What the hell?' he muttered.

By now his staff officers had rushed to his aid and were crowding round him.

'I saw someone in here,' Hugo snarled. 'Guard the door.'

Fighting his dread, he forced himself to close the door behind him. Now he was alone with whatever deadly presence was in the room. His sweaty hand slithered on his revolver. Stiff-legged and breathing heavily, Hugo searched the room, tingling with superstitious dread.

If only he could think straight. If only he weren't so drunk. Could it be the vodka? He'd been over-indulgent lately. Perhaps one of his guests resembled Marietta. But the door had been locked. Swearing, he strode outside, slamming the door shut behind him.

He had a raging hangover the following morning, and the telephone rang incessantly, but as soon as he could, he locked himself in his office and searched his room and his safe.

It did not take Hugo long to discover what was missing. Bile flooded his mouth and fear nibbled at his nerve-endings. He felt as if a strong steel band was being slowly tightened around his chest. Whoever had robbed his safe had enough evidence to destroy him at the war's end, the letters from Heydrich and the Führer alone would be sufficient evidence to have him hung as a war criminal. But he would be safe in South America. Then he remembered that the title deeds to his ranches had been in the safe. They had been stolen. Even worse, the intruder knew where to find him.

Who knew his safe combination? Who would want to destroy him? There was only one answer ... and he had seen her and looked into her eyes ... but she was dead. Even in broad daylight, he could not shake off a terrible premonition of doom.

Hugo spent the day on the telephone to the Camp Commandant. What he learned made him feel sick. Only six people had been released from Lichtenberg Concentration Camp over the past five years. One of them had been housed in the same bunkroom as Marietta ... Greta Brecht, the records stated. Had Marietta managed to exchange places with her?

Another terrible thought occured to him ... if Marietta were alive, could she be working with the Resistance here? Was Marietta the agent Edelweiss? Had he been locked in mortal combat with his step-sister for the past two years? She always won ... she always had. That treacherous thought unnerved him.

His anxiety brought painful cramps in his chest, his ulcers played up, and a disgusting, itchy rash spread over his hands that same day, and he began to feel cursed.

Walther and Emma Bock lived on a small farm, ideally placed a few miles from the mine, near to the small village of Nové Dvory, along the banks of the River Ohre. It was prime property, situated near the main highway, only twenty-five miles from Prague and four miles from the camp. This was Bock's reward for successfully designing and making the complicated hydraulic system that operated the roof of the rocket ramp. It was Friday, May 4, this was Walther Bock's exeat weekend and he was at home.

The Americans had crossed the Czech border some hours ago, according to Marietta's contacts, but they were still forty miles away. The Germans had surrendered in Holland, Denmark and north Germany. The end was very near.

Marietta had made up her mind to contact the Bocks just before dawn. She approached the farmhouse apprehensively. The nearer she walked, the more scared she became. Her mouth was dry, her legs leaden as she crept through the herb garden towards the pretty thatched cottage. The shutters were open, smoke drifted from the chimney and through the window she could see Emma Bock pouring coffee from a blue enamel pot. Marie pushed open the kitchen door and paused in the doorway. She had a revolver in her hand which was pointing at Walther's fat stomach.

'Good God!' Emma said, looking more affronted than scared.

Walther made a lunge towards her, but Marietta held her ground, and as her finger tightened on the trigger, he reluctantly raised his hands.

'Sit down and put your hands on the table,' she said. 'Both of you.'

'Who are you?' Emma said, angrily.

'I represent the Czech People's Liberation army,' Marietta said. 'You have two hours to vacate these stolen premises. You may only take what you can carry, no vehicles, no livestock, no horses. I cannot guarantee you safe passage through Czechoslovakia to Bavaria.'

'You're crazy,' Emma said. 'The war's not over yet. Get out of here.'

'Not crazy, just a day or two premature,' Marie said softly.

'Wait, Emma. Keep quiet. Why are you here?' Walther's tough brown eyes were alight with curiosity. When he frowned, his black brows met on his forehead. He was a giant of a man, well over six foot, with a huge pot belly. Emma was a stout woman, with greying blonde hair, a large red face and watery grey eyes.

'You expected to be evicted one day soon. Am I right?' Marietta looked directly into the woman's eyes.

Emma nodded tearfully. 'We've worked so hard to build up the farm . . .'

'But it was stolen from Czechs,' Marietta said. 'All *Volksdeutsche* will be expelled . . . at best you will be destitute . . . but you might be killed by the mobs. After that there will be the Russians. You know as well as I do that feelings will be running high. What have you saved? Can you get your savings out of the country?' While she argued, she was hating herself. Why was she helping such scum?

'We can't,' Walter said flatly. 'No one can. We'll be finished. The job will come to an end. Five years of hard work for nothing.'

'I can offer you an American contract. Safe passage for both of you within the next few days. A good salary, a pension, housing and transport supplied, and you'll be working with Professor Alesh. But first you must help me.'

'Put your gun away,' Walther said. 'I can't discuss this looking into its barrel. I don't trust women with guns. Sit down and twist your finger round a coffee cup. It'll be safer for all of us.' He grinned facetiously. 'We're interested in saving our skins. To say nothing of my career. Who wouldn't be? Now talk.'

*

Hugo and his closest aides, together with the scientists, technicians and SS guards inside Richard's Mine, were standing on a specially-constructed platform near the firing station. The time was 9.30 a.m., on Saturday morning, May 5. Five days ago Hitler had committed suicide and Admiral Doenitz appointed his successor. The Third Reich was dying. Most of Eastern Europe was under the domination of the Kremlin. Much of Germany would be, too. Unless . . .

If they could fire one missile carrying an atomic warhead at London, or Paris . . . it would be enough to show the West the awful destructive power at their command. Then they could demand favourable peace terms. With the V-3, they could force the Soviets to remain east of the Czech borders.

Count Bernadotte, vice-president of the Swedish Red Cross and a nephew of the King of Sweden, had been approached by Himmler three times in the past two months to try and bring about a better peace settlement. On each occasion he had told the Nazis that the Allies would not negotiate. They insisted on unconditional surrender. This time, Himmler had informed Count Bernadotte, they had a weapon of awesome power, which they were about to demonstrate to him. In the face of these threats the Count's aides were meeting with Himmler at midday on the Bavarian border. Firing was scheduled for noon, and split-second timing was essential.

Hugo's pent-up anxiety kept his palms sweating and his heart hammering and it was an effort to maintain his composure.

Before them stood the missile. White and shining like alabaster, its pencil-shaped nose was almost six stories high. Hugo gloated at this magnificent sight. Here stood a fitting monument to *Woden*, God of nocturnal storms, who once ranged the sky in pursuit of fantastic game. *Woden* it was who granted heroism and victory and ultimately governed man's fate. The sign signified the unchaining of the brute forces of the world. It was a fitting name.

Hugo winced from a painful twinge in his stomach and watched Professor Ludwig turn to the control panel. He bent forward and pressed the buttons which would set in motion the intricate hydraulics system that opened the circular ceiling that covered the central well.

There was a long wait. The seconds passing as slowly as hours. Then the scientist tried again. Hugo felt himself sweating with fear as the roof panels remained tightly shut. At last, Ludwig hurried over to Hugo and gave the Nazi salute.

'A slight delay, Herr Colonel. If we could reassemble in an hour's time. A mere technical hitch, I assure you. We have a very good lunch waiting for you and our guests.'

'We can't delay,' Hugo hissed at him. 'Himmler is waiting. The missile must fire on schedule.'

'Regretfully, Herr Colonel, there is no alternative.'

At 3 p.m., after a lengthy lunch which Hugo had been unable to eat, the guests and technicians reassembled in the crater and the ceiling opened smoothly. Seconds later, the rocket fuel was ignited behind transparent barriers. Hugo held his breath and gazed in awe, anticipating the slow rise, followed by a swift soar into the heavens. To his fury, the missile remained grounded. By 5 p.m. Hugo's face was pinched with anger and fear. Despite Ludwig's protestations, it was clear that the missile was not going to be launched. 'Another hour,' the scientist pleaded.

'Very well.' Hugo stood, hunched and brooding, staring at the missile as if willing it to move. By 7 p.m. he was still waiting. His own fear of failure was increasing his fury.

'Sir . . . Herr Colonel . . .' Ludwig said, approaching him cautiously. 'I think we should call off the demonstration. It appears that the fuel has been tampered with. We have made tests . . .'

Hugo watched him carefully. Why this smug glint of subtle triumph? Suppressed suspicions surged out of Hugo's subconscious. Why had Ludwig agreed to launch the rocket with a nuclear warhead? Why had he not bleated about the sinful loss of life, as he usually did? *Because he intended to sabotage the launch?*

Hugo felt ice cold fury stiffen his limbs as he walked towards Ludwig and the missile. At that moment, every act of sabotage tumbled through his mind in a kaleidoscope of images, and he blamed the professor for every one of them. Ludwig was a traitor. He'd been bought, just as Alesh had been bought, and probably at the same time, only Ludwig had agreed to remain at the mine.

He grabbed his gun and took aim at a spot between Ludwig's frightened eyes. As his finger tightened on the trigger, a massive blow struck his arm. The bullet fired harmlessly into the ceiling as the gun was knocked out of his hand.

A moment of disbelief stunned Hugo. In that instant of shocked incredulity, he turned to the Russian prisoner who had attacked him and found himself stared at Bill Roth. He gasped. Then he smiled.

'You're dead, Roth,' he whispered and grabbed his knife. As Roth lunged towards him, he positioned the blade and saw his guards aim their guns on Roth. At that same instant, the mine was plunged into stygian blackness. Hugo felt Roth's hands around his throat, choking him, and they both fell to the floor.

Bill drove his fist forward into the darkness, blessing Schwerin for his efficient timing in short-circuiting the electrical wiring. Now none of the guards could fire for fear of killing each other, but each Russian had marked his man and knew exactly where to go. Hearing the sickening crunch of bone and teeth, Bill lunged in again. All his longing and suppressed aggression blew his mind like dam walls breaking. He was punching, kicking, feeling for Hugo's eyes, using his fists and his fingers and his boots to claw the life out of the beast. For a while he went crazy, but Hugo was fighting back with every trick at his command. He was cunning, skilled and deadly. Bill could feel warm blood on his hands, making his fingers slip and slide over flesh. Whose blood? He had no way of knowing. Then he felt the knife in Hugo's hand. A sudden slash to his neck brought blinding pain. A warm trickle ran over his ear. A split second later he was sprawling over Hugo, smashing his head against the floor. He heard the knife clatter on hard stone nearby, and he kicked it hard away from them.

As if far away, he heard a crash and saw a sudden flare. The blast came a split-second later, followed by a roar like thunder. The floor trembled with the shockwave. What the hell was that? Had the mine blown? Had they failed . . .? Bill had no time to think. He felt the numbing pain of a blow on his back. And then another. And then he felt nothing.

Chapter  78

IT WAS ALMOST DAWN. Marietta fought off her tiredness and sat bolt upright. It was pitch dark, but as she remembered where she was, panic surged. Had she fallen asleep? She fumbled for the matches and candle. In the first flicker of light her anxious eyes took in the Bocks, snoring gently on the sofa. Thank God! The candle had burned out, that was all. Or was it? She heard a distant sound again. Glancing at her watch she saw that it was ten minutes past four. She listened, stiff with fear. Had there ever been a time when she was not gripped by tension, she wondered? Right now she felt as if two giant hands were pressing against her ribs, making it hard to breathe.

All at once she heard the sound quite plainly. Troops were marching towards the farm. As she listened they turned in at the gate. The Americans were a hundred miles away. Had their mission failed? Was this the Gestapo? She prayed for Bill's safety as she checked the windows. Shadowy figures were moving purposely around the house at the front and the back, cutting off any chance of escape.

The sudden, loud hammering on the door woke the Bocks who sat up in terror. Too late to run. Her heart was beating wildly as she drew back the heavy bolts.

She gasped. It took a few minutes to grasp the reality of the scene. The man at the door was wearing the uniform of a sergeant in the US forces. Behind him, a group of GIs peered curiously at her.

'Oh!' she said. 'Oh, heavens . . .'

'Occupation troops, Ma'am. This chicken farm has been commandeered. You may keep one room for your own use. You have half an hour to vacate the rest of the premises.'

She began to laugh. She stepped forward and put her hands on the sergeant's shoulders. Then she kissed him very solemnly on both cheeks. 'Have it all,' she said. 'Every last chicken and egg. I am a Free-Czech agent working for Major Schofield in London. Please take us to your commanding officer. He will be expecting us.'

Slowly Bill became aware of a call echoing through the blackness. It seemed to come from far away, as if he was at the end of a long, dark tunnel.

'Lay down your arms. You are surrounded. The war is over. I repeat, General Alfred Jodl signed the unconditional surrender this morning at 2.41 a.m., May 7. It's over. Come out with your hands on your heads.'

American voices!

'Thank God!'

'Okay friends.' Surely that was Franz. 'It's been over in here for the past two days. This section is in Allied hands. We're coming out.'

Bill felt a surge of relief. He tried to sit up, but he could not move. What's wrong with me? Was I shot? Am I paralysed? he asked himself in panic. He tried again, but excruciating pain made him immobile. He couldn't move a limb. Every breath was agony. He seemed to be choking. What was wrong with his lungs. He tried to scream, but only a feeble groan emerged from his lips.

'Who's there?'

Someone had heard him. He groaned again.

'Bill?'

Surely that was Louis' voice? 'Louis,' he groaned. 'Help me.'

'We're looking for Major Roth, British Intelligence,' someone called out. The voice sounded American, but waves of pain and nausea were making it hard to concentrate. Bill groaned again.

'Help me dig him out from under this rockfall,' Louis yelled.

The next thing Bill knew, he was looking up into brilliant sunlight, and swaying around madly. He moved his hand, half afraid that he was paralysed, but it moved, and he thrust it over his eyes.

'This one's coming round,' he heard. 'Here comes the ambulance.'

He felt himself being jolted to the ground and he realised he'd been on a stretcher. An American medical orderly bent over him with a flask of water. Bill drank and spluttered. The good news was sinking in. They'd made it. He looked up and grinned.

'Bill ... Bill darling ...'

'Marie,' he croaked. 'I can't see in the sunlight. Come down here.'

Suddenly her shadow covered his face. She was kissing his forehead and his nose, and his eyelids.

'Move aside, please. I'm a doctor,' he heard. As the doctor flung back the blanket, he heard Marie gasp.

'Oh my God ...'

'Severe bruising, scratches and cuts, he's concussed, but with luck there's no major damage. Couple of cracked ribs by the feel of it. He'll survive. Sorry to break up the reunion, but I've got orders to get him back to hospital immediately. Were pulling out ... back to Bavaria. The Russians don't want us in Czechoslovakia.'

'He's lucky. He was buried alive and we didn't know where he was.' Louis' voice.

'Hi, Louis,' he said hoarsely. 'Thanks for getting me out.'

'Louis. Dearest Louis. I'm so happy. Both of you safe ... Oh, thank God ... thank God ...' Marie was sobbing. Bill wished he were strong enough to get up and hold her.

Marie leaned over him, her eyes were watery and the tears were splashing on his face.

'No more crying, darling,' he said. 'We'll be back in Baltimore in no time. It's over. The future is for us.' He smiled happily as they lifted him into the ambulance.

'Try to make him understand why I have to go back,' Bill heard Marie whisper, as he lay on the stretcher with the door still open. 'Tell him about the vows I made to Grandmother on her deathbed, and my promise to Father. I can't run away, especially since they both died. They trusted me.' Her voice broke off in a sob. 'Make him understand what it is to be a Habsburg. Oh, and Louis. Tell Bill I love him.' The door slammed shut. Bill sat up cautiously, his head throbbing. He'd get after her, somehow, just as soon as he got out of the ambulance.

A wedding was about to be held at St Margaret's, Westminster. Lord Stephen Schofield, war hero and close relative of the royal family, was marrying none other than London's own 'Plucky Princess'.

For days past, the newspapers had resurrected stories of Princess Ingrid's endurance and dogged bravery as she toiled eight hours a day in the aircraft factory and went on to cook at the troops' canteens after hours. She had become a very special heroine.

The war was all but over. It was May 7, 1945 and early that morning, at 2.41 a.m., in a small red schoolhouse in Rheims, German troops had surrendered unconditionally to General Eisenhower, the Allied Supreme Commander.

The war was not officially ended yet, but Londoners, drab and tired after years of spartan discipline and self-sacrifice, needed to celebrate. What better reason could they find than this fairy tale romance.

Just after dawn on May 7, crowds began forming in Parliament Square. At 11 a.m. they were rewarded by the sight of Ingrid, in a beautiful lace gown, diamonds glinting on her fingers, her eyes sparkled with fun as she stepped from a Rolls

Royce, a gift from her husband-to-be, the newspapers stated.

Ingrid could hardly believe this was real as she walked slowly up the aisle on the arm of Gwen's brother. She looked down at the beautiful lace gown, traditionally worn by Schofield brides, and sighed contentedly. On her finger was a pure yellow diamond set amongst emeralds and her veil was laced with pearls. She smiled softly as she remembered the night long ago with Hugo at Sokol Castle, when they had studied the old Princess's list of eligible men. How she had longed to marry one of them, and now she was doing just that.

What a long way it was to the altar and as she walked towards her future husband, she thought of Bill, the only man she had ever truly loved. She had a moment of butterflies in her stomach as her eyes met Stephen's. She had never known for sure if he believed her story. Now it didn't matter, he was marrying her.

An hour later Ingrid emerged and waved to the cheering crowd as she walked with Stephen through an archway of naval swords. Most of the Foreign Office and SOE had turned out to throw confetti. Half of London seemed to be there, too. Ingrid smiled and blew kisses and threw flowers from her bouquet into the crowd.

'Good old Ingrid,' one of the factory girls yelled. 'Remember us.'

'Good luck, Ingrid. We'll never forget you.'

Gwen, her bridesmaid, helped her into the car. Then she was smiling and waving and clutching Stephen's hand.

'I'm going to make you very happy, my darling,' Stephen murmured in her ear.

Still in her splendid white lace wedding gown, Ingrid was cutting a four-tier wedding cake, at the Dorchester, together with Stephen, whose arms were around hers. The happy couple smiled into the camera. Ingrid had never looked more radiant and she knew it. The band struck up the Blue Danube waltz. Ingrid took the floor to the applause of their one thousand guests. She drifted around in a happy daze, enjoying the acclaim and the knowledge that apart from the loss of Bill, everything had turned out absolutely splendidly.

'I can't wait to soak in the sun,' Stephen whispered in her ear. 'I'm going mouldy after five years of this damned awful weather.'

The prospect of leaving Britain for a while was the plum in the pudding, unaware of how many strings her husband had had to pull to get permission to travel abroad. It was all marvellous, she thought, as she wandered from group to group, accepting the kisses, the admiration, the good wishes and compliments.

Stephen was looking for her. 'Time to change, darling. We have a boat to catch.' He caught hold of her and pulled her against him with unaccustomed recklessness and for a brief, thrilling moment she was reminded of Bill. Quickly she closed her eyes and her heart. Thoughts of Bill were not allowed. Not ever, but in her heart of hearts she knew she would never love any other man.

'The most beautiful bride in the world, my darling. I'm longing for tonight,' he murmered against her ear, and she sighed softly.

She turned away and gazed at herself in the mirror. She saw a young, vivacious, beautiful girl, with tears running down her cheeks. How absurd! She quickly wiped them away. She took a glass of champagne and lifted it in a toast towards her reflection. 'To you, Ingrid,' she whispered. 'Well done! You won through after all.'

Andrea was sitting at her battered desk in a prefabricated hut, in the displaced persons' camp. She looked tired and thin and very pale, but her dark eyes glowed with caring. She was dressed in an overall with a red cross on the pocket, underneath she wore a shapeless, woollen skirt and blouse donated second-hand from Britain. Her hair was growing fast, but she kept the dark curls in a tight bun. She looked hauntingly lovely, but that was of no interest to Andrea. She hadn't bothered to look in a mirror for a long time.

In the camp she was respected for her compassion, her determination and her quiet acceptance of their hardships. She had started to work for the Red Cross only days after arriving at the camp. She found that work maintained her sanity.

It was 7 a.m. on the morning of May 7. Andrea shook hands with an elderly Polish farmer and promised to set in motion the complicated routine search for his missing son, through the archives of the liberated concentration camps.

When she had finished her dictation, she opened the door and motioned to her next applicant. As usual, almost a hundred sad people were sitting on the benches outside. Goodness knows what time they arrived, but when she began work at seven, there was always a long queue waiting.

It was the turn of an emaciated, white-haired woman. She had to be assisted by a Red Cross nurse. Andrea began her usual questions.

By noon, Andrea had dealt with twenty cases, all of which seemed hopeless, but sometimes miracles happened and Andrea never stopped hoping. Daily, heart-broken survivors filed through the office and she tried to find their missing relatives or help them to establish their identities.

When she showed the next applicant out, she saw a man sitting at the end of the bench. She froze. A terrible surge of hope washed through her and she nearly passed out with the force of it. 'Can it be . . .?' She whispered to herself. She ran her tongue over her dry lips and tried to stop shaking. The man was walking towards her. A stranger, yet his eyes were Louis' eyes. She framed his name in a whisper.

'Louis? Could it be you? Am I going crazy?'

'I'm looking for my wife,' Louis said gently. 'My beloved, brave wife, who has endured so much, but is still so beautiful and so full of compassion for others. I've come to take her home. It's her turn to be cared for.' His hand reached out to touch her hair.

'Louis . . . Oh, Louis.' Moments later they were clasped in each other's arms. For them the war was over at last.

Chapter  79

HUGO STOOD IN HIS OFFICE at Sokol Castle gazing at the smouldering ashes of files and papers. He had been up all night and he was exhausted. His face was unshaven, his tie loosened and his black ceremonial uniform, which he had decided to wear to take leave of Sokol Castle, was creased and covered in dust. He turned to the window. A mere seven miles away he could see the smoke and flashes of exploding shells from the front line. The Russians would be here in a matter of hours. It was time to go, but first he had something important to do.

It was May 13 and the war had been officially over for five days, but in a last ditch stand, German troops had succeeded in holding up the Soviet advance, while German and *Volksdeutsche* families were being evacuated.

The war was lost and so was his dream of power and greatness and a vast European Empire. But he was not wiped out, as so many were. He had six magnificent ranches in the Argentine, where Freda was getting their home organised.

But would he be safe there? He knew the answer to his question. There was nowhere in the world far enough away from Marietta. She would find him because she wanted her revenge. Why else had she taken those incriminating letters from his safe? She knew where to find him, she had the deeds to his land. Hugo stood staring out of the window, unable to rid his mind of his nagging anxieties.

He had planned a fitting revenge himself, he thought with a soft smile. Right now, Sokol castle was as lethal as a grenade. One match was all it would need. The thought of all those priceless treasures and works of art being destroyed, almost made him regretful, but better they were destroyed than left in the hands of his step-sister. Marietta was not going to get her full inheritance back. Not ever.

Hearing footsteps, Hugo was filled with superstitious dread. Was she already here, dressed in her white gown, as she appeared nightly in his worst nightmares. He called out gruffly: 'Who's there?'

There was a timid knock on his door. Most of the building had been evacuated, but there was supposed to be a skeleton staff on duty. Where the hell was his adjutant? Hugo grabbed his revolver, strode to the door and flung it open.

Miroslav Kova stood there shivering with fright. God, how he stank! Hugo wrinkled his nose with distaste and aimed his gun at a point between Kova's eyes.

'I have something you want, General,' Kova whined.

Hugo laughed and his finger tightened on the trigger.

'I have Edelweiss.'

Hugo put down his gun and stared hard at that oafish face. Marietta! His mouth dried with longing. With her dead he would be safe. He would wait out the seven years the lawyers required to officially recognise Louis' death and then return as the prodigal to claim Marietta's and Louis' massive estates.

He turned his attention to Kova ... could he be speaking the truth? Why had he come here ... risking his life? He must want something very badly. Then Hugo remembered that Kova did not know that his daughter had hanged herself in her cell.

'What do you want?' Hugo asked.

'We had a deal ... my daughter for Edelweiss. I have the agent locked in my cellar.'

'How can I trust you?'

'You don't have to trust me, I have to trust you. If I deliver

Edelweiss into your hands, you must tell me where my daughter is. Most of the camps are liberated and I must go to her.' He looked up pleadingly. 'Is she still alive?'

'Yes,' Hugo lied, eyeing Kova speculatively. Was it possible the fool thought his daughter would have been allowed to live after he fled with the agent? But he'd noticed that simple people always hoped, even when there was no basis for their optimism. Kova's hands were shaking and his cheeks were red-veined. Clearly his brains were pickled in alcohol. Yet he had tricked Marietta. How was this possible? Hugo knew that he could not afford to ignore the peasant's offer. It took him only a second to discover that Kova was unarmed.

'Let's get going,' he muttered, pressing his gun against Kova's back.

His driver was still on guard beside the car in the abandoned courtyard. He would have to kill the boy, for there must be no witnesses to what he was going to do.

'Guard him well,' he muttered. 'I'll be back in a minute.'

What he had to do would not take long. He had been planning his leave-taking for weeks past. He hurried to the vaults of the castle and set light to the fuse. Within ten minutes Sokol would be ablaze. By the time he returned to the car, smoke was already beginning to escape.

'Take the highway north,' he muttered, peering over his shoulder.

'Sir, the Americans are within fifteen miles of Prague.'

'They've gone ... pulled out this morning,' Kova muttered. 'Edelweiss told me. She came to the abattoir driving the Bocks' van. She said she was going to Sokol Castle, but she'd run out of petrol.'

'And out of luck,' Hugo thought, with a silent chuckle.

The abattoir was silent as a grave. There were no animals in the yard, no men, only the stink of death. Hugo felt wary of Kova now. Prickles of apprehension ran up and down his spine.

'Tie his hands behind his back,' he ordered the driver.

Kova was wet with sweat. 'But General, I told you all I want is my little daughter.' He muttered on as his wrists were bound. 'Wait here,' Hugo told his driver. 'If you hear a shot come at once, and come armed.'

Their footsteps echoed on wooden floors as they walked through the old building to the filthy cobbled pen, deep in manure.

Kova chuckled. 'I pushed her down into the cellars where I store the carcasses, but this time I bolted the door to the sewers. There's no other way out.' He led the way to the killing shed and pointed down through a large grid with an iron ring in the centre.

'Pick up the grid with your foot,' Hugo ordered, keeping his gun trained on the sweating man. Kova managed to slip the grid aside, but lost his balance and fell.

He looked up, grimacing with pain. 'If you untie my hands,' Herr General.'

'Get on with it,' Hugo grumbled.

Kova pushed the grid back with his feet.

'Get over there.' Hugo waved vaguely at the wall.

Kova rolled to the wall, panting. 'She's down on the right, tied to a chair.'

Hugo bent over the grid. Out of the corner of his eyes he saw a sudden movement as Kova lunged his feet towards a switch. Then his head seemed to explode from a massive blow.

'A man on his own has to learn to be inventive, General von Hesse,' Kova was saying.

Hugo blinked and shook his head which ached abominably. Where was he? What was happening? Then he remembered and looked around for Marietta, but there was no sign of her. Had he fallen?

'A very tricky device and my own invention. I intend to patent it when things get back to normal. The toughest bull is stunned for at least three minutes, von Hesse. Long enough to cut its throat, but don't worry, I won't cut yours.'

'What the hell was the fool prattling about?' Hugo struggled to sit up, but found that he could not. Anger set in when he saw that Marietta was not here. He had been tricked. His fury dimmed the pain in his head. Then he blacked out again. Minutes later, he sighed and groaned. Then he opened his eyes. It felt as if he'd been hit with a sledge-hammer.

'Are you all right, General von Hesse? Speak to me,' Kova said, and chuckled.

Hugo surfaced slowly. The first thing he saw was Kova's face, only inches from his own. He tried to pull up his hands to push him away, but gasped with pain. Looking down, he saw that he was naked, his feet and hands bound with wire that was cutting into his flesh. His hands were attached to his feet by a wire rope. An ox couldn't break it. Panic welled up inside him. He was trapped. Looking round in the dim light, he saw that he was in Kova's obscene cellar, surrounded with stinking carcasses hanging on meat hooks.

'Untie me, Kova, or you'll never know where your daughter is.' Hugo hung on to the hope that he could still talk the man round.

'My daughter's dead, you swine. She hanged herself because you and your men foully abused her, in front of her father. You're about to pay for that, von Hesse. You're going to wish you'd never set eyes on my girl, or on me.'

'I was doing a job. It was the war. Don't you understand? These things are necessary in wartime. You were a traitor. But the war's over, Kova. We can put all that behind us. I'm a very rich man. We can do a deal.'

'I want you to appreciate the sheer brilliance of my inventiveness . . .' Kova was saying. 'I had to be clever, after the troops took my Slav workers for their labour gangs. I was alone. How could I cope with these huge oxen?'

'Kova, untie me. You'll be well-rewarded, I promise you. Name your price, man.'

'I hit on the idea of a bolt fired from an adjusted crossbow in the roof. All I have to do is to position the beast and kick the switch at the bottom of the wall. The animal is stunned and I can cut its throat without struggle or pain. Did you know that fear and anguish taints the meat? My meat is always sweet and fresh. Yours, on the other hand, will be very tainted.'

'Listen to me, Kova,' Hugo pleaded. 'I'm a very rich man. I have ranches in South America. You can have what you want of mine. Think of the lovely girls you can buy.'

'You'll rot here, von Hesse. It will take you days to die. I'm an expert in death. It's my trade.' He bent over Hugo, still laughing. The smell of him was horrible and his spittle landed on Hugo's mouth.

Hugo could hardly breathe. It felt as if his chest was being puffed up by gigantic bellows that were bursting his lungs. His throat was constricting, his hands were slippery wet, and it felt as if his head had been staved in. A trickle of warm liquid ran around his neck and he guessed it was blood from the wound.

Kova lurched towards him, pointing a sharp meathook at him. His expression was deadly.

'Just shoot me,' Hugo gasped.

'I wouldn't waste a bullet on shit like you. Normally the carcasses are skinned, von Hesse, and, of course, dead by the time I get to this stage, but in your case I'm changing the routine. You're only stripped, not skinned. Your skin isn't worth anything.' He laughed briefly. 'Well, here goes. This is how I do it.'

Hugo felt his head being yanked up by his hair. Gasping with fear, he stiffened his body and hung on, so that he could not be bent forward.

With a brief, impatient gesture, Kova knocked him sidelong and Hugo fell on to his face. He screamed as he felt the hook prodding his back around his shoulder blade.

'No . . . no . . . no . . . ' he gasped. 'Don't . . .'

The pain was terrible as the sharp steel lunged into his flesh. He screamed again and again as it was pushed home. This couldn't be happening. It was insane. Only the pain was real. He was dimly aware of Kova pulling on a chain. He screamed again at the tearing agony in his shoulder and his chest. He was being pulled up to a sitting position.

He passed out again and Kova let him slump back on to the ground. A bucket of cold water brought him to his senses.

'I want you to understand what's happening,' Kova said softly. 'Next I haul up the beasts with my block and tackle.' Hugo could hear himself screaming, but the sound seemed to come from far away. He was dimly aware of footsteps ... shouts and shots. The body of his driver fell through the grid, to land beside him. Nothing seemed real except the pain that was consuming him. He had no more strength to scream. He felt he was on the shore of a gigantic lake ... waves of pain were washing through him.

'That's better,' Kova said. 'There's no point in screaming, von Hesse. This is no-man's land. The Czechs have fled, the US troops have retreated, the Germans have gone south and the Russians haven't arrived yet. Your step-sister, Edelweiss, has gone back to Sokol. I gave her the petrol she needed, you see. She's a fine woman. You, on the other hand, are a piece of shit. 'Now, up you go. You can hang there till you rot.'

Kova pulled at the block and tackle. Hugo felt his muscles and tendons and flesh tearing away in blinding agony, but some held and he was dragged up and up, hanging from the hook, until his feet left the ground and his body hung awkwardly from his dislocated shoulder, revolving slowly in the air. He groaned, unaware of his blood and urine dripping on to the floor until there was a large pool under his feet.

The pain was more than he thought a man could bear. He was propelled out of time and space into a world he had never known, where a second lasted an eternity. He was only dimly aware that he was swaying backwards and forwards, just like the carcasses around him.

'Sweet dreams, von Hesse,' he heard. 'Think of my daughter. It must have been good to rape her. She was a virgin and pretty, too. I bet you enjoyed it. For two pins I'd cut off your prick, but I wouldn't want you to bleed to death. Too quick by far.'

Hugo groaned and lapsed into unconsciousness. When he came to he was alone. The agony was all-consuming and he knew that it would never leave him, but only get worse until he died. He'd been told of men put to death on meat hooks in Hitler's cellar. They'd lived for days, he'd heard.

Chapter  80

MARIETTA'S HEART WAS POUNDING, her mouth was dry and she could scarcely breathe for the lump in her throat as she crossed the bridge over the Vltava River towards her home. The ramparts over the bridge and the east gate were still standing. She could see the swastika flying high above. Well, she would have that down soon enough.

She knew what to expect. She had been warned by the Resistance wives who had hidden her for the past few days, until the last of the troops and *Volksdeutsche* refugees had left the area. But it was still a shock. She stood in the courtyard, gazing at her ruined home with tears streaming down her cheeks.

The East Wing of Sokol Castle was entirely burnt out. The walls had been built to last and they might well remain as they were – blackened and jagged, like ancient, eroded teeth – for the next few centuries, she thought. Bulldozing those walls would take time and cost a fortune. Marietta waited for a while, biting her lip, until she pulled herself together. Then she crept up the main steps, picking her way across fallen debris and blackened rafters, to the main hall. There was nothing here. The interior was chaotic and dangerous. The roof was half open to the sky and around the gaping hole, half-fallen, sooty rafters, flapped dismally in the wind. The floors were choked with charred lumps of wood and fabric, some still smoking. She guessed that the recent downpour had put out the blaze. Everything was gone ... the library with its rare manuscripts and books, the paintings, the works of art, the antique furniture, centuries of accumulation of priceless objects had been totally destroyed.

She wandered from room to room, gazing around fearfully until she reached the older part of the building, where the troops had been stationed, and which had not been touched by the fire.

Here, Sokol looked what it was, an abandoned army garrison with its cracked and dirty windowpanes, peeling paint and broken doors. Would she ever get it back to normal? The probable cost was intimidating. What viable reason could she find to justify such expenditure? People would need homes, jobs, the country would need communications, industry and all the infrastructure destroyed by the Nazis. They would not need castles, nor works of art. Why should she stay? Why not give them what she had and go? That thought was seductive. Why not?

Peace would mean many things for many people, but for her, if she stayed, it would mean a lifetime of learning to live without Bill.

Unless ...

She walked along century-old corridors, noting the missing art treasures, the cracked and damaged marble floors, the ruined sculptured ceilings, until she reached the family gallery where many of the portraits remained. She could guess why, too, for most of them were of sentimental value and not worth looting.

There was a portrait of her grandmother, painted as a young woman, at the end of the gallery. She was dressed in a black riding habit and sitting side-saddle on a white stallion. What would grandmother do now, she wondered, gazing long and wistfully at the painting?

Marietta was startled by the sound of heavy vehicles rumbling across the bridge into the courtyard. Running to the window, she saw a convoy of German lorries move swiftly to the main door. Her stomach knotted until she noticed the red stars painted over the swastikas. A bunch of ragged Czech partisans, led by Jan, tumbled out of the lorries. They looked exhausted.

Hurrying outside, she saw Jan was taking the steps in leaps and bounds. His face was stern, his eyes bleak and unforgiving.

'Countess, I salute you for your patriotism and your courage. You are a brave woman. But you should understand that I cannot guarantee your safety when the Russians get here.'

She flushed angrily. 'I'm a patriot, as you are. I fought as hard as you did.'

Jan took her arm and led her away from his men. He flashed a badge at her. She read: *General Jan Zykov, The Czech People's Liberation Army.* 'For the time being, I'm in charge here,' he said quietly. 'But who knows if I'll survive the post-war upheaval. It's bound to be rough. You must trust me one more time, as you always have done. You are the daughter of a Nazi who was given a hero's funeral . . .'

'You know the truth of the matter,' she retorted angrily.

'Don't waste time, my friend. You are the step-sister of a known war criminal who ran the Reich security from your home. Furthermore you, and certain Allied agents, conspired to deprive the Soviets of the nuclear and missile research in Richard's Mine. I've come here to warn you only because we were comrades. And there's another reason. I admire you too much to see you throw your life away for some absurd sense of duty. We fought together for ideals, not possessions. There was a difference, you'll agree. Please believe me, Marietta, it's time to go. Besides, most of your estates will be appropriated within two to three years. There's no future for you here. Believe me.'

'Yes . . . of course,' she said, in a small, tired voice. 'Strange, but I had thought I would be needed. I want to be alone for a few minutes, please.' Not wanting Jan to see her bitterness, she turned and walked slowly back to the gallery.

'So there you have it, Grandmother,' she said, looking up earnestly. 'I wasn't a very good link in the chain after all. We are passing into history . . . you and I.'

She felt puzzled and a little lost. All her life, she'd been hemmed in by responsibility and protocol and the burden of being a great heiress, a Habsburg and of royal blood. Like a fool, she had only considered her loss, not her gain. She sat on, frowning as she considered her situation.

'So what now?' she said, looking up sadly. 'What next?' Her grandmother's painted features gave her no reply.

There was nothing left to do. 'I'm free!' she whispered, feeling uncertain and lonely.

The old empty walls echoed back her words: 'Free ... free .. free . . .' Free to marry Bill!

She stood up, now strangely light-headed. 'Free!' She tried out the word again to see if it felt real.

The portraits of her ancestors seemed to be watching her disapprovingly. 'It's no good blaming me,' she said. 'I have no choice in this matter. You may gather dust here, which is fine for you, since you are only portraits and old bones down in the mausoleum. But I am alive. I lust for life ... and for happiness,' she added solemnly. 'And it has been a long time coming to me.'

She heard Jan running down the passage, calling her name. He caught hold of her arm and pulled her towards the hall.

'Please ... hurry. Soviet troops are close by. Roth has arrived to fetch you. I couldn't let him in ... I don't want my men to see him. He's waiting across the bridge. Here's a safe conduct for both of you. Go south ... it will be safer, but go quickly. I'll send an armed escort with you.'

She hugged him, laughing at his shocked expression. Turning, she ran along dusty corridors and burst into the sunlight. High above, on the castle ramparts, she could see the Czechs hauling down the Nazi flag, but she hardly spared them a glance.

The sky was dazzling, birds were singing, fish were leaping in the gurgling river, and her heart leapt with them. A strange feeling was growing inside her, making her want to laugh and cry at the same time. 'Bill ...' she called. 'Bill ...'

There he was ... sitting in a jeep, parked across the river. He was heavily bandaged and he looked grey with fatigue, but his eyes lit up when he saw her. Marietta raced across the bridge without looking back. The past had no meaning for her any more. They would create their own home and their own future on the firm foundation of their love.

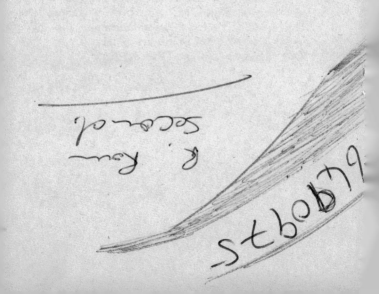

R. Row
Second.

9640957

SUMMER HARVEST

Madge Swindells

'a spellbinding read' Sarah Harrison

Set between 1938 and 1968 in a land where gruelling poverty rubs shoulders with remarkable opulence, and moving from the Cape to London and the West Coast of America, SUMMER HARVEST is a family saga in the finest tradition.

At the heart of the story is Anna, a woman as strong and passionate as she is ambitious, who fights her way up from near destitution to become one of the Cape's most prominent and powerful businesswomen. Only love eludes her. For Simon – a poor farmer when they marry – has too much masculine pride to stand on the sidelines while Anna plunders her way to a success that threatens tragedy and loss.

'Anna van Achtenburg mirrors the strengths and the weaknesses of her beautiful, harsh country: the toughness, the dazzling material success, the moral dilemmas, the tragedy. I was gripped from start to finish.'
Kate Alexander, author of *Fields of Battle*

Other bestselling Warner titles available by mail: